PORTRAIT IN BROWNSTONE

By Louis Auchincloss

The Indifferent Children

The Injustice Collectors

Sybil

A Law for the Lion

The Romantic Egoists

The Great World and Timothy Colt

Venus in Sparta

Pursuit of the Prodigal

The House of Five Talents

Reflections of a Jacobite

Portrait in Brownstone

Louis Auchincloss

PORTRAIT IN BROWNSTONE

HOUGHTON MIFFLIN COMPANY BOSTON
The Riverside Press Cambridge

FOURTH PRINTING

COPYRIGHT © 1962 BY LOUIS AUCHINCLOSS
ALL RIGHTS RESERVED INCLUDING THE RIGHT TO
REPRODUCE THIS BOOK OR PARTS THEREOF IN ANY FORM
LIBRARY OF CONGRESS CATALOG CARD NUMBER: 62–8116

The Riverside Press
CAMBRIDGE • MASSACHUSETTS
PRINTED IN THE U.S.A.

For Blake and Shiela Lawrence,

*with all my love and thanks for the long
summer visits to Lake Champlain
where this story was conceived
and much of it written.*

PART I

The Denisons of Fifty-Third Street

Ida: 1950

I HAD EVEN reached the point of wondering if Geraldine Brevoort's suicide, so long dreaded, might not prove in the event a relief, but like everything else about Geraldine, when it came, it came with a nasty twist. She had plagued me living; now, apparently, she would plague me dead. In the preceding weeks, night after night, she had called me on the telephone to pour out her bile and her terrors, in maudlin, drunken rambling, to complain about God and the manager of her hotel, the rudeness of taxi drivers and the magnitude of tips, and to express her undying resentment against the fancied indifference or fancied jealousy of her long-dead parents and our long-dead uncles and aunts. If Derrick happened to be about, I would go upstairs to the telephone in my bedroom. I was afraid that if he heard her squawking cry: "I wish I were dead!" he might exclaim too loudly: "I wish you were, too, Geraldine!" For it was Derrick's theory that Geraldine was trying to torture me by insinuating that my home was built on sand, my serenity (as she called it) on illusion, and that if I had attained any peace of mind, it was only because I had never known ecstasy, only because I had never *lived,* as she, Geraldine, had lived. And it was certainly true that Geraldine, with her shabby past and her shabby secret, vacillated between the inconsistent claims that I was rich because I had looted her happiness and poor because I could never hope to share her lost youth. To her, I would always be the little brown cousin who had worn her hand-me-downs and still envied her the glamour of a debutante year in which no fewer than eight men had proposed.

That last night it went on interminably. I stared into the mirror over my desk as I offered the mechanical words of consolation and wondered if they seemed as weary and bored as the apprehensive eyes that stared back at me between the dark circles and the waves of grey hair that Geraldine liked to describe as my "rocking-chair brigade."

"But, Geraldine, I *never* said I was any better than you, I never even thought it, no, I didn't, dear . . . No, *listen* . . . I only said I minded your drinking because it makes you ill and unhappy . . . No, I didn't say it was immoral . . . I *didn't*, Geraldine, you're putting words in my mouth . . . My dear, I know I've had an easy life, no one is more aware of it than I . . . I'm *not* being smug . . . Look, dearie, why don't you let me come and spend the night with you?"

Of course I knew she would never consent. She might fool the nurse about her drinking, but she could never fool me. And it struck me, still talking, that there was something ignoble about the way I was always building up a record that would exonerate me on the ultimate day of disaster, like a quartermaster keeping a log that nobody would ever want to read.

"I know you have a nurse, Geraldine, but what's a nurse? . . . Of course I want you to live, dear, I want you to live for years and years . . . No, you're wrong, you still have wonderful looks . . . Minerva Denison was saying just the other day, if Geraldine would only take off twenty pounds she'd be as lovely as the day she came out."

Really, was there no end to pity, to family loyalty, to my childish habit of respectfulness for slightly older cousins? The lower Geraldine descended into the pit of drink and

self-pity, the more sentimentally, it seemed, I deferred to
her, until the stout painted creature with the whiskey breath
who lived entombed in two little rooms full of bibelots and
junk at the Algar, husbandless, childless, friendless, treated
me with more condescension than she did the maid whom
she paid to come in and drink with her! Here was the result
of what Derrick called my fetish about the past. He complained that I attributed his success to Uncle Linn Tremain
who had given him his start, a debt which, in Derrick's version of my credo, had been passed down, unamortized, from
Uncle Linn to Geraldine, so that the cluttered little parlor
at the Algar was now the chapel in which the orisons of our
joint gratitude should be daily offered. Well, perhaps there
was something in it. Perhaps I *had* been a fool.

"Then why don't you come here? . . . No, seriously, why
don't you, Geraldine? . . . Don't be silly, of course Derrick
wouldn't mind . . ."

Derrick loomed up in the doorway, holding a cigar. The
dim light in the vestibule over his broad shoulders gave to
his thick mound of grey hair a more than usually magisterial
look.

"Derrick most certainly *would* mind," he called across the
room. "Derrick will not have that woman in the house!"

I quickly covered the mouthpiece. "Derrick, hush! Do
you want her to hear you?"

"I don't care! I will not have that woman in the house!"

"But she's ill! Desperately ill!"

"She has a nurse, hasn't she?"

"Not a very good one, I'm afraid."

"Then get her another."

"Derrick, how *can* I? At this hour?"

"I don't know, and I don't care. All I know is that as long
as I'm living in this house, that woman is not going to come
here. I promise you, Ida, I'm serious!"

I took his opposition so for granted that it shocked me suddenly to consider that I might have invited Geraldine only in reliance upon it. Since my sixtieth birthday, over a year before, my powers of self-analysis had uncomfortably sharpened. And I had so counted on an old age lulled by the slapping waves of fatuity! "Here I am, dear," I continued into the instrument. "I had to close the window. It was blowing in. Perhaps you're right. Perhaps it's better and more restful if you stay where you are and take a sleeping pill . . . No, darling, it has nothing to *do* with Derrick, he's at a bankers' dinner, anyway . . . Yes, of course I'm sure . . . Well, Geraldine, really how you *insinuate* things . . . No, I'm not cross . . . What?"

I listened for a moment until I realized that I was hearing the dial tone. Geraldine had hung up.

"I don't think you appreciate how ill she is!" I exclaimed, turning angrily on Derrick. "I've told you that we ought to commit her!"

"She's not that nutty."

"She complains that the hotel allows corpses to be stacked in the corridor!"

"That's only delirium," he retorted with a shrug. "Once you had her under lock and key, and off the booze, she'd calm right down and unspring herself. And then tell everyone you'd done it out of spite!"

"I don't care!" I protested miserably. "I only care what's good for Geraldine. She won't let me go to her, and you won't let her come here. The only thing to do, then, is get her to a hospital, and if she won't go, she must be committed!"

"I tell you, it won't work," he said decisively. "I think you'll have to take my opinion on that. I've talked to the lawyers, and you haven't. Geraldine has an expensive psychiatric nurse whom *I* pay for and who's supposed to know all about her case. That should be quite enough. And now I suggest you go to bed."

"But, Derrick, I don't trust that nurse!"

"Then get a new one," he said with a yawn. "*In* the morning. If you ask me, you're making a great deal of fuss about a querulous, selfish creature who has drunk herself into her present predicament. I'm sorry," he continued, turning at the door and raising his hand to quell further protest, "I have no patience with this modern, morbid preoccupation with the mentally ill. If you wish to wear yourself out for Geraldine, that's your prerogative. *I* prefer to keep my strength and energy for those who can still profit by it. Good *night,* my dear."

I sat up late that night, uneasy and foreboding. It gave me little relief to recall how often in the past I had had the same premonition. Dr. Valdez, Dorcas' psychiatrist, had told me that to apprehend a death was subconsciously to wish for it, but if such was the case, I had learned to live with my subconscious. All I could do for Geraldine was to let the same heavy hands of the past press upon my shoulders that pressed upon hers. The old brownstone house and I were the sole survivors on Fifty-third Street of that crowded, organized family childhood that she and I had so intimately shared. Derrick had always wanted to move uptown, but the compromise that we had reached, after he had started to make what he called "real money," was that if he would keep my family's house, I would give him carte blanche to build as he chose in the country. Even at that, he had cheated a bit, for when the old stoop began to crumble, he had taken it off and installed a front hall of grey limestone with a showy marble stairway that always embarrassed me. And, of course, I could not prevent his buying the house next door and cutting through doorways to his new library and study. But the rest of the house was much as it had been half a century before

when Mother, breaking away from the stiff parlor tradition
of an earlier New York, had managed, with surprisingly few
dollars, to add a touch of French eighteenth century to the
dark Victorian things.

Below in the hall I heard the front door close and, a minute
later, the click of Hugo's evening shoes on those marble stairs.
Ordinarily he took the elevator to the top floor which he had
converted to his apartment, but when he saw the lights in
the front window he would stop in to chat.

"Hello, Ma! What keeps *you* up?"

"I was just thinking."

"Good Lord! That bad?" He came over and kissed me on
the cheek. He rarely kissed me except when I was sitting
down, for he hated measuring his height against that of any
woman even a fraction of an inch taller than himself. Hugo
was by no means a small man, and a temper as dark as his
hair and eyes more than compensated for any question of
size, but he had always resented a fate that had made him
shorter than his father. "You should have been at Aunt
Irene's. No nonsense like that with her and Uncle Chris."

"I imagine not," I said with a faint smile. "Actually I was
a bit worried about Cousin Geraldine." Hugo was the only
one of my family who still cared in the least for Geraldine.
She was at her best with him, because she loved to hear about
the social world.

"Is she bad?"

"Oh, you know, the same. Except every day it seems a
tiny bit worse. How long can it go on, do you think? How
long can a person be terrified of dying and want to die and
not die?"

Hugo straightened up at my tone. "See here, Ma, do you
want me to go round and check on her?"

"Oh, no, darling, that's not necessary at all. There's nothing you could do. Besides, you need your sleep."

"Need my sleep?" He laughed, the old high explosive laugh of all my mother's family. "I'm thirty-five, I'll thank you to remember. Can't you ever face the fact that your darlings are grown up? Grown up? Hell, they're middle-aged. Do you realize Dorcas will be forty in two years?"

"Will she?" How could Dorcas be middle-aged before she had had her youth?

"And yet you never let any of us do anything for you. Not, I grant, that you'd get much. Dorcas thinks of nothing but *her* children. But try your bachelor son. Seriously, would you like me to go and sit with Cousin Geraldine? I can sleep on the sofa there."

"Oh, darling, no, she's got a nurse!"

"A reliable one?"

"Oh, perfectly reliable. Please, dearest, go to bed."

"I will, if you will."

I rose, and as we put out the lights, I reflected that however much I had always fussed over Geraldine, I wouldn't give her a single one of my child's hours of sleep. No, I whispered grimly as I started up the stairs, not even to save her life.

I slept deeply that night, and, as usual, without dreams. I did not even hear the telephone, and I was awakened at eight o'clock by Derrick, already dressed, standing at the end of my bed and calling my name. I always regained all of my senses at the moment of waking and took in immediately the gravity of his expression.

"What's happened?"

"We needn't worry any longer about commitment," he said in a tone too dry not to have been rehearsed. "Geraldine went out the window half an hour ago. She fell eight stories. The hotel just called."

I sat up sharply. "And the nurse?" I cried in agony. "Where in God's name was that nurse?"

His gaze never flinched. "The nurse was in the bathroom."

One thing that I had to admit about Derrick was that he always knew when to shut up. To have pretended the smallest concern about Geraldine would have been ignoble; to have apologized for steps not taken would have been to invite a bitter storm of reproach. For the years had taught him that I was not of those who are disarmed by surrender; I had, on the contrary, a tendency, born of my very lack of confidence, to rub things in. I got up and dressed in two minutes while he stood there, silent.

"Where are you going?" he demanded, as I started to the door.

"To the Algar, of course."

"Not till you've had breakfast. There's nothing you can do now. I've got the office on the job, and they'll have a lawyer and an undertaker there." Derrick was immediately easier as soon as he could identify anything with his office.

"There's no need!" I cried, on the verge of tears. "I can take care of everything!"

"Nonsense!" he retorted firmly. "There'll be all kinds of details you shouldn't be bothered with. Besides, according to the will at my lawyers', I'm Geraldine's executor."

"*You* are!" I exclaimed in astonishment. "*Your* lawyers have Geraldine's will?"

"They have *a* will," he said with a shrug. "It was executed years ago, after Freddy died. But until someone turns up with a later one, I shall at least make noises like an executor." He took a step towards me as if to grasp my hand, but then appeared to think better of it. "I know your heart is full of bitterness, Ida. But Geraldine is dead, and all that can wait. You and I have a job to do. Let's do it together."

I caught my breath and struggled with the impulse to shout at him. But what was the use? What was the use of gestures? I sighed at last and nodded. "Of course, you're right. It's disgusting of me to think of myself at a time like this. If you're the executor, you must do as you see fit. I don't suppose, though, that poor Geraldine left much to 'execute.' "

We went down together to the dining room where Hugo was waiting for us in pajamas and a kimono. He usually had breakfast in his own apartment, but he had come down when his father telephoned. He got up to kiss me, without waiting for me to sit, and for just a moment I clung to him.

"What ghastly news," he murmured. "Poor Ma."

"I'm all right, dear," I said quickly and took my seat. "It isn't so much Geraldine's death I grieve for. It's her life. Let's all have coffee. Nellie!" I called.

But Nellie was already there with the coffee urn, and we drank in silence. Derrick turned to his newspaper, and I saw Hugo eye him with disapproval. In moments of tension they always fought.

"Shall I go with Ma to the Algar?" Hugo asked.

"It won't be necessary, thank you. I'll take her."

Hugo continued to stare at his father's paper. "When? After you've finished the *Times?*"

"When I've finished my breakfast, thank you," Derrick retorted testily, unfolding his napkin and turning the front page of the paper. Sensing Hugo's eyes still on him, he looked up suddenly and snapped: "I can't do more than all the king's horses and all the king's men, you know. I can't put Geraldine together again, can I?"

"And I daresay you wouldn't if you could!"

Derrick met his son's angry eyes with a retorting glare. He was obviously relieved by the excuse to speak his mind. "It's quite true, I wouldn't. If ever I knew a useless human being, it was she. I can see nothing to be gained in false sentiment about her death."

"Nothing!" cried Hugo. "I quite agree, nothing! But you

might at least recognize that Ma loved Cousin Geraldine. Don't let *her* see how you feel."

"Hugo, *please!*" I murmured, but my protest was lost in Derrick's answering roar: "I think I may be allowed to express my feelings in my own home! Everyone else does!"

"Do you insinuate that I stretch my privileges?" Hugo demanded, flaring up immediately. "Do you imply that I'm not welcome? It's very easy for me to find other lodgings, you know."

"Look, Hugo." Derrick paused now to regulate his exasperation and make it a more effective instrument of his antagonism. "You don't have to play that game with me. You know perfectly well that you're welcome here. You know also that, as far as I'm concerned, you may leave whenever you wish. Any issue that may exist on that subject is entirely between you and your mother. But I expect to do as I like in my own home. And I expect those who share it to accept that."

I imagined that if Hugo could have been sure of making the smallest dent in his father's feelings, he would have left. As it was, there was no point in his abandoning a free apartment.

"Darling," I said soothingly, "you can help me by not fighting with your father. I think we're all on edge."

Derrick and I went straight from the dining room to the waiting car where his faithful Hans, in tucking the rug over my knees, murmured some inarticulate words of sympathy. It touched me, for Hans, a former convict of whom Derrick, in his practical fashion, had made a slave by the simple expedient of employment, regarded himself as Derrick's chauffeur and only incidentally as mine, just as he regarded the big black waxed and shiny Cadillac as his master's exclusive property. Certainly, it was a point of view to which I had no objection. I hated the ostentation of the Cadillac.

We were met at the door of the Algar by the manager, a lawyer and a detective. Derrick always enjoyed the little hubbub that was apt to follow his arrivals in the big car.

"Why don't you go right up to Geraldine's rooms?" he asked me. "I can take care of things down here while you look through her desk. There may be a last note or a memo with funeral instructions."

"Not before I've seen her!" I exclaimed suddenly. I turned to the manager. "Where is she?"

"We've laid her on the day bed in the back office."

"Ida," Derrick protested, "please don't go in."

"Oh, it's all right, Mr. Hartley," the manager assured him. "The head was not damaged at all."

"Take me to her!"

I followed the manager quickly to a dark little room in back and found myself standing by what was left of Geraldine. The body, broken by its fall, swollen by the stoutness of the last five drinking years, rose in a mound under an old brown blanket. Only the head was exposed and the dyed, braided golden hair. As so often is the case, Geraldine had regained in death something of her old beauty. I saw again in that long oval face, in those marble cheeks, in that delicate straight nose the magnificent luster of the Edwardian belle, and I remembered, with a sad, sick jealousy and agonized regret, how Geraldine had dominated our childhood world of cousins. I would have broken down had it not been for the manager's voice.

"I trust Mr. Hartley will look after the press," he was whining. "Naturally, he will care as much as I do that nothing be said about this."

"It is of not the slightest importance to me what the newspapers print," I said abruptly. "I'll go to Mrs. Brevoort's rooms now, thank you."

In Geraldine's apartment I closed the door firmly in his

face. It was suddenly unbearable to have to share her death with any more humans to whom it meant nothing but its method. Alone in the little living room, at least, I was alone with a past that had loved her. Her father, who had been my Uncle Victor, Mother's favorite brother and the most charming of the Denisons, with his slanting eyelid and walking stick, smiled down from a portrait too large for the wall space, surrounded by the remnants of his little art collection: Vibert, Detailles, Walter Gay. Guarding the door to the bedroom was the big Indian elephant screen that had so fascinated me as a child. And everywhere, on the floor, on the sofa, on chairs, abounded the dolls that Geraldine had so passionately collected and clung to: big, floppy dolls in pajamas that nobody had seen since the 1920s, dolls in crinolines, dolls in dirndls, Raggedy Anns, eighteenth century marquises. Propped up on the back of the sofa and leaning against the wall was a huge pink cushion with the embroidered legend: "Don't worry, it never happens." I went over quickly to turn it and then sat on the sofa and allowed myself the bitter luxury of tears whose sincerity I even doubted myself.

I knew that Geraldine kept her papers in two drawers at the bottom of her desk. Into these she had thrown what she wanted to keep, helter-skelter, but as she had cleaned it out before her move to the Algar, I had now only a small bundle of old documents and the random accumulations of three years. The latter were quickly sifted: unpaid bills, addresses of drugstores that were not fussy about prescriptions, names of cleaning women who would gossip as well as clean, and copies of indignant letters about city smells and street noises to the *Herald Tribune*. The older papers were tied more neatly in a bundle: Geraldine's first divorce decree, the court papers of her legal squabble over Freddy Brevoort's trust, galleys of a slushy yarn about a rum runner and a debutante with green fingernails that Geraldine had written for a pulp magazine in the early twenties, and then, unexpectedly and touchingly, a letter that my mother had written her when Geraldine had left Talbot Keating. Geraldine had always been Mother's favorite niece, but Mother had understood her and, unlike myself, had known how to give advice without offending.

"We're all of us selfish," the long slanting handwriting warned Geraldine. "It's a Denison characteristic, and there's precious little we can do about it. But I find people don't mind so much if we're selfish and pleasant. It's being selfish and cross that they never forgive!"

I felt a stab of jealousy at the thought of how Mother would have loved to have had a daughter as beautiful as Geraldine. But would anything have been worth the aftermath? "When the tide goes out," Mother used to say of old age, "it's *your* beach that's left." Mother's tide had not gone out, for she had died too young, but I had my vision of what a clean, gleaming beach hers would have been. Poor Geraldine's, on the other hand, had been strewn with old bottles and seaweed and dead crabs and odd spiked things tossed from the deep, and . . . and the paper that I now spotted beneath Mother's note, bearing the letterhead of a law firm and a date in March of 1935, just fifteen years before.

Dear Mrs. Brevoort:

You have asked our opinion on the legal consequences of the following state of facts: Plaintiff, as a young woman, received a proposal of marriage from Defendant, which she declined because he had been paying marked attentions to her cousin. Defendant and Plaintiff's cousin were subsequently married, but some years later Defendant told Plaintiff that his marriage had been a mistake and that he was still and had always been in love with her. He promised to get a divorce and marry her if in the meanwhile she would become his mistress. Plaintiff, relying on his promise, entered into the proposed relationship. Defendant, however, never thereafter took any steps to obtain a divorce and at last told Plaintiff that he had never intended to do so. Does Plaintiff have any legal redress?

As a practical matter, Plaintiff does not. No action could be based on the promise of marriage which Plaintiff knew that Defendant was in no position to fulfill. There is, we suppose, a conceivable action in seduction, but Plaintiff's knowledge of Defendant's married state would make any recovery most unlikely. Undoubtedly advantage has been taken of an unfortunate woman, but it is one of those wrongs for which our law provides no effective remedy.

Even at such a moment, when all my childhood and early years seemed to shrink into the grotesque accumulation of that room, when the back of that absurd pillow with its admonition against worry seemed to grin at me in its base joy at my disillusionment, I was able to repudiate the "advantage" taken of that "unfortunate woman." I had known Geraldine for a hypocrite and an egotist, but *this!* I saw the room and its accumulations suddenly as anybody might have seen it, stripped of the associations in which the past had wrapped it for me. Now it was merely cluttered and shabby, and Uncle Victor's portrait a slick fashionable dated job, and Aunt Sophie's porcelain chipped and bad Victorian. But what was worst of all was that there seemed not only no taste but no principles, or at least no principles that weren't everybody's principles. I was suddenly abandoned in a wasteland of moral equality where tact and kindness and self-sacrifice and greed and lechery and simple selfishness were so many cactuses of the same size and barbs, and Geraldine and I were one at last — and nothing. Yet the only real surprise which that letter had contained for me was that she should have written it.

When I heard the door open and saw Derrick before me I did not bother to wipe away the tears. I simply stared at him reproachfully.

"I'm glad you're giving in to it," he said with conventional sympathy. "It's bad to dam things up."

"Oh, yes, I'm giving in to it."

"I don't suppose you've had a chance to see if there's another will?"

"There isn't," I said briefly.

"Then it's all yours."

"*What's* all mine?"

"This apartment. All these bibelots. The papers you're going through." He shrugged. "The whole damn estate. Of course, it's no fortune, but I figure, after taxes and everything, it ought to amount to some four hundred thousand dollars."

My first dizzy reaction was that it must have been a gesture of conscience on Geraldine's part. "But don't I have to share it?" I demanded. "Shouldn't it be divided equally among all the cousins?"

Derrick seemed amused. "I always count on you, Ida. You never let me down. You can convert a windfall into a duty the very minute you hear of it. Who but you could imagine that it was an obligation to turn over the money to a parcel of cousins who didn't give a damn about her?"

Another idea struck me. "Derrick, did you say you *knew* about this will?"

"Certainly. She told me about it the winter I took over her investments, just after Freddy Brevoort died. It seemed to me perfectly appropriate. You had been very kind to her, and she had no children of her own. Besides, I made most of that money for her."

"And was *that* why you wouldn't let me commit her?" I demanded, rising from my seat. "Because you thought she might get well again and be so angry she'd change her will?"

It was Derrick's particular pride that his face never betrayed him. He surveyed me now with a dispassionate stare and shrugged again. "I'm not so hard up that I have to play little tricks like that. I assumed that Geraldine had changed that will a dozen times."

Had he? I would never know. It was true that the money was not important to him, but the smallest sum would have been more important than Geraldine. I handed him her letter from the lawyer.

"Read that. I'm beginning to wonder if, between us, we didn't do rather a job on Geraldine."

But if Derrick had been able to face my first attack, there was nothing in my second to make him quail. When he had finished the letter, he tossed it back on the desk with a grunt.

"So she even went to a lawyer," he muttered. "I might have guessed it. Geraldine could never believe that the machinery of the state wasn't constructed especially for her own petty complaints."

"Is that all you have to say?"

His face showed a mild surprise, but that, too, was premeditated. "What more is there to say?"

"What about *me?*" . .

"But you knew all about it, Ida!"

"I didn't know that Geraldine intended to marry you!" I exclaimed passionately. "I didn't think it was you who had turned her down!"

I thought that I could make out for the first time a sincere astonishment on Derrick's features. "What *did* you think?"

"I thought she threw you out because she wouldn't take *my* husband!"

Derrick stared for a moment and then emitted a low whistle. "And you'd rather believe *that?* Rather than that I never wanted a divorce?"

"Yes!" I cried. "I'd rather believe that you and Geraldine

were in love, and that she was big enough to give you up, than that you seduced her with a lie and that she plotted to take my husband! What decent woman wouldn't?"

Derrick sat down on the sofa and was quiet for several moments. Perhaps he was reflecting that in all the years of our marriage I had never spoken to him so violently. "So that's it," he said at last. "That's what you are. A decent woman."

"You find it out just when I discover that the term is meaningless!"

"And what does a decent woman do now? Leave me?"

"Of course I'm not going to leave you," I said, exasperated at his obtuseness. "Why should I leave you for something that happened fifteen years ago? I'm not such a sentimental fool. Not now, anyway. No, there's nothing you have to *do* about this or even think about it." I pointed to the letter on the table with a trembling hand. "I shall burn it, and as far as you're concerned, that will be the end of it. You can go on about your own life as if nothing at all had happened."

"And you?"

"Oh, Derrick, what do you care? Leave me *be!*" I got up and walked to the open drawer and took out the last bundle of papers. "I have work to do."

"I want to know what all this means to you," he insisted stubbornly. "After all, I'm responsible, no matter how long ago it was. How do you know I can't help you?"

"Can you mend a broken past?" I demanded bitterly. "A broken past that never existed?"

"Why did it never exist?"

"Because it was only in my own silly mind." I threw down the bundle of letters and walked to the fireplace to pick a cigarette off the mantel. "Geraldine was right. She's always been right." I turned to him defiantly. "I've seen the world with the eyes of a child. Always. Mother and Uncle Victor and Aunt Dagmar and *all* the Denisons. What gods and goddesses they were to me! And how Geraldine always sneered at me and said that everybody was carrying on with everyone else, even her own father, and that Aunt Dagmar drank whiskey in her bedroom!" I gave a little helpless laugh at my own naïveté and at the seeming absurdity of bringing it all up after so many years. "I daresay they all did!"

"I very much doubt if your Aunt Dagmar drank whiskey in her bedroom," he observed judiciously. But then he appeared to consider. "At least she never showed it if she did."

"Oh, what does it matter, who cares? She's been dead these last twelve years!"

"*You* care!"

"Well, I'll get over it. It won't kill me."

"You make me wonder."

"Only it *does* seem to me," I went on, with a sudden resurgence of indignation, "that if Geraldine cared enough to want to marry you, you might have been a little kinder to her at the end!"

But Derrick simply shrugged as he rose. "She didn't want to marry *me*," he retorted quietly. "She wanted to marry *your* husband."

The door that he closed on me seemed to shut out more than the present. It shut out my own past and left me with Geraldine's. For a few terrible moments I thought it was going to stifle me, that those grotesque dolls would end by convincing me that truth lay in their placid leers or else drive me out the window after their defeated mistress. I had already reached the door, on my way to the lobby to call after Derrick, when I finally got hold of myself.

"No, no!" I whispered hoarsely. "I don't care if you *are* dead, Geraldine! Your whole life was rotten! And I'm still alive!"

It seemed for a moment that Uncle Victor might be going

to wink from his portrait. But no, Uncle Victor also was dead. I picked up Geraldine's copy of my little printed pamphlet, *The Ancestors and Descendants of William K. Denison and Dorcas Fuller,* and, turning to the page which contained the dates of her birth and of her two marriages, I carefully inserted the date of her death. The first trembling in the old jerry-built castle of my evasions was over. It had shaken me badly. But now that the bricks were tumbling and one great tower had disappeared in a roar of dust and masonry, I felt, in the very core of my misery, a little stir of elation. I wanted to see it all go. I wanted to rave and shout over the general ruin from a last tottering turret until I, too, should fall into the wreckage and be buried in the rubble with whatever stern lesson might have been turned up in the bricks of that ancient past.

2

Ida: 1901

AUNT DAGMAR TREMAIN dominated our childhood world on Fifty-third Street, but behind Aunt Dagmar there was always Uncle Linn. We became more conscious of him as we grew older and learned in what esteem our parents held this tall, silent, sardonic, whiskered gentleman who was known to be brilliant in finance and supposed to be brilliant in everything. He had inherited the cultivation and independence of parents who had left an ante-bellum New York for the Florence of William Wetmore Story and the Robert Brownings. There Uncle Linn had lived as a young man, dabbling in painting and sculpture, and haunting the studios of those American artists who created towering marble figures for monuments and painted pictures of crowded and bloody historical scenes. It was typical of his prudence and detachment that he should have destroyed every item of his own early work and that he should have married his Italian mistress, not on the birth of his daughter Livia, but only on the ultimate birth of a son. The poor gratified creature's subsequent death (a Nunc Dimittis, as Mother used to call it) had freed Uncle Linn to return with his small family to New York and to the downtown world of stocks and bonds for which nature had all along intended him. There he found himself and his fortune, and he was already a rich man when his purchase of Grandpa Denison's little banking business brought him to Brooklyn and to Aunt Dagmar.

It was a family legend, despite the Italian lady, that Aunt Dagmar was the first and only passion of his life. Of course, when I was little, she was already in her fifties and inclined to be plump, but I could still piece together the beauty that must have dazzled Uncle Linn. It was a beauty that photographs never captured, the moist, shiny-eyed beauty of a nereid in pre-Raphaelite painting with long, blown hair that somehow managed to be neat, and skin of pinkest pearl. Although she was tall, like all her family, and magnificent in simple reds and blacks, she had the rather lovable inclination of a fussy generation for too many scarfs and lace handkerchiefs and lockets and frills. Aunt Dagmar's heart was as soft as her person, and I don't think anyone but her stepdaughter Livia ever really disliked her.

When Uncle Linn met her, she had passed her thirtieth year and was serenely keeping house for a widowed father and those of his younger children who were still unmarried. He proposed to her on their second meeting, and, being refused, crossed the East River every Saturday afternoon for three months to call on her. Aunt Dagmar was bewildered by such persistence; she had resolved not to marry while her father lived, and suitors had long since stopped coming to the house. But Grandpa Denison had had one stroke and was determined to see her settled before his next, and Uncle Linn, aided and abetted by the united Denisons, at last, amid storms of tears, prevailed. The boat to Europe was nearly missed when Aunt Dagmar, a still sobbing bride, insisted upon a final visit to the family homestead.

The sobs continued. Even after the honeymoon and her establishment in the French Renaissance mansion with the pink façade and big grey pedimented windows that Uncle Linn built for her on Fifty-third Street between Fifth and Sixth Avenues, Aunt Dagmar pined for her native Brooklyn. Had she had children of her own, the homesickness might have passed, but she didn't. Uncle Linn's answer was to bring over her family one by one. First came Uncle Will Denison, the oldest brother, who was given a junior partnership in Tremain & Dodge and moved his wife and six children into a house two down from Aunt Dagmar's. Then Uncle Philip, the bachelor brother and auctioneer, took over a floor of the Tremains' house and lived there until his marriage to Mrs. Clyde enabled him to build an even larger one on the corner of Fifth. Third came Uncle Victor, the doctor and favorite brother, who established his family and practice in the street, and last of all, my mother, Lily, the adored "baby," who persuaded my father, Gerald Trask, to take a job in a trust company of which Uncle Linn was a director and move into the brownstone that Uncle Linn had bought to ensure Aunt Dagmar's sunlight. Small wonder that the street became known as "Denison Alley."

It must have been Uncle Linn's hope that if he ever rid Aunt Dagmar of her homesickness, her heart would turn more wholly to him. But she was one of those lovely, vexing creatures who never fully mature and whose primary affection is reserved for siblings. For a long time Uncle Linn watched with a bemused and tolerant eye while his wife reconstructed her adult nursery around him. It had the incidental advantage, of course, of providing a host of children with whom his own delicate and adored son, Charley, could play. Aunt Dagmar's love for Charley, indeed, almost compensated her husband for the other things that she failed to give him. But after Charley's death his stricken father began to see the Denisons with an increasingly critical eye. He was perfectly willing to smile at their jokes and go to their parties and even to foot their bills, but they bored him. To tell the truth, human beings bored him. Uncle Linn had had his brief fling with passion and lived on for such slight diversion as his business offered. With stocks and bonds, a daily game of whist at his club and here and there the purchase of a picture, he could just get by.

His in-laws were just the opposite. They never seemed to feel the need to get off into corners and hug things to themselves. Even a small desire for privacy they regarded as almost anti-social. "Tell your Aunt Dagmar, she'll be so amused," Mother was always saying to me, or "What a pretty dress, do run across the street and show it to Geraldine." To want to be alone was to be a "moper" and to break a cardinal rule, like gushing too much or whining too much or reading too much or praying too much. Excess was "sloppy," as I learned to my pain, for I was the sloppiest of the little band of cousins who bicycled in the Park and sat on the stoops in spring evenings, shouting and giggling back and forth. To me immoderation, however wicked to my uncles and aunts, contained the secret of all the delights of living. When Mother or Aunt Dagmar gave me a present, I wanted to hug them dramatically in return, and at the least bad news, or the death of anybody, I wanted to sob and sob. If I liked doing something, I wanted to go on doing it; I wanted to see Ellen Terry *every* Saturday matinee in *Cymbeline,* and I wanted to read Marion Crawford and Mrs. Humphrey Ward right through the night.

"Ida Trask," I can hear Mother saying, "don't you think you spend enough time in school without sitting all afternoon in this dark library? What are you reading? Tennyson? But all his most beautiful passages are about the out-of-doors! Aunt Sophie tells me that Geraldine is organizing a picnic supper in the Rambles. Why can't you think up things to do, like Geraldine?"

Alas, why not? Geraldine was the golden-haired darling of the block. All the grownups took an unreasoning pleasure in her sly, soft, flattering impertinence. Only to the juniors of her own sex did Geraldine allow peeps of a less lovable side of her nature, and I, being closest to her age, had the privilege of an uninterrupted view. She was always pulling my pigtails or sneering at me because she had silk stockings or real pearls and I didn't, and once, at Aunt Dagmar's Christmas party, she went so far as to push a book off a table while I was reciting *Oenone* to make me forget my lines. When she needed me, on the other hand, she could turn me into a confidante as dedicated as any in French tragedy by the simple expedient of taking me up to her bedroom and letting me try on the dresses that the indulgent Uncle Victor was always buying her. These sessions were apt to end in my doing her homework, though she was in a class above me at Miss Irvin's School.

My bitterest lesson in the art of not being "sloppy" came partly through Geraldine and partly through the death of Queen Victoria. The sunset of that long and glorious reign had cast its dramatic glow across the wintry Atlantic to our awed breakfast table, and Mother and I had followed with an absorbed interest the bulletins of the royal decline.

"I wonder if we should cancel Dagmar's birthday party," Mother said to Father on the morning of the final one. He glanced up from his paper with a faint smile.

"I should think ex-colonies are exempt from court mourning."

I would have been shocked by the idea of even a family party on so tragic a day had it not occurred to me that it would be the perfect opportunity to recite Lord Tennyson's dedication to the *Idylls of the King* which I had just learned by heart. I quickly conceived the hushed, even tearful silence that would fall over the assembled family as I rang out:

> *Break not, O woman's heart, but still endure,*
> *Break not, for thou art royal.*

Oh! In a sudden, suffocating fit of emotion, I hurried through breakfast and joined Geraldine and Elly Denison to walk to school with Miss Brown, wondering how I could get through the day and reciting the opening lines over and over with moving lips. But at school something more awe-inspiring than even Queen Victoria's death awaited me.

Miss Irvin herself was in the front hall, our large, red, bespectacled deep-voiced headmistress whose twin passions were discipline and poetry. As we passed her to enter the assembly hall for morning prayers, she touched me on the shoulder.

"Miss Gilder tells me you've learned the dedication to the *Idylls*. Do you really know it, dear?"

"Oh, yes!"

"Do you think you could recite it at assembly? Before the whole school?"

"Oh, Miss Irvin! The whole *school?*"

"You needn't if you don't want. I can read it aloud. But I thought it would be so much nicer to have it recited."

"Oh, yes! Oh, yes, please, I will!"

Miss Irvin nodded and gave me an approving smile, as if to show that we were now equals, and then led me down the aisle between the rows of seated girls to sit by her until the entire school was present. Then she rose.

"Girls, you have all heard the sad tidings about the Queen of England. She was a great sovereign and a great woman, and with her we have lost one of the most illustrious of our sex. I am now going to call upon Ida Trask to recite Lord Tennyson's dedication to the *Idylls of the King*. He dedicated them, as some of you know, to the memory of the Prince Consort, her beloved husband, whom she survived through four lonely decades."

How glad I have always been that I responded so promptly and so uncharacteristically to Miss Irvin's challenge! In a

way, the whole rest of my life has been an anticlimax. For
I never once faltered, not over a single word of that long
dedication. It rang out loud and noble and clear, from the
slow, mournful start:

> *These to His Memory — since he held them dear,*
> *Perchance as finding there unconsciously*
> *Some image of himself — I dedicate,*
> *I dedicate, I consecrate with tears —*
> *These Idylls . . .*

to the organ peal of the final words of consolation to the
royal widow:

> *The love of all thy sons encompass thee,*
> *The love of all thy daughters cherish thee,*
> *The love of all thy people comfort thee,*
> *Till God's love set thee at his side again.*

The big pale room of upturned faces ceased to have any
relation to a school. It was like a sloping field of daisies that
led my eyes away to a wild broad sea and across it to a grey,
fog-enshrouded morning on the Solent with flags at half
mast on the long line of misty ships and the muffled roll
of drums. I, Ida Trask, was at one with this somber pageant
of the death of kings. And I realized, with a perfect clarity,
then and there, that it was only by the wings of poetry that
I could be carried so far above the little world of all my
cousins. In the respectful silence that followed my recitation
I caught sight of Geraldine's face and saw that it was as awed
as even I could have wished. Miss Irvin rose and cleared her
throat.

"And now God's love *has* set her at his side again. Thank
you, Ida."

All that morning I was listless and languid in my classes.

I accepted the congratulations offered me with a weary little smile that I thought very effective. I was the great artist, exhausted by my performance and happier than I had ever been in my life.

The family were always very good about each other's accomplishments. That night, before the grownups' dinner at our house, when the children trooped into the parlor to offer their birthday greetings to Aunt Dagmar, each of my uncles and aunts congratulated me in the heartiest fashion. I was beginning to be afraid that I was preempting the attention that properly belonged to Aunt Dagmar when my father called for silence, and Geraldine opened the skits with a take-off of Maude Adams in *As You Like It*. Everyone found it terribly funny, but I knew that its only purpose was to show off Geraldine in tight pants. In the applause that followed, Mother came over to whisper to me.

"I have a birthday request from Aunt Dagmar. She would love it if you could recite 'Annabel Lee.' "

I gasped. Would they have asked Melba to sing "After the Ball"?

"Wouldn't she like the dedication? I'm all ready with it."

"It's just a bit long and sad for a birthday party, don't you think, darling? And 'Annabel Lee' is Aunt Dagmar's *favorite* poem."

" 'Favorite' or 'only'?" I retorted under my breath and walked gloomily to the middle of the room to comply. I was so indignant and disappointed, however, that I forgot my lines in the middle and had to be rescued by Mother who cried: "That's enough now, dear! We're having a soufflé, and we've just got time for two more. Elly, will you sing us 'Loch Lomond'?"

I ran up to my room, burning with humiliation, and fell sobbing on my bed. Mother this time must have sensed something of my misery, for she came upstairs after dinner before her guests had gone. Standing in the doorway, seeming even taller in her white dress, she gazed down at my sullen features with a mild reproach. Mother was not in the least feminine or soft, like Aunt Dagmar; she had a handsome, firm, rather square face and a very erect figure. But those calm, clear grey eyes were surprisingly capable of pain.

"Darling, you're not in bed."

"I'm just going."

Mother came over and sat on the edge of the bed. "You think nobody appreciates you, I know. But if you could have heard all the nice things they were saying downstairs about your recitation in school, your ears would have burned. I was so proud!"

"No, you weren't!" I cried miserably. "All you want to do is laugh at the silly things Geraldine does!"

"That's only at parties. People *like* silly things at parties."

"Well, I hate parties!"

"Hate them all you want, dear, but you must learn about them. Then they can't hurt you. Because you're my bright Ida. Ten times as bright as Geraldine ever dreamed of being. And don't worry. In the long run brightness may get you further."

I sat up suddenly and flung my arms around her neck. I must have rumpled her evening dress, but Mother knew when demonstrations had to be allowed. "But *you* like parties!"

"So will you some day."

"Never!"

"Never's a long time. You'll see."

"Never!"

I clung to her as I felt her pull away. But I knew she had to go downstairs.

"Never!" I repeated for the third time.

And I never have.

3

Ida: 1903

LIVIA TREMAIN was the maverick of Fifty-third Street. In the first place, she was not a real cousin, being only Aunt Dagmar's stepdaughter, and then she was half Italian and a Catholic and went to Mass with the maids. She had lustrous black hair and large dark eyes and had been educated — insufficiently — in a convent in New Jersey. She was pretty, in a tough, pouting way that Aunt Dagmar was afraid would not last, and stupid, in a tough, pouting way that Aunt Dagmar was afraid would. She was never in the least congenial with her stepmother or with her stepmother's family and exhibited to the adults on our block a truculence that they found very exasperating. I heard Uncle Victor once telling Mother that if she had the name of an ancient Roman, she had the character of a "wop."

Yet they tried their best with her. She was included in every party and treated like a true if difficult Denison. They planned to give her a place in New York which she could never have had without them, for despite the fact that Livia, after her brother Charley's death, was Uncle Linn's only child and presumably an heiress, the rumors about her birth did little to recommend her to the society of that day. Mother and Aunt Dagmar might have overcome the prejudice had Livia cooperated with them, but Livia had no taste for cooperation. At sixteen she tried to elope with Uncle Linn's groom and at seventeen with the boy at the desk of the Southampton Beach Club. In the latter case they got to New York before they were apprehended, and the episode was duly reported in the public prints. This settled, once and for all, the question of Livia's social career, and at nineteen she found herself isolated in a world that she had never understood, living with a stepmother who bored her and a father whom she bored, with nothing better to do of an afternoon than loll about the old playroom at Uncle Victor's where Geraldine and I did our homework, popping postcards from Aunt Sophie's collection of European royalties into the magic lantern.

Geraldine and I, however, were young enough to be impressed by her, particularly Geraldine. She and Livia were opposites in many respects, one so blond and Anglo-Saxon and generally loved, and the other so dark and Mediterranean and generally disliked, prototypes, if you will, of the heroine and villainess of Victorian fiction, but in another, more basic respect they were very much alike. Livia was redeemed in Geraldine's eyes by the very thing that damned her in those of our parents.

"Do you ever hear from Eddy?" Geraldine asked her one afternoon, looking up from the page of *Colomba* that I was helping her to translate.

Livia did not even turn her eyes from the magic lantern. "Eddy?"

"You know, the boy at Southampton. Surely you haven't forgotten him already!" Geraldine's tone wavered between incredulity and admiration.

"I don't even know where he is."

"You mean he's not at the club any more?"

"Are you kidding? Trust my old man to see *he* got the sack."

Geraldine clapped her hands. "It must be thrilling to be the cause of someone's losing his job."

"Oh, Geraldine!" I reproved her. "How can you say anything so silly? It would be horrid, and you know it."

"You!" She whirled fiercely on me. "You only say that because nobody could ever lose a job over you!" She turned back to Livia. "But would you write Eddy if you knew where he was?"

"What would I write him about? Nothing goes on around here."

"You could tell him you were thinking about him."

"Oh, *thinking.*" Livia's shrug seemed to evoke the instinct of generations of Italian lovers.

"You mean you don't even think about him?"

"No, I guess not."

"Don't you even think of the things you used to *do* with him?"

Livia turned at last from the magic lantern. "What do you mean by that?"

"I mean the things you did that night in the hotel before Uncle Linn caught you and brought you home!"

Livia frowned for a second, but then shrugged again and smiled pityingly. "Look, little girl, you're too young for that kind of talk."

"I am *not!* I'm fifteen and a whole year older than Ida, and, besides, my father's a doctor. Oh, Livia, *tell* me about you and Eddy!"

She ran across the room and sat by Livia and put an arm about her waist to coax her, and Livia smiled and kept shaking her head, but after a few minutes of this persuasion she leaned down suddenly and whispered something in Geraldine's ear which made her gasp and then burst into hysterical giggling. When she had recovered, Geraldine sent knowing glances in my direction, to tantalize me, but I had no wish to be enlightened. I knew there were two worlds, the dry, brisk daylight of my own parents and that darker, more rustling hemisphere of Livia's adventures, and if I hardly felt a member of either, at least the first was familiar. When Geraldine, irked by my seeming indifference, ran over and seized me by the shoulders to whisper something in my ear, Livia jumped up.

"Leave her be, Geraldine! She's too young!"

Geraldine, however, simply laughed shrilly and tried to force her lips into my ear. I had pushed her away and was covering my ears when Livia pulled us roughly apart.

"I said leave her be, Geraldine! Do you want to get me in trouble?"

"I'll thank you not to lay your big hands on me in *my* house!" Geraldine screamed in one of her sudden fits of temper. "I'll say what I want to whom I want when I want!"

"Not to Ida, you won't."

"Who's going to stop me?"

"I am!"

"*You!*" Geraldine was reckless in her fury. "Why your parents weren't even married when you were born!"

I gasped in horror, but Livia simply slapped her face and strode, with a last contemptuous shrug, from the room.

I had hoped that the scene would end Livia's visits to Uncle Victor's, but that slap must have satisfied her resentment, for the next day she turned up again as if nothing had happened. Geraldine, who had been terrified that her remark would be repeated to Uncle Linn, was only too willing to forget the episode. Besides, the Christmas holidays had started and her brother Scotty, who was crazy about Livia, was down from Yale, and Geraldine cared about Scotty as much as she could care for anyone. He was an amiable young man, very grave when he was grave, and very gay when he was gay, whom I worshiped in the dumb, besotted way of my fourteen years. The nicest thing about him was that he never snubbed me or his sister or tried to drag Livia away from us down to the parlor where they could be alone. He would sit in the playroom while Geraldine and I worked and laugh and make gibes at Livia to which she returned her flat retorts, accompanied by the sullen pout and repeated shrug that Mother had taught me to associate with house-maids and their followers.

"Why are you always peering into that old magic lantern?" Scotty asked her once. "Isn't it for children?"

"It may interest you to know that my *father* has a magic lantern which he's constantly looking through. It helps him to study paintings."

"Oh, I suppose it's all right for Uncle Linn. Great men have to relax with simple things. But why do you relax, Livy? Were you exhausted by your manicure this morning? Or your drive with Aunt Dagmar?"

"Pretty fresh, aren't you?" Livia said scornfully. "What do *you* do at Yale but sit around the Porcellian Club and drink whiskey and talk about girls?"

"The Porcellian Club's at Harvard, old dear."

"I'll thank you not to call me 'old dear.' Who cares where a silly boys' club is, anyway?"

"A lot of people care. Uncle Linn may not, but then he never went to college."

"No. He had to go to work to support all you Denisons!" Scotty gave a hoot of laughter. "That's what happens to 'malefactors of great wealth'!"

"*To what?*"

And so it would go, while I listened, entranced. Scotty had very ordinary American blond good looks, but to a girl of my age he was simply dazzling. Father always said that Scotty's was a tragic type because his youth would last only as long as a butterfly's and that by twenty-five he would be heavy and pompous, and I admit that Father's prediction came true, but Scotty's shining eyes continued to appeal to women long after he had passed that fatal quarter-century mark. He was desperately sincere, desperately anxious to please his own fond but rather cynical father, desperately determined to make his mark and do all the right things in the right way. When one expected him to talk about Yale and football, one was surprised to be met with a long, confidential discourse about himself and his innermost problems. Scotty had few reticences, because he could not believe that his emotional tangles were not fascinating to everyone. In my case, at least, he made no error.

He was waiting at the bottom of our stoop one afternoon when I came out on my way to his family's.

"Tell me something, Ida," he said, tucking my arm under his. "Have you any notion what Livia thinks of me?"

"Oh, does Livia think?"

"Cut it out. I mean, does she like me?"

"I thought all the family liked each other."

"Shucks, Ida, you know what I mean!"

"I guess she likes you as well as she likes Dicky or Peter."

"No more than *that?*"

I relented as he squeezed my arm. "Perhaps a little."

"Don't you think a girl *could* like me?"

I blushed furiously. "Oh, I suppose."

"Could *you*, Ida?"

"How could I like you like that?" I cried in agony and mortification. "Aren't we cousins?"

"What difference does that make?"

"Oh!" Scandalized, I escaped from his grip and ran up the stoop at Uncle Victor's as his laugh rang out below.

Sometimes his bickering with Livia took a more serious turn, and they had bad quarrels. The worst of these occurred on a rainy afternoon when he and Livia and Geraldine and I were sitting as usual in the playroom. I had been looking in the magic lantern at a postcard of Florence, and Livia, after pushing me aside and squinting at it, asked me what it was.

"Why, it's the Duomo," I said, surprised.

"Duomo?" she repeated irritably. "But that just means cathedral. I can *see* it's a cathedral."

Scotty put his eye to the glass. "But Ida's quite right. It *is* the Duomo. That's what it's called."

"*What* Duomo?"

"Why the Duomo in Florence, of course! You ought to know *that*. Weren't you born there?"

Livia flushed and looked very cross. "I haven't been there since I was a child."

Scotty, however, could be very obtuse. "But everyone knows the Duomo in Florence. It's famous, like Notre Dame or St. Peter's!"

"Well, I guess I'm nobody then!" Livia exclaimed, flaring up. "And thank you so much, Mr. Scott Denison, for taking such pains to make it clear!"

"Oh, Livy. I say! I didn't mean to hurt your feelings!"

"Of course you didn't *mean* to. None of you *mean* to. Because you don't think I have any. You all look down on me because my mother was Italian!" Livia suddenly began to sob. "And I *hate* you all so!"

I was astonished that she did not slap him as well, the way she had slapped Geraldine. She simply continued to sob until Scotty, murmuring consolations, came over to put an arm around her heaving shoulders. My hand was suddenly jerked, and Geraldine pulled me out the door and turned on me with excited eyes.

"Can't you see they want to be alone?" she hissed. "Can't you tell when you're *de trop?*"

"You mean — you mean?" I gaped. "You mean they're *in love?*" Being "in love" to me was something quite different from being "crazy about" or being "attentive to." It was a grave, grown-up thing, even a painful thing, having little relation to what I had imagined to be going on between Scotty and Livia.

"Of course they're in love, you ninny! But I'll murder you if you tell anyone!"

I was far too removed from Scotty's sphere to resent Livia as a rival. Indeed, it was actually more exciting to think of my hero as being in love. But I still found Geraldine's vicarious excitement distasteful. If she had cared more about Livia or even her brother, I could have understood, but as it was, I was sure that what she really wanted was the thrill of conspiracy.

"Why can't I tell anyone?"

"Because the family would break it up. They'd say they're too young. And, besides, they all hate Livia."

"Oh, Geraldine! Hate?"

"You know they do. Because she likes boys. Can you imagine anything so stuffy?"

I wasn't sure. It seemed to me that there might be a lot of difference between liking boys and liking Scotty. But it was Geraldine's secret, and I was honor bound by our code not to repeat it without her permission. When she had exacted the necessary pledge, she told me more. It appeared that Livia and Scotty had been corresponding regularly while he was in New Haven and had done so through Geraldine.

"Why do they have to write?" I demanded. "Don't they see each other often enough? What do they have to say?"

"Oh, all kinds of lovey-dovey things. Can't you imagine?"

I could not imagine Livia saying lovey-dovey things. But surely there was no harm in their writing, and if the overdramatic Geraldine could only be convinced of this, and in turn convince Livia, there would be no further need for secrecy and hence no need for me to feel uncomfortable about keeping it from the family. The opportunity to clear the whole thing up occurred unexpectedly one evening at Aunt Dagmar's, while she was reading aloud, as she did twice a week, to Geraldine and myself.

I always felt that Aunt Dagmar reading aloud to us would have made a charming subject for a Sargent painting. I saw it posed with Aunt Dagmar in her green velvet robe which blended with the deeper green of the huge stuffed sofa, one long white hand, thinned a bit by the artist, resting on a pillow while the other supported the book. She would be seen in profile, her best view, which brought out her exquisite aquiline nose and the fine rise of her light, greying hair, while Geraldine, with golden locks and mutely admiring eyes, would be staring up at her. But, best of all, I had fixed on a pose for myself that was bound to steal the canvas. I was to be sitting up straight in the middle of the sofa, all intense and listening, a small brown thing made interesting and perhaps even a touch sublime by her evident passion for the words being read. That day they were from *Sense and Sensibility*, which was as far as I had been able to drag my aunt and cousin up the steeps of good literature. But it was better, anyway, than *Lorna Doone*, Aunt Dagmar's favorite, and in the chapter where Elinor Dashwood assumes, on discovering that Marianne has written a letter to Willoughby, that they must be engaged, I gave a little cry of surprise.

"Is it so terrible for a girl to write a letter to a man she's not engaged to?"

Aunt Dagmar paused to consider this. "I suppose it must have been, then."

"But not today?"

"No, I don't suppose it would be so bad today."

"Would it be all right for Livia, say, to write Scotty at Yale?"

"*Does* she?"

I squirmed at the sudden pain of Geraldine's pinch. "Oh, no, I don't say that!" I exclaimed hastily. "But just supposing?"

"Yes, I think it would be all right," Aunt Dagmar replied judiciously. "Provided she didn't write so many letters that it interfered with his work. Besides, they're cousins."

"Not really," I pointed out.

"No, but for all practical purposes."

"You mean they could get *married?*" I had to move quickly to avoid Geraldine's darting hand.

"Well, I don't know about marriage," Aunt Dagmar said, frowning, "but that's not something we have to worry about for a long time yet. Scotty's only a freshman." She glanced with sudden suspicion at Geraldine and then at me. "Isn't that so, girls?"

"Oh, of course!" I agreed. "I was just thinking that Livia is like Marianne. So impulsive. And Scotty is surely as handsome as Willoughby!"

"But Scotty's a *good* boy," Aunt Dagmar insisted gravely.

"And Ida's a ninny!" Geraldine exploded at last. "As silly as Marianne and as dull as Elinor!"

"Geraldine, my *dear!*" Aunt Dagmar was starting to talk on the odiousness of comparisons, particularly of Geraldine's, when she was interrupted by the arrival of Mother to take me home. They always had a few words to say to each other first, and Geraldine and I were sent out to the landing. There she turned on me furiously.

"You dirty sneak!" she started right off. "Now see what you've done!"

"I only wanted to find out if it was all right for Livia to write Scotty!" I protested. "And now you see it is! So we don't have to be secret about it any more."

"That's all *you* know!" Geraldine retorted. "You've roused all Aunt Dagmar's suspicions. She was pumping you, but,

like an idiot, you couldn't see it. You'd have blabbed out
everything if I hadn't pinched you!"

"Everything?"

"Well, you may as well know it: they *are* going to get
married! Now do you see the importance of keeping your
big mouth shut?"

I stared in consternation. "They are? Oh, Geraldine,
shouldn't we tell?"

"If you do, I'll never speak to you again in my whole
life!"

"But what if it's wrong . . . ?"

"Wrong?" she interrupted me with a bitter sneer. "Wrong
for you, you mean. Because you're jealous. You're jealous of
Livia! You want Scotty all for your own dirty private
dreams!"

I flushed and turned quickly away. Yet to be accused of a
grown-up emotion like jealousy gave me a little throb of
elation. For to be recognized as having a stake, however
small, in Scotty — was that not to be recognized as a woman?
Just for a moment I trembled at the excitement of my vision,
just for a moment, before the great shadowy owl of shame at
my own presumption glided down to overwhelm me. I turned
back to Geraldine, resolved to do anything in expiation.

"All right," I said grimly. "I'll be quiet. You have my
word."

Geraldine surveyed me appraisingly. "Will you help?"

"Try me and see."

"Tiptoe over to the door, then, and tell me what they're
saying."

I hated to eavesdrop, particularly on Mother, but I had
given my word, and I tiptoed, sick at heart, to the door.

"She's doing it out of revenge, you can be sure of that,"
I heard Mother say. "It's her obvious way to get back at us
all. I don't say it's planned out. I say it's instinctive."

"But you're so suspicious, Lily. You've always been suspicious."

"And I've been right as many times as I've been wrong. You'll have to admit that!"

I heard Aunt Dagmar sigh and the scrape of Mother's chair on the floor as she rose. I hurried back to Geraldine.

"Well?"

"They were talking about some lady who's out for revenge. They weren't talking about Livia and Scotty at all."

"You're sure?"

"Oh, sure."

And I was. It never occurred to me that anyone of my generation, even one as much older as Livia, could be a subject of such adult concern. Geraldine, impressed that I had shown the courage to eavesdrop, revealed the next day that Livia and Scotty were planning to elope and, after a civil wedding, to come back and throw themselves on the generosity of their fathers.

"But what about Yale?" I protested, scandalized. "Will he be able to go back to Yale?"

"Would that be the end of the world? He can go to work for Uncle Linn and make oodles of money!"

I knew there was no point discussing it further with Geraldine, and I turned away from her in dumb dismay. My father and all Mother's brothers had been to Yale; it was a thing that happened to men, like shaving and going "downtown." Uncle Linn, of course, had not, but then Uncle Linn was a "great man," an exotic figure, like a President, to whom a log cabin or a charge up San Juan Hill were equally permissible. I felt the quickened heartbeat of my adventurousness, the nervous excitement of being suddenly allied with Geraldine and Livia against the family and Yale. But being allied with Geraldine and Livia also involved being allied with the smothered giggles and smacking sounds that occurred behind the closed door if Livia and Scotty were left alone, and I flushed deeply at the thought of what my shame and humiliation would be if Mother's grey, reproachful eyes should ever be fixed on me with the knowledge of what I had concealed.

I couldn't sleep. I couldn't do my homework, much less Geraldine's. The remarkable power of the united adult world in our block was that it seemed to draw forth revelations without even soliciting them. Geraldine, for example, knew that I was wobbly, yet she still told me things. And I, while determined to honor my word, was still too wretched not to seek assurance, from the very persons from whom the secret was to be kept, that it need not be a secret at all.

My little brother, Christopher, had had a bad throat that week, and Mother had been too preoccupied to notice that I had something on my mind. But towards the weekend, when he was better, her normal perceptiveness returned. As she was putting place cards on the dining room table one evening, I followed her restlessly about.

"Mother, is it really so important for boys to go to college?"

"What sort of boys?"

"Oh, boys like Dicky and Peter Denison." I paused. "And Scotty."

"Well, if they want to get ahead in life, it is."

"But Uncle Linn never went to college, and *he* got ahead."

"Yes, that's perfectly true," Mother conceded, pausing to pick up two cards that evidently would not go together. "But those were different times. Besides, Uncle Linn lived in Italy, and that was almost as good as going to college."

"Why?"

"Because it has so many museums and picture galleries."

I considered her theory and rejected it. After all, she was not really meeting the point I wanted to make. To get ahead a young man was supposed to go to college and not to marry until he had graduated.

"But Uncle Linn got married in Italy, didn't he?"

"What has that to do with it?"

"Did *his* wife keep him from getting ahead?"

"No, she died before . . ." Mother stopped herself. She had spoken too fast, and now, of course, she would have to cover up. "I daresay she was very sweet, but not the kind of woman who would be a help to a man in New York. Of course, she was Italian."

"So is Livia!"

"Only half. Besides, Livia was brought up here."

"You mean Livia *wouldn't* keep a man from getting ahead?"

Mother gave me a brief glance. She was much too smart to think that any child on the block was unaware of the family attitude towards Livia, but she was not going to let me trick her into admitting it. That was the eternal game between grownups and children. But at least Mother knew it was a game and minded the rules. "Livia has a bit of growing up to do," she observed in a more judicial tone. "One of these days she's going to discover that life is a great deal easier for girls who try to make people like them."

"Then will she be able to help a man get ahead?"

"Then perhaps she will."

"Even a man who hasn't finished college?"

I remembered afterwards that Mother had stopped placing her cards and was gazing at the middle of the table. It should have been my warning. "A man?" she queried. "I thought we were talking about boys. What sort of a man?"

"Oh, a man or a boy, what's the difference?" I shrugged. "Like Uncle Victor or Scotty. Or even Father."

"You've mentioned Scotty twice now," Mother said sharply, turning to me abruptly and putting down her cards. "Is there something between Livia and Scotty that Aunt Dagmar ought to know about?"

"Oh, no, not at all, how can you *think* so?"

"Come with me, Ida." Mother took me down the hall into the parlor and closed the door so that no maid could hear. "It happens to be your misfortune that you're a very bad liar. Now tell me what this nonsense is all about."

"Oh, Mother, I can't!"

"You can't? What do you mean, you can't?"

"Because I gave my word of honor!"

"Your word of *honor?*" Mother's tall, indignant figure loomed over me, and I felt shriveled and shabby. "How could you give your word of honor not to tell Uncle Linn and Aunt Dagmar something that vitally concerns them? Or something that vitally concerns Uncle Victor and Aunt Sophie? What sort of honor is that?"

"*My* honor. And Geraldine's honor."

"Honor! When Aunt Dagmar gave us the very house we live in? Not to mention your pony and all those matinees at Ellen Terry."

"Oh, I know, I know!" I wailed wretchedly.

"It's not, of course, that Aunt Dagmar *expects* anything in return," Mother continued remorselessly. "What she does, she does out of pure love and kindness. But don't you think we might at least *try* to do something for her in return? Don't you think we might help her in the difficult job of being a good stepmother? Must we all stand by and see two silly children like Livia and Scotty ruin their lives because Ida Trask has to hug her sacred 'honor' to her bosom?"

Even when I felt I was right, I could never stand up to Mother when she was angry. As it was, my collapse was total, physical as well as spiritual. I fell on the sofa and wept and told her everything, in a wonderful orgy of confession. I felt my breath coming back as the facts tumbled out before Mother's expressionless stare, and when I had completed the sorry tale there remained for me only to grovel in the ultimate humiliation of begging:

"You won't tell anyone I told?"

"Not if I can help it."

"You promise?"

"I don't have to promise, Ida. I said I wouldn't. But you can congratulate yourself that you've saved your cousin Scotty from blasting his career before it's even started."

"And what about Livia?"

"Livia?" Mother for the first time betrayed the full extent of her contempt. "Girls like Livia should be put away in homes!"

"Homes? Whose homes?"

"Well, not ours! But never mind about that. I've got to go and see Uncle Victor."

My family operated with speed in a crisis, and the very next day Scotty arrived from New Haven, and drama throbbed behind the closed curtains of Uncle Victor's house. Geraldine hurried over to tell me in awed tones of the great happenings; she enjoyed the climax of disrupted plans quite as much as she would ever have thrilled at their fruition. It seemed that Uncle Victor and Scotty had been closeted for two hours in the former's office, that Uncle Linn Tremain alone had been admitted, and he only for a brief visit. Geraldine had tried to listen at the doorway and been discovered and banished by her horrified mother, but not before she had distinctly heard the sounds of Scotty's sobbing. Across the street, Livia had been confined to her room and allowed to see nobody. Geraldine never once accused me of treason, as Mother had let it out that a friend of Scotty's at Yale, in a fit of conscientiousness, had divulged the secret to Uncle Victor. I had to bear my new and now seemingly intolerable load of remorse alone.

But worse was to come. The next day was Sunday, and as Mother and Father were lunching out, I was sent, in the usual way, to Uncle Victor's where I had to sit through a somber meal with Scotty and Geraldine and their parents. I found myself a bit embarrassed for Scotty, who made so little effort to conceal the ravages of his emotional crisis. His eyes were red and tearstained, and his shoulders from time to time shook with a dry sob. Decidedly, there was nothing stiff about his upper lip, but I reminded myself that Frenchmen, even as soldiers, were not ashamed to cry, and I would have indulged in the warmest fantasies of consoling him had I not been haunted by the terrible vision of what his feelings would have been had he known the identity of his betrayer.

Uncle Victor did not share my attempted tolerance for such emotionalism. He was obviously disgusted with his son, who, even to my admiring eyes, seemed crude and juvenile beside the long grey elegance of the paternal figure. After a particularly gulping sob Uncle Victor slapped the table.

"If you can't control yourself, please go to your room. What a spectacle for the girls."

"The girls know perfectly well how I feel!" Scotty exclaimed, glaring at his father with suddenly rekindled rebellion. "And why shouldn't they? Would you want to have them think I can give up Livy without a pang?"

"You might try at least not to be such a baby."

"Victor," Aunt Sophie protested. "Haven't you been hard enough on him for one day?"

"Daddy expects me to tear a girl out of my heart as easily as . . . well, as easily as I'd pluck a flower out of my buttonhole."

"That will be enough, Scott!" Uncle Victor's drooping eyelid fluttered in indignation. "You will forgive me if I fail to plumb the depths of an emotion that can express itself in such stale images. You may leave the table. But please remember you're taking the three o'clock for New Haven and that I want to see you in my office first."

Scotty stamped out of the room, and his mother quietly followed.

"Sophie!" Uncle Victor called sternly after her, but for once in her life she ignored him.

"Daddy, what did you *do* to him?" Geraldine demanded excitely. "How did you ever make him give her up?"

I imagine that she and I owed the revelation that followed to Uncle Victor's irritation at the independence of his usually submissive spouse and his consequent need to justify himself, even to a jury of two young girls.

"I didn't *do* anything," he replied testily. "It was only necessary for Uncle Linn to convince your impetuous brother that his bride would be disinherited if she married him. As Scott is hardly in a position to support her himself, what could he do but give her up?"

"He could have quit college and taken a job!" Geraldine cried stoutly.

Uncle Victor's eyes rested on her for a quizzical moment. "Which is exactly what he offered to do," he replied with an ominous moderation of tone. "And that is what we discussed this morning. I told him that if he left Yale, *I* should disinherit him. Which would have meant, of course, that he would be asking Livia to starve with him. Your brother may have acted like an ass, Geraldine, but he's still a gentleman. He saw, of course, that he had to give her up. For her sake, if not his own."

"But what about her?" Geraldine cried. "What did she say?"

"Oh, she was all for taking her chances with Scott." Uncle Victor's shrug contained no hint of admiration at such a choice. "She was all for love or a world well lost. No doubt it's her warm Mediterranean blood."

"I think that's magnificent!"

"Do you? Do you, really?" Uncle Victor was icy. "Perhaps

you will understand one day that all grownups can do for youth is to protect it from irrevocable decisions."

"But *you* could have supported them!"

"Support Scott and that . . . !" Uncle Victor stopped himself in time and flung down his napkin impatiently as he rose from the table. "Try not to be more of a goose, Geraldine, than God made you."

My last sight of Livia for decades was in the evening of that same Sunday when Mother sent me to Aunt Dagmar's to return the last R. W. Chambers novel which she had borrowed. Stride, the old butler, let me in, and I ran, as I always did, up the circular marble stairway with the low, pink steps, but I stopped abruptly on the landing when I heard Livia's voice from the parlor. She was shouting at the top of her lungs, and the raucous sound that throbbed in the air and hurled itself against the great tapestry of the marriage of the Emperor Maximilian was as shocking in that still, ordered house as the bursting of a sewer pipe. I made out that she was addressing her father.

"But I promise you one thing! As soon as I get my hands on any money of my own — and I will one day — I'll pay you back for every bloody cent you've ever spent on me. As for *your* money, you can keep it. I don't want it! You can give it to *her*. All I ask of either of you is that you send me away where I'll never see you again!"

I crept to the door and peered into the big, dark room. Aunt Dagmar was standing before the fireplace, looking into the fire. As I watched, she took the poker and moved one of the logs. Uncle Linn was sitting in a high-backed chair, his hands clasped to the arms, also looking into the fire. Neither seemed to be paying the least attention to the ranting, gesticulating maenad in the middle of the room. She might have been a singer who was being tried out for an evening party and whom they had already decided would not do. In

my misery and pity I turned and fled down the stairs to the
front door, thrusting the novel I had come to return in the
hands of the silent but comprehending Stride.

After that terrible Sunday life resumed, at least for the
non-guilt ridden, its normal course. Livia was sent off on
a trip to Europe with Uncle Linn's sister, Miss Tremain, a
sober, severe, dark-garbed figure from whom she ultimately
escaped with the aid of her first husband, their Italian
courier. Scotty went back to New Haven and was allowed
no weekends in New York for a year. And I was left with
my tortured doubts as to whether it was jealousy or spite or
simple weakmindedness that had induced me for the first
time to put my hand into the spinning wheel of life on our
street and bring it, however briefly, to a halt. Nobody suspected my anguish. Mother had too little time for the immediate past to conceive what I was enduring. I knew of no
outlet but confession and nobody to whom I could confess
but Geraldine. One afternoon, when she had asked me up
to her room to see a new dress, I grimly decided that my
moment had come, only to discover that it had already passed.

"Geraldine," I began somberly, "I have something to tell
you. Something that will make you despise me forever!"

"You don't like my dress?"

"No. It was I who told on Scotty."

"Mummy says I shouldn't wear gold because of my hair.
But I think it's fun every now and then to overwhelm people.
Don't you?"

"Geraldine!" I exclaimed. "Listen to me! I was the one
who told about Livia and Scotty."

"And just like you, too," she said indifferently, holding the
dress up to her neck and shoulders and gazing affectionately
at the image in the mirror. "You always were the most filthy
sneak."

"But you don't understand!" I was determined to reap my just punishment. "They'd be married now if it hadn't been for me."

Geraldine turned to stare at me for a moment. "Yes," she said, taking it in at last, "I suppose they might be. Well, that's one good turn you did. In spite of yourself!"

"A *good* turn?"

"Certainly. Don't gape so. It makes you look like a frog." Geraldine resumed her contemplation of herself. "Daddy was right about all that. Livia is common."

I bowed before the bleak finality of the term. We had all been brought up on the creed that Venus herself would have been impotent before it. "But mightn't she have learned?" I faltered.

"You can't learn not to be common," Geraldine retorted. "She'd have dragged Scotty down to her level." I recognized Uncle Victor's phrase. "And they'd never have had any money, either. Uncle Linn isn't the kind to forgive. Besides, he doesn't like Livia. After all, he wasn't even *married* when she was born."

And so I discovered that whichever way I turned, matters came out for the best. Or for what my family thought the best. Sometimes it seemed to me that they were the universe and I a passively observing atom with no power to affect what it observed. At other moments, with the raw egotism that underlies shyness, it occurred to me that I might have been the sole reality and the family, in fact the whole Fifty-third Street world, the simple product of my fancy. For if I had no power to affect, I could still be affected. If Scotty and Livia managed not to influence each other's lives, they both still influenced mine.

That neither, unlike myself, was really malleable was borne out by their subsequent histories. Had they married each other, briefly or not, it would have made little difference in their patterns. Scotty never finished Yale; he left in his junior year to marry into the chorus of *Daisy, Daisy,* and, after an expensive annulment, became a customer's man in Tremain & Dodge. He married twice more, once to a beautiful woman who was unfaithful to him and then to a plainer and richer one who was not. He became a famous figure on Long Island as perpetual president of the Glenville Golf and Tennis Club, which he managed with loving efficiency and at whose bar his widening figure was a symbol of cheer and hospitality until his death there of a stroke in his early fifties. Livia exceeded him in marriages. She became a wife four times, always in Europe, and her last husband was a German count who put her eye out in a fist fight. Uncle Linn left his money to Aunt Dagmar for life and then to Columbia, but the trust fund that he had earlier set up for Livia was enough to keep her in minor titles. I met her on the street shortly before Geraldine's death, almost half a century after the episode with Scotty, and I did not at first recognize her. She was dressed smartly in black and was very thin and elongated. Her hair was purple, and her nose had a large but elegant hook. She stopped and put a hand on my arm and murmured in a low, throaty tone: "Don't you know me, Ida? I'd know *you* anywhere."

"Livia!"

"I've been to the dogs since last we met, but I've come back. Could we lunch, dearie?"

We lunched, of course, and talked, as might have been expected, exclusively of the past. It fascinated me that Livia should have done with it just the opposite of what Geraldine had done. Where the latter, in her last years, had turned it over and over in her memory to detect new slights and injustices on which to blame the whole sad collapse of her present, Livia preferred to see it as a garden of lost innocence down whose ordered and brightly colored paths she delighted, as an old woman, to stroll. She talked of Aunt Dagmar and her father and Uncle Victor and Aunt Sophie and my parents as if they were characters in a big crowded, lovable, moralizing Victorian novel that one had adored reading in school. She made them seem even further back in the past than they actually had been; they stood up in her conversation as quaint and stiff as figures in daguerrotype. They were more loving, more kindly, more strict, more righteous, than their originals. Livia had had to construct in her fantasy a Fifty-third Street world from whose too tight embrace she, a bright, hopeless, fascinating, doomed maverick, had been compelled to flee. "I had my own little benighted wings," she told me in that voice of semi-cultivation that is often developed by a life of sin, "and I had to try to soar." It was her revenge on a world of Denisons to have turned it into a fairy tale.

4

Ida: 1904

THERE WAS only one other person on my small horizon, besides Livia, who resisted the organizing influences of Fifty-third Street, and that was my father's mother, Grandma Trask. But where Livia had been unquestionably wicked, Grandma was unquestionably good, and it was therefore conceivable that one might attain a species of independence under her proud little banner, if only in the privilege of being able to take sides, on rare occasions, with a relative who was not related, at least by blood, to one's mother and who disagreed with her in every known particular. The trouble with Grandma, unfortunately, was that she never seemed to take notice of her would-be allies, particularly when they were girls of a rather gushing fifteen. She was a small, immaculate, formal woman with a high, lustrous, black wig and a face that was like a white mask of frozen features, without a single line or wrinkle. Everyone always said that she had been a great beauty, and I can imagine that those large, clear, still, blue eyes, however chilling to importunate grandchildren, must have been alluring to young officers in days of civil war. Mother and Father took me to see her every Sunday in the neat, still brownstone house on Brooklyn Heights where she lived with two maids and four cats, and although the cookies at tea had no icing and her anecdotes were repeated with the Sunday and season, like lessons in church, I was awed by the grave dignity which made her seem as "difficult" and "special" as I thought grownups should be. It was hard for me to believe that she had a weekday existence.

I have since understood that her special quality for me consisted more in what she was not than in what she was. She was *not* a Denison, and hence belonged to none of the cousins in Fifty-third Street. When she came to Aunt Dagmar's on Thanksgiving and Christmas in black lace with long pendant diamond earrings, walking in measured steps, a Chinese shawl, symbol of festivity, wrapped tightly about her trim little figure, her eyes fixed gravely in turn on each member of her daughter-in-law's large family, I felt as proud of her as if she had been some Oriental princess or dowager empress come to shed a patch of her glamour on her admiring granddaughter. I could not see that my cousins were laughing behind their hands at her wig or that poor Grandma's plain, literal turn of mind and total lack of humor insulated her from the other adults much as deafness isolates its victim from the cheer of a family board. All I could see was that my maternal aunts and uncles made a great fuss over her, and that some of that fuss seemed to contribute to my own puny stature. Geraldine might have long, braided hair and her brother Scotty a real pearl stickpin, but I was the only one to boast a Grandma Trask!

My pleasure in Grandma's rather stately appearances at Aunt Dagmar's was further enhanced by knowing, from Mother's and Father's conversation at home, that she had but a small opinion of Mother's relations. To Grandma, apparently, the Denisons were a pushing lot who had taken possession of her only son and dragged him from a Brooklyn that had been good enough for his parents. To that "unseemly scuttle across the East River" she ascribed each subsequent disaster, from Father's failure to do better in his trust company to the early failure of his liver. Mother used to say that Grandma condemned in the Denisons the very qualities of gaiety and openheartedness that she had distrusted but never dared to criticize in her own husband. Grandpa Trask, it seemed, by dying young, had become sanctified and was now mourned in the perennial black and evoked by the host of relics required by a Victorian tradition.

Mourning, however, to Grandma's generation, was too common to be always associated with gloom, and she led a brisk, busy life which included an annual trip to Europe with her old and good friends, the Jerome Robbinses. She and the Robbinses departed and returned each year, as closely as possible, on the same day. They went to London where they stayed at Brown's Hotel and to Paris where they stayed at the Vendôme, always in the same rooms. The only variety in their trips was in the different watering places which they visited in their long and ultimately vain effort to restore Mrs. Robbins' flagging health. The family joke used to be that Mr. Robbins had never seen Europe except with his back to the horse, as he always occupied the seat facing his wife and her devoted companion.

When Mrs. Robbins finally succumbed, early one spring, to the ailments that had so stubbornly resisted every spa, Grandma's trip to Europe was canceled for the first time since the Franco-Prussian War. All the next winter she grumbled about the inconvenience that her friend had caused her, and as another Europeless summer loomed, her plight seemed pitiable indeed.

"It seems such a shame," Mother said one night at supper when Father had just returned from a visit to Brooklyn. "Why on earth shouldn't your mother and Mr. Robbins go to Europe together as they always have?"

"But they are."

"They *are?*"

"Certainly." Father glanced at me for a second, and I thought he was about to wink. "As you say, why shouldn't they?"

"Well —" Mother's eye also fell on me, and she was silent, but it was the silence of deep reflection. "It's really only the boat, I suppose, that makes any matter. There's something about two at a table that looks so . . . so connubial."

"And think of those deck chairs, side by side," Father continued with a small smile. "And down in the hold, Vuitton trunk by Vuitton trunk."

"Ida," Mother said suddenly, "how should you like to go over with your grandmother this year? You could join us in Baden-Baden. Wouldn't it be fun to be on your own for a bit?"

"Oh, Mother!" I cried, breathless with excitement.

"Come now, Lily," my father protested, "if Mother needs a chaperon, we'll *all* go with her. I won't send a fifteen-year-old girl to do our job."

"Who said anything about a chaperon? I never heard anything so absurd. I simply thought it would be nice for your mother and Ida to have a chance to get to really know each other. Besides, your mother's not going till the end of June, and we're supposed to join the Herndons at Genoa on the eighteenth."

I could hardly believe anything so tremendous was going to occur, that something wouldn't happen to prevent it, such as Grandma's getting ill, or even dying, like poor Mrs. Robbins. There was not only the excitement of going abroad with Grandma, which held infinite possibilities in its sheer novelty, but there was the excitement of being left alone with Christopher and his nurse and the maids during the two weeks between Mother's and Father's sailing and Grandma's. It was one of the nicest things about Mother that she always understood and never resented such feelings.

"You must run the house so well," she told me, "that when Aunt Dagmar comes in the afternoon to check up, you can give her tea like a lady and have nothing to do but gossip!"

So occupied was I at home that it was not until the afternoon of my departure, when Aunt Dagmar took me down to the big, white, clean Cunarder to meet Grandma, that the full strangeness of the forthcoming trip burst upon me. Nobody had told me that Mother, in one of her economizing moments, had prevailed upon Grandma to share her cabin with me! When the whistle blew, and Aunt Dagmar left us, Grandma and I stared at each other suddenly like two children at a party who have been told to make friends.

"Come, Ida," she said at last in her flat tone, "we must go up on deck and wave goodbye to the Statue of Liberty."

Up in the air and the sudden sea breeze Mr. Robbins joined us in what I remember as a captain's cap (I don't know why he was entitled to it) and pumped my hand and let me look at the boats in the harbor through a huge black pair of binoculars. Later, at dinner, when I was allowed a glass of champagne, I began to feel, a bit giddily, that the trip might work out, after all. If it only hadn't been for sharing that cabin! I doubt if any bride ever approached the nuptial chamber with more apprehension than I approached Grandma's that night. Would I have to witness the dismantling of the famous wig? Or did she sleep in it? Once again it was Grandma who took the initiative. Poor woman, she must have dreaded that moment as much as I.

"You will get ready for bed first, Ida. In the bathroom. Take your things."

When I came out, I saw to my astonishment that Grandma, using a sheet and several towels with the dexterity of an accomplished seamstress, had hooked up a little tent that enshrouded her dressing table. She remained within its protective cover long after I had gone to bed, with only a muffled lamp, and I was beginning to wonder if she was going to sleep there, when the sheet was finally pulled back and Grandma emerged, like a sheik, in a big white cap and a billowing white wrapper, more clothed than when she had gone in. I sighed in relief and went to sleep. The trip had started well.

Mr. Robbins walked me around the deck in the morning and every morning thereafter. He was a short man with very short legs, a high bald dome and a long nose that gave him a rather intellectual appearance in contrast to his bright, natty clothes. He walked fast and talked briskly and wore a pince-nez with a flowing ribbon. He ran a streetcar company in New York and used to hold forth with great knowledge, but rather fatiguingly, about the transit problems of the city. He was the most impersonal man I have ever known; I doubt if there was much difference between his conversations with me and those with my grandmother or any other of his fellow passengers. I remember his telling an anecdote about the construction of the Third Avenue Elevated to a gentleman who simply walked away in the middle of it. Mr. Robbins, nothing daunted, perhaps not even noticing, completed the anecdote to the next gentleman who greeted him. Mother used to say that his habit of talking for his own benefit came from years of traveling with two women who never listened to him. But I was flattered to be treated as a grownup and considered boredom a perfectly reasonable price. Besides, Mr. Robbins bought me a small present every morning after our walk at the ship's store.

In the dining room we sat at a table for three, and at dinner Mr. Robbins would drink a great deal of champagne, very fast, throwing his head back as if he were gargling, which he said was the only way to drink it. He would then become rather disputatious and take evident pleasure in seeking to disillusion Grandma about the financial leaders of the era, in whose reputations for wisdom and generosity she had a persistent, peasantlike faith.

"Jim Herndon!" he would exclaim, naming the railroad executive whose yacht Mother and Father had boarded at Genoa. "Don't talk to me about Jim Herndon! I was a director of the Rhode Island Shore Line when he took over. Of course, he expected to find us a bunch of rubber stamps. Quite!" Here Mr. Robbins took another gulp of champagne. "Well, your friend Jay Robbins set him straight on that one. Oh, my yes! When I found what he was doing with our preferred stock, I said: 'Mr. Herndon, is it your intention to loot the company?' Well, he frowned and blustered like Jove, but when he learned that I was going to lay the minutes of the meeting before the Attorney General, I can tell you his voice became sweet as honey. "Perhaps you and I can have a little talk, Mr. Robbins.' 'Certainly, Mr. Herndon,' I said, 'we can have that little talk right here before the board. Unless you'd prefer to ask the Attorney General in now?' Well, you should have seen him back down. You should have heard his 'Yes, Mr. Robbins' and 'No, Mr. Robbins'! He knew when he had an honest man to deal with!"

"But you didn't remain on that board long, did you?" Grandma observed dryly.

"Of course I didn't!" Mr. Robbins retorted, banging down his glass on the table. "I tell you, Herndon wanted rubber stamps. He got rid of me as soon as he dared. But as long as I was on that board, he didn't loot that company, I can promise you that!"

"He probably had no intention of doing anything of the kind. You probably simply misunderstood him."

"Amelie!" Mr. Robbins retorted in high exasperation. "You don't know anything about business!"

"I may not know anything about business, but I think I know something about people. Mr. Herndon happens to be a friend of my son's. As a matter of fact, Gerald and Lily are guests on his yacht in the Mediterranean at this very moment. I hardly think that a son of mine would care to travel with a man who 'looted' companies."

"What does Gerald know about business? Gerald's a trust

officer. In the crowd he and Lily play with, all that matters is how big a house a man has and how good a dinner he serves. What's it to them if he's a crook?"

"A *crook,* did you say? You insinuate that *my* son is on board the yacht of a crook?"

"If he's on Herndon's yacht, he is."

And so it went, back and forth, until Grandma made her stately withdrawal, after a single demitasse in the lounge. It was apparent even to me that they enjoyed these arguments. In the morning, meek once more, Mr. Robbins would mumble apologies for the champagne-incited rebellion of the previous night, and Grandma would nod, rather ungraciously, as if she had expected it all along. But I am afraid that she admired Mr. Herndon, whom she did not even know, more than she did Mr. Robbins. The latter was a small tycoon in an age of titans, and Grandma believed in titans.

It was unfortunate for Grandma that Florence Polhemus should have been on board. Miss Polhemus was the person she most respected in the world. She lived in Pierrepont Place in a square brownstone three-storied box with red velvet curtains looped over the windows so as almost to exclude the beautiful view of the East River. She had never married, according to legend, because of insanity in her family. She was very sweet, in a mechanical, repetitious way, and Mother always said that she was pretty, though it seemed to me an absurd term to use in relation to a woman past her seventieth year. Whenever I met Miss Polhemus at Grandma's, she told me that she, too, would have been an Ida, named for her mother, but for the circumstance of her birth in the capital of Tuscany where her father had been minister.

"Why does she always tell me the same thing?" I asked Grandma once.

"Because you always have the same name."

"But doesn't she remember she's told me before? She can't be very intelligent."

"You mustn't say that about Miss Polhemus," Grandma reproved me. "She has a million dollars."

How I remember Grandma's tone as she said that! For her there was no need of hypocrisy. When I think what pains Mother and all the Denisons took to emphasize the homely virtues of their rich friends and to praise the little-known acts of generosity and kindness for which they *really* loved them, I cannot but admire the simplicity of Grandma's attitude with its suggestion of an unsophisticated, unashamed early New York reverence for birth and property. The Polhemuses had outranked the Trasks in Brooklyn at the time of Grandma's marriage, and for her they always would. She would no more have considered herself the equal of her spinster friend because she had married and became a mother than would a matron of the court of Louis XV have presumed that her fecundity had placed her any nearer to the virgin daughters of France.

While making my tour of the deck with Mr. Robbins on the third morning out we encountered Miss Polhemus. She had evidently been ill, for it was her first appearance on deck, and her maid was tucking her into a chair. She stared at us blankly as we approached her chair and then gave a sudden little cry.

"Why, Jerome Robbins. I had no idea *you* were on board!"

"But I go every year on the *Mauritania*."

"You *did*. Of course, I know you *did*. But I didn't know you still do."

"That's my biography, Florence. I did, and I still do. And I shall continue, so help me, for the little time I may be spared."

I always minded when old people talked of the little time they had left. One of the things that I liked about Grandma was that she never did. Mr. Robbins and Miss Polhemus continued chatting for several minutes while I turned away to the railing. When she called me back, I thought she seemed flushed and excited.

"How is your grandmother, Ida?"

"Very well. Have you been seasick?"

"No, I have *not* been seasick," Miss Polhemus responded in a very definite tone. "I'm as old a sailor as your grandmother. Will you tell her that I shall wait upon her in her stateroom tonight if she is free?"

"Oh, I guess she's free now."

"I said tonight, my dear," Miss Polhemus insisted with a hint of mild correction. "I have no wish to intrude upon her while there are other calls on her time."

She nodded rather frostily to Mr. Robbins, but I did not know why until that night when I had gone to bed and Grandma received her visitor. They sat at the far end of the cabin, and spoke in hushed tones, but I could hear them distinctly.

"You must have been *so* upset when you discovered Jerome Robbins on the boat," Florence Polhemus began.

"Upset? Why should I have been upset?"

"Well, of course, nobody could think for a minute that you *arranged* it. I don't mean that. But in view of all the years that you and Carrie and he went abroad together — well, let us say it has an unfortunate appearance."

I remember distinctly that there was not even a hint of unpleasantness in Miss Polhemus' tone. There was an invincible sweetness about her, an unsurmountable attitude that one must, of course, agree with her, before which my poor grandmother could only crumble.

"How *does* it appear?"

"Surely, Amelie, you don't need an old maid to explain such things?"

"You mean that anyone could possibly think —!"

I shut my eyes quickly as both heads turned on the same impulse to make sure I was asleep.

"I have never considered what it is that people think," Miss Polhemus continued serenely. "I was brought up to believe that certain things looked badly and certain things looked well. *Why* they looked badly or well was never the point."

"You mean it's as bad for a woman my age to go to Europe with an old man as it would be for two young people?"

"Worse! A woman your age should know better!"

"Now, Florence, you're being absurd! Don't you know that after seventy there are things —?"

"Please, Amelie. I'd rather *not* know!"

"But, my dear, it's too ridiculous. I suppose I should be flattered!"

"*Amelie!*"

In the pause that followed, Miss Polhemus must have stared my grandmother down, for when she spoke again it was in an even sweeter, firmer tone.

"I came in tonight as a friend, as I'm sure you recognize. And I know you'll take my advice, as I would take yours. Isn't that the way things have always been between us?"

"I suppose so," Grandma answered sulkily. "But what can I do about it now? Get off in a lifeboat?"

"You should do nothing that would attract the least attention. But you and Jerome must not stay at the same hotel. And you must not allow him to handle your passport or to make the arrangements about your luggage. If he dines with you in Paris, you must have Ida with you. You must never travel on the same train, and you must return on different boats."

"But I'll have to rearrange everything!" Grandma protested with a wail.

"That, my dear, is a mere detail," Miss Polhemus said, rising.

When she had gone, I realized how much she had upset her friend. For Grandma had actually commenced her preparations for the removal of the famous wig without first erecting the protective tent! She brought out a small wooden stand, evidently to place it on, and two little silver brushes. I realized in sudden fascination and horror that there must be a whole nocturnal ceremony of brushing, adorning, perhaps even washing the wretched thing, and that it was to be my awe-inspiring privilege to be a witness. I closed my eyes just in time as Grandma turned sharply around to check on me again, and I did not reopen them until the dread business of dismantlement was already in process. Grandma, using all ten fingers, slowly raised the wig, held it for a second above her head to be sure that it was clear and then moved it to the stand and started to work on it busily with both little brushes. What appalled me most, as it had appalled the witnesses to the execution of Mary Stuart, was not to find that she had *no* hair, but to see instead the long, sad, thin, grey wisps. Grandma's profile seemed suddenly that of a very old and broken woman, an impression created not only by the grey wisps but by the unaccountable and dismal fact that she was weeping. Grandma was actually weeping! It was not that I thought of her as hard, but simply as a being with whom tears had no known relation. And now, like a child, she was weeping at the disruption of her plans, at the break in a pattern that was probably the only thing that made sense out of the chaos of her widowhood. I ached to run over and fling my arms about her, but I knew that she would never forgive me for seeing her so exposed. I could only lie there miserably and watch that sobbing figure brushing fiercely at the high pile of shiny black locks in front of her. And when she had finished and dabbed her eyes with the corner of a handkerchief, I found she had still another surprise in store for me. She put on a nightcap that had locks of sewn-in black curls along its border! Grandma was now ready for every contingency of marine disaster.

In the morning she seemed herself again, except that she was more preoccupied than usual at breakfast. When I was about to leave the table, she put her hand suddenly on my arm and asked me in a very grave tone: "Tell me something, Ida. Should you mind terribly spending three weeks in Paris before joining your mother and father in Baden-Baden?"

I hesitated unhappily. The novelty of being with Grandma had begun to wear off, and I was already homesick for my parents. But I remembered what Miss Polhemus had said about the value of my company to Grandma, and I hated to disappoint her.

"Oh, I don't know. What would I do in Paris?"

"It won't be very gay for you," Grandma conceded, "but you can learn a great deal about French history from Mr. Robbins. He's quite an expert, you know. And when we get back to New York . . . I'll give you . . ." Her words, after the pause, came in a rush: ". . . my little ruby bracelet that you used to admire. Do you remember it?"

"Oh, Grandma, no!"

Nothing could have convinced me more vividly of her desperate need than this sudden, shocking bribe. We faced each other with startled eyes, and when I recovered, I knew that our relationship was altered.

"I don't need a present, thank you, Grandma," I said a bit primly. "If Mother will let me, I'll be glad to stay."

"You're a good girl, Ida," she said with an immediate humility that made me wince. "Of course, I was silly about the bracelet."

That afternoon she had a long conference in the lounge with Mr. Robbins, which I could observe from the table where I was playing solitaire. They consulted papers and maps, and he seemed a good deal agitated and cleared his throat continuously. I learned afterwards that they were reorganizing their whole summer trip to conform to Miss Polhemus' specifications. Poor Mr. Robbins had to change his hotel in Paris, and the trips to Dinard and the château country were canceled. It was decided that they would spend their time in the French capital and see each other daily, but under certain definite conditions. And one of those conditions, undoubtedly the most stringent, was that *I* should always be present.

Paris in 1904! Who does not think of trim carriages in the leafy Bois and big, plumed hats and the blurry greens and whites of Renoir and of Yvette Guilbert and an elegance the more haunting in retrospect for being doomed? But I think of these things only with a conscious effort. The memory that is first conjured up is of the somber, paneled dining room in Grandma's hotel and the discreet clink of glasses and chink of silver as a dozen Americans ate silently and chewed long. Paris to me will always be a grey, damp city where old people talk — incomprehensibly — of love.

After only a few days in Paris the daily pattern asserted itself. Mr. Robbins would call at our hotel in the morning, and he and Grandma would chat for half an hour in the courtyard. Then Mr. Robbins would take me out for a walk. I would come back to the hotel to lunch alone with Grandma, and at three o'clock Mr. Robbins would call for us in a Victoria, and we would drive in the Bois, or sometimes on expeditions as far as Saint-Germain or Saint-Cloud. In the evening we all dined at the hotel, and Mr. Robbins always brought Grandma an orchid.

It was a slow life for a girl, but I was used to being alone with my elders, and it was a strong principle of the Denisons that the pleasures of children were incidental to the conveniences of adults. What I liked most (or, perhaps I should say, what bored me least) was the morning walk with Mr. Robbins. His hobby was Cardinal Richelieu, and his knowledge of seventeenth century Paris was copious and detailed. We spent a great deal of time poking about the Palais Royal, the Louvre and the old hotels of the Place des Vosges. I was reading and adoring *The Three Musketeers*. Richelieu to me was a fascinating villain in sweeping scarlet who was always tearing about Paris in a great rumbling coach, escorted by guards with red tunics and white crosses who were ambushed at every turn by the king's musketeers. There was little in common between my cardinal and Mr. Robbins' dry statesman who had established the first post office and the French Academy. In fact, at times it seemed to me that he was doing to Richelieu what adults did to everything, that he was changing him from a figure of glamour into one who had tried to strip history of what little glamour it possessed. But at least we were each interested in a man in red robes, and as we slowly paced the gardens of the Palais Royal, we had each our picture of him.

It was after one of these walks that Mr. Robbins gave me an envelope for Grandma. I handed it to her just before we went in to lunch, and she read it in the foyer. She seemed very upset during our meal and afterwards, before going back up to her room, she said: "You will tell Mr. Robbins, Ida, that I have a headache and cannot go out this afternoon. But I suggest that you go and give him a letter that I will leave at the desk."

Mr. Robbins drew up promptly at three o'clock in the Victoria. The project for that afternoon was the Cluny Museum. He seemed much put out about Grandma's headache and coughed nervously as he read the letter. He then made the first personal remark that I had ever heard him make prior to his consumption of the evening quota of champagne.

"Women!" he exclaimed. "Women! If there's a way of

complicating a simple situation, trust a woman to find it!"

I was old enough to know that when adults made remarks like this, they were not referring to family but to romantic relations. There was no implication that Mr. Robbins could not trust women like Mother or Aunt Dagmar. But there was a definite implication that Mr. Robbins could not trust Grandma, and therefore their relationship had to be romantic.

"Have you put *your* faith in Grandma?"

"I've asked her to be my wife!" he exploded. "If that's not putting your faith in woman, I'd like to know what is!"

"And she won't?"

"She doesn't believe in second marriages," he said gruffly, already regretting his indiscretion. "Of course, she's entitled to her point of view. I daresay it does her credit. But, for myself, I could never see the point of eternal mourning."

"Did Richelieu ever marry?"

"Of course not. He was a priest."

"Do you suppose that was why he was such a great man?"

Mr. Robbins slapped his hand on his knee. "By golly, it wouldn't surprise me in the least!"

As it turned out, the rejection of Mr. Robbins made little difference in our daily round. He continued to drive out and to dine with us as if nothing had happened. Grandma and I were alone only at lunch, for she breakfasted in her room. These lunches were always the same. Grandma ordered the table d'hôte and made me drink Perrier water instead of wine. But she allowed me to select what I wanted from the pastry tray which almost made up for it. My awe of her had been reduced by her proffered bribe of the ruby bracelet, and the day after my discussion with Mr. Robbins, I asked her bluntly: "Why don't you marry Mr. Robbins?"

Grandma was startled, but I could see at once that she was not as startled as I had expected her to be.

"I don't know if that's a proper question for you to ask."

But I knew that she was only dodging me, and I repeated: "Why don't you?"

"In the first place, it would not be loyal to your grandfather. He was a very fine and good man."

"But how can you be loyal to someone who's dead?"

"He seems dead to you, Ida, because you never knew him."

"But he's still dead, isn't he?" I protested. "Hasn't he been dead for years and years?"

"Years and years seem longer to some people than to others."

"If you died first, do you think he'd never have remarried?"

I saw by the grave way that she settled her blue eyes on me that I had really startled her now. My indiscreet speculation had put a solid period to our discussion, and I could never again get Grandma to revert to it.

I wrote my parents, who had finished their cruise and were now in Baden-Baden for Father's cure, all about Grandma and Mr. Robbins, and my letter had a greater effect than I could have possibly foreseen. They agreed at once that one of them should go to Paris and see that Grandma did not jeopardize her happiness for an outdated scruple. Mother felt that as an in-law she was less intimate with Grandma and could present the case more effectively, and Father, whom an attack of asthma had robbed of much of his energy, finally agreed. She gave neither Grandma nor myself any notice, but simply arrived one evening before dinner. I cried out with surprise and joy when I saw her tall figure in a dark traveling suit by the desk, and she turned, smiling, to take me in her arms. Mother was never one for public demonstrations, but she always knew when to make an exception.

She and Grandma, for all their differences, had a definite mutual respect. Grandma appreciated Mother's practical contributions to Father's business and social life, while Mother admired Grandma's independence as a widow and the way she was able to fill her life without appealing to the sympathies of a married son. But to her the limitations of Grandma's social and religious thinking were the limitations of a quaint and bygone era. Mother treated Grandma with the outward respect and inner amusement of a British admiral greeting an Indian rani. They formed an odd couple together in the ensuing hot July days: Grandma so small and black and dignified, a being indifferent to and unaffected by weather, and Mother, so tall and towering in white, with her veil tucked up under her big feathered hat and beads of perspiration on her brow and under her eyes. Nobody could be more impressive than Mother in the right clothes, at the right time. The long lines of the Edwardian dress and the wide-brimmed hats were perfectly adapted to her strong, straight figure, and with her easy gait and swinging parasol, with her loud, high laugh and fine boldness of demeanor she was a striking figure on any boulevard. But at the same time, perhaps from her very bigness, she seemed more affected by changes in weather and temperature than other women of her generation. When Mother cried "Brr!" and flung a scarf around a neck or "Whew!" and mopped a dripping brow, there was a naturalness in her gesture that made it an attractive contrast to her otherwise neat and ordered look. This note of the commonplace, or even sometimes of the faintly comic, was why she even looked well in the absurd black bathing suits and long stockings of the period. Grandma would not have appeared in one of them to save her life.

Our Paris routine continued the same, except that Mother now joined us on the afternoon excursions, full, as always, of comment and suggestions. But in the mornings, while I was out with Mr. Robbins, she had a series of long talks with Grandma. Much later she told me about them. Poor

Grandma, it appeared, was suffering from an apprehension common to her generation; she was afraid of confronting Grandpa with Mr. Robbins in the next life. She visualized the encounter against a background of highly specific detail. She and Mr. Robbins would be walking uptown home after church on Sunday and would run smack into Grandpa. She told Mother that she was afraid that Grandpa would laugh at Mr. Robbins. It was probably just what he would have done.

"But have you never thought that *he* might have married again?" Mother interposed.

"He? Who's he?"

"Mr. Trask, of course."

"My dear Lily, surely you're not implying that your father-in-law could have been guilty of bigamy?"

"I don't mean that he married again *here*. Obviously, we know he couldn't have done that. I mean that he may have married again *there*."

Grandma became very grave at this. "I don't think it's right, Lily, to make fun of sacred things."

"Who's making fun of them? I'm perfectly serious. Why shouldn't Mr. Trask have married again in the next life? Why, for that matter, shouldn't he have married Mrs. Robbins?"

"Carrie Robbins was an invalid!"

"Ah, but not *there*."

"I must say, Lily, I had no idea you had this whimsical turn of mind. Of course, people don't marry in heaven!"

"You mean, there are no marriages there? I hate to think that."

"I mean there are no marriages *performed* there."

Mother now made her crushing point. "If there are no marriages performed there, it's because God doesn't permit them. And if He doesn't permit people to *get* married, why should He permit them to *be* married?"

"Then you and Gerald won't be married there?"

I imagine that Mother looked away at this. Though she never boasted about it, she regarded her own marriage as uniquely happy and not to be compared to others. "I'm sure that Gerald and I will be very good friends there," she said lightly. "At the least. But that's *your* point, Mrs. Trask, not mine. I believe that marrying *and* marriages exist there. Aren't all things possible in heaven?"

Grandma became very thoughtful, but she said no more on the subject that day. However, it came to be tacitly understood between them that the topic could be reopened each morning. After only two sessions Mother had led Grandma out of the thickets of her religious difficulties, and was clearing a quick path through the underbrush of practical considerations. Did Grandma want to know how Gerald would feel about her remarriage? Why, he was all for it! *For* it? Grandma really stared. Did Lily mean that he knew about it? That they had been discussing it?

"Why, ever since poor Mrs. Robbins died!" Mother exclaimed boldly. "Even before, if the truth be told. I know that sounds terrible, but it's the way we are. You may as well accept it."

"But I never discussed any such things about *my* mother," Grandma replied, deeply disturbed. "Not even with my own sisters. I never heard of such a thing!"

"Times have changed."

"Not for the better, I fear."

"But it's only because Gerald loves you, Mrs. Trask!" Mother protested with an opportune demonstration of feeling. "He loves you and wants you to be happy!"

One by one, Grandma's poor little objections, like gawky, conscripted farmers, were summoned up, drilled, reviewed and dismissed. There was no escape on the broad, clean parade ground of Mother's determination, where the least misstep sounded like the retort of a pistol. Grandma's final scruple was the simplest of all. She believed that it was a wife's absolute duty to leave all she had to her husband, and how could she leave the little pile of securities that she had salvaged from Grandpa's extravagance away from his own son and grandchildren?

"But, bless my soul, Mr. Robbins would never hear of it!" Mother exclaimed. "He's far too much of a gentleman. As a matter of fact, though I hate to mention it, if you married him, it would probably be to Gerald's advantage. After all, Mr. Robbins has no children of his own."

Everybody in the family always thought that Mother did a wonderful job that summer. Father used laughingly to describe it as the time when she made an "honest woman" of her mother-in-law. But I have often wondered if she didn't overdo it. She meant well, of course; she meant enormously well. She could not bear, sensible, practicable woman that she was, to see Grandma lose an innocent happiness for a handful of ridiculous scruples. But Mother, like all of her family, never made allowance for the power of her own personality. She took it too much for granted that no woman of Grandma's generation could be dominated by any woman of hers. She did not realize how much of her mother-in-law's seeming strength was simply reserve and dignity. Far from home and faced with a strange, bewildering problem, Grandma allowed herself to be taken in hand by her big, kindly, reassuring, fast-talking daughter-in-law. But I doubt very much if, left to herself in Brooklyn, she would ever have married again. Marriage to her meant Grandpa and love, and that had been over three decades before. All that she wanted from Mr. Robbins was the continuation of the schedule of bygone summers, lightly flavored with the atmosphere of an indefinitely protracted courtship. She liked her daily drive and her daily orchid and her daily argument over the bottle of champagne. She liked to talk about friends and relations to the waltzes of a three-piece orchestra at tea time. And it could even add to the delights of the situation if some of Mr. Robbins' old friends, as the romance prolonged itself, should see fit, sitting in their club windows, to describe her whisperingly as "cruel." Wasn't it all that Mr. Robbins really wanted, too?

But, no, they could not be allowed so little. The old have in common with children that if something is fun, it is bound to be stopped. Grandma and Mr. Robbins had to do the sound, sensible, up-to-date "Denison" thing. Miss Polhemus was much less demanding than Mother; she insisted only that they be proper. Mother insisted that they be happy. When Grandma had at last been induced to yield to the respectful importunity of Mr. Robbins, she was frightened by the burst of congratulation in the messages from relatives and friends. Aunt Dagmar cabled from Long Island, and Uncle Victor and Aunt Sophie came up from Dinard and Uncle Philip from the château country. The Denisons seemed to be claiming poor Grandma as one of their own. She became Mrs. Robbins in the private episcopal chapel of one of Mother's expatriate friends in the presence of her son and daughter-in-law, two of her daughter-in-law's brothers, a granddaughter and Miss Polhemus, who wept copiously throughout the ceremony. Grandma wore a dark brown dress, which was as far as Mother could make her depart from her habitual black, and a round straw hat with yellow flowers. There was something faintly macabre about such a note of gaiety over her expression of sober resolution, and when she leaned down to kiss me at the chapel door, I wondered if her rather bleary, preoccupied eyes had even recognized me. I remember speculating if Mr. Robbins would now see her without her wig. Perhaps, poor woman, it was what she was speculating herself. Perhaps it was exactly what her second marriage meant to her.

But I feel sure now that Mr. Robbins never saw the wig removed. When they returned to New York and settled in his house in Manhattan, Grandma brought over a few favored pieces of furniture from Brooklyn and put them in her own bedroom. This became her private domain and her only one; the rest of the house she left as it had been in the days of the first Mrs. Robbins. It stands to this day, occupied by an antique dealer, and whenever I pass it, I think of Mother's description of Mr. Robbins as a man with one million, and of his house as a slice off the house of a man with many. For its narrow grey limestone façade, no more than twenty feet in width, is covered with grinning lions' heads and balconies for flowerpots supported by squatting ladies, and topped with a giant dormer studded with bull's-eye windows. Nobody passing it today would believe that it had not been built by the most pushing parvenu. Yet I know how little the houses of that era sometimes expressed the souls of their occupants.

I tried at times in the ensuing years to recapture some of the intimacy that Grandma and I had enjoyed in Paris, but I never really succeeded. She had retreated to her old position as the rather stately head of her little family, and I was no longer especially favored. Perhaps she was embarrassed to consider all that I had seen and heard. But I often felt in the lower pitch of her voice when she addressed me and in the extra flicker of her smile in my direction when I took my leave that I at least reminded her of a period of very special emotion. When Mr. Robbins died, she gave me his notebook about Richelieu with a card on which she had written: "For dear Ida, in memory of happier days when she was *such* a comfort to her Grandma."

It was so like her to think of needing a "comfort" in "happier" days. Grandma never quite trusted happiness. Certainly there was very little of it in her second widowhood. Mr. Robbins left her the income of his whole estate, but stipulated that the principal should go to two of his nephews on her death. It was a handsome provision for a second wife, but nobody could persuade Grandma of that. She felt that he should have trusted her to leave his money back to his family. In a curious mood of retaliation, she cut her expenses to a minimum, remaining in the town house winter and summer with only one old servant, in order to save out of her Robbins income a small pile of money to leave to her Trask grandchildren. Perhaps it was thus that she tried to make up to Grandpa for her great and sole disloyalty. But the surname on her tombstone bears witness to this day that in the crisis of her later years she succumbed to the philosophy of Fifty-third Street. It seemed to me at my impressionable age that I could only follow suit.

PART II

The Coming of Derrick

5

Derrick: 1911

WHEN Derrick Hartley came to New York in the fall of 1911, he was twenty-seven, and, having buried both his parents, was possessed of a small competence. He had graduated from Harvard and worked for five years in a Boston trust company before the final illnesses, in quick succession, of his father and mother, and the ensuing necessity of salvaging what he could of the family property, had brought him back to the village near Concord where he had been born. Now it was over; the little white house on the green, to which his father had moved on retirement from ecclesiastical duties, and all the china and furniture, a modest lot, had been sold, twin marble slabs erected in the cemetery plot and the past seemingly liquidated. Derrick had been fond of his parents, but he had never professed himself a man of intimacies or dependencies, and he kept one eye, and sometimes two, on the future. There were obvious advantages, from an unsentimental point of view, in facing it disencumbered. He prudently invested the small proceeds of his father's estate, made arrangements by correspondence to share the Tenth Street flat of a bachelor friend, ordered two suits from an expensive tailor and resigned his position, with many diplomatic expressions of good will, at the trust company. He was at last ready for Wall Street and Linnaeus Tremain.

He had not seen Mr. Tremain since he had been a boy at Shelby School and a friend of his son Charley, but he had never forgotten the cool, appraising, yet not unkindly eye with which that tall, trim, slowly moving gentleman had seemed to take in every boy, every building, every master, as if to put them up on some auction block in his mind where one felt sure they would fetch but a small sum. Derrick had sat with him on the porch of the parents' house all one Sunday afternoon and had been fascinated at how quickly and surely Charley's inert, cigar-smoking, lazily questioning father had laid bare the very heart of the institution.

"I approach everything in life as if I were going to buy it," Mr. Tremain had explained. "Both things spiritual and things material. It's a useful little habit that I recommend. Even God has His price, you know. It may be faith or prayer, rather than cash or credit, but it's still a price."

Derrick at home had been used to the daily, almost hourly deference to the distinction between flesh and spirit. It was exhilarating at last to hear it categorically denied. It seemed to him a very splendid thing to be, like Mr. Tremain, in absolute control of one's tiny corner of the universe, and not a gangling, sheepishly smiling sentimentalist like his own father who always had a cowlick in his hair and dandruff on the shoulders of his black suit. It was the affliction of Derrick's life that the Reverend Hartley, whose parish abutted on the grounds of Shelby, should have been asked, out of the headmaster's courtesy and neighborly spirit, to preach at the school chapel once a term. He was known to the boys as "Reverend Tug" because of a sermon in which he had drawn a parallel between a Christian and a tugboat. Were not both engaged in God's work of pushing others ahead? Derrick knew, of course, that he owed his scholarship in Shelby, a church school, to the proximity of his clerical parent, but he sometimes wondered if it was worth it. Not until Mr. Tremain had told him that some of the most successful men in the business world were sons of New England ministers did it occur to him that there might be an asset side to the "Reverend Tug."

Charley, always a frail boy, had died of pneumonia the following year, and there had been no occasion for Derrick to see the stricken Mr. Tremain again. But that image of silent competence, so free of cant, had remained in mind through the rest of school and college days, and, afterwards, at the trust company, Derrick had always been alert to any reference to the New York investment house of Tremain & Dodge. Though relatively small, its reputation had penetrated to Boston, and Derrick often heard Linnaeus Tremain spoken of as an "artist" among underwriters. Apparently he had never been known to visit a plant or factory or to read any more about one than its bare financial statement. No market crisis had been allowed to interrupt his trips in search of Italian primitives or even his late afternoon whist at the Knickerbocker Club. A glance at the ticker tape seemed to tell him all he needed; he could see a forest in every tree. As Derrick gradually put the picture together, it became his fixed conviction that Tremain's was the studio where he must learn his art.

When he sent in his card, on his first visit to Wall Street, after settling himself in New York, he had scribbled on it: "I wonder if you remember me from Shelby?" It came back with the message, "I remember you perfectly. Please wait," and wait he had to, for an hour. At last he was ushered into a dark, rather small office with linen-fold paneling and three small brilliantly colored religious paintings with lights over them. Mr. Tremain did not even look up. He was examining a stamp through a heavy magnifying glass with a stout silver handle. Derrick interpreted the pose as favorable to himself.

The old ham, he reflected, as he sat himself, uninvited, before the desk. I bet he's been rehearsing it for the past hour.

Mr. Tremain looked as lean and gaunt as he had looked a dozen years before, but his long, thick hair had turned a snowy white and his dark skin was even browner. The clear, almost childish, light blue eyes over the aquiline nose now fixed their gaze on Derrick.

"Would you like to see a Laga Canal 'blue' issue of 1887?" he asked abruptly. "I believe this is one of three specimens in existence."

Derrick rose to take the proffered glass and leaned over to squint at the dusky profile of Queen Victoria. He knew nothing of stamps and was sure that Mr. Tremain would be waspish if he pretended to. He simply nodded and resumed his seat.

"I've come to ask you for a job, sir."

"Presuming, no doubt, on your friendship with my dead boy?"

Derrick looked up in astonishment to catch the flash of hostility in those suddenly kindled eyes.

"I should have presumed before now had I been going to. I've been out of Harvard five years."

Mr. Tremain stared back at him for a moment and then nodded. Evidently he was satisfied, but Derrick, with a quick breath, vowed that *he*, at least, would not soon forget so wanton an insult.

"Tell me about yourself," the older man continued with a shrug. "I mean, the part after school. I remember that your father was a parson and that you had a scholarship. You were a prefect, too, weren't you? And then you went to Harvard?"

Derrick briefly described his career in Cambridge and at the trust company. "Of course, I realize it doesn't amount to much," he concluded with a candor that invited no rebuttal. "The only thing that might interest you is my resolution about working for your firm. It seems to be a case of Tremain or nobody."

Mr. Tremain looked critically down at his long white

folded hands. "You mean if I don't give you a job, you won't go to work at all?"

"Not while my money holds out."

"Then I hope you are rich, Mr. Hartley. For I tell you frankly, I haven't an opening. And I may not have one for a year."

"I can wait a year."

"But I can't promise you one even then. I might die or retire. If you wait for me, you may wait till Doomsday."

"I guess that's my lookout."

Mr. Tremain's eyes narrowed in what might have been either surprise or irritation. It was difficult to tell. As Derrick had first surmised, he was a real ham.

"Would you mind explaining this remarkable compliment to me? If it is a compliment?"

"I want to learn about money from a man who knows about money without being impressed by it. Or by anyone who has it. I want to learn from a man who wouldn't hesitate to say: 'To hell with you!' to anyone he damn pleased. And just because he pleased!"

"Dear me. And you think *I'd* do that?"

"Look at the way you told *me* off."

"But, my dear Mr. Hartley, you happen to be a very unimportant young man."

"I won't always be."

"Perhaps not. But you are now. Do you think I'd walk down to 23 Wall Street and tell Pierpont Morgan to go to hell?"

"I think you'd be quite capable of it."

Mr. Tremain laughed cheerfully. "Well, I see your game, and I like it. You're trying to describe me as you think I want to see myself. And you're probably laughing up your sleeve at me all the time. Why not? It's perfectly fair. But what *I* must consider is that if I take you on, I'll never get rid of you. I can see you're the type that sticks. You'd expect to be a junior partner and then a senior partner. I daresay you'd wind up as my executor and liquidate my estate!"

"Why not?"

"Oh, come, Mr. Hartley, now you're overdoing it," the older man said dryly. "I don't like that. You may leave your name and address with my secretary, but I repeat: I have no openings, and I don't expect any."

Derrick was good to his word about seeking no other employment. When he left the office of Tremain & Dodge, he went uptown and made his plans for the waiting period. His friend Harry Prime, a gentle and amiable bachelor who worked for a small, quiet law firm of old name and diminishing status, was glad to continue the arrangement about his apartment, and Derrick set aside from his capital the goodly percentage of it which he estimated would be needed to defray the expenses of a year in New York. He then settled down to enjoy himself, for he knew that it was not in his nature to prepare for a job by reading economic tracts. He was a man who had to work altogether or play.

Fortunately, New York in 1911 was an amusing place for a bachelor to play. Society was still homogeneous, and Derrick found that his looks, his self-assurance and his Shelby and Harvard connections brought him invitations to a number of dinner parties and receptions. He and Harry would dress for the evening over a glass of sherry and stroll to a bar on Sixth Avenue where, standing under a monumental painting of a Roman banquet, they would eat oysters and drink a Martini cocktail. From there they would progress to one of those stately dinners where the excellence of the food and the variety of the wines, the profusion of scented flowers and the gleam of silver and gold over square yards of damask went far to make up — at least to young eyes which, as Derrick quite recognized, were still dazzled — for the general mediocrity of the conversation. He found that for a few weeks, or even months, he could be content to sip Moselle or champagne while the ladies on either side of him chattered across his white shirt about servants. He was free to indulge in fantasies that he was as rich as his host, with a centerpiece that had belonged to Napoleon and a Gainsborough duchess over the mantel. Afterwards, back in the apartment, he and Harry would discuss their host, and whether the money had been earned, married or inherited, over a glass of brandy. In the morning he would take long walks, or ride in the Park, and every afternoon he practiced billiards at the Harvard Club.

One night he found that his dinner partner was a large, vigorous, friendly woman called Mrs. Gerald Trask. She was the kind of woman who easily elicited confidences, and when he had told her about his ambitions for a job in Tremain & Dodge, he was startled to discover that she was the younger sister of Mrs. Tremain.

"I should think Linn could use a young man like you in his shop," she observed. "I know if anyone cared that much about working for *me*, I'd find a place for him."

"Of course, your brother-in-law can pick anyone he chooses."

"Not quite. And, besides, enthusiasm is a rare flower. I'll tell him you ought to be plucked."

"Will he take your advice?"

"I can't say. The poor man is singularly afflicted with sisters-in-law. But he and I are rather special. At worst, it will do you no harm."

It didn't. On the following Saturday afternoon, when Derrick was at the billiard table of the Harvard Club, surrounded by a silent, smoking group, he happened to make a brilliant shot, and there was a little burst of applause. As he turned to acknowledge it, he spotted Linnaeus Tremain, expressionless except for a grim wisp of a smile about the corners of his lips, standing at the edge of the group. At the end of his game Derrick went over to him.

"I understand that you live entirely for pleasure now," Mr. Tremain remarked gruffly, taking a tightly clenched cigar from between his teeth. "I hear you have become a society playboy."

"Whose fault is that?"

"My word, you *are* a bold one. But tell me, do you think you could analyze a financial statement as sharply as you made that last stroke?"

"If somebody would let me try."

"Well, I suppose 'somebody' mustn't be responsible for your continued idleness," Mr. Tremain said with a little grunt. "I shall expect you in the office on Monday morning. At half past eight."

It was a moment for jubilation, even for impertinence. "So Doomsday's here at last!" Derrick exclaimed with a little shout of laughter, and brandishing his cue, he returned to the billiard table.

As he had hoped and expected, he liked everything about Tremain & Dodge, from the great high-ceilinged front hall of yellowing marble, with its ponderous brass chandeliers and row of cashier's windows, to the comfortable paneled offices of the partners, the black oak conference room with its ticker tape machine on a malachite stand and the long gallery of whiskered portraits beneath which old grey-coated clerks, seated on stools at high tables, made entries in ledger books in an atmosphere of Victorian fidelity. Derrick worked exclusively for Mr. Tremain, as he had wanted, and the long hours interfered with his social life, but that had been a fill-in at best and easy to give up. All his attention was now absorbed by his job and the fascinating study of his new employer. Derrick had a feeling that Mr. Tremain's mind never wandered far from Wall Street. Whatever he was doing, whether presiding over a dinner table surrounded by his wife's guests and relations, or bargaining for a tryptich at Duveen's, or playing whist at the Knickerbocker Club and puffing silently at a long cigar, Derrick suspected that the back of his mind was a jigsaw puzzle of mergers and reorganizations and new ventures over which his subconscious or half-conscious self was always languidly presiding, in the relaxed but confident search of the right price. Compared to the brief ecstasy of such discoveries, his travels, his paintings, even his lovely wife were but shadows. Had Charley lived, it might have been otherwise, but Charley had not lived, and the greater part of his father's heart must have died with him.

Derrick, on the other hand, was no artist; he was interested in what the business would do for him. He wanted elementary things, like money and power. But he enjoyed the means quite as much as he expected to enjoy the ends, and his mind embraced affectionately each tool of his ambition, the small as well as the large. It was not only the work in the office that fascinated him; it was the office itself. Derrick loved to figure out the deficiencies of the file system and to calculate to the penny the cost of surplus office boys and stenographers.

"If we ever *do* make you a partner," Mr. Tremain would grumble whenever Derrick pointed out such things, "one of the conditions will be that you take over our housekeeping."

"How much longer do you think you can afford to wait?"

"A good bit longer than you think!"

Their relationship was pleasant, at times almost intimate, but curiously lacking in affection of any real depth. They needed each other too much and understood each other too well. Derrick knew that the older man's hardness was a front for a repressed sentimentality which was in turn a front for a deeper layer of hardness. What he wanted was another son, and he respected Derrick for eschewing the role at the same time that he deplored his being neither sufficiently mawkish nor sufficiently calculating to attempt it. Mr. Tremain had buried his only love, and Derrick did not believe that his would ever be born. It was a bond, but not an easy one.

On Sunday nights the Tremains had family supper in the big red French Renaissance house on Fifty-third Street, and Derrick was soon a regular guest. Mr. Tremain called it "family supper," but Derrick soon made out that the family was all his wife's. The Denisons talked very fast and ribbed each other and were always laughing, and the Sunday evenings were lively. There Derrick met again Mrs. Gerald Trask, who winked at him conspiratorially, and her handsome, affable brother, Dr. Victor Denison. He noted that Mr. Tremain was amused by his brothers-in law, but evidently had no very high regard for their intellectual capacities, while they, although respecting his brains and success, clearly found him heavy going at a party. For Mr. Tremain usually said very little or else spoke at considerable length, both habits incompatible with the kind of breezy repartee in which his wife's family specialized. But Derrick began to suspect that the Denisons were capable of more design than he had first apprehended when he found himself for the third consecutive Sunday seated next to Ida Trask.

She was a junior at Barnard and passionately proud of the fact. To go to college, she told him straight off, she had had to overcome a formidable and united family opposition. Actually, as her mother had already explained to him, this opposition had amounted to little more than friendly scoffing. Mrs. Trask did not really disapprove of college for women, but she decidedly disapproved of bluestockings, and Ida's tendencies in this direction had to be watched. Derrick, listening now to Ida, agreed with her mother. He liked her large, worried, limpid brown eyes, the heart shape of her face and the fine, high line of her cheekbones. But he could not equally approve her general lack of gracefulness and the excitement and volubility of her conversation. She was in the throes of a reaction to what she regarded as her family's worldliness and complacency, and she loved to chatter of the abolition of slums and the raising of educational standards. She was much upset when she discovered that Derrick did not share her enthusiasms.

"But don't you *care* that there are people in Harlem who sleep twelve in a room?"

"Care? Of course I don't *care*. I deplore it, I condemn it, whatever you want, but I don't care. I don't enjoy my dinner tonight a whit the less because of it. Do *you?*"

"I think I do," she answered thoughtfully. "I think I really do."

"Well, it's wasted worry," he retorted. "It does nobody any good. I make a point of caring only about the things I'm responsible for. The things I can *do* something about."

"Everything else can go to rack and ruin?"

"I didn't say that. I can promise you that if I owned any buildings in Harlem, my tenants would *not* sleep twelve in a room.

"Only nine, I suppose."

"Now, Miss Trask, that's hardly fair. You penalize a man because he's honest. I'm a relative stranger in New York, working in a humble job. You come of an influential family with every sort of social connection. But what are *you* doing about Harlem? You're looking extremely pretty, in what I imagine to be a very expensive dress, eating your aunt's excellent dinner and posing as a friend of the masses!"

"But Aunt Dagmar *gave* me this dress!" she protested excitedly. "And can *I* help it if she has a good cook? And . . . and . . ." She paused in perplexity and then flushed as he burst out laughing. "And what's more, I think you're horrid!"

But he was quite satisfied that she did not. He could see that she wanted nothing better than a man to convert, and he deduced from the eagerness with which she went about it that the candidates had so far been few. In the short time that those things take he found himself regarded as Ida's property at her aunt's Sunday night suppers. She would jump up now, when he came in, to appropriate him and pick up the argument where they had left it the week before.

"I thought you'd be interested to know that I talked to Professor Stookey — he teaches American history — about your theories on how the railroads got their land. He doesn't agree with you at *all*. *He* says — and I believe he's one of the first men in his field — that being a pioneer is no excuse for being grabby. He says it would have been better if we'd taken more time developing our natural resources and done it in a more orderly way. After all, what was the hurry?"

"Hurry? *You* might have been in a hurry if you'd been in a stockade with Indians outside whooping for your scalp. And a mighty pretty scalp it would have made, if you'll allow me to say so."

"Don't shift the argument," she retorted in a tone that, for all its primness, betrayed a throb of pleasure. "And, by the way, Professor Stookey thinks we treated the Indians abominably. After all, whose land *was* it?"

"The buffaloes', if you come right down to it. From the way he talks, your Professor Stookey sounds like a socialist. I'd like to have seen *him* out there when the Wild West was being tamed. Him and his 'little more time' and his 'abominably treated' Indians."

"Professor Stookey is as much of a man as you are."

"Has he ever run a business? Has he ever hired labor?

I'll bet not. Unless maybe he once sold cosmetics behind a counter. I'm sorry, Ida, but I hate that namby-pamby type of idealist. No wonder he ends up teaching girls!"

"*Well!* I suppose you think women shouldn't be educated, either."

"Not by the likes of Stookey. What do women want to know about railroads? What do your mother or your aunt know about them? Haven't they got on all right?"

"But Mother and Aunt Dagmar belong to a different generation."

"And a generation that has nothing to be ashamed of. I'd a damn sight rather have your mother with a rifle alongside me in that stockade than dear, mincing Mr. Stookey!"

"You're quite impossible."

Impossible or not, on the first Sunday when the Tremains were out of town, Derrick found himself invited to supper by Ida's parents. He even wondered if Mrs. Trask had not sent her sister to the country to provide her with the occasion for asking him. He was learning that the Denisons were capable of concerted action. But he still had no idea of declining the invitation. He was beginning to like Ida, despite her theories, which he was sure would pass with time; he certainly liked her mother, and as a lone bachelor he liked the family atmosphere in which the Tremains and Trasks and Denisons enveloped him. A man could be independent, after all, and still miss the reassurances of family life.

The Trasks, he discovered, lived in an ordinary five-story brownstone house with a high stoop, in the same street with Mrs. Trask's sister and brothers. They were obviously not rich, like the Tremains, but they lived very comfortably. Derrick guessed that Mrs. Trask had a flair for making a little money go a long way. Looking about the living room, he noted that she had created a rather expensive French eighteenth century atmosphere by the judicious use of a sofa, three good chairs, a tapestry, an ormolu mirror and a gilded clock. And she had been too smart to make the mistake of asking Derrick alone. There were six other guests, and he was not even seated next to Ida.

At dinner he discussed with his hostess the difference between a New England and a New York conscience. Mrs. Trask said that the New York woman had the more difficult time, for her conscience required her to be not only good but in fashion, which was a great strain. It was easy enough to be good, she maintained, in last year's hat. Derrick laughed and thought what a pity it was she had thrown herself away on her quiet, asthmatic husband who spent his evenings reading English history in the smooth, soothing prose of nineteenth century authors. What if she had married a man like her brother-in-law? Or himself!

After supper he took a seat by Ida in the living room and found her full of curiosity as to what he thought of her parents in the atmosphere of their own home. For all her indignation at what she called their "lack of social consciousness," she was obviously proud of them and accepted his polite comments as literal truths. Derrick admired the competence with which Mrs. Trask must have handled her gushing and at times explosive daughter. Clearly she gave her a good bit of rein, let her read and study what she wanted and laughed at her with a devastating good-nature, but she always knew when to pull her up. There had been, for example, the awful coincidence of Ida's initiation into the sorority, Kappa Kappa Gamma (described by her mother as "Wrapper, wrapper, pajama") which had fallen on the same night as her grandmother Robbins' birthday party. Ida, to whom election to the chapter had been the great event of a lifetime, had pleaded with tears for permission to absent herself from the family dinner. Her mother had been adament.

"I have no objection to your joining a sorority if you care that much," Mrs. Trask had told her. "But taking on new obligations and commitments does not mean that you can shake off old ones. Your grandmother's birthday was a fixed date before Barnard was even founded."

Ida's voice had still an edge of resentment as she told the story to Derrick that first evening at her family's.

"You can imagine what I went through!" she exclaimed. "Having to explain to the other girls that I was skipping my initiation because of Grandma's birthday!"

"Did they understand?"

"Well, they were very nice about it, I admit. But I don't think many of them came from the kind of family that takes birthdays quite so seriously."

"No? What *do* they take seriously?"

Ida looked up in surprise at this mocking tone. "Well, do you assume, if they don't take birthdays seriously, that they don't take *anything* seriously?"

"No, but I think gracious living requires attention to detail, and gracious living is a woman's job. Your mother knows you can't pull too many bricks out of that wall before it caves in."

"And Grandma's birthday party — or rather my presence at it — is such a vital brick?"

He shrugged. "It's a brick."

"You mean you actually *approve* of Mother's making me go?"

"Yes, I guess I do."

"And you'd do the same thing with a daughter of yours?" She dropped her eyes at a sudden sense of the boldness of such a reference.

"I would. Sororities are all very well, but they're hardly part of a grown-up world."

"Like birthday parties? What would you say if you had a

son, and it was a question of his initiation at the Porcellian
Club?"

"That's a different thing entirely."

"I *see!* You really believe in the double standard, don't
you?"

"I make no secret of it."

Ida was very silent and thoughtful for several moments
after this, but he was confident that he had lost no real stature
in her estimate. He had no doubt that, except in the case
of a few unnatural spinsters, all feminist chatter in women
was a kind of parlor decoy to titillate and attract the opposite
sex. He believed that women took up their cudgels only for
the delight of flinging them down, that all they sought on
the battlefield for equal rights was the ecstasy of surrender.
Nor was there anything in Ida's subsequent conduct to shake
his convictions. At the Tremains', the following Sunday
night, she was more than usually proprietary in his respect,
misquoting him loudly to support her side in argument with
her Uncle Linn and strewing her conversation with such
phrases as: "But Derrick says —" He took her twice in the
course of the next two weeks to walk in the Park, and it became his regular practice to call at the Trasks on Saturday
afternoons. Mr. Tremain spoke of this development, in a
gruff voice, as they were leaving the office together one evening.

"You're seeing a good deal of Ida Trask."

"Is there any objection, sir?"

"Oh, no. So long as you realize that you may be raising
expectations. My sister-in-law may have an easygoing manner, but when it comes to the point, she can be a very firm
woman."

"I can well imagine it. Don't worry, sir. I shall not trifle
with Ida's affections."

"Good." Mr. Tremain cleared his throat in relief. "Then

that's all I need say. Except that she's a good girl, Ida. She's the best of the lot of them."

Derrick had appeared self-assured, even casual during this brief interchange, but his brows were knit when he parted company with Mr. Tremain at the door of their building, and he declined a lift in the Electric in order to walk. He knew perfectly clearly, as he strode up a dusky Broadway, that if he continued to see Ida after so straight a warning, it would be tantamount to a proposal of marriage. Mr. Tremain might have intervened more to warn a favorite employee than to gain a husband for a favorite niece, but the fact remained that he *had* intervened. Derrick, as the lawyers put it, was "on notice." But did he really mind? That was the only valid question. Wasn't Ida Trask as good a wife as he was apt to get? He had expected more time, it was true, to make up his mind, and he was a man who hated to be hurried, but Ida's virtues were incontestable. With the fulfillment of marriage all her silly ideas and half-baked notions could be expected to blow away, and with a bit of discipline and care about her dress and weight, she could easily become a very handsome woman. She was certainly intelligent and fundamentally clear minded, and the natural submissiveness of her female nature could be counted on to check her tendency to intellectual independence and provide the perfect complement to his own need for possession. For Derrick minced no words with himself; he wanted a woman who would be his property, spiritually as well as physically, and he knew the New York social scene already too well not to understand how few of such women it offered. Ida admired him and was perhaps already in love with him. He felt sure that she would not be fickle. Did he love her? Probably not, but when *had* he been in love, and how long did a man have to wait? She never bored him, even when she was being silly; that was the great thing. He liked the big friendly family setting of which she was a part and the social opportunities which its ramifications so abundantly offered. He liked the prospect of children, and Ida seemed strong and healthy. The only thing that she would not bring him was money, but was she not a niece of the man through whom he expected to make it?

At the Metropolitan Museum, the following Saturday afternoon, he found himself alone with Ida in the Egyptian room, staring up at the great pink seated figure of a pharaoh who stared bleakly back.

"That was my kind of civilization," he remarked. "Not even a hint of sentimentality."

"But they were always thinking about death."

He looked at her in faint surprise. "Is that sentimental?"

"It's egocentric, isn't it, which comes to the same thing. What is a pyramid but a monstrous valentine?"

"Sent by a man to himself?"

"Posthumously."

As they laughed, he felt a small twinge of jealousy at the sudden thought that she might, in some ways, be quite as clever as he.

"Now that you've destroyed the Egyptians for me," he said, a bit brusquely, "what will you put in their place?"

"Must it be something unsentimental?"

"By all means."

"But sentimentality isn't always bad! It may be just the lace frill around a genuine feeling. Or don't you believe in genuine feeling, either? Must we all be granite all the time?"

Her smile faded as she looked up at him, and her eyes for a second earnestly searched his. Then, abashed, she looked away and quickly shrugged. Derrick smiled, and taking her by the hand, turned her around.

"Does this answer your question?" And leaning forward, he kissed her on the lips.

She jumped away from him with a smothered "Oh!" and walked hastily to the next room where there were people. Stopping abruptly before a glass case of earthenware jars, she pointed to different specimens, and delivered, in a sudden inarticulate flow of words, an improvised lecture on Egyptian pottery. But despite her evident reluctance to discuss what had happened, it was easy to see that her agitation betokened a bursting happiness, and when he handed her into Mr. Tremain's Electric that was to take her home, she gave his hand a confiding little squeeze.

There was no Sunday supper the following night, for both the Tremains and Trasks had gone to Long Island for the weekend, but the next Tuesday he received a little blue note from Ida that fairly throbbed with the suppressed, seething excitement of the girl who knows that only formalities now stand between her and her ultimate happiness.

I can't be at Aunt Dagmar's next Sunday because Mother is sending me to Atlantic City with Grandma Robbins who has been ill and needs a change of air. But if you go, you'll meet my cousin, Geraldine Denison, and then, of course, you'll never even notice I'm not there. Don't have such a divine time with her, however, that you forget to give just one little thought to your poor lonely friend, treading the boardwalks by a cold grey Atlantic and dreaming of old Egypt and valentines!

The "one little thought" that he devoted to Ida that Sunday night was the reflection of how right she had been in predicting that he would have a "divine time" with her cousin. For there was no question about it; Geraldine Denison was the most beautiful woman he had seen in his life. She had a golden, breath-taking, erupting beauty; she swooped upon the little family party and upon her Aunt Dagmar with a rasping cry of love like a bird of paradise. When Derrick had recovered from the shock of his first impression and could observe her more closely, he made out that her face was thin and oval, her skin of a marble whiteness, her eyes, large like Ida's, but grey, clear and restless, now evasive and now very direct, and that the impression of gold was all from her marvelous hair, which she wore long and straight, rising in front to a small pompadour. Geraldine, like all the Denisons, was tall, but she moved with a grace that Ida never approached. She managed to seem fragile when she was probably strong, helpless when she was almost surely able to look out for herself. But where she differed most strikingly from her aunts and cousin was in the obvious pleasure that she took in her own femininity.

"I know I'm a terrible substitute for Ida," she murmured to Derrick at supper, betraying, in her very first words, that she had been "warned off." "Ida's so full of books and facts and figures. It's really quite frightening. Everyone says I'm just a butterfly compared to her. But there you are." She smiled in mock pity. "For one whole evening you'll have to put up with a butterfly!"

"Why haven't I met you before? Where have they been keeping you?"

"Oh, I've been abroad. Aunt Dagmar gave me a trip to Paris for my birthday. You see, I'm like Amy in *Little Women*. I'm the niece who gets what she wants."

"Did you get what you wanted in Paris?"

Her grey eyes seemed to debate the possible impertinence of this. "I don't think I really wanted anything in Paris."

"What you wanted was here?"

"Oh, yes, there are lots of things I want here."

"What kinds of things?"

"Well, for example, I want to redecorate my room in beige, instead of pink. And I want to have my aquamarines reset. And I want terribly to see my portrait by Zorka in the exhibit for the hospital fund." She paused to smile again.

"You must understand that I'm entirely trivial. I'm not a bit serious, like Ida."

That she should mention Ida a second time could only mean that she was pointedly flirting. "You're serious about the things you want, anyway," he suggested. "So am I. And they're the only things worth being serious about."

"That sounds frightfully immoral and rather like Oscar Wilde."

"Except that I mean it!" he exclaimed in a louder voice. "If you don't get what you want in this life, you're nothing. You're not even pitiable!" He flushed suddenly as he realized that he had spoken too violently, and now moderated his tone. "I'll bet you've figured out already who's going to give you each of those things you said you wanted."

"Well, perhaps I have," she mused. "I think Aunt Dagmar will give me my new bedroom."

"Because you came back from Europe when you were supposed to?"

She laughed good-naturedly. "Has Ida been talking? It's quite true, Aunt Dagmar didn't want me to stay any longer in Paris. Neither did Mummy and Daddy." She paused, and Derrick concluded that there must have been an adventurer, probably a penniless count. "And I imagine that Uncle Linn will take care of my aquamarines," she continued, gazing at him with widened, quizzical eyes. "And that leaves only the exhibition. But, everyone's already been, so I guess I must go by myself."

"Unless you go with me. Tomorrow afternoon."

"Why, Mr. Hartley! Don't you work?"

"Only when I'm not taking beautiful girls to see their portraits."

"Oh, shush! Of course I couldn't *think* of letting you." When she changed the subject and began to talk about his work in her uncle's firm, he knew that she meant to go with him, and he clenched his fists in excitement under the table. "Tell me," she was saying, in the mild, quizzical tone that young ladies reserved for the "serious" topic; "it always seems to me so unfair the way you bankers treat the poor little inventor. After all, when you stop to think of it, none of the great fortunes ever seem to go to the man who really thought the thing up, if you see what I mean?"

As he proceeded to explain the rewards that were necessary to induce men to risk their capital and the superior function of the investor to the inventor in modern society, he became gradually aware of disapproving glances around the table. Mrs. Tremain twice interrupted him with direct questions to Geraldine, and Dr. Victor Denison made several efforts to make the conversation general. Only Ida's mother betrayed nothing. Derrick smiled grimly and continued to address himself exclusively to the lovely creature on his right, but his throat was constricted with a sullen defiance. It was evident that the Denisons thought him good enough for Ida, but not good enough for Geraldine. Well, they would see!

After dinner, as the gentlemen joined the ladies, Derrick was crossing the living room towards Geraldine when he heard his name called by Mrs. Trask in a tone that he could hardly ignore. He turned and saw her pointing, with a smile that recognized, without mocking, his helplessness, to an empty chair beside her.

"Come, Derrick, you can't have Geraldine to yourself all evening. It's hardly gallant of you to make us older women fight for our rights."

"I had not imagined that this seat could be vacant," he replied with a smile that he hoped matched hers. "I didn't have the presumption to look."

"That's better," she said with a chuckle. "Much better. Good manners is the only rag between us and the apes. Let's keep it there."

It was only too clear that she meant to fix him at her side

for the balance of the evening, and there was nothing that he could do about it but grumble to himself that such maneuvering must fail of its ultimate goal. Mrs. Trask would elicit from him neither apology nor recantation. For Derrick knew already, with a clarity unique even in his clear mind, that what had happened to him that night was something that had never happened to him in the twenty-seven years of his life. It was as if he had been playing up to that moment with a pack of cards from which the aces had been drawn. Now it was a different game. There was a bright glow within him that made the unuttered remonstrances of Ida's mother seem like snowflakes landing on a window, observed from within. Hard on Ida? Of course it was hard on Ida! But he clenched his fists in his lap again at the leaping idea that with Geraldine he could go to the top of the world!

Mrs. Trask must have taken in his attitude — perhaps she had observed those clenched fists — for she said, still smiling: "Geraldine is our Freia. When she's away, we all seem old. Like the gods in *Rheingold* behind that scrim."

"She's the most beautiful girl I've ever seen!" he said stoutly.

"My poor Ida!" Mrs. Trask exclaimed, raising her hands in a half-joking gesture of dismay. "It's always been that way. Geraldine dazzles all the men. If we go to Paris, Ida comes home with an album of post-cards and Geraldine with a proposal from a duke!"

"*Did* she have a proposal from a duke?"

"Oh, I guess he wasn't quite a duke. But he was better than those portraits in the Louvre which were all my Ida got." Mrs. Trask's grunt indicated that her own tastes were closer to her niece's. "However, duke or count or whatever, he was only an interlude for Geraldine. Everyone's been an interlude since Talbot Keating."

"Who is Talbot Keating?" But he knew about the Keatings, and, of course, she knew that he knew. He could measure his own ineligibility against the name alone.

"He's a very handsome, very rich but very idle young man who has wanted to marry Geraldine for the past two years. She thinks, and her parents agree with her, that he lacks a real purpose in life. That he needs more drive. So it was arranged that she should go abroad while he took a job in a bank. And after that they would see."

Derrick could not help admiring the speed and decisiveness with which Mrs. Trask's mind worked. Faced with a crisis, she promptly unsheathed the weapon of a family secret. She did not resent his being dazzled by Geraldine; she regarded it, on the contrary, as entirely natural. But that did not mean she had given up the fight.

"And what have they seen?" he demanded.

"I imagine it's still too soon to tell. But everyone seems to think that young Keating has done very well in the bank."

"Well?" Derrick repeated with a mild sneer. "For a whole month? Or even two? Then there's hope indeed!"

Mrs. Trask shrugged. "You know how it is. After all, you're not a boy. Very little is expected of the young Keatings of this world."

"And very much of the young Hartleys?"

"I don't think that's altogether fair," she came back at him with her first undisguised note of reprimand. "My brother-in-law gave you a job, and my whole family has welcomed you as a friend."

He flushed before that penetrating gaze. "I'm sorry," he murmured. "You've all been very kind. You especially."

"Because we *like* you, Derrick. It's as simple as that."

He rose when he saw Geraldine rise, bade good night abruptly to Mrs. Trask and crossed the room to take his leave of Mrs. Tremain. There was no better or even kinder way of letting Ida learn what had happened than by making it thus coarsely plain to her assembled family. He found Geraldine in the hall with her parents, and all four went out together. Dr. and Mrs. Denison lived just down the block, and Derrick was allowed to walk with Geraldine to their stoop. The time was brief, but it was long enough to ascertain that he might call at three the following afternoon and take her to the art gallery. She conveyed this information in a quick, low tone that would not carry to her parents, and he was faintly surprised that a girl of twenty-two should feel the need to be so furtive. Afterwards, as he strode the two miles down Fifth Avenue in the thickening drizzle, he laughed aloud to discover, at this late date, that his inner turmoil could make the damp, dark shop fronts a spring garden of riotous color. For his joy was more than the joy of the first stirrings of love; it was the joy of discovery that love, after all, was real and that the poets had been prompted by something more than their ambition to write memorable verse. Derrick was not dismayed by the late arrival in his life of the goddess who had so long slighted him; he was delighted, on the contrary, to meet the guest of honor, in whose coming after so long a wait, he had ceased to believe. For it was she, was it not, upon whom the ultimate success or failure of the party depended? Wasn't that the whole message of poetry? It was regrettable, certainly, that poor Ida should have to be hurt and his career in Tremain & Dodge jettisoned, but false starts were better soon corrected, and with Geraldine, the world could still one day be his.

6

Derrick: 1912

No sooner had the maid at Dr. Denison's opened the front
door the following afternoon than he heard the swish of
Geraldine's skirt in the dark vestibule and caught the scent
of her perfume. She just touched his hand and hurried down
the stoop to the waiting hansom cab.

"You're very prompt," she said as they started off. "I like
that in a man."

"I've been sitting at the bottom of that stoop all day."

"Really? And to think nobody saw you!"

"I wore different disguises. Sometimes I was a pigeon and
sometimes an English sparrow."

"Come to think of it, there *was* a rather aggressive little
sparrow around here this morning. He drove all the others
away."

"I can't brook rivals."

"Are all the men downtown so fanciful? It gives me such
a new idea of Uncle Linn's office."

"They're fanciful when they're in love."

She turned to him quickly, too quickly, her lips tightly
pursed, her high brow contracted in a pouting frown. Fast
as he had been, she was still ready for him.

"If you're going to be silly, Mr. Hartley, I'm going straight
home."

"Do you call it being silly when a man's dead earnest?"

"I call that being silliest of all. You can be that way with

Ida if you want. That's as it should be. But you and I are simply acquaintances — friendly acquaintances, I hope — who happen to be going together to an exhibition of pictures. Now — is that understood?"

"I tell you what's got to be understood, Geraldine," he retorted, emphasizing her Christian name which she had not yet asked him to use. "I'll tell you just once, and then we'll talk about the exhibition or anything else you want. I don't belong to Ida, and I don't intend to belong to Ida. I think you're the most beautiful and wonderful girl I've ever met, and I want to marry you. There! Now shall we talk about your portrait?"

Geraldine stared silently ahead for a moment. "I think we'd much better," she said, at last, but her voice trembled. "They say Zorka's made my neck too long."

"That's typical. There hasn't been a normal neck since Boldini."

"And, apparently, there's something wrong about the mouth. Isn't there always something wrong about the mouth? Oh, dear!" She plunged her hands petulantly into her muff. "You've got me all upset! Why can't we *get* there?"

"Don't worry. I promise to be good."

And he was. At the gallery they talked only about the pictures, briskly and artificially. The neck in Geraldine's portrait *was* too long, and the mouth a sullen red blob. It was a conventional painting of a society girl in a white ball dress, standing before a mantel. The only thing that struck Derrick about it was the faint hint of a lurking fear in the eyes, but the rest of the painting was so bad that he concluded that this must have been an accident rather than the effect of any subtletly or penetration on the artist's part. When they had made a single tour of the room, Geraldine asked to be taken home, and she slipped out of the hansom and darted up her family's stoop like Cinderella returning from her ball. But not, however, before he had extorted permission to call the following Sunday. He paid the cab and, once again, walked the two miles home, even more elated this time than the first. For he was convinced that he was making progress. If she had taken him up initially for the satisfaction of flirting with Ida's beau, she must have been aware by now that she was caught in a game of someone else's choosing.

On Sunday afternoon, as he walked down Fifty-third Street to the Victor Denisons', he was aware that Ida might have been watching him behind her window curtains, and he turned defiantly to scan the unexpressive tan front of the Trasks' house. He had not written to Ida, but it had not been from fear. To have apologized would have been to insult her. A gentleman could only assume — whatever he might suspect or even know to the contrary — that a kiss such as theirs in the Egyptian Room had meant as little to her as to him. There were certain crises when brave men and cowards had to behave in the same way.

Geraldine and her mother received him in the back parlor that had been furnished in Indian fashion with the relics of Dr. Denison's early traveling days. Gleaming scabbards and pieces of Oriental armor hung on the wall amid the heads of water buffalo and tigers, and the floor was strewn with shaggy bearskins. The chairs and settee were of dark, elaborately carved wood, like grotesque New England porch furniture, and two great painted screens showed various steps in the domestication of elephants. Over the mantel was the single Western motif in a portrait of Mrs. Denison by Madrazo, looking very solemn and long-nosed and holding a large red rose. Geraldine sat in one of the dark chairs by the tea table and dispensed hospitality with an easy, if somehow defiant, gracefulness, while her mother, looking strained and unhappy, talked about the weather. Nobody else was there, and nobody came.

"I wonder if your father wants his tea," Mrs. Denison speculated at last, and when Geraldine simply shrugged, she rose abruptly and left the room. No sooner was Derrick reseated than her daughter leaned stiffly back in an evidently premeditated pose of self-command.

"I think I should tell you that I asked Ida Trask to come in this afternoon. Unfortunately, she had another engagement."

"I thought you understood that references to Ida do not embarrass me."

"Because you're quite shameless!"

"On the contrary. I've been very much ashamed, but I have no intention of being ashamed forever. It isn't as if we'd been engaged."

"But you admit you made up to her?"

"I paid her some attention — yes."

"And the moment another girl came along, you dropped her flat!"

"The moment *you* came along."

"What assurances would *I* have that I wouldn't be treated the same way?"

"You'd have two. In the first place, you're a hundred times prettier than Ida."

"Poor Ida! Really!"

"And in the second, I love you." Geraldine shook her head in quick deprecation, but he went firmly on. "I never loved Ida, and I never told her that I did. We have no obligations to each other."

"But did you never kiss her?"

Derrick smiled. There were moments when Geraldine seemed the very portrait of feminine sophistication and others when she might have been fourteen. "If I had, do you think I'm the kind who'd tell?"

"And what does Ida think of all this?"

"I haven't the presumption to guess."

"I bet she's utterly wretched!" Geraldine exclaimed with a little wail. "It's all the most dismal mess!" She stamped her foot in sudden petulance under the tea table. "Why did I have to go to Aunt Dagmar's that night? Why did I have to meet you in the first place?"

"Because you were bored with Talbot Keating," he answered promptly. "Because you wanted to meet a man who would really care for you." He seized her hand suddenly and pressed it hard, and she stared at him with a paralyzed horror as if she realized that he was going to kiss her, there and then, under the horns of the water buffalo, and that he might not have finished before her father came in. He read this in her eyes and more, that she yearned now to have him do it and get it over with, to have him add the scandal of his presumption to the scandal of his inconstancy and confound them both in irredeemable sin. He leaned over, half rising from his chair, and then drew back as Dr. Denison appeared in the doorway.

"My dear Hartley, I'm delighted to see you," he murmured as he strolled in. "Geraldine, my dear, you know how I like my tea." He sat down and pulled up each trouser leg carefully, as affable and easy as his wife had been nervous and uncomfortable. He was as handsome, for a man in his mid-fifties, as was Geraldine for her own sex and age. He had thick grey curly hair and Geraldine's wide clear eyes in a long, smooth oval face. One eyelid drooped in a way that Derrick had heard was supposed to be fascinating to women. But he evidently intended to stay.

Geraldine busied herself with the tea things while the doctor embarked on a discussion of the great differences between Derrick's profession and his own. Yet the leisurely way in which he plunged his thumbs in the pockets of his grey vest, his little cough as he surveyed a well-shod foot, his air of faint but perennial amusement, suggested much more the exchange and the ticker tape than the angry reds and gleaming whites of the emergency ward.

"You financial boys have it all over us doctors. If one of you slips up, what happens? Some poor devil loses his money, isn't that about the gist of it? But when a doctor slips up — and even the best of us do, you know — it may be the same poor devil's life."

"But you have one great advantage," Derrick pointed out. "If the poor devil's dead, he can't complain."

"True! And you don't even give them ether when you take their money!" The doctor tilted his head back and opened his mouth as if to laugh, but no sound emerged. "Maybe it all evens up in the end. But there's another thing I envy about Wall Street as I get older, and that's the respect you pay to age. Take Linn Tremain, for example. I'll bet all of you young fellows downtown consider him a sort of financial Nestor."

"It's true, we do."

"Whereas I'm sure all the interns at St. Luke's refer to me as an exploded old quack."

Derrick laughed spontaneously at the probable accuracy of the doctor's idea. But at the same time it occurred to him that the man who could see this was no fool. "You forget a very simple thing, Doctor," he said. "In my field, if the old man is still around, he's probably rich. Opinions may vary about who's a good doctor, but a man who's made a fortune is always a good money-maker. What other criterion do we have?"

"Gracious me, is that what comes of working for Linn? So young and such a cynic!"

And so it went, back and forth, for half an hour, while Geraldine sat looking from one to the other with an apprehension that seemed to take both sides at once, until Derrick, realizing that he had been blocked by a major diplomat, rose to take his leave. But as he turned to Geraldine, the evident relief in her evasive eyes angered him, and he blurted out: "Will you ride with me tomorrow in the Park?"

He turned again, before she could answer, to her father, who was smiling cryptically. "I'm quite aware, Doctor, that I am not entirely welcome in this house. But it's absolutely vital for me to have a talk alone with your daughter. If she met me in Central Park, and if she left me there, would it be all right for us to ride for an hour?"

"A 'last ride together'?"

"In a fashion, yes."

Dr. Denison put his head back to execute again his soundless laugh. "My dear fellow, do you really think a girl Geraldine's age needs her father's permission to go riding with a young man in the Park? I should like to see the fix I'd be in in this house if I started laying down that law!"

Derrick swung immediately back to Geraldine. "How about it then? Tomorrow at three?"

She appealed in a worried glance to her father, but for what answer it was not clear. His only response was a faintly irritated shrug. "At three," she murmured and turned to the mantel as the good doctor, reverting again to the contrast between financial and medical men, escorted Derrick slowly to the door.

The next morning Derrick went to Mr. Tremain's office and told him the whole story. The latter listened silently, touching the tips of his fingers together, his lips pursed, his head slowly shaking.

"I won't say I haven't heard about it," he said at last. "You've got them all really down on you now."

"Mrs. Tremain's family?"

"Yes. And a formidable lot they can be, I assure you."

"I don't care a rap about them, sir. I only care about you. Are *you* down on me?"

Mr. Tremain squinted at the window for a silent moment. Then he faced Derrick again with a sterner stare. "What's between you and Ida?"

"A bit of tomfoolery. A kiss. That's all. I'm sorry about it, sir, but I can't go back to her now, feeling as I do. Would you want me to?"

"Oh, no! *No!*" Mr. Tremain hit the desk in sudden emphasis. "Poor Ida, she's had enough without that. Don't you dare quote me to any of the Denisons — they'd have my skin for it — but as long as this thing has happened, you may as well go after Geraldine and grab her if you can. She's not worth a quarter of Ida, but I'll admit she's a stunner. And if anyone can make anything out of her, it's probably you!"

Derrick never forgot that afternoon. He was not a man normally sensitive to nature, but the dark and light greens of Central Park under the pale sky of an early spring, the slowly prancing horses with their smartly cut tails and Geraldine in black riding clothes with a tall black hat, was always in later years to be re-evoked for him by a Constantin Guys or a Toulouse-Lautrec. Geraldine had never been more animated. She talked without stopping about Paris and parties and what the man at Cartier's had said about her aquamarines and how she didn't like Southampton because there was sand in everything. Derrick smiled at the thought of how it would have bored him had he not been in love; a drugged man can laugh at pain. And Geraldine was at her best with trivia. She faced the world, her world, with the bright eyes of a little girl before a mountain of ice cream and spun sugar. He could imagine her idea of a serious discussion — was it possible, did Derrick think (and here she undoubtedly would pucker her brow and stick her chin forward to indicate a bold candor), for a man and woman to be . . . just friends?

And he began to realize, as their ride progressed, as his soul smoothed itself out, "a long cramped scroll" in the phrase of the Browning poem suggested by her father, that such was precisely the topic that she was now trying to introduce. Between him and his urgency she was piling up, with nervous, darting hands, a makeshift wall of parasols and hatboxes and gloves and tissue paper. What she planned to use for cement was Platonic love! With a shrug and a snort he swept the wall away.

"Of course, we're just avoiding the real topic."

"Oh. Derrick!" she pleaded, with panic in her eyes. "Don't! I'm having such a good time!"

"I know you are. And I'd be perfectly willing to have you go on talking as long as you want, if I thought I'd have another chance to see you. But *will* I?"

"See me? Of course you will. How ridiculous."

"It's not ridiculous!" he said, and the roughness of his tone made her immediately spur her horse forward. "Your parents are obviously determined to keep me away from you, and I'm equally determined that they shan't. If you'll agree to treat me as you would any other eligible beau — like Mr. Keating, for example — I'll agree to go on talking about friendship between the sexes as long as you like. But will you?"

She reined her horse in and faced him now with an expression of condescending reproach. "I don't know what you mean by an 'eligible beau,'" she retorted, "and I think it's highly impertinent of you to mention Talbot Keating's name."

"All I want to know is whether you'll go riding with me again next Sunday."

"I refuse to be pinned down like that. Really, Derrick, you're the limit!" As her horse moved into a trot she called back to him: "Why can't you be like other people?"

He kicked his horse to catch up with her. "Why can't I be treated like other people?"

"You are."

"Not by your father. Oh, I don't blame him, of course. I suppose it's only natural for him to look higher. You could marry a duke. Or even a millionaire." He laughed crudely, in sudden, sheer good spirits as he caught up with her. "Only I guess you'd have to marry the millionaire first!"

She pulled up to a walk, her eyes alive with anger. "I think you're perfectly horrid!" she cried. "What have I ever done to you that you should insult me?"

"I'm only admitting I'm no catch," he protested. "But just give me time. I'm going to make as much money as your Uncle Linn ever made. And *he* was the one who brought the Denison's over from Brooklyn!"

Geraldine opened her mouth for a moment, but then closed it and turned her gaze serenely to the tops of the trees by the bridle path. "I think you're the rudest man I've ever met," she said in a remote, reflective tone. "*And* the most mercenary."

"Why? Because I call a spade a spade?"

"No. Because you assume that my family are after a 'catch.' As a matter of fact, at the risk of spoiling you, I may as well admit that they agree with you. They think you *will* make as much money as Uncle Linn."

His heart bounded. "Then what's wrong with me?"

"You're Ida's beau." She turned to make a little mocking face at him. "Or should I say, Ida's 'eligible beau'?"

"But I'm not!"

"Oh, but you are. In Daddy's eyes. And in Aunt Dagmar's. And in Aunt Lily's. I assure you, I've been told, in no uncertain terms, to keep my hands off you!"

"But there's nothing between me and Ida!" he cried in exasperation. "Nothing at all!"

"Nothing? Do you call kissing nothing?"

"For pity's sake, is there *no* privacy in Fifty-third Street? Or do the Denisons have public confessional?"

"It's just like *The Mill On The Floss*," Geraldine continued in her maddening superior tone. "Only there Philip hadn't even kissed Lucy. Or if he had, George Eliot doesn't say so."

"So now we take our morals from George Eliot! An old drab who lived in open sin for twenty years!"

"She did not!" Geraldine exclaimed indignantly. "She and Mr. Lewes simply shared a home. It was very daring, of course, but basically I'm sure everything was all right."

"You can't really be so naïve as to think —!" But he stopped as he made out the lively interest beneath the stubbornness in her averted face. Obviously, she would be relieved and delighted to spend the rest of their ride discussing the nature of George Eliot's relationship with Lewes. "Look, Geraldine. If I were to give you up —"

"Give me up!" she retorted angrily. "What do you mean, give me up? Do you think you own me?"

"Give up pursuing you, then. Do you think if I did, I'd go back to Ida?"

"I'm sure I don't know, and I'm sure I don't care. The point is, I can't go riding again, or anywhere again, with a man who has been so markedly attentive to my own first cousin."

"Then you had no business leading me on in the first place!" he exclaimed hotly.

"Leading you on?"

"You know perfectly well what I mean!"

Tears of real anger welled up in her eyes. "I think you're the horridest man I've ever met. And if I did . . . flirt with you . . . just for a few minutes, it was wrong of me." She shook her head emphatically. "Very wrong of me."

"It was the best thing you ever did in your life!" he cried. "You saved Ida, and you saved me. And you saved yourself from Talbot Keating — that's what I'm going to prove to you."

"Never!"

"Are we both to miss everything because of Ida?"

"You kissed her, Derrick!"

"Oh, Geraldine, *really*," he groaned.

"You *did!*" She shook her head violently. "And Aunt Dagmar called me in and gave me such a bawling out as you never heard in your life. And so did Daddy. And Aunt Lily looked at me with those reproachful eyes of hers, which was even *worse*. They said I'd always had all the beaux, and now I had to take Ida's. They made me feel so *awful*. Oh, Derrick, you can't imagine. And I *promised* I wouldn't see you again!"

Derrick, watching that stubbornly shaking head, felt a sudden desperate bafflement. He could hardly believe that the hard swift vessel of his passion was going to founder on reefs of such obviously cardboard scenery, but something in the pit of his stomach warned him that so it might be. "Geraldine," he pleaded, "listen to me. Listen to me this once. You are the only woman I've ever loved. The only one. What you and I could have together might make us different people. Real people. Happy people. I've had my glimpse of it now, and I know. You're surrounded by family who live by the morals you find in children's books: what you owe to Ida or Talbot Keating and who gave who his word. Don't you see you can't *live* that way? Or love that way?" He was addressing himself to the back of her head, but he knew by the rigidity of her posture that she was listening. It was the time to take his ultimate gamble. "I can't compete with any of them on Fifty-third Street. It's not my territory. And I can't compete with Talbot Keating in offering you possessions. But if you would come with me for an hour to my apartment, I could try to show you what love is."

She turned quickly around, her face very white and drawn. "Oh, Derrick," she murmured in a horrified tone. "Don't *say* things like that. Please!"

He rode up abreast of her. "I have to. I have to prove to you that you're a woman. As well as a niece and daughter."

"Oh, I'm a woman," she said softly in a different voice. "I promise you, Derrick, I'm a woman."

"Show me," he said, and stretched his hand across to her. She looked at him for a moment and then at his hand and then slowly reached out her own.

As he grasped her fingertips, the thing happened that changed his life. Or at least so it seemed at the time. Later, he was to speculate that it had simply caused Geraldine to do on impulse what she would have done anyway on reflection. Her horse shied to the left, and as she lost her balance and fell towards him, he caught her round the waist and lifted her from the saddle. So far, fate might have played into his hands, for there was an old if rather hackneyed note of romance in his gesture, and Geraldine was not impervious to such notes. But there was nothing out of Walter Scott in what happened next. His own horse shied, and Derrick, not an experienced rider at best and unused to his extra burden, tumbled with a screaming Geraldine to the mud of the bridle path. They both rose to face each other, with nothing damaged but Geraldine's coat and their relationship.

She turned away without a word and walked quickly down the bridle path towards the shed where they had leased the horses. The latter were already out of sight.

"Geraldine!" he called, hurrying after her. "Forgive me!"

She did not turn, and when he caught up, he saw that she was staring grimly ahead down the path, very pale and set. But when he tried to take her hand, she lashed at him suddenly with her riding crop and hissed the word "Beast!" She was evidently on the verge of hysteria, and there was nothing he could do but bow his head and pause to let her go ahead alone.

The oddest thing about the whole sorry business, he reflected later that night over many solitary brandies, was his own premonition, despite all that his reason told him, that his cause was hopeless. Of course Geraldine cared about him, and the objections of her family were trivial. How, then, was it not a situation where sex and boldness and youth were bound to prevail? How could the doemstic principles of Dr. Denison and his two sisters, like the pretty, cuddlesome bunny rabbits of Beatrix Potter, not scamper away before the first rumbling growl of the real world? Surely the clue had to lie in Geraldine herself and not in her paternal aunts. Derrick knew very little of nerves from his own, but his mother had been a prey to their disorders, and he had seen as a child how fear could paralyze any instinct, even that of self-preservation. Geraldine, he was sure, would have made love with the devil himself — unless Aunt Dagmar had classified the devil as "unattractive." Somehow, perhaps because of her own mother's quivering abdication as a parent and rumored solace in drugs, she had set herself limits of conduct, had staked out the area of permissible frolic with little replicas of those very bunny rabbits that had just come to mind. Perhaps she now gazed at him over her artificial border with eyes of tremulous distrust. If he could only get at her, if he could only fix her attention entirely on himself and away from her family for a few days or even hours, he was bound to prevail. But how could he get the time?

How indeed? In the next two weeks she was always "out" when he called at Fifty-third Street, nor would she even come to the telephone or answer his letters. Half crazed with anger and frustration, he found, for the first time, no relief in work.

Mr. Tremain, who knew all, stopped by his desk one morning and placed a sympathetic hand on his shoulder.

"You'd better give it up, my boy. Young Keating's at the house every day now. Dagmar tells me the engagement is going to be announced next week. It's just as well to get the damn thing over with."

Derrick did not even look up until he heard the older man's sigh and retreating step. He had never been able to endure the least expression of sympathy from others. The following Saturday afternoon he climbed the stoop of the Victor Denisons' house, determined to stand in the doorway until they permitted him to see Geraldine or sent for the police. As he was about to ring the bell, however, the door opened, and Ida Trask came out. The little vestibule that contained their startled meeting was at once a tight, suffocating box of embarrassment.

"Hello, Derrick."

"Hello, Ida. You're looking well."

"Oh, I'm fine." Her voice was low, but unresentful. She moved to the outer door and then turned suddenly back, a hand on the knob. "Don't go in, Derrick," she pleaded. "For your own sake. Talbot Keating is there with his mother. It'll be so miserable for everyone."

He looked into her dark, troubled eyes and read there only kindness and solicitude. It struck him for the first time that, for all his attempts to be honest, he had not faced the magnitude of his unkindness to Ida. It was an immediate solace to him that she should see him in his present misery. "Thanks for the warning. I know it was kindly meant. But if one was born a mule, one must lead a mule's life."

Ida nodded quickly and hurried down the stoop without again turning back. Derrick watched until she had crossed the street, then shrugged ruefully and pressed the bell. The Irish girl who opened the door looked scared when she recognized him and blurted out that Miss Denison was not at home.

"Look, Bessie," he said in a firm tone, "I *know* Miss Denison's at home and that Mr. Keating is with her. I want you to be good enough to step into the living room and ask if she will come down and let me put her one question. Surely that's reasonable. Wouldn't you do as much for one of *your* young men?"

The girl hesitated and blushed and stammered out something about her instructions, but as Derrick simply stood there, staring at her, she finally turned and ran up the dark high straight stairway into the blackness of the landing. The murmur of voices which he could just hear from the upstairs living room ceased as she went in, and he next heard Dr. Denison's voice alone. A few moments later there was a step on the landing, a masculine step, and a handsome, but rather florid young man in tweeds came slowly down the stairs. As he approached, Derrick could make out that he was smiling, probably in embarrassment.

"I'm Talbot Keating," he announced, halfway down, and then had to proceed, rather foolishly, to the bottom in silence. He put out a hand that Derrick grasped briefly. "Geraldine thought I'd better see you. Look here, old man, I know this is hard on you. No one knows it better than I. But the thing is — well, Geraldine and I are engaged."

"Since when?"

Keating looked surprised at the sternness of his tone. "Well, officially, I guess only since yesterday. But there's been a kind of understanding for a year."

"Would you think me very presumptuous if I asked to have my dismissal from Geraldine herself?"

Keating's eyes avoided Derrick's stare. "Isn't that a bit rough on her?"

"I think she owes it to me. Just that and nothing more."

Keating shuffled his feet and then shrugged and went back up the stairs. Derrick could hear his voice in the living room followed by Geraldine's shrill "But I won't!" This in turn was followed by a buzz of family argument, and at last he heard her quick step and his name called from the landing.

"Derrick Hartley!"

He went to the bottom of the stairs and looked up. Her outline was tall and white and forbidding against the dark landing.

"Yes, Geraldine."

"I'm engaged to Talbot Keating! *Now* will you go?"

"Yes!" he shouted back up at her in a sudden explosion of wrath. "I'll go and I won't come back. And I'll always remember you didn't even have the guts to come down these stairs to dismiss the man you'd led on!"

As he strode back up Fifty-third Street to Fifth Avenue he felt a certain rude exhilaration that every Denison was probably watching his retreat from behind the shelter of second-floor curtains.

If Derrick had been unable to work while his fate was uncertain, this was no longer the case after it had been sealed. If it had seemed to him, for one long dazzling week, that his future might contain not only a partnership in Tremain & Dodge but marriage to the most beautiful girl in New York, one of these destinies, at least, was still open to him. For three months after his last visit to Fifty-third Street he worked downtown until midnight almost every night, relaxing only on Sundays and then only on walks. When he read in the newspaper of the wedding of Miss Geraldine Denison and Mr. Talbot Keating at Saint Thomas' and the brilliant reception which followed at Sherry's, he felt, with a relief that surprised him, that his heart could now come out of mourning. He started to go to parties again and to play billiards at the Harvard Club. Mr. Tremain never referred to the matter but once, when he asked gruffly if everything was now "all right." Derrick had simply nodded, and that had been that. But it was tacitly agreed between them that Derrick had better come no more to the family Sunday suppers.

The first member of the Denison family that he was to see again was Mrs. Trask. He was summoned to Mr. Tremain's office one day at noon to find Ida's mother sitting by her brother-in-law's desk. She seemed as cheerful and self-contained as ever, greeting Derrick as if no shadow had ever dimmed the pale sun of their friendship.

"Linn has been helping me with my little investments," she said. "We do it once a quarter, and I always feel that I'll get richer if I come downtown myself. I didn't want to leave without saying hello."

"I'm glad you didn't, Mrs. Trask."

"I'm not sure you deserve it, though. You never come to see us any more."

"You never ask me."

"Well, that's soon remedied. Come dine on Saturday, will you?"

"I shall be delighted."

There was no refusing a woman who was such a sport. She seemed to be saying: "I don't hold Geraldine against you. Any man could lose his head over Geraldine. But she's gone, and you and I are realists, and how about Ida? If she suited you once, can't she suit you again?" And couldn't she? He had miscalculated once, because he had not thought himself capable of the sudden flame of feeling that Geraldine had kindled. But could it be kindled again? Didn't he, at last, really know himself? And hadn't Mr. Tremain said that Ida was worth four of Geraldine?

On Saturday there were eight for dinner, and as on his

first evening at the Trasks', Derrick was not seated by Ida. She looked flushed and uncomfortable and constantly avoided his glance. Had her mother not warned her that he was coming? Anything was possible with Mrs. Trask. After dinner he went to the living room ahead of the other men and walked deliberately to the corner where Ida had retreated with her needlepoint. She could hardly stop him from sitting beside her, but she leaned more closely over her work.

"I want to thank you for warning me that day at Geraldine's. You were right. It was miserable for all."

Ida's voice was very sad and low. "I'm sorry for the pain it must have caused you."

"That's all over now."

"Oh, yes, everything's over now."

"Everything?"

"Everything," she replied with quick emphasis, pulling her needle through the material. "We all get over our disappointments." She was still flushed, but she forced herself to go on. Evidently it was a point that had to be made. "I mean, you're not the only one," she explained.

"You mean that *you*'ve got over me."

"Please, Derrick." Her voice trembled. "Let's not go into the past."

"But if I want to? If Geraldine was only an insane infatuation?"

"Derrick!" She looked up now and glared at him fiercely. "What do you think of me? That I'm a tap to be turned off and on?" Her breath came in a gasp. "How can I make you understand that there can never be anything again between you and me? I can forgive you Geraldine. I could forgive any man Geraldine. The only thing I could never forgive would be your trying to come back to me!"

Across the room, as her words hung in the air between

them, came the long high peal of her mother's laugh. Someone must have told a really good story, for Mrs. Trask was
sitting with her head tilted way back and her shoulders were
shaking. It seemed to fill the room, that laugh, like a cool,
splashing stream, eddying about to clean out every corner of
the dust and litter of hesitations and sensitivities, filling up
every vacancy with its clean and bubbling demand, its
despotic normality, and Derrick was surprised to feel the
stirring of a regret, faintly kin to remorse, that the fine, pale
candle of Ida's scruples was so sure to be doused by it.

PART III

Ida Between Worlds

7

Ida: 1912

I was always ashamed of the tremor of excitement with which my heart greeted any news of illness in the family. It was not that I really wanted anyone to be sick, but my relatives, when stricken, seemed less superior, and my assiduousness at the bedside, in contrast to the reluctant visitations of the others (for the Denisons had a horror of maladies), made up in my mind, at least in part, for the shyness and awkwardness which I stubbornly insisted that my family deplored in me. Never was this shame more burning than on the day when my poor father's increased apathy and lassitude were at last diagnosed as the symptoms of a virulent liver disease. My mother, so strong on other occasions, went almost to pieces at the news, and the tumult of her restlessness, of her hoarsely whispered telephone calls to doctors, of her ordering about of nurses, threatened to destroy the peace and quiet so necessary to the patient's unlikely recovery. When Aunt Dagmar suggested that I give up Barnard to help keep order at home, I was only too glad to comply with her wish. By hard work and sacrifice I might be able to make some reparation for having, even for a minute, considered Father's illness in the light of an interruption from another preoccupation. I could sublimate the sufferings of Ariadne to the tender ministrations of Florence Nightingale.

I speak, of course, with a detachment and insight acquired in later years, but even at the time I wondered if Mother's perfunctory acceptance of my sacrifice of college might not have sprung from her intuitive understanding of my mixed motives.

"When this is all over, and your father is well again, we'll take a trip to Europe," she promised me. "We might even charter a little yacht and do the Greek islands. That would be a lot better, wouldn't it, than hearing some old maid with a pince-nez lecture on Helen of Troy?"

I recognized Mother's picture of Barnard and made no comment. For I had every intention of ultimately enrolling myself among the academic old maids of her fantasy, and despite the mockery in her tone, I was moved by the idea of Helen's legendary beauty finding a state of preservation in the soft tones of a withered virgin lecturer. The only way that I had been able to reconcile myself to the horror of Derrick's desertion had been in cultivating the hope that the dismal chapter of love was now over for me and that the balm of a long grey institutional life might one day assuage any lingering pain. Who had I been to presume to look to such a man as Derrick? Did he not, in his male strength and egotism, belong to the kind of female that Geraldine represented, a Rossetti Guinevere of pale willowy weakness? I was deservedly crushed for my boldness by the armored heel whose very armor had attracted me. It was suitable that one who had shivered in pleasure before such ruthlessness should now shiver in pain. If I could only succeed in robing myself in the gown of learning and in spending a lifetime with beautiful and soul-lifting things, even under the shadow of the menacing male figure who had cast me aside but who had given me a kiss that I would always remember, might I not be seizing as much happiness as I had any right to expect?

But now it appeared that I might not be permitted even this. For, however humble an ambition, what was it but variation, and was not variation the very crime that Mother's family could always detect? And did it really matter, if one varied, whether one did so as a king or as a peasant, as a great actress or an old-maid dean? I felt in our house, and even in Uncle Victor's, that Derrick had been forgiven and that the family thought it only a matter of time before I would take him back. Their attitude was the harder to combat in that it was never expressed. Nobody asked me to see Derrick; nobody had the indelicacy to praise him to me. Everybody simply assumed that he would continue as a part of the Denison pattern of life, and how could that be unless he was incorporated into the family? I had thought that Father's illness might bring postponement. As it turned out, it brought acceleration.

My sickbed duties consisted largely in reading aloud. Father had an inexhaustible enthusiasm for nineteenth century fiction, and he preferred me to Mother as a reader because I did not keep stopping to fuss over his bed or medicine table or to close a window or to check up on a nurse. I read Jane Austen and Trollope by the hour while he lay silent and still, his large, dark sad eyes fixed on me and the book. He was heartbreakingly patient and cheerful. I think he minded dying only on Mother's account.

"Ida," he said quietly, on the afternoon that we finished *Ayala's Angel,* "I think it's time we had a little talk. I'm not much on little talks, but we can't altogether avoid them."

"You're not supposed to tire yourself," I protested, more in alarm for myself than for him. "Can't it wait till you're better?"

Father's smile was charming. "Oh, but when I'm better, we'll never do it! We'll talk about silly things. What have the healthy to do with facts?"

I clasped my hands on top of the closed novel. "We'll talk about anything you want."

"Let us start briefly with myself." He turned his head away

and stared up at the ceiling as if to find his words there. "There will always be people who will tell you that I was dominated by your mother's family. If nobody else does, your grandmother will. And, of course, it's perfectly true. But I want you to remember that I chose it that way. Your mother's family are the kindest, fairest people in the world. If I had it to do over again, I'd do it the same way."

"But surely Grandma understands that!"

"No." His lips parted in a faint smile. "Grandma prefers independence to happiness any day, God bless her. Each to his taste. All I want you to understand, Ida, is that my life has been my own doing. For better *and* for worse. Perhaps I should have had the guts to get out of the trust business and go into teaching. Nobody tried to stop me. Certainly not your mother. But I preferred my little rut, and I bless those who made me happy in it. In life you can be a leader or you can be led. It doesn't make much difference which you choose, as long as you *do* choose. My life could have been a tragedy if I had decided that I was the victim of a family plot. I didn't."

"But you *are* a leader," I protested. "All the family look up to you and respect you."

"They respect me, of course. As I say, they are very fair. But that is enough about me. To come to *you*." He reached out a thin hand to put on mine. "You could be a leader, my dear."

"Oh, Father, me?"

"Yes," he insisted, "I'm quite serious. Everyone thinks you're like me, and that little Christopher's like your mother, but everyone's wrong. Chris is basically the conformist, and you . . . well, I can easily see you as a radical dean or a window-smashing suffragette."

"You're making fun of me!"

"No. It would simply be a matter of making you mad

enough. But you could also be passive. Oh, yes, I see that, too. If you married Derrick, for example, *he* would always be the leader."

"I'll never marry Derrick!"

"What is the use of unilateral resolutions?" His tone was dry, and he closed his eyes. I saw that my violence had tired him, and was silent. "They can always be revoked, anyway. I'm not suggesting that you marry Derrick. I'm suggesting that if you did, he would be the leader. But there's nothing wrong in that. It's just as good a life to be Mrs. Derrick Hartley as to be a radical professor. The only thing to remember is that it's *your* choice. My worry about you, Ida, is that you might slide into it. Into being passive. Or even into being active. Without knowing that you were committed."

"Do you think I *should* marry Derrick?"

Father closed his eyes again in protest against such a rejection of all subtlety. "I think you should recognize there's no reason you shouldn't."

Which was all I could get out of him. Father, even when well, detested the didactic and rehearsed ahead of time his rare bits of advice to reduce them to the fewest possible words. Now, too, a little stir in the corridor betokened the daily visit of Grandma Robbins. She always paused for a moment on the threshold to apprehend with one quick, bird-like glance if her only child was still alive and then moved with a rapid rustling of black skirts to the bedside. She was so totally intent upon Father that she did not even nod to me, and, putting down the Trollope, I silently left the room. I found Mother in the corridor where she always hovered during Grandma's visits, not wishing to tire Father with the presence of two women at once, but always at her post to be able to drag off her mother-in-law at the first hint of fatigue in the patient's voice.

"You have a visitor downstairs," she told me, and I was glad for the darkness of the corridor. "Put on a dash of powder before you go down. You look done in, dear. I told him you were reading to your father, but he said he'd wait. He's been in the living room half an hour."

"Oh, Mother, is it Derrick? Why didn't you tell him to go?"

"Because he didn't come to see *me*. Do you want me to pick your friends for you? Is that my Barnard girl?"

"Must I go down?"

"Of course you must! If you don't want him to come to the house, tell him so yourself!"

"You know I wouldn't dare," I murmured resentfully, and hurried down the stairs to get it over with.

Derrick and I sat in the living room amid the peculiar hush that sickness gives to a dark house. Yet he appeared to feel no constraint; he talked about himself and his business and how clever Uncle Linn was and even about Galli-Curci and her mad scene in *Lucia*. I sighed with relief as irrelevancy succeeded irrelevancy. Yet I could hardly bring myself to comment except in monosyllables. My world had shrunk to the sickbed upstairs and to my shame at my preoccupation with Derrick. I longed for him to go away and leave me to the lesser discomfort of missing him.

"Don't you think it's rather artificial to go on like this? When we're both thinking the same thing?"

"But I *want* to be artificial!" I protested in alarm. "Artificiality is an art."

"And one you've been taught by masters."

"I don't suppose that's a compliment, but I shall take it as one."

"Why do we have to be so stiff, Ida? Here you are, and here I am. I feel about you exactly as I did that day in the museum, and I believe you feel the same way about me." I made a gesture of protest, but he went straight on. "If there's such a thing as common sense, why shouldn't we be married?"

"You never asked me!"

"But you knew I was going to!" he insisted boldly. "I was just about to when Geraldine hit me. And if you were really fair, you'd admit that was your fault. Who went off to visit Granny and left me in a house with measles?"

"Measles?" In spite of everything I smiled. "Is that what you call poor Geraldine now?"

"What else? She gives a high fever, but she can't be caught twice. If you had a business mind, you'd see that I was a more valuable property after Geraldine than before."

"I'm not worried about your value, Derrick. I'm sure it's very high."

"Then you'd better marry me."

"Before another Geraldine catches you?"

"No, I tell you, I'm immune. You'd better marry me before some Geraldine in striped trousers and a bowler hat catches *you*."

"Oh, me." I shrugged at the absurdity of his idea. "I, too, am immune." I managed to look at him steadily for a moment. "Because, you see, you were *my* measles."

He laughed loudly, and the noise seemed to rattle the whole still house. "But you don't have to get over *me!*"

"Ah, but I do," I said gravely, shaking my head. "It's just exactly what I do have to do."

"Why, for pity's sake?"

"Because you don't love me."

Derrick rose and paced up and down the living room rug. When at the furthest end from me, he turned suddenly, like a cross-examining lawyer. "Why do you think I want to marry you? Surely not for your money?"

"Nor for my beauty," I answered meekly. "I'm afraid you only want to marry me for my family."

"My dear girl, you're absolutely out of your mind! A man doesn't marry to acquire in-laws. If anything, that's what keeps him a bachelor."

He seemed so burstingly alive, so noisily alive at just that moment, in contrast to the approaching death upstairs, that I clenched my fists in a sudden agony of wretchedness. How could I talk about my family when it was disintegrating on the floor above? Surely he was right, and I was out of my mind to think that any young man could want a family that consisted of a dying man, a distracted wife, a moody, muddled girl and a small boy!

"Why do you want me, then?" I asked with a stifled sob.

"Because you suit me."

"Is *that* love?"

"You may well ask." He shrugged philosophically. "Is your suiting me love or was measles love? What I feel for you, Ida, is much pleasanter and deeper and more lasting."

"I'd rather be measles!" I cried in petulance. "What girl wouldn't? Please, Derrick, go now. I can't stand any more of this!"

He came over to take my hand. "I'll go, of course," he said quietly. "And when I come back, don't worry. I shan't be importunate. I'm not a man to beg. But I can talk about the weather and the high events of Fifty-third Street as long as the most garrulous of the Denisons!"

I was hot and ashamed, when he had gone, to find that, like the heroine of *Pride and Prejudice,* which I had read the week before to Father, I was regretting already that my rejected suitor so obviously meant his words about refusing to beg.

In the next weeks Father grew weaker and weaker, and finally there was no further question of reading aloud. Mother would hardly leave his room now, and the household chores and the visitors were turned over to me. I would not have gone out at all except that Aunt Dagmar insisted that I drive with her in the afternoons. None of the family forgot about youth, even in the presence of death, and Father's illness was considered in the light of its ultimate effect on everyone, including myself. Aunt Dagmar had a very good idea that filial grief was not the sole cause of my apathy, and those afternoon drives were designed to shake me out of my morbidness.

Even the automobile assisted her plans. Aunt Dagmar's Brewster, with its tiny round engine and huge roundish wicker body, its cushions and tassels, reminded me of a luxurious Easter egg basket in the window of a Fifth Avenue shop. Perched inside like a big handhome nesting bird, a picture of ease and indolence, its owner would deliver her sprightly lectures of practical advice. Aunt Dagmar, more dependent on servants than any woman I have ever known, who could be induced to walk a block a day only under the most peremptory orders of her doctor, yet maintained successfully in our tolerant family her reputation for vigor and energy.

"I'm going to give you a tip, my dear," she told me on the terrible day when the doctors had withdrawn our last hope. She reached for my hand with her two black-gloved ones and brought it over to her lap. "It's never too soon to face the fact that your position in the world has changed."

"Oh, I know," I murmured. "We shall be very poor. Mother may have to sell the house."

"What do you think *I'm* for?" Aunt Dagmar demanded irritably. "There'll be no selling of houses while I'm around. I'm not talking about a vulgar, useful thing like money. I'm talking about your *position* in the world. You're not a *jeune fille* any more, my dear. You've got to help your mother now. You've got to take over, until she pulls herself together. You've got to run your little family."

"I'll do my best."

"Of course you will. You're a good girl, and you always have been. As your Uncle Linn says (though don't spread it about) you're the best of the lot."

Compliments from Aunt Dagmar, however exciting, always filled me with a bottomless sense of my inadequacy. "If I can ever be a tenth of what Mother is, I'll be happy."

"You can be more than that, my dear, if you have the help *she* had." She paused significantly. "If you have the help of a good, strong man."

"Oh, Aunt Dagmar!"

"Now hush up, till I've finished. I know you're not going to like it, but I want you to hear me out. Derrick Hartley has the respect and affection of all of the family. He lost his head over Geraldine, and he behaved badly. No one denies that. But he took his disappointment like a man, and I think he's learned his lesson. He's hard working, he's bright, and your Uncle Linn and I, in spite of everything, think that he's fundamentally steady and dependable. I haven't much doubt that one day he'll be a partner in the firm. Maybe even the senior partner. He's not a young man to be easily stopped."

"But I don't want to marry a man just because he's not easily stopped!"

"Will you be quiet?" Aunt Dagmar raised her voice severely. "Nobody's asking you to. All I'm suggesting is that if you're turning him down because of Geraldine, you're a ninny."

"But he loved her, Aunt Dagmar! He still does!"

"Men are inconstant creatures, Ida. I *know*. But they're also creatures of habit. If Derrick wants to marry, Derrick will settle down. Now, if you don't care about him, that's another thing. But *if* you care about him and let your pride — your vanity, I should say — deprive you of a good husband, and your mother and little Christopher of a man to take care of them, you're worse than a ninny. You're downright irresponsible!"

"Oh, Aunt Dagmar, *please!*"

"I know it hurts, my dear, but it's my duty. Your happiness may be at stake. Now answer me one question. I needn't say honestly, for you've always been, if anything, too honest. Do you love Derrick?"

"You know I love him!" I wailed bitterly. "Everyone in Fifty-third Street knows I love him!"

"Then may I tell him not to despair?"

"Oh, despair. He won't do any despairing. He's probably out riding with Ellie Denison now."

"He's doing no such thing! He's sitting right in my living room, waiting for me to come back and tell him if there's any hope!"

At this I started to weep, and Aunt Dagmar wisely dropped the subject. But she knew, and I knew, that the decision had been made. I loved him, and I had not positively asserted that he had no hope. In such matters silence has always been properly taken for assent. How could I stand out against my whole family, with their shining panoply of common sense, as well as my own somber, preoccupying love? I knew, even then, that my red danger signal was in the simple fact that I loved Derrick most when he loved me least, but with no one to help me, how was I to persuade Aunt Dagmar of anything that would have struck her as so foolish? Father would have known and understood, but would he have counseled me to act on instinct? When had he so acted himself?

Aunt Dagmar promised me that I should have all the time I wanted, but I knew that I would not get it. I knew that she would speak to Derrick that afternoon, and Derrick was not one to wait. He had the consideration, however, to let a week go by before he called. Consideration? Or was it cleverness? At the end of that week I was beginning to be sick at heart that he might have changed his mind again. Or that he might not come before Father died.

When he came, I went down to meet him in the old back parlor, and he walked across the room to take me in his arms.

"You're a great one for regretting things, Ida, but you're never going to regret this."

We knew Father had only a day to live, and I see the scene now as a Victorian engraving. But it was hardly Victorian, at such a moment, for me to kiss Derrick as desperately as I kissed him. It may, however, have been Victorian of him to assume the demeanor of gravity that he did, as if to avoid the insincerity of announcing his small flame as a bonfire. The Victorian novel usually ended in the embrace to which I clung, and that, no doubt, is the reason that I, like Father, have always so loved Victorian fiction. But in taking Derrick as I took him, in full knowledge of my passion and his coolness, I was surely being as crafty as he. If he owed me anything for what he had done to me, I had wiped the slate clean.

8

Ida: 1922

MY BROTHER, Christopher Trask, was living in the old family brownstone with me and Derrick in the winter when Derrick, who had been hitherto a most indifferent father, first began to take any real notice of our daughter Dorcas. Indeed, Christopher was the first to point this out to me, as he pointed out many things that year. Too little was happening in his life, and too much in mine, and he did not miss one of my minor catastrophes.

"I have the feeling," he told me, "that the destinies of Tremain, Hartley and Dodge are being controlled by a prim little girl of nine on her morning walk to school with Daddy."

"You think they talk about business?"

"I think *he* does," Christopher replied. "I've walked behind them on my way to the subway. Derrick's lips are always moving, and he gesticulates with his left arm in that jerky way of his when he's making financial decisions."

"And what does Dorcas do?"

"Oh, she nods. Very wisely, the little minx."

"But I think that's rather cute, don't you?"

Christopher shrugged. "I wonder if I really believe in the American legend that successful fathers naturally adore their daughters. Isn't it a question of default?"

"By their wives, you mean?"

"Well, hardly by their brothers-in-law."

It was not like Christopher to be so biting, nor was he

with anyone else. But Mother was dead, and he was much alone, and it was only natural that an older sister, who exasperated him by her very failure to play the maternal role which he would have passionately resented her least attempt to play, should bear the brunt of his inner dissatisfactions. I was glad, anyway, to be of that much use to him, for Christopher had used up too much of himself in his desperate effort to enlist in the war. He had been first under age and then underweight, and he had succeeded in getting to France only as an ambulance driver and then at the very end of hostilities. Mother's death, the day after the Armistice, had intensified his sense of anticlimax to an almost unbearable degree. He had not wanted to return to a New York that would have made him feel too desolately an orphan and had remained in Paris for two years, conscientiously cultivating the young artists and writers who came to be known as the lost generation. But Christopher, despite an unpublished novel and some dabbling in cubist painting, never became a true member of the left bank. His candor had too little egotism; it was the candor of good manners and not of self-revelation. And for all his Denison charm and thin, dark, tense good looks, he was, like all my family, basically reserved. He must have stood apart as Uncle Linn had stood apart in Florence half a century before. And then, too, he dressed too well to be ever quite lost. Wall and Fifty-third Streets were waiting for him.

When he returned he went straight into Tremain, Hartley and Dodge, as Uncle Linn's firm had been renamed on his death, and came to live with us in the old house that he and I now jointly owned. The arrangement had been meant to be temporary, but it had extended itself for a year, partly, I fear, because Christopher, for all his exasperation with my nerves and messiness, sensed how much I needed him and was too kind to push me off. Derrick was constantly away on business, in spirit as well as body, and his hours were late, and I clung to my unattached younger brother to throw before the sardonic but basically sympathetic court of his judgment the little problems of my days and nights. Besides, he was wonderful with the children, buying them presents and taking them to the circus and zoo. He seemed to understand Dorcas' damp, steamy moodiness and little Hugo's violent fits of temper which so terrified me, and he never, like Derrick, showed the least preference between them, even when they fought over him and demanded his opinion in favor of one or the other. He was faithful, too, in his calls on Aunt Dagmar, the inconsolable widow whom only he could console, and on all the aunts and uncles in the block. In fact, Uncle Victor, who, more than anyone, had filled Father's place in my life, warned me that the family were taking advantage of Christopher.

"That's the devil of being the youngest of a generation. Chris was too little to get the good of Dagmar and the rest of us when we were at our best. And now that we're beginning to be querulous old crocks who want attention, he's the only one who isn't married and can't get away."

I knew that Uncle Victor was right, for I had seen the trapped look in Christopher's eye at the Sunday night suppers that Uncle Victor had taken over during Aunt Dagmar's mourning. I knew that it pained him not to be a more real part of life in the old house where our adoring mother had once made him the central figure. He suffered from the young veteran's loneliness and inertia, and it was clearly my job to take Mother's place and push him, as she would have done, out of a nest that was filling with my own noisy brood. But I kept postponing the decision. I would say to myself: "Any day now, he'll meet the right girl," or "How do I know that he won't be moved to the Boston office?" I tried to persuade myself that it was not worth his while to leave me for the real reason that I wanted a buffer between myself and Derrick.

It was the critical year of our marriage. It had taken me a decade to learn that I could never change Derrick, and now that I had learned it, I was afraid, not of what he, but of what *I* might do. His self-sufficiency had had the effect of encasing my feeling for him in a cold-storage cellar where all of its strength but not all of its sweetness had been perpetuated. I no longer liked many of my thoughts about Derrick. I did not like, for example, my habit of dwelling on his refusal to take any part in the war. He had claimed his family as dependents and had told me blandly that he could do more good in Wall Street than in a trench. Perhaps this was so. I am certain, anyway, that he believed it. Derrick was no coward. But why should *I* have minded, unless I had minded his not taking his chances with Christopher and the other men? And if I had wanted him to do that, was it not possible that I had wanted him to be killed? There was a thought to ruin a night's sleep for one of my masochistic disposition. Also, I disliked my growing tendency to note and remember Derrick at his least becoming moments, as when he bowed from the waist to a rich banker's wife or when he tried to impress my uncles with how much better Uncle Linn's firm was being managed than in the old days. I shrank increasingly into silence as I recognized my own inclination to cry out against his beliefs. For once I had started, how did I know where I might end?

The crisis came when he fired Scotty Denison. Scotty's first two marriages had collapsed, and he had not yet met Minerva, who was to save him. Uncle Victor had decided that a job in the Tremain firm might help to keep him off the bottle, and pressure had been successfully placed on Derrick. But the latter had warned the family that Scotty's job would not survive the first evidence of his drinking in office hours, and he was good to his word. I heard of it only when Scotty called to entreat my intervention.

It was painful, no doubt, for Scotty to have to go begging to a younger female cousin, and one who had followed him about in his childhood with adoring eyes, but it was still more painful for me to have him do it. And my pain continued, too, after his had worn off, for, taking in my discomfort, his confidence returned, and some of the old, gay, boyish, cheerfully condescending Scotty began to peep out from behind the round red contours of the pompous, middle-aged failure.

"I know I don't come up to Derrick's lights, but we can't all be Derricks, can we?" he protested. Seeing my nod, he ventured a wink. "What sort of a world would it be if we were? A pretty cutthroat affair, I wager. I don't mean that Derrick isn't doing a splendid job, but how did my having a nip at lunchtime hurt him?"

"I'm sure we can fix it somehow."

I resolved to speak to Derrick that night while he was dressing for dinner. It was unfortunate that it should have been for a dinner given by a customer that I had declined at the last moment because of Hugo's croup. He was an undersized child, and his coughing that winter had been very violent, and I hated to leave him even with the most competent nurse. But I should have anticipated that Derrick's anger at my maternal agitation (which he always construed as a rejection of himself) would preclude the least chance of my receiving a sympathetic ear.

He was in his dressing room, in black trousers and undershirt, shaving before his full-length, mahogany-framed mirror. Dorcas, with the plump, demure look that she adopted now when under her father's aegis, was intently engaged in putting the pearl studs in his stiff shirt front.

"I can imagine what's on *your* mind," Derrick said without turning, and the smile whose edge I could make out in the mirror was his stubborn smile. "I can guess who came to weep on whose shoulder this afternoon."

"Oh, Derrick, he was *so* pathetic."

"Let him be pathetic at his own expense, then. Not at mine."

"Couldn't you give him some position where he'd be harmless?"

"I could make him a messenger." He turned abruptly when he caught the reflection of my impatient shrug. "No, I'm serious, Ida. We have messengers older than Scotty. Or I could put him in the mail room or even on the night switchboard. It would keep him out of trouble."

"I mean something dignified."

"We don't have 'dignified' jobs," Derrick retorted flatly, turning back to the mirror. "Not the way I've set up the office. We have responsible jobs and menial jobs, and they don't mix. I refuse to give Scotty the least opportunity to bring discredit on us. Now if it's a handout he wants, I'm willing to consider that."

"He'd never take it!"

"Then he's most unreasonable. He's too proud to work and too proud for charity. I'm afraid he's too proud for me."

"You make things so black and white. All he wants is to be tided over for a bit. The firm used to do that kind of thing all the time. I remember how Uncle Linn would . . ."

"My dear," Derrick interrupted dryly as he sharpened his blade against the strap, "you never really knew your Uncle Linn. You only knew the family legend of him."

I was turning to the door, my lips closed tightly to avoid any open expression of resentment in front of Dorcas, when I heard her exclaim: "Cousin Scotty's a drunk! Isn't that so, Daddy?"

"Go to your room, Dorcas!" I cried in a tone that I had never used to her before. "Go and do your homework. And

I never, never want to hear you talking like that again!"

"But this is my time with Daddy!" she protested, shocked and frightened. When I turned back, she reached out to take hold of the suspenders hanging from Derrick's waist.

"Do what your mother says, Dorcas," Derrick said gruffly, and she ran to the door, pausing at the threshold to ask, in a timorous voice: "Mummy, are you sick?"

"Go ahead, Dorcas," her father said.

Alone with Derrick, I crumpled in a chair and gave myself up to a bit of weeping. He gazed at me silently a minute and then shrugged and continued to shave.

"Do you know something, Ida? You've never heard of feminine guile. You've been brought up in a family where the women get their way by raising their voices. It doesn't happen to work with me. But do you know what might?" I shook my head sullenly. "If, when I came home after a hard day's work, you didn't start wailing about Scotty's job. If instead you put on your best dress and went out to dinner and made me proud of you. And then, on the way home, if you put your head on my shoulder and shed a little tear about Scotty and said you understood my position, but wasn't it a pity... Well, who knows what might not happen?"

I suppose that was my chance. I wiped my eyes and blew my nose and even considered it. "I don't really think I'm the geisha type."

"That's just it! You think if you ask for something, you're being a whore. That's all you learned at Barnard. A lot of claptrap about women's rights!"

But he was wrong. Utterly wrong. I would have been willing to play the geisha had I only known how. It was the fear of being ridiculous that prevented me, or, worse than ridiculous, presumptuous. The Geraldines of this world could be geishas, not the Idas.

"I didn't really want you to do it for *me*," I said sadly as

I got up again to leave. "I wanted you to do it for Scotty. Or for the family."

"And do you think I've done nothing for them?" he demanded, angry again. "Who's kept the firm together? Well, if my wife won't recognize it, at least my partners will. Have a look at *that*." He took from his bureau and handed me an engraved letterhead which announced in big block type the names: "Hartley and Dodge." I stared for a moment before I realized what it meant.

"But where's Uncle Linn's name?"

"We've taken it out. The firm has decided not to carry the names of deceased partners." As he looked at me now, with a first faint furtiveness, I realized, in a thrill of temper, that even he was nervous. He had not known before how to break this to me and had taken a quick advantage of his own impatience. "Besides, Hartley and Dodge is shorter and easier to remember."

"To *remember*," I exclaimed, as the full outrage of what he was doing filled my consciousness. "What have you to do with memory? Have you asked Aunt Dagmar about this?"

"Of course I haven't asked Aunt Dagmar! What business is it of Aunt Dagmar's? Honestly, Ida, your disloyalty is positively psychopathic. You'd rather see the name of a dead uncle on the door than a living husband's!"

"It's not a question of my loyalty to you," I insisted, humiliated to find the tears again in my eyes. "It's a question of *our* loyalty to Uncle Linn who gave you your start. Who made you what you are today!"

"Your ignorance of the business world is exceeded only by your ignorance of your family's role in it," he retorted coldly. "Obviously, there's no point in our continuing this discussion."

The following day I spent in an agony of apprehension, for Aunt Dagmar, despite the note of entreaty in my voice on the telephone, would not see me until the late afternoon. She had changed greatly since Uncle Linn's death, to which she had reacted with a querulous resentment. She seemed to feel that a providence which had denied her children owed her the reparation of preserving her husband at least to his ninetieth year. She stayed home all the time now, receiving visitors with a rather peevish air and making lists of relatives who might wish a pair of Uncle Linn's cufflinks, or a drawing, or even a page of his stamp book. It exasperated her that Derrick, her co-executor, paid so little attention to these details.

"It doesn't surprise me in the least," she said, when I had stammered out my news. "I only marvel that he didn't do it the day of the funeral. Linn always said he'd end by swallowing us up."

"Aunt Dagmar, I'm so sorry."

"Sorry!" she exclaimed fretfully. "He was your choice, wasn't he?"

"I sometimes wonder," I murmured dismally. "You were all so for him."

When Uncle Victor came in from next door, for his daily call, she told him my news while I hung my head.

"Oh, I say, Dagmar, that's too bad!" he exclaimed. "The man was never quite a gentleman." Then he took in my stricken countenance. "Forgive me, Ida, that slipped out. Derrick is a brilliant man, I know, but he goes a bit far at times. He's young, of course. You should learn to curb him. That's a woman's job."

This was too much. I got up, one hand on my lips and hurried from the room. Aunt Dagmar called after me, with contrition in her voice now, but I did not heed her. When I got home, I went upstairs to my little green living room and shut myself in. There, at last, I could give in to my misery. For the shadowy, secret thing which I had always dreaded without making out all of its contours in the misty corners of my fantasy had finally happened, and there was none of the relief of despair in its happening, but only further terror. I had destroyed Fifty-third Street. I had destroyed the family. It had been in the cards that I would do it; everyone, even Geraldine, had always suspected me of being the agent of dissenting forces. Poor Mother, with her sad, hurt eyes, had known that she had produced a Trojan horse. And Derrick had promptly seen that *I* was his way in. Well, Derrick would have my help and sanction no longer. The family could choose between him and me, and if they chose him, which I felt sure, in their own perverse fashion, that they would, I could retire like Scotty, and Livia of old, into the limbo of those who were unable, and in the end unwilling, to keep up the eternal Denison appearances.

Christopher came home before Derrick, and it was he who discovered me in my state of disheveled collapse.

"Hello!" he exclaimed. "You look as if you'd run through Hell with your hat off."

"Oh, Chris, have you heard? About changing the firm name?"

"Congratulations, Mrs. Hartley!"

"Don't make fun of me," I wailed. "Doesn't it shock you?"

"Shock me? Why should it? I don't like it, I confess. I'm a bit of a stickler for the old things, and Uncle Linn was very good to me. But Derrick's right. Let the dead bury the dead."

"You don't really believe that! You're just saying it because you're afraid I'll do something crazy. Well, you're right. I'm going to leave him."

Christopher came over and sat down on the sofa, leaning forward towards me, his knees tight together and his hands clasped over them. He was still smiling, but the sarcasm had gone from his voice, if not his words. "If you're talking about divorce, you'd better get a first-class lawyer. Your grounds seem a bit wobbly to me."

"Please be serious!"

"But I am. I doubt if any court would give you a penny of alimony or custody of the children. Though I suppose Derrick might let you take Hugo."

"But I don't want alimony!" I moaned. "Let him keep the children and the house and everything. I'm no good to anybody. I may as well crawl into some little hole and die."

Christopher stared for some moments at the carpet as if he were looking for something and then shook his head regretfully. "Poor Ida. She's so far down in that old bog of self-pity I don't know if we can still get her out." He jumped suddenly to his feet and pretended to be pulling someone from an imagined swamp in the middle of the floor. It was infuriating, it was absurd, but it was the best possible treatment for me, this elaborate pantomime before which it was impossible to sustain any mood more harmful than irritation. At last he simulated a recovery of the body and shook his head again dubiously. "Pretty far gone, I'm afraid. But we'll see what a drop of whiskey can do."

I sat morosely on the sofa until he returned with a flask and two small glasses. After one of these I was sufficiently revived to tell him about Aunt Dagmar and Uncle Victor.

"But don't you see they're getting older?" he pointed out. "They don't see things the way they used to. They take themselves more seriously. They take themselves almost as seriously as *you* take them. What is Derrick, after all, but an up-to-date Denison? If Mother were alive, wouldn't she give you the dickens for pulling a scene like this!"

"Then is honor to go for nothing?" I demanded bleakly. "Is tradition and family feeling to go for nothing? Is gratitude to go for nothing?"

"Are marriage vows to go for nothing?" he came back at me. "Are maternal duties to go for nothing?"

I brooded over this, reflecting sourly that I was no longer in a position to answer back with the privilege of an older sister. "You think Mother would have expected me to take this lying down?"

"I think she would have expected you to take it. I doubt very much if she would have recommended the posture."

"And you? How will you take it?"

"That, my dear Ida, is my affair. It so happens that I am not wedded to Derrick."

I had another few sips of whiskey, and when Derrick came home I was quite calm. I even went to the dinner party given by Mr. Dodge to celebrate the firm's change of name, and I confess that I was not displeased by the embarrassment which my silent, unexpected and rather grim presence caused my husband and the others. But there was no disguising my capitulation. That day was the most important in my life, at least until the day, twenty-eight years later, when Geraldine went out the window of her hotel. Father had told me that I could be a leader or be led, but that it was vital that I should choose. I had not chosen until that night, but I chose then.

One thing, however, happened to cheer me in my new passivity and make me less somber in the months that followed my talk with Christopher, and that was his resignation from Hartley and Dodge. He told Derrick that he had borrowed the money from Aunt Dagmar to purchase a stock exchange seat and start his own firm, and he told me that the time had come when he had to be on his own, clear of the family. I have no doubt that both reasons were valid, and, indeed, he moved to an apartment the very next month, selling his half of our house to Derrick. But I have never had the smallest doubt that the real reason for his leaving was his disgust at Derrick's treatment of the shade of Uncle Linn. It was like Christopher to make no open protest. "If somebody can't see a point of honor, there's no point explaining it," he had always said. He has led his life ever since in his own neat, brisk, successful fashion, more disciplined than I ever dreamed of being, both in big things and in small. Even now he will stop his car to rub a bird stain off the hood, and he still brings an extra shirt to his office to put on after lunch, but the good side of this particularity is that his kindness and his decency are always scrubbed and ready for use. It has been my consolation through the years that he sees Derrick with my eyes. For thus I have always had the sense of an inarticulate ally. If Christopher and I have learned to act like Denisons, we both still feel as Trasks.

9

Ida: 1950

I DID NOT ASK any of the men of my immediate family, after Geraldine's funeral services, to go to the interment in the Denison plot in Brooklyn, but when Dorcas, conspicuously large and tweedy in the sober little group that had gathered on the church steps, plucked my elbow and asked in that voice that she never bothered to modulate if it was all right "now" for her to go back to the country, I felt that I could no longer postpone the little lecture which I had been preparing for her.

"I won't keep you more than an hour. I'd like you to go with Cousin Minerva in her car and then come back with me."

"But Daddy's not going," she protested in surprise.

"Neither is Mark." Dorcas' husband had already left with Derrick for a downtown world removed from the irrelevancy of death. "They leave the mourning to us."

"But I should get back to the girls."

"Why?"

"I told Lucy I'd go to see her basketball team play."

"Well, you'll have to be a little late, that's all."

I walked to the first of the hired limousines which was to take me and Christopher, leaving her no decent alternative but to go with Minerva Denison, who, standing beside us, had heard my directions. But I was not fooling myself. I knew that it was going to be difficult to scrub off the effect of the years in which I had given in to Dorcas. The soaked hull of our relationship was covered with the barnacles of all that she had taken for granted. I had let her believe that Mark and life with Mark and children by Mark were her sole duties. I was only now, in my new thinking since Geraldine's death, beginning to see how insulting my sense of her limitations had been.

Christopher and I, in the car, plunged as always, when alone together, into the past.

"I keep going back in my mind to that winter when Derrick and I first met," I told him. "The winter, too, when he first met Geraldine. Do you think she'd have had a happier life with him?"

"Well, she couldn't have a much worse one, that's for sure."

"What about him? Would he have been happier?"

Christopher smiled, recoiling instinctively at my tone of self-indictment. "She might have done a better job with his social life. At least until she started drinking. She might have charmed all those butter-and-egg men."

"*I* tried."

"Oh, Ida!" He burst out laughing and slapped a hand on his knee. "I remember you at those dinners. Vaguely sweet. With a remote smile. Like a cultivated Greek slave at a Roman banquet. It must have been pretty hard for Derrick to bear."

The car stopped for a red light, and ahead of us I could see the hearse growing smaller down the long street until it turned the corner.

"You blame *me*, then," I said morosely. "For everything."

"I don't know what you mean by everything. I blame Derrick for being hard. You were never hard, Ida."

It was a small tribute, but it helped to mollify me. Christopher looked more and more like Father as he grew older, with the same gentle brown eyes, the same clear skin and fine features. But, unlike Father, his hands were always on the move, to tighten his tie, to straighten a hair, to scratch the corners of his chin, to gesticulate. He had made a fortune in his brokerage firm; he had married a beautiful and much photographed woman, and at fifty he was still a competent polo player. He had taken the advice that Father had offered me and chosen to be a leader. But he was still a Trask who by force of will had turned himself into a Denison. And how could that be, when the essence of being a Denison was precisely that one didn't try?

"Hard?" I queried. "Do you think Derrick is really hard?" I paused to consider it. "Perhaps he was, to Geraldine."

"Wasn't that Greek meeting Greek?"

"I don't mean *then*. I mean years later, when they had their affair."

Christopher's mouth fell open. "Oh, you knew?"

"Of course I knew. Even shutting my eyes as tightly as I could, I knew."

He closed his lips the way Mother used to when something distasteful was mentioned. *"De mortuis* and all that, but let's face it, Ida. She was a pretty bad girl. And as for Derrick . . . well, it was long ago. Best forget it." He rubbed his hands together in the Denison gesture of dismissal that applied to the awkward, the unpleasant and the inevitable. And how better could one do than dismiss them? I felt perverse and ashamed.

"But it was much worse than just knowing about it!" I exclaimed. "I *encouraged* it. I thought it was my punishment for marrying Derrick when he was still in love with her. Do you know, I even helped her decorate the apartment where they used to meet? With Mother's things! Can you imagine what Mother would have thought?"

Christopher at this gave a real whoop of laughter. "But

she'd have absolutely adored it!" he cried. "Did you really? Poor Ida, how *like* you."

"How sloppy, you mean?"

He threw up his hands. "But the very cream of sloppiness! Mother would have treasured it!"

"Sloppier than adultery?"

"Oh, no." He frowned, serious again. "But then Geraldine was always fundamentally the sloppiest of us all. Even Mother, who had a weakness for her, knew that."

It was absurd, but Christopher's judgment came to me as if from another world, as if Mother and Aunt Dagmar had sent me a message of cheer. "Did you really think, poor foolish Ida," they seemed to be asking, "that we didn't know how hard you tried? Could you honestly have thought that we didn't see through Geraldine?"

"It's sloppy, you know," Christopher warned me, when we turned in the gate of the cemetery, "to be always worried about being sloppy."

As we walked behind the coffin to the Denison plot where my grandparents lay under a brown obelisk and Aunt Dagmar under a brooding angel and Father and Mother under their simple twin grey slabs, I slipped my arm under Christopher's and was comforted by his answering squeeze. To the dead, at least, I had done my duty. I could face those tombstones and whisper with courage, even with presumption, so long as Christopher was beside me: "I *was* a good daughter. I *was* a good niece." The realization that my failures were all with the living made of the graveyard a preface and not an epilogue.

"He cometh up, and is cut down, like a flower . . . In the midst of life we are in death."

My prayers were for Geraldine, but my tears, as I stood through the rest of the brief service, were for Mother and the thought of what she would have done with the years that

Geraldine had wasted. She would have helped me to bear my disappointment at Derrick's disappointment in me. She would have taught me to realize that my refusal to become the woman he wanted was due as much to stubbornness as to pride. She would have kept me from transmuting the mere tastes of my forebears into moral principles. She would have driven into my stubborn mind that Derrick had not chosen me for my emotional depths or even for my intellectual heights, but because he wanted a partner to bear his children and to grace his triumphs. Without Mother I had stood apart, to preserve my honor, a shabby old rag clutched in two desperate fists, exposing Dorcas to his possessiveness and Hugo to his misunderstanding. There seemed, at that moment, little enough to choose between Geraldine and me.

But Geraldine was dead; what remained of her was being lowered into the earth by four men before my eyes. I turned away with Christopher and looked up, as we walked, at the cloudless grey sky of that warm winter day.

"Well, that's that," I said. "Whether I did too little or too much, and no matter what my motive, that's that."

"Are you exorcizing her?"

"No, I'm learning to live with her."

"You're just in time. Ghosts are the hardest to live with."

Going back, I sent Christopher with Minerva and took Dorcas with me. I glanced sideways at her as she stared moodily out the window of the car. She was still resentful that I had made her take a morning from her children.

"Is it true that Cousin Geraldine left you all her swag?" she asked without turning.

"Yes. What do you think I should do with it?"

"Well, I suppose it makes sense to get it over to the grandchildren as soon as possible. There's no point just giving it to Uncle Sam in estate taxes."

I considered the different strands of rudeness that went

into her advice. Not only did Dorcas take for granted that I existed only to assist her children; she assumed that I had little time to exist.

"If Geraldine had wanted to leave her money to your children, presumably she would have done so. She left it to *me*."

Dorcas glanced at me briefly as if to determine whether this was a poor joke. "Of course, you may do as you like with it," she said, throwing her cigarette out the window. "Only why ask me, then?"

"Because I thought you might suggest something that was fun."

"Fun? Well, wouldn't it be fun to do something for my poor girls? Daddy's interested in nobody but little Derrick."

"He didn't always prefer boys."

"Well, he's getting old, Ma, let's face it. Mark says he's becoming bogged down with details. You ought to get him to take more time off."

"Ought? Why ought I to? Why should I concern myself with what happens at the office?"

"Well, of course, if you're going to take *that* attitude, I don't suppose anything matters." Dorcas shrugged and turned to stare again out the window.

"Oh, but I think some things *do* matter," I insisted. "I think, for example, loyalty matters."

"Loyalty to whom?"

"To one's father."

Dorcas turned back quickly with angry eyes. "What about to one's husband?"

"Mark owes the same loyalty that you owe. To your father."

She had become so accustomed through the years to my accepting, at least by silence, her own values that my smallest independence of judgment now struck her as treachery. "Isn't it for Daddy's good to keep him from wrecking his own firm?"

"You exaggerate. He's not wrecking it. And even if he were, it would not be your place — or Mark's — to stop him."

Dorcas gave a little cry of outrage. "You think I'm undutiful? Is that it?"

"I think you may not realize how much your father, as he gets older, is going to need you."

"Why won't he have you?"

"Because I've failed him," I said simply, "and you haven't. *Yet.*"

I was surprised to see something like fear creep over her face. "How have you failed him?" she demanded.

"Oh, in many ways. More even than I know. He's a lonely man, dear. And he's built too much of his life around you."

"But I never asked him to!" she cried in a sudden fit of excitement. "I never wanted him to! As a child, I never suggested he take me on those fishing trips, with all those men. And do you think it was fun, at dances, when I wanted a boy to take me home, to find Daddy waiting for me, at the foot of the stairs, smoking his eternal cigar?"

Her cheeks were now mottled with indignation, and her bosom heaved. Emotion had never been becoming to Dorcas.

"I know you never asked for your father's affection," I assured her. "And I can well imagine that you didn't want it. But, after all, you accepted it. As you have accepted all the benefits that flowed from it."

"What benefits?"

"All kinds of money that Hugo has never seen. Not to speak of Mark's partnership in the firm."

"Mark made that on his own!"

"He might have. But the fact remains that your father put up his capital. The fact remains that your father has groomed him to be his successor."

"If Daddy ever retires. But *will* he?"

"If Daddy chooses not to retire, that's Daddy's affair," I reproved her in a more severe tone. "You have got into the habit, my dear, of blaming everything on Daddy. Maybe he deserves it. But his deserving it has nothing whatever to do with your duty to him. That may not seem fair, but since when has life been fair? Daddy is *your* responsibility."

I was prepared for anything but what happened now. I was prepared to have Dorcas rap on the glass and tell the driver to stop and let her out. I was prepared to have her excoriate me and bring up childhood injuries to thrust in my face. I was even prepared to have her retreat haughtily, as she had done as a little girl, behind the high barrier of her exclusive intimacy with Derrick and tell me that I did not understand him. But I was decidedly not prepared to have her burst into hysterical tears and continue sobbing for the rest of our drive. When I tried to talk to her, she simply shook her head, and when I tried to put my hand on hers, she huddled away from me into her corner and sobbed even louder. I would not have minded had I thought it was merely her old resentment. But it struck me oddly that Dorcas was not thinking of me at all. Something that I had said about her father seemed to have aggravated a wound that had already been festering. It was too bad — if it *was* too bad. But it was going to take more than Dorcas' sobs, to which the years had accustomed me, to drive me back to my role of silent watcher.

PART IV

Dorcas' Men

10

Dorcas: 1934

DORCAS decided, after her graduation from Barnard, that it was time for what her father called a "stocktaking." She had a favorite vision of herself as too young and too helpless for such assessments, as a quivering furry creature crouched in the palm of some vast protective hand, but she knew perfectly well that such fantasies were for her private amusement and not for getting ahead in the bleak world of fact. For the latter, alas, a quite unamusing detachment was needed, and when she had finally induced herself to step back and take that stock, she had had to conclude regretfully that her principal assets seemed to be a clear mind and robust health. Her father, in transmitting to her his natural endowments, had, in his usual fashion, overdone the job. With his health he had given her too much of his figure; she was too tall, too long strided, too broad in the shoulders and hips, too reminiscent of one of those exercising blond fräuleins in a Nazi poster. And with her good slice of the paternal mind, she had also been burdened with a slice of the paternal temper which took the unlovely form of bursting into tears when her feelings were hurt or even stamping her feet on the floor. It was her particular grievance against her brother Hugo that he refused to regard these fits as involuntary.

"You think they're attractive," he insisted. "Basically, you think they're feminine and rather appealing."

"I do not!"

"Oh, but you *do*." Hugo loved to analyze her coolly, with small, glinting, sibling eyes. "You want to seem volatile and romantic, when really you're just as mean and calculating as Daddy."

"You judge everybody by yourself!"

"Ah, but I have *other* qualities. A sense of humor, for example. And a lively imagination. The imagination to see that you're going the wrong way about getting what you want."

"And what, may I ask, do you assume I want?"

"A great big hairy man!" His raucous laugh cut short her gasp of protest. "Oh, please don't deny it. Spare me that. But can't you see that your error is in assuming there's only *one* way to be feminine? Nature made you big and strong, and you try to be small and messy."

"I'm no messier than you are. I peeked into *your* room this morning!"

"Just like you to be spying on me. The poor fellow you finally catch had better come to me for a tip-off. *I* could tell him how much aggression lies under those layers of would-be passivity."

"I imagine I could prove of equal help to the future Mrs. Hugo Hartley."

"I'll bring her to you!" he exclaimed in glee. "I'll be glad to! If she won't have me, knowing the worst, I don't want her!"

Hugo's razor sharpness in family arguments made him respected, not only by their mother and Dorcas, but by their father. For with Hugo none of them had any assurance of a basic family affection to blunt his wit. He probably cared about Ida, in his own sardonic way, but it was perfectly possible that the pains which Dorcas had seen him take in the selection of his mother's Christmas and birthday presents had been for the real purpose of bolstering their alliance against

Daddy. Dorcas had taken freshman psychology at Barnard and understood the division of her family into rival pairs of father-daughter and mother-son. But the peculiar feature of the Hartleys was that her father had lacked the patience or tact, upon the ultimate awakening of his latent interest in Hugo, to overcome the latter's prickliness. Hugo had little use for Johnny-come-latelies, and the father who had been too busy to accept the offer of a favorite toy or teddy bear was not to enjoy, on mere demand, the confidences of the college man. The resulting constraint between him and Derrick had settled the mantle of paternal affection more heavily upon Dorcas' shoulders, and she had taken to repeating every night her resolution that she would not be "Daddy's girl" all her life.

For there was no point denying to herself that Hugo had placed his icy fingertip on the very palpitating pulse of her greatest problem. She had failed, at least so far, with other men. She had an unfortunate inclination to seem either eager or hostile. If a man attracted her, she either made too much of him, with many exclamatory interruptions, head shakes and sudden, pointless laughs, or made too much of herself by being disputatious or even contradictory. Sometimes, disgusted with her two extremes, she would relapse into daydreams and waste valuable time at parties in fantasies of movie stars when there were attractive men right at hand. She had always been the kind of girl whom other girls introduced to their brothers, and now she saw herself in danger of becoming the kind whose married friends ask to supper without providing a beau. The first casualty of her stocktaking was her plan to go to graduate school. She decided that she had wasted enough time on the art and literature of dead days. She would take advantage of the shorthand and typing that she had learned in the summers and become a secretary.

Her father had no objections; in fact, he seemed relieved that she was giving up the idea of a master's degree in the fine arts. He believed that women, if not wives and mothers, should occupy useful, subordinate positions in the business world. But Dorcas' trouble came when she announced at dinner that she planned to look for a job in a publishing house.

"I had hoped that you might consult me first," he said in the slow, deliberate tone that marked his swelling irritation. "I was thinking of offering you a job in the office. I thought it might amuse you to be our receptionist for a while."

Dorcas breathed quickly and smiled in what she hoped was a disarming manner. Anything connected with the office was the highest imaginable honor. "I'm sorry, Daddy, but wouldn't you rather have me go into something that has a future for women? After all, you couldn't very well expect me to be a partner in Hartley and Dodge, could you?"

"You might be some day. A limited partner."

"I'm sure it would have to be very limited!"

"You don't understand me, Dorcas," he said, clearing his throat testily. "If I should die and leave you an interest in the firm, you would become what is called a limited partner. It would do you no harm in the meanwhile to learn something about business."

Dorcas knew that the moment had come to get up and give him a kiss. Of course Hugo would be nasty about it, and call her a hypocrite, but she had to learn not to mind Hugo. After all, did the fact that one saw the fitness of one's gestures make them any less sincere? As she leaned down to kiss her father's leathery cheek, she gave her brother a defiant glance. "I can't bear it when you talk about dying, Daddy. All that won't happen for ages and ages, when I'm an old woman. It has nothing to do with the kind of job I take now." She went back to her seat and smiled down the table at him.

" 'What shall Cordelia do? Love and be silent,' " Hugo quoted mockingly.

"A lot of girls take jobs for the chance of meeting young men," her father continued in a mollified tone, and she saw Hugo wink at their mother. "I don't know what part that may play in your plans — I can't imagine why it should play any — but if it does, there's a much better chance of meeting a worth-while fellow in my shop than in any publishing house."

"Why do you say that?"

"Because the young men who go into publishing are men who can't stand competition. If you can call them men at all. Poor creatures who haven't the guts to live in an attic and write. So they 'publish.' " Her father made a grimace as he uttered the word. "With a small salary to amplify a small trust fund they live delicately in a world of 'nice things.' "

"But if Dorcas came downtown, Daddy, how could you be sure she'd go for the right young man?" Hugo intervened. "How do you know she wouldn't fall for an elevator boy or a pink, pimply file clerk?"

"I think you're both horrid!" Dorcas protested angrily. "You can't believe a girl has anything in her mind but getting married. I want a job that's *interesting*. Isn't it better to read manuscripts by people who may one day be famous authors than take dictation about stocks and bonds?"

"If you want to read, there's always the Public Library," her father retorted. "Better than these modern novels about sex in Chinatown."

"That's not the point, Derrick." Ida came unexpectedly to her daughter's aid. "Dorcas wants to be connected with a living organization. It's not just books. It's publishing. I wish I'd done something like that myself at her age."

Dorcas always felt disloyal to her father in accepting her mother's assistance, but she was in no position now to reject allies, so she gave Ida a grateful look and stared uneasily into her plate. Derrick continued to grumble about the cheap standards of the publishing world, but his grumbling took a general form, and she knew that the individual issue, for the moment, was closed.

The next two weeks were devoted to job hunting. She was determined to use neither letters nor references, but simply to make the rounds of the publishing houses. She had two offers, but at a very low salary, and it was not until she called at the Brandon Press on Madison Avenue that she found what she was looking for. This company, as she had learned from her talks at other houses, was owned by Jack Brandon, a steel heir who had started it with the rich liberal's proclamations that its future standard would be quality alone, but since then he had lost interest, and it had settled back into the routine of general publishing, that broad, grey sea of humdrum emotion on which gleamed the occasional atoll of a thoughtful book. But there was money in the firm, and the young editors had a reputation for being eager and able, and fourteen days had taught Dorcas that this was all one could expect.

Her interview with Mr. Robin Granberry did not start well. He seemed more concerned with what he could tell her about herself than with any information that she had to offer. In fact, as he hardly allowed her to say a word, she could only stare at his long, lanky body and long lanky hands, at the black suit that needed pressing and the brown sweater with its large stain in front. He had thick black hair that fell across his forehead and a face, long like his body, with a sensitive white skin that bore the red welts of careless shaving habits. But he had beautiful eyes. Dorcas decided that one might forgive a disorganized appearance for such a pair of dark, restless, worried eyes. Like a deer's, she thought and immediately regretted the phrase as if those now jeering eyes would pounce on it and tear it out of her mind.

"You don't have to tell me what you want," he was saying in a tone unpleasantly like Hugo's. "I'll tell *you*." She was struck by how much he had to be doing as he talked, pulling his hair, rubbing an itching elbow on the table, turning his swivel chair. "You're an English major, and you *adore* Herman Melville. You fancy yourself picking a new *Moby Dick* out of the scrap basket where some Philistine editor has flung it. You take it to Mr. Brandon who promptly gives you *my* job. Then Melville comes to town and falls madly in love with you, but you won't let him leave his wife, so he commits suicide, and you win the Pulitzer prize by publishing his love letters. Isn't that the gist of it?"

Dorcas was flustered, but she reminded herself that that was just what men like Mr. Granberry wanted. She felt that her father would have been proud of her answer: "I can type and take shorthand, Mr. Granberry. Try me!"

"You can. Of course you *can*. But *will* you? That's the point. Or every time I give you a letter, will you gaze at me with eyes of soulful reproach because it's not a page of *Omoo?*"

"Well, is it wrong for a girl to want to make something of her job?" Dorcas exclaimed. Hearing herself go so far, she surrendered to the balance of her temper. "I suppose you're the kind of man who thinks a stenographer should always stay a stenographer! That menials should know their place!"

"On the contrary," he said, taken aback. "I consider myself an advanced liberal. Rather on the pink side, if anything. I simply consider that stenographers should be stenographers *while* they're stenographers. Forgive me if I have my doubts as to whether you'd be content with such humble fare." He paused now to study her application card. "I see that you attended Miss Irvin's School and that your father is the Hartley of Hartley and Dodge. Are you sure you wouldn't be more comfortable in a stock-exchange seat?"

"Look, Mr. Granberry. Either try me out or let me go."

He studied her for a moment and then smiled in grudging approval. "I like that upper class quiver of your nostrils. Perhaps, after all, you might give us a needed tone. Could you start tomorrow?"

Dorcas in the weeks that followed decided that she had every reason to congratulate herself. She acted as secretary for Mr. Granberry and another young editor and had been promised an early opportunity to try her hand at jacket blurbs and press releases. She found that she could type as well as anyone else in the firm and that her services were in great demand whenever she had free time. Only the office itself disappointed her. The great two-storied room where she worked, with its huddled center group of typewriter desks and its lawn of an emerald rug, surrounded on three sides by the glassed-in cubicles of the junior editors and on the fourth by a gigantic bookcase rising to the ceiling and packed with dust jacketed volumes, had no relation to the publishing house of her fancies with its quiet, dignified aspect of considered disorder. She could not imagine, for example, Charlotte Brontë or Thackeray coming to the offices of the Brandon Press. And if they had, would anyone have recognized them? A classic, in the eyes of her fellow workers, could go no further back than Joyce.

Granberry, himself, as if to rectify the unseemly intimacy of their initial dispute, made every effort to treat her formally. He would barely look up when she came in for the morning's dictation and would throw her the opening lines of his first letter without so much as a word of greeting. He obviously meant to appear too absorbed in thought to be aware of the very existence, much less the sex, of his amanuensis. But at the same time he was incapable of resisting the urge to show off; he had always to interpolate, to explain to Dorcas, respectfully waiting, pad in hand, the role that *he* had played in the negotiations leading to this very letter, to fill in the background that she might comprehend how beautifully his scheme fitted the facts and, incidentally, how vividly he could describe the characters involved. Robin Granberry wanted approval — from the Brandon Press, from its shareholders and authors, even from Dorcas Hartley. She understood, as she watched him strut about his little office, declaiming his correspondence, or slumping in his chair, a leg dangled over the arm, that he was a man who could never have enough applause.

"I guess you really told them off that time, Mr. Granberry!" she learned to exclaim, or: "I'd love to see their faces when they get *that* letter!"

And Granberry would shrug and turn away as if he had barely heard, as if her excited comments were of no more significance than the jingle of her charm bracelet as she whipped over a page in her dictation book. But that he paid her more attention than his demeanor admitted was proved, after she had been working there only a month, when he casually handed her a pile of manuscript, some chapters from Ely Bliss's work in progress. Bliss was a wordy, nostalgic young novelist of Iowa farm life, who was then enjoying a phenomenal vogue. Dorcas had heard in the office that Granberry owed his editorship to his Swarthmore friendship with Bliss, and she was intensely flattered that her opinion should be sought. She took the manuscript home and read every word of it that night, staying up late to rehearse aloud her detailed report to Granberry. But when she appeared, pale and excited, in the doorway of his office the next morning, he simply scowled.

"No dictation just now, Dorcas," he grumbled. "I've got one sweet bitch of a hangover. I was out with Bliss last night."

"So was I!"

"You were?" His face looked utterly blank. "My God, I must not remember anything."

"Oh, I don't mean *really*. I mean I was reading the book."

"What book?"

Nothing, however, was going to deter her. Sitting down, uninvited, before his desk, she started off on her piece: "I think Mr. Bliss writes with great beauty of style. Sometimes I feel that the length of his descriptions impedes the reader who is primarily fascinated with the story. On the other hand, it is very difficult to know where to cut."

"Cut! Did I ask you to cut?"

"You asked for my opinion, Mr. Granberry. I think I would cut in the love scenes. Why, when there are so many beautiful things in the world, is it necessary for Mr. Bliss to emphasize the sordid side of sex?"

"Because that's precisely the beautiful side!"

"Oh, Mr. Granberry! You can't believe that!"

He uttered a groan and covered his face with his hands. "Please, *please!* It's a bit early in the morning to face Kate Greenaway hand in hand with Mrs. Humphrey Ward! Has it never struck you, my dear Miss Hartley, that there might be *some* things you hadn't experienced? *Some* things Mummy didn't tell you?" He looked up at her now with a sudden irate resentment. "And who the hell do you think *you* are to set yourself up as the arbiter of what is beautiful and what is sordid? To me the really sordid things are probably just the ones you like! Moonlight and handholding and soul kisses. Ugh!"

Dorcas closed her lips tightly, for she felt them trembling. "If you have such a low opinion of my critical faculty, I wonder why you thought me worthy of even peeking into the sacred pages of Ely Bliss."

"Because, God help us, it's women like you who make up the reading public!"

She strode out of his office and back to her typewriter. She worked very busily and inaccurately all that morning, and by noon she had decided to resign. It was hardly fitting that she should stay a day longer after being so grossly insulted. It was certainly hard that what should have been her proudest moment, the delivery of her first report, should have turned instead into her bitterest humiliation, but it was not her fault if the publishing world was full of brutes. She was still banging furiously at the keys when she felt the final impudence of a hand on her shoulder and whirled around to face Granberry.

"Will you kindly keep your hands to yourself!"

There was instant silence from the adjoining machines as the other girls delightedly stopped to listen.

"I was simply trying to attract your attention," he replied, unruffled. "I spoke to you twice, but you didn't hear me. Would you be good enough to let me take you out to lunch and apologize for my very bad manners?"

She nodded quickly, but made no attempt to speak. It was quite bad enough that her eyes were already full of tears.

"Shall we say twelve-thirty?" he continued in the same tone, and when she simply nodded again, staring straight ahead, he turned back to his office with a little shrug and a smile for the benefit of his approving audience.

At lunch in the booth of a Third Avenue bar, over sandwiches and beer, he explained himself, on the whole, very graciously.

"We must learn a mutual tolerance, Dorcas. I don't want you to get huffy and quit. You're too good a worker, and you've got too good a brain, if a bit encumbered with minor prejudices. There's a place for you at Brandon, and I don't mean just as a secretary. You could be a copy editor. You could be in charge of dust jackets. You might even ultimately run our publicity. Only don't *ever* get the idea you could work with authors. It's not your line."

Dorcas, mollified by his tone and warmed by the unaccustomed midday beer, was easily resigned to the diminution of her prospects. "Why couldn't I?" she asked mildly. "What's wrong with me?"

"As a businesswoman, nothing. As an editor everything. You don't have the first notion of why a man like Ely Bliss sits down at a typewriter to pound out his little fantasies of guilt and hate and yearning. And why should you? Leave the job of handholding to the frustrated writers, like myself. The woods are full of them. What this firm really needs is a good housekeeper. Why shouldn't it be Dorcas Hartley?"

It was not exactly what she had dreamed of as a publishing career, but what had she really wanted of Brandon but the chance to meet men, and who but a man, a brilliant man, however erratic, however uncreased his trousers and sour his moods, was taking the trouble, right then and there, to offer her his friendship?

"I'll try," she murmured docilely. "I'll try to learn to be a housekeeper."

The following Monday a new arrangement was proposed by the office manager whereby Dorcas would work full time for Granberry, as his assistant and secretary, and before the day was out her life was entirely altered. The telephone was to be her medium and not the typewriter; she was to call hotels and magazines and radio stations; she was to organize cocktail parties and lunches; she was to plan the visits of out-of-town authors, and above all she was to guard Robin Granberry's calendar and see that he kept his appointments.

He needled her badly; that she found out right away. She did not comprehend, indeed, how he had previously managed without her, either in his business or his private life. For she even had to compose his letters to his old mother and warn him when he had asked two girls for dinner on the same evening. He treated her as a friendly if sardonic lieutenant might treat an efficient if sometimes officious sergeant: democratically, companionably, affably, at times waspishly.

But there was always the lieutenant's bar between them. However much Dorcas tried to see their relationship in the light of Jane Eyre and Mr. Rochester, she had to admit that there seemed little future with a man who asked her to his apartment to cook his supper when another girl had stood him up and who addressed her as "Hartley."

"What is Mr. Granberry *like?*" her mother was always asking.

"He's handsome when he's not being ugly. And bright when he's not being stupid. And divinely agreeable when he's not being rude as hell!"

"He sounds interesting."

"Don't worry, Mummy. He's madly in love for the moment with a neurotic poetess called Vera Stiles."

"Is she attractive?"

"How does one tell? She wears her hair in her face."

What she omitted to tell her mother was that when Robin was nice to her, he was nice in a way that she had never experienced before. He might expect her to take Vera's place and cook his supper at the last moment, but if the supper was good — and Dorcas blessed the paternal creed of self-sufficiency which had made her adept in the kitchen — he would light a cigar, pour a glass of brandy, sprawl on the day bed and begin to ask questions about herself and her family. His curiosity seemed inexhaustible; he explained it as the craving for fact of a frustrated writer. It had never occurred to Dorcas that another human being would listen to her, *really* listen. She was inured to the glazed eye of the girl friend that lit up only in anticipation of the story to be belted back in return for the story that one was telling. But Robin wanted to know everything about her and her mother and father and brother and even about her great-uncles and aunts. He loved what he called the "Denison Saga" and claimed that it was perfect material for a novel, far better than his own bleak boyhood in Syracuse that he had been "working up" on weekends for the past two years.

"My novel is about my father," he told her, "but I'm not sure I wouldn't do better with yours. I like the whole idea of his relationship with the Denisons. The merger of two different types of social climber."

Dorcas was torn between her delight at his candor and her sense of outrage at what he said. It was thrilling to hear anyone speak so disparagingly about a father of whom she had so long stood in awe, but such thrills were followed by pangs of guilt and remorse. One by one her inhibitions gave way before the beaver jaws of Robin's conversational habits, and she began to be afraid that her moral standards would be eroded along with her prejudices. For to Robin nothing about himself and certainly nothing about herself seemed immune from analysis or jokes. He took a perverse joy in assuming that she could not be shocked.

"In families like yours," he told her, "the daughter is always proud of her father's attention. It proves that she has filled the void left by her mother. For Mummy, of course, always seems to her a frigid failure. To Hugo, on the other hand, Mummy's frigidity is the symbol of Mummy's honor. It proves that she has never been willingly violated. What you each want, basically, is a virgin parent of the opposite sex."

But there were times when his mood was sour, and he was simply abusive. He would watch her with a little smile as if he were seeing how much he could make her take. And finally, one night, when she was tired and angry, and full of a dull depression at the cerebral quality of their relationship, she got up immediately after supper to take her leave.

"Where on earth do you think you're going?" he demanded.

"To the movies."

"The movies? Who said we were going to the movies?"

"We're not. I have a date."

"A *what?*" He fell back on the sofa with his arms over his head. "I never expected to hear a graduate of Miss Irvin's School use *that* term! With whom, may I ask, do you have this 'date'?"

"No, you may not ask. You know too much about me already. I have to keep some little private corner for myself."

"And that little private corner is the real, true, pulsating you, isn't it, Hartley?" he cried mockingly, jumping up and catching her hand. "Is that what you're trying to tell me?"

"It's none of your business and don't call me Hartley!" She shook herself loose from his grip and went to the door. "And you can do the dishes yourself for once. *If* you know how!"

He hurried over to place himself between her and the door. "I hate people who brood over their grudges and then suddenly explode! Why can't you give a guy a little warning? Why can't you say: 'Look, Granberry, you egocentric heel, do you think a girl has nothing better to do than cook your supper and listen to you jaw?' How was *I* to know that all this time you've been *seething?*"

"But I haven't!"

"Of course you have! And I was an ass not to see it. What does a girl your age want with good talk? She wants corsages and movies and 'dates'!"

Dorcas tried desperately to reassemble the remnants of her dignity. "I like to be made to feel like a woman once in a while," she protested. "Maybe it's silly, but girls *are* silly. At least, most of us are. Of course, I can't speak for your neurotic poetess. But I'll bet you never made *her* clean dishes. I'll bet she never has! And I'll bet her apartment's a pigsty."

Robin, with a suddenly judicial air, considered the violence of her conclusion and then shook his head. "You're wrong there. Vera's neatness is her only discipline. But come back and sit down. Just for a moment. I won't keep you from your little date." He took her by the hand and led her firmly back to the sofa. "Now tell me what I must do to make it all up. Of course, it's fun to nurse a grudge, but a generous nature should scorn that kind of fun. Do you have a generous nature, Hartley? I mean, Dorcas?"

"Well, I try."

"Then stipulate my penance. Shall I stand in a hair shirt on the snow-piled steps of Canossa?"

She was about to dismiss it all as another of his jokes when a better idea, suggested by his image of the penitent emperor, occurred to her. "You can come to a family supper!" she exclaimed in excitement. "That's it! You can meet my mother and father. You're always asking about them, but you've never met them!"

"Exactly. It's like a James novel. I make them out entirely from your point of view."

"But that's not fair to them!"

"It's probably fairer than you think. You see, I regard myself as a trained reader. I make allowance for your astigmatism."

"But life isn't a novel!" she protested.

"No, but we can try to make it one, can't we?"

She paused, baffled, unable to believe that he was as suddenly serious as he looked. "Anyway, it's your penance," she insisted. "To come to family supper on a night of my choosing. I'll let you know tomorrow. You'll be bored, but that's part of the penance. Do you agree?"

"I believe it's an error of style to change in a novel from the third to the first person. There's no telling what crudities may ensue. But, of course, if it's my penance, I must submit."

When she left his apartment, she sat alone through two hours of a neighborhood movie that she detested in order to be ready in the morning for any cross-examination about her "movie date." But he never mentioned it. He always seemed to sense intuitively when she was ready for him.

They were just four at dinner on Friday, and Dorcas' father maintained a silence that she could only interpret as ominous, while her mother kept up a little splashing rivulet of comment on books and publishing firms and whether Robin believed there were any "really great" authors still writing. Dorcas was surprised at how politely he answered. Looking about the dining room that she had accepted from her childhood as a handsome room, she saw it as she imagined that Robin must see it, and wondered for the first time if her mother had any taste at all. Had she not simply left the things as Grandma Trask had left them: the dark Piranesi prints of Roman domes and colonnades, the high-backed, Italian chairs, the imitation Sheraton sideboard with its overload of silver plates and candelabra? Was it not all too crowded, too self-consciously stately? Surely her grandmother, with her reputation for style, had filled it with flowers, painted the walls a lighter color, done *something*? It came upon Dorcas, with a flash of pride at her new perspicacity, that her mother lived in the house more as a daughter than as a wife, and she wanted to finish dinner so she could tell Robin. But now her father had entered the conversation, and her heart fell at the instant prospect of trouble.

"Hitler's still living, and he's written a great book. At least, some eighty million people would *call* it great."

"Does that make it so?" Robin's tone was suspiciously mild.

"Well, I suppose 'great' is a pretty vague term, but it's certainly a book that's had an impact on history. You can't deny that."

"I wouldn't try. But surely the ravings of a lunatic can hardly qualify as literature."

"A pretty smart lunatic, I'd say."

Robin's little smile hardened into something closer to a sneer. "Tell me, Mr. Hartley," he pursued in the same mild tone, "I've heard that men in the financial world are divided in their views on Hitler. Is it really so? Is it possible that a sane man could regard him as anything but evil incarnate?"

"Evil incarnate is a pretty fancy phrase," Derrick retorted. "I don't go in for fancy phrases myself. I'm not a publisher. Hitler's a rabble rouser and a fanatic, of course. And I don't propose to defend his conduct towards the Jews. But as a businessman I'm trained to view things in terms of their alternatives. The alternative to Hitler was communism."

"Which you think is worse?"

"Which I think is a hell of a lot worse, Mr. Granberry," Derrick emphasized severely, turning his full glassy stare on Robin. "I know your generation likes to flirt with communism, but you'll find out one day that Stalin's gang of thugs make Adolf Hitler and Co. look like the Colonial Dames!"

"I'll still take the thugs!" Robin exclaimed with a shrill burst of laughter, and Dorcas realized that the roughness of her father's tone had removed the pretense of manners between them.

"At least, Daddy, the communists have an ideal," she protested hastily. "Just because that ideal hasn't always been lived up to doesn't mean it has ceased to exist. But Hitler has no ideal. It's all just hysteria and hypnosis and silly saluting."

Her intervention, however, seemed only to make her father unreasonably angry. "I'm glad you find Stalin's slaughter of ten millon peasants a mere matter of not living up to an ideal!" he exclaimed heatedly. "I'm glad you prefer it to saluting. I suppose it's old-fashioned of me to place a somewhat higher value on human life."

"Human but not Jewish!" Robin cried. "Isn't Hitler's treatment of the Jews merely something you don't 'propose to defend'!"

"I'll choose my own words in my own home, young man!"

"Derrick, my *dear!*" Ida intervened hastily, for Robin had flung down his napkin and seemed about to get up. "Mr. Granberry, I beg of you, please let's talk of something else. Isn't it bad enough to have all Europe about to explode without blowing up ourselves? Derrick, you hate communism and dislike Nazism. Mr. Granberry, I suspect, dislikes communism — at least the way it's produced in Russia — and hates Nazism. Is there really so big an issue between you? Now, I'd like to know who Mr. Granberry considers the greatest novelist: Ellen Glasgow or Willa Cather? Or perhaps you consider neither great?"

Dorcas had to admire the way her mother forced the answers out of Robin and kept her topic in tepid discussion until Nellie came in to announce that Mr. Hartley was wanted on the telephone. Once out of the room, Derrick never returned, and when dinner was over, and they were crossing the hall to the living room, Robin stopped and abruptly bade his hostess good night. Dorcas followed his swiftly retreating figure down the stairway into the front hall.

"Robin! What are you *doing?*"

He did not even turn. "I was asked for dinner, and I've *had* my dinner."

"But you can't just eat and run!"

He turned so suddenly that she collided with him. "Would it be better if I stayed and gave your father another chance to insult me?"

She paused, wretched. "Where are you going?"

"To have a drink. As a matter of fact, I'll probably have several drinks."

"Don't you think *I* need one?"

"Come along then!"

In the taxi he reached over and took her purse from which he calmly removed the little wad of bills. After counting it carefully, he nodded and gave the address to the waiting driver.

"Twenty-five dollars. We can afford La Rue."

She was careful not to reveal how much she minded. Of course, he would simply tell her that she was "bourgeois" and sneer at her middle class rules, and she was determined that she was not going to spoil anything more that night. But it surprised her that her father's principles should be so tenacious in their grip. She tried to shake off her feeling about the money in the exuberance of her enthusiasm over everything else: the corner table, the gay, crowded room, the familiar music.

"I love La Rue. And nobody ever takes me any more!"

"All you have to do is pay the bill."

"Oh, please, Robin, who cares about the bill?"

" *You* do. It's written all over you."

"Well, for heaven's sake, who's talking about it? Oh, look, here comes our waiter. Do you think I could have a stinger? Please?"

Robin, however, was moody all evening. He drank a great deal of whiskey and made venomous remarks about the girls on the dance floor, speculating on which ones had been to Miss Irvin's and what their relationship was with their partners. He refused to dance even once, for all Dorcas' urging.

"All right," she said at last wearily. "Let's have it out. Let's get it over with."

"What?"

"What you think of Daddy."

He drummed his fingers on the table and whistled, out of tune, to the music. "Do you want it straight?"

"Do you ever serve it otherwise?"

"Very well." He moistened his lips. "I don't think I mind so much his being a dyed-in-the-wool fascist. I expected that from the business milieu in which he lives. What I really mind is that he isn't content just to blow off steam like the other old dodos. He really *cares* about destroying the opposition. He's a tyrant of the ancient Tartar type. He's not really cruel; he just happens to like chewing bones."

Dorcas managed a nervous laugh. "Well, there! That wasn't so bad, was it?"

"For you or for me?"

"Oh, for me, of course. I'm sure you enjoyed it immensely."

"Didn't *you*? We all love to hear nasty things about our parents. It makes our imaginary debt to them seem smaller."

"Must you be psychological about everything? I'm simply trying to be objective about Daddy. He is rather a tyrant, of course. He likes to have things his own way. But aren't many men like that?"

"Not in America. It must be terribly hard on your poor mother to be the only dominated wife in the Park Club!"

"Don't take Mummy for granted. She's not as dominated as you think."

"She hasn't totally surrendered, if that's what you mean. There are still little oases to which she flees. Women's groups and gentle gossip and charitable works. Harmless little copses of fatuity where the monster cannot penetrate. Yes, I caught a kind of hunted gleam in her eye when she looked at me. Some dim awareness that she was once a woman."

"That *you* brought out in her?"

"Why not? I'm a man, aren't I? You don't have to

chew bones to be a man. Whatever your father may think."

"Do you imply that Mummy was *flirting* with you?"

"Basically, yes. Why do girls always think of their mothers as sexless?"

Dorcas felt tired and depressed. She might have been willing to have her parents ridiculed had Robin not lumped her with them. If he had ridden up to the family threshold, bearing the smallest resemblance to a Lochinvar, on anything remotely resembling a white charger, no matter how spavined and broken-winded, had he declared, or even so much as hinted: "Your parents may be illusions, but *I* shall be your reality!" how gladly she would have clambered on that steed, and even Hugo's mocking laugh would have meant nothing as they galloped off. But no, he appraised and sneered and shrugged and then left her with her family. He had not even once commented that night on the house or on the dinner, nor had his eye distinguished so much as a picture on the wall or a carpet on the floor to laugh at or to praise. Usually he noticed such things, but evidently her home was a bourgeois blur of vulgar values. There was nothing in it to hate and surely nothing to love.

"I suppose my family's very dull," she said despondently. "It's hard for me to see it because I'm dull, too."

"Now don't take *that* attitude," he cried in disgust. "Fight back! You shouldn't allow anyone to say the things I've said about your parents. You ought to tell me I'm a pipsqueak hack editor who's eaten up with envy of your father's dough. Which, incidentally, I am. And then you ought to demand the money I took out of your pocketbook and march out of here, leaving me to wash dishes to pay the bill. If you're born a lady, *be* a lady, for God's sake!"

It was simply too much, and Dorcas solved all her problems by bursting into tears.

"What a horrible day!" she wailed. "Everything I do

seems to be wrong. I don't *want* my money back! I only want a dollar so I can get home!"

Robin, visibly appalled for once, signaled the waiter frantically for the check, and in the minutes that elapsed before it came, alternately consoled and chided her, distracted by the widening circle of attention that surrounded them. But Dorcas, refusing to acknowledge anything he said, whether desperate entreaty or fiercely whispered abuse, simply continued to stare down at the table and violently sob. In the taxi she pushed him roughly aside when he tried, as a last resort, to give her a peck of a kiss on the cheek, and dashed into her family's house on arrival without even turning to bid him good night. It had all been rather terrible, she decided, climbing the stairs, but it had been a greater scene than she had thought herself capable of. In bed, lulled alternately with feelings of shame and pride, she went soon to sleep.

When she arrived in the morning at the office, she was fully determined to go straight home if Robin so much as mentioned the events of the previous evening. But he didn't. With a subtlety (if such it was) that surprised as much as it relieved her, he was very dry and businesslike and even, towards the end of the day, took occasion to pick her filing system to pieces. It was a lecture, he warned her sharply, that was long overdue. After this their friendship was renewed, but not quite on the old basis. He never addressed her now except by her Christian name, and when he asked her to dinner, it was to take her to a restaurant and not to a meal cooked by herself. He never referred to Vera Stiles or to any of his other girls, and their relationship, losing its resemblance to that of lieutenant and sergeant, began to assume the proportions of a marriage where the husband respects, if he no longer loves, the wife. Yet Dorcas drew a bleak encouragement from the fact that their principal topic of conversation had shifted from her family to himself.

He talked a great deal now about his unhappy childhood in Syracuse. "At least," he would say, "I have *that* qualification to be a twentieth century novelist." His father had left his mother, one of those sweet, passive creatures who invite abuse and betrayal, and gone to New York for a life of dissipation which had ended in a violent death. Robin at the age of seventeen had been able to collect the life insurance that put him through college only by giving half of it to his father's mistress who had threatened to inform the company that the insured had died, a suicide. When Dorcas let it be seen that she was shocked, he showed the quick temper of a bad conscience.

"It's all very well for *you* to take a high moral stand. You can afford it. The only chance I had to go to college was to get my hands on that money. My father owed it to me. He'd never paid a penny to support me or Mother."

"I quite agree that your father owed it to you. But it wasn't his money. It was the insurance company's."

"As I say, you can afford these subtle distinctions. I couldn't!"

"I don't see anything subtle about that. You were telling a lie to the insurance company!" She was sorry as soon as she had said it. It was her old habit of blurting things out. She was so used to the whiplash of his tongue that she had forgotten how little experience he had had with hers.

"Lie!" he retorted, furious. "How do you know it was a lie? How do you know that my father hadn't died by accident and that *she* was lying? How do you know she hadn't pushed him out that window?"

Dorcas had on the tip of her tongue to say: "All the more reason not to pay her for it," but she checked the utterance. The unwonted exercise of such self-restraint gave her an instant, exhilarating sense of maturity. So *that* was how it was done! If one loved a man, one learned to deceive and flatter. Love? *Was* it love? She was on a giddy peak surrounded by grey abysses of hysterical laughter.

"How stupid of me!" she cried. "Of course! She was only trying to cheat you out of your rights! You paid her not to lie. As a matter of fact, you saved her from committing a crime."

Robin looked startled for a moment, and then suspicious, but he ended by greedily accepting her reassurance and piling her new theory, a wobbling boulder, on top of the jerry-built structure of his contrived excuses. Dorcas felt superior to him for the first time, but it was not a superiority that tarnished her image of Robin the man. It was simply that she knew she was experiencing for the first time the superiority that every woman feels when she learns to deal with the masculine moral need to have his cake and eat it. As Robin went on to describe to her the novel that he was writing about his father, she reflected that, if published, it might make painful reading for his mother. But this, too, called for silence. What, after all, did she care for Mrs. Granberry? Was she any more real to Dorcas than the mistress who had swindled the insurance company? The point to remember was that she and Robin were suddenly coming close. At least, he was coming close to *her,* and was that not closeness?

The crisis that was to bring them together at last, however, came over Ely Bliss's defection from the Brandon Press. Dorcas and Robin had twice dined with him in restaurants, and she had observed with a silent distrust the author's almost hysterical egocentricity. At neither dinner had he addressed more than a few words to her; he had simply poured forth to an abjectly attentive, sympathetically smiling Robin the hour-to-hour grievances of his daily round: the flutter of his heart, the ache in a tooth, a neighbor's loud radio, a wrong telephone number, the laundry's "emasculation" of his shirts and the idiocy of critics who insisted on comparing him to Thomas Wolfe. When she had protested to Robin afterwards that Ely Bliss seemed eaten up with self-pity, he had merely retorted: "But that's what makes great literature. Except when it's translated into fiction, we call it compassion."

But what he utterly failed to see, and what Dorcas intuitively understood, was that a man like Bliss was incapable of even a transient loyalty. He existed to distrust. When the contract for his new novel, of which Dorcas had read the extract, was being prepared, Robin told her that Bliss had objected to the option clause.

"Shall I strike it?" she asked.

"Certainly not. We can't afford to let these purveyors of sexual fantasy put *everything* over on us. From time to time it pays to pull them up a bit."

Dorcas smiled at the contrast between the gently smiling Robin of the dinners with Bliss and the peremptory editor before her now. "But you've always said these options are worthless," she pointed out. "Nobody tries to hold an author to one. Why isn't this a cheap way to oblige him?"

"It's true they're hard to enforce legally. An author can always dig out some juvenilia and throw it at you as his 'next book.' But they do constitute a moral obligation, and that means something in the publishing world. However much your father might sneer at the idea!"

"*I* can't help sneering at the idea of Ely Bliss recognizing any moral obligation."

"You just have it in for him because he pays no attention to you. So like a woman!"

Dorcas, adhering to her new discipline, finished typing the contract without further comment and mailed it to Bliss. But her worst misgivings were justified a week later when she was awakened by her mother at midnight to say that Robin Granberry was on the telephone and insisted on speaking to her.

"I'm afraid he's not quite sober, my dear."

Dorcas brushed past her and ran down the corridor to the telephone.

"What is it, Robin?"

"It's that bastard, Ely," the high unsteady voice came over the line to her. "Do you know what the son-of-a-bitch has done? He signed up with Doubleday!"

"Oh, Robin," she murmured. "Are you at home? I'll be right down."

She refused to listen to her protesting mother as she dressed; she simply kept repeating that her friend was in trouble, and that she had to go to him. She ignored Ida's ultimate threat to arouse her father and fled down the stairs into the street. As she stood in the icy night air under a street lamp and frantically hailed a taxi, she murmured to herself: "God forgive me, but it's the happiest day of my life!"

Robin was alone and more than half intoxicated, and told her morosely to go home and mind her own business, but when she refused and continued to sit placidly on the sofa, he sulkily poured her a drink that was much too strong and began to sob. She listened sympathetically as he moaned that he was bound to lose his job at Brandon and that he had never had a proper break in his life.

"Nonsense!" she exclaimed briskly at her first opportunity. "Nobody at Brandon thinks as much of Ely Bliss as you do. They'll be sorry to lose him, of course, but losing writers is an everyday affair. How many times have you told *me* that?"

"But not Ely," he muttered, shaking his head. "There's only one Ely."

At last she divined that what he wanted was not encouragement but consolation. He wanted to twist and writhe on the luxurious bed of his new agony, to relish every turn of his rack, to glory in the unrivaled magnitude of his wretchedness. Dorcas changed her method, and listened with moistened eyes, when she was not pouring drinks, to his catalogue of the abominable perfidies of Ely Bliss. She then heard a new Robin's complaints against his mother, his deceased father, Syracuse, Swarthmore, the Brandon Press, her own parents, and, at last, rather flatteringly, herself. He ended by drunkenly accusing her of being a Philistine, a slyboots, a hypocrite and a designing bitch.

"You even got me drunk," was his final retort, "so you can go to bed with me."

After this he became silent and sleepy, and Dorcas helped him to remove his coat and trousers and to lie down on the bed. She then lay beside him and took his head in her arms, and so they spent the night.

When she awoke in the morning, he was no longer beside her, but she heard him moving in the bathroom and in a few minutes he came in, cleaned and shaved and wearing a new grey suit that she had not seen before. He looked as oddly spruced up as a schoolboy for Sunday chapel and quite as cantankerous.

"I suppose you think I have to marry you now."

Dorcas felt only a surge of hilarity, of sudden, irrepressible gaiety. "Do you think Daddy's waiting in the street with a shotgun? Oh, *do* look and see!"

"Well, if he thinks he can buy you a husband or even scare me into it, he has another think coming!"

"You don't understand my father," she said, sitting up suddenly and getting out of bed. She walked to the bureau and straightened her blouse and dress. "Will you *look* at me!" She took his comb and pulled it through her rumpled hair. "He wouldn't waste a dollar on you, much less a bullet. Even if I were pregnant, which, under the circumstances, would be odd. And if I *did* marry you, in spite of everything, he'd never give you a penny. Never! He's quite remorseless."

When she turned around, she saw that the trapped look had gone from his face and that he was staring at her with tensely searching eyes.

"Do you mean that?"

"Certainly I mean it. If that's not fair warning, I guess a girl's never given it."

"But do you promise me, Dorcas Hartley, that if you married me, you would turn your back on your father's money?" She had never seen his eyes so glittering. "Do you promise me," he continued, in the same desperately serious tone, "that you would be *my* wife? That you would aid and comfort and console me?"

Some instinct told her not to be as serious as he. "Didn't I last night?"

"But would you *always?*"

"Always is a long time."

"Would you for a long time, then? Would you for ten years?"

"Is that all you think you'd need of me?"

"Dorcas!" he cried, taking a step towards her. "Will you marry me?"

It was part of the fantastic exhilaration of the moment that she should then discover that her mind saw clearly in a crisis. To have accepted him now would have been to put him in a panic before the day was over. She raised her hand forbiddingly, but she kept her tone gay.

"This is hardly the time or the place for a proposal," she warned him. "You'd only say again that I'd trapped you into it. And please get one thing absolutely straight. I don't want a husband who feels even the tiniest obligation to marry me. Nothing happened last night, but it wouldn't make any difference if it had. You are free, Robin. Absolutely free!"

His eyes dimmed with what she hoped was disappointment, and he laughed in his old sarcastic way. "My God, you're a clever woman, Dorcas. A chip off the old block!"

"I won't try to have the last word with you," she retorted. "I know I'd be bound to fail. All I can do is tell you where I stand." She turned to the door. "And now I think I'd better go home and change. I'll see you at the office."

"Mind you're not late!" he shouted after her down the hall. "It would be very bad taste for you to presume on whatever happened — or didn't happen — last night."

Her exhilaration persisted in the taxi, and the cold, thin, granite-bitten winter air on her cheeks, the grey, slowly moving restlessness of early morning streets, the sexlessness of the huge waking city so oddly in contrast to the sticky warmth of her own body and unchanged clothes, all of these things, together with her sense of the enormity of having been out all night and her unexpected indifference to what her parents might say, united to press down upon the happiness in her heart and to delineate and make more explicit every nob and bump of which it was composed. Robin had slept in her arms, and Robin had proposed to her! Whatever regrets, even horrors, should assail him now, he had made up with a few words for all his months of ungallant behavior.

The front door in Fifty-third Street opened before she could fit her key in the lock, and there stood Ida, in her nightgown and pale flannel wrapper, worn and tired.

"Mummy! You haven't been to bed!"

"Of course I have," Ida murmured, closing the door behind her. "I just happened to wake up early and went to your room to see if you were in. When I found you weren't, I came down to see if you'd left a note. That's all, darling. Really."

"Oh, Mummy, what a fib! You were afraid the maids would see me, and you've been sitting here all night. How ridiculous!"

Dorcas sat down on the little pink marble bench under the stairway by the big green plant. She felt elated, indignant, superior — and pitying.

"Is Mr. Granberry — feeling better?"

"Mr. Granberry's feeling fine!" She knew the misinterpretation that her mother would place on her note of triumph, but she was still irritated by the deepening dismay on Ida's countenance. "Really, Mummy, there's no point going on as if I were a fallen woman! Or as if Daddy were going to turn me out in the snow. I'm over twenty-one, and I know what I'm doing. It's not like when you were a girl. Today a woman can *be* a woman."

But Ida seemed quite unconcerned with the implication as to what *she* was. "Are you going to marry Mr. Granberry?"

"It's not impossible," Dorcas replied with a shrug. "But if I do, it won't be because of last night."

"I think being married to him might make an interesting life."

Dorcas' pride shivered into splinters on the unexpected pavement of such ready acceptance. It was as if she heard already the faint strains of an organ in the dusky hallway, and she jumped up, feeling panic in knowing what Robin's panic would have been.

"Oh, come, Mummy, one thing at a time!"

"Just remember, my child. If you want to marry Robin, there's no reason we can't work it out."

Dorcas' tears of mingled gratitude and exasperation were checked by her father's step on the stairway. He was wearing the red velvet dressing gown with the yellow brocaded tassels that gave him the air of a doge.

"What does this mean, Dorcas? What do you think you're doing, coming home at this hour? Have you been all night at that man's apartment? It's a disgrace, that's what it is. A dismal disgrace. In my day no decent woman would have ever spoken to you again!"

"Derrick!" cried Ida. "Please. Someone will hear you."

"Let them. A fat lot Dorcas cares what people think."

"Aren't you taking rather a lot for granted, Daddy?" Dorcas demanded indignantly.

"I'm only drawing the conclusions that any father would draw," he retorted coldly. "But that's where the resemblance to other fathers ceases. Another father might disown you if you didn't marry Granberry. I shall disown you if you do."

Dorcas found at once that she was trembling all over. For it was suddenly terrible that her father was not concerned with what might or might not have happened in Robin's apartment. He brushed it aside, as he brushed aside anything that could be encompassed in the limits of a single hour or day, and went directly to what he considered the only issue. "I'm very sorry about that, Daddy," she cried in a harsh voice that sounded new and strange to her. "But I'll have to take the consequences. Robin and I are engaged."

"You damn little fool!" he shouted. "Can't you see he's nothing but a cheap neurotic who wants to live off you? Can't you see you're taking on the support of a moral infant?"

"Robin will never touch your money."

"If he won't touch it, it's because he's afraid of it. And if he's afraid of it, that's worse. My God!" He stamped his foot with a disgust so obviously genuine that her heart sank. For the curtain that seemed to be crashing between them was no longer the mere curtain of parental admonitions and attitudes. She grasped suddenly that her father was quite capable of drowning his love of her in the boiling sea of his hatred of Robin, and with this new concept came a weary sense of abandonment. For where in all of this crazy scene was Robin?

"When I think of what fathers go through," he continued, striking his forehead. "And what for? To hand the product of twenty-two years' labor over to a fuzzy-minded radical who despises her family for every decent thing they stand for. Well, let him despise my money all he wants. He sure as hell isn't going to see a penny of it!"

"We'll never ask! Not if you come and beg us!"

Her father turned and walked quickly back up the stairs. As she stared irately after him, she felt her mother's hands on her shoulders.

"Darling, don't worry. I *promise* you he'll come around!"

"But I don't *want* him to!" Dorcas hissed fiercely and ran into the kitchen and up the back stairs to her room.

Robin did not come to the office till noon and then he went directly to her desk.

"Was it awful?" he whispered.

"Awful?" She looked up calmly. "No. But if I want to be a good girl and please Daddy, I won't ever see you again."

"And what do you want to be?"

"That depends on what *you* want."

"Let's get out of here."

She followed him to the drinking fountain in the vestibule.

"The reason I'm late," he said hurriedly, "is that I've been looking up marriage requirements. We could be married in forty-eight hours in the Municipal Building. Are you willing to tell your family to go to hell?"

She looked carefully into those brown, furtive eyes and decided that they gleamed with a new intensity and resolution.

"Am I to do all that," she asked gravely, "for a man who's never even told me that he loves me?"

"Yes!" he cried with his high peal of laughter. "It's the last stand of an old bachelor! No mush!"

"No mush," she said, shaking her head ruefully. "Very well, no mush. But you must let me tell you that I love *you*. I have to do that if I'm going to marry you."

And, oddly enough, as he kissed her gently and briefly on the lips in that corridor that was so rarely and luckily empty, as he squeezed her hand and smiled, as he started, crudely and verbosely, to hold forth on licenses and medical requirements, she felt, with tears of uncertain happiness, that the person to whom she had been unfair was not Robin, and certainly not her outrageous father, but Ida, the neglected Ida, who had had the heart and the simple kindness to wish her an interesting life.

11

Dorcas: 1935

AFTER a week of constrained honeymoon in Virginia, where Robin displayed a great deal of temperament and Dorcas an equal share of passivity, they came back to New York and to his apartment. He flatly objected to her making any changes in it, but here Dorcas became insistent and, with her mother's help, she ultimately persuaded him to allow her to introduce a degree of color and comfort into the bleak decor of his two rooms. For Ida, by refusing to acknowledge a break, had managed to gap it, and, by treating Robin as a welcome son-in-law, had ended by making a friend of him. Derrick, however, continued adamant, and Dorcas never went to Fifty-third Street. She would have more resented his attitude had it not been for her mother's assurance that it was bound to change, an assurance, however, that was by no means altogether comforting. It gave her the pressed feeling that she had to build her happiness on a firm foundation before her father should intervene to knock it down. Such an attitude might have struck her as uncomplimentary to her own husband, had she not already understood that one could love a man without deeming him a match for one's father. Dorcas was proud even of the proprietary aspect of her conjugal love. At last she had something of her own.

In many ways he was an outrageous husband. He snapped at her and criticized her and left her alone when he wanted to dine with his authors. He made her quit her job and then complained about the loss of her salary. He was rude about her "banal chatter" at cocktail parties and disgusted when she said nothing. He never stopped to consider her mood when he wanted to make love, and he scoffed at her "spoiled" upbringing without acknowledging her efficiency as a cook and housekeeper. But he accepted her. That was the great and redeeming fact. He accepted her, as a now integral part of his existence, as someone who had come to stay. Beneath all his grumbling and abuse she thought she could dimly make out an undercurrent of relief that he had, at last, pulled it off, that he was, and never again could not be, a married man. And when he complained about the loss of a freedom that she did so little to curtail, she was subtle enough to perceive that his sense of confinement grew more from his gradual comprehension of her permanence than from any desire to be rid of her. This comprehension alone might be enough to build a marriage on. Dorcas, the wife, and Dorcas, the defiant daughter, were full of new confidence. If she was submissive to Robin, she was already aware that it was a voluntary submission.

When his mother came down from Syracuse to meet her, she was agreeably surprised to find her a dowdy, affectionate, talkative, dear little woman, with opinions as Philistine as any which Robin derided in her own parents, and she made the discovery that formidable persons do not always have formidable relatives. Robin interpreted her enthusiasm correctly.

"I should have kept Mother hidden," he told her afterwards. "If a husband is to be respected, his wife should never know there's another woman in him."

"Even when it's such a nice one?"

"No!" He raised a clenched fist above his head. "He should be a god!"

"But, darling, you *are*."

He gave her the little mocking smile that accompanied

his moods of acutest perception. "You're really becoming a damnably clever woman. You're learning to manipulate me like clay. Or at least you think you are. But don't be too sure that I haven't a hand on that potter's wheel. How do you know it isn't my super-subtlety to be shaping you into a shaper of me?"

"I don't."

"Married life is a kind of masquerade, isn't it? As long as I pretend to be strong and you to be weak, it's just as good as if I *were* strong and you *were* weak."

"But I *am* weak," she insisted with sudden vehemence. "I lean on you. I depend on you."

"In a way." The expression in his eyes became curiously sad. "You're what I might call an aggressive dependent. If I fell, it would be with your weight upon me. But I should be crushed in the process, and you'd get up and dust yourself off and find another man."

"Never!"

"Oh, Dorcas, my *dear!*" He shook his head and raised a finger to his lips. "What a word to use! You forget, I have the clairvoyance of a failure."

"You're not a failure!"

"I'm afraid your conversation has degenerated into a series of passionate denials. Never try to make feeling do the job of sincerity. It makes for a fearful din."

She knew that he hated to be taken too seriously, and she did not now pursue the subject. Such discretion had been attained only after repeated efforts. She was learning that the world to Robin was only fascinating if half revealed. He wanted always to pause before a half-closed door, to dangle a question mark, to play with a supposition. Her habit of flinging doors open and throwing up sashes was acutely distasteful to him. If she had to move at all in the house of his imagination, she was learning to do it on tiptoe.

She was learning, indeed, so fast that at the end of two months of marriage she was beginning to believe that hers might be a happy one. But this dawning conviction was cut short by another discovery. She was pregnant. Even in the mixed shock of first realization she did not fool herself that Robin would be pleased. They had planned not to have a child for two years, and she now wondered if he would want one even then. But she was not prepared for the full violence of his reaction. He ranged up and down the room, repeating over and over in a high, dry, distracted tone: "Of course, we can't afford it. We'll have to move. We'll have to get a new apartment, and where do you think the money's coming from? Your father? You know I'd go on relief before taking a penny from your father."

"We could get it from Mummy."

"How like a woman!" he jeered. "To judge the degree of larceny by the pocket you pick from."

"But it's different," she protested miserably. "It really *is*. Mummy has money that she inherited. It has nothing to *do* with Daddy."

"I refuse to go into that kind of middle class logic-chopping. It's the butchery of every moral standard."

"I wouldn't take any money if it was for *us*," she said, with tears in her eyes. "But it's for the baby. What has the poor baby ever done to Mummy or she to it?"

He stared at her with wildly exasperated eyes. Just because it was so eminently the moment for him to kiss and reassure her, of course he wouldn't. She sighed and turned away as he continued to rant.

"I'll bet it wasn't an accident at all! I'll bet you *planned* it. You're all alike. You *pretend* you want to look up to a man. You pretend you want a lord and master. But all you really want is a stud. So you can fill your home with squawking progeny that will shout him down!"

She knew that he was feeling sorry already for his unkindness; she could sense the self-punishment in the very shrill-
ness of his tone. She even recognized that he wanted to
apologize and to tell her that he would not mind the baby
so much, after all. But it was a case where the deed was
everything, the feeling nothing. Instead of welcoming her
baby, he had babbled petulantly against the laws of nature.
For the first time, she saw him as just a bit ridiculous. She
loved him, of course, but she had judged him. And she
knew it.

"I can manage in this apartment," she said dryly. "It will
all be much easier than you think. You'll see."

At least he had not suggested an abortion. It was something. And two nights later, when she had got up from bed
to be sick, he propped himself up on one elbow and called
into the bathroom: "If you really want a new apartment, I
don't mind borrowing the money from your mother." He
laughed a bit wildly. "I suppose I can be big about something!"

His grudging attitude accelerated the inevitable reconciliation with her father. Had he been nicer about the baby,
she would have been less undone by Derrick's congratulations. The morning after Robin's offer about the apartment,
Dorcas called to repeat it to her mother. Two minutes after
their talk was over, her telephone rang.

"Dorcas, this is Daddy. Please don't hang up. I'm so *proud*
about the baby!"

"Oh, Daddy, darling! *Are* you?"

"If you're a generous girl, you'll forgive me. And the
best way to forgive me is to let me make you a present of the
new apartment. To hell with this idea of a loan. Tell Robin
I'll buy the apartment in *his* name. Will that make it easier?"

"Oh, Daddy, what a beautiful idea!"

"And, darling, I can't wait for my first grandchild. I have

a funny feeling it's going to be a boy. Do you know what? I think a grandfather is what I was always meant to be! I've made my mistakes with Hugo, but I'm not going to make them with this fellow. I promise!"

"Oh, Daddy. I'm going to cry. Goodbye!"

When Robin came home that night, she had worked herself into what she hoped was a state of near hysteria.

"You don't want the baby!" she shrieked at him. "You don't want the baby, and you don't want me! I'm going home to Mummy and Daddy, and I'm going to have my baby there, and I'm going to call it Derrick Hartley!"

"Even if it's a girl?"

"Even if it's a girl!"

Robin put his briefcase on the desk and pretended to look over the morning mail. She stared at his back, breathing in sobs. When he turned, he had a rather grim smile.

"If you're making a scene because there's something you want, why not tell me? Isn't it simpler?"

"I'm going home!"

"If you've made up your mind, why make a scene?"

"Because I *want* to make a scene! Because I want you to know what a selfish brute I think you are!"

She stamped her foot in a rage that was only half simulated and started to hit the table by the sofa with both fists. Robin came over at last and caught her hands. His smile was gone, and he looked tense and tired.

"Stop that!" he cried. "Do you want to have a miscarriage?"

"Yes!"

"Stop it, you fool!"

She pretended to give in to his strength and threw herself down on the sofa to weep.

"All right," he said wearily, "what is it?"

"What is what?"

"What am I to do to make up? Haven't I promised to let you have the new apartment? What else must I do?"

She opened an eye to consider his chastened look. "You can help me make our peace with Daddy." When he said nothing, she instantly sat up. "He promised to put the apartment in *your* name. I think the least you can do is thank him for it!"

"So that's it." He shook his head with a dry bitterness and turned again to the morning letters. "I might have guessed. Very well, Dorcas. I shall make my peace with your father. And I'll do it handsomely, never fear." There was a slight tremble in his voice. "But I'm afraid I'll always remember that you made me do it."

"That I *asked* you to do it!" she corrected him passionately. "And why not? Daddy's *proud* I'm having a baby!"

After a week at the hospital Dorcas brought her nine-pound son, Derrick, and a nurse to stay with her parents in Fifty-third Street. Absorbed with her baby, she had allowed herself to be persuaded by the arguments that he would be better looked after, that there was more room for the nurse, that it would be easier for Robin who would not be awakened by the baby's feeding. And Robin himself had added his voice to her family's; he seemed to get on with everyone now. He had been so jubilant over the birth of a boy that he and Derrick had actually danced a jig together in the hospital corridor. Dorcas, hearing of this, had closed her eyes in sleepy content and wondered if her family troubles were over.

But, of course, she knew all the time that they had just begun. The period in the hospital had been a period of suspended hostilities, a doped, blessed, euphoric time, that she knew, nonetheless, was euphoric. The smiling, cooing masks at the bedside were bound to come off, in due course, and she would see again the worn, familiar faces of apprehension and jealousy. But there was still a difference, a wonderful difference from other times, and that was in the presence of the damp, red, heavy, sucking and screaming bundle that would grow up to be an ally and protect her from the aggressive loves of spouse and parent. Dorcas was conscious of the survival of her objectivity even in her moments of most intense maternal satisfaction. Watching Robin's eyes while she fed his son, she was perfectly aware that the sight was distasteful to him. He had wanted to be a husband, and he had, at the last, wanted to be a father, and now, by God, he had pulled off both jobs. He had shown the world the master sketch, and the details could be filled in by students.

She was much more painfully conscious of this attitude when she had moved to Fifty-third Street. He called in the evenings after work, but he barely stayed a half hour. The house bored him, her family bored him, the talk about the baby bored him and, worst of all, *she* bored him. For at home in the months of her pregnancy he had never had to make conversation with her; he had simply talked about himself and his day while she worked on baby clothes. Now, seated stiffly in a chair by the bed in a room which they had never shared, he seemed to find nothing to say. He could hardly wait to get back to the alcoholic ease of his renewed bachelor evenings.

"Tomorrow they're letting me get up for dinner," she told him one night as he was leaving. "I hope you'll stay. You can go right afterwards."

"But I'm dining at the Jack Brandons'!"

The mention of his employer's name was intended, of course, to arrest all further protest. But Dorcas was not at all sure that he was really dining at the Brandons'.

"Oh, they'll understand. My *first* night down. They've had babies."

"Of course I realize my career's of precious little importance to the Hartley family," he said bitingly. "But however poor a thing, it's still mine own."

"You *know* how important your career is to me!" she exclaimed, the quick tears in her eyes. "But I'm sure Mr. Brandon wouldn't expect you to go under the circumstances. He probably only asked you because he thought you were lonely. May I call him up and ask him?"

"Certainly not!" Robin cried, jumping to his feet. "I'll do it myself, thank you. Since it means so much to you!"

"No, no," she wailed, shaking her head in misery. "Not if you feel that way. I'll *hate* it that way!"

"It's all decided," he said coldly. "I shall be here tomorrow at seven."

Dorcas felt very low that night after he had gone. She knew that what he could least endure was the sense that he might be missing a good time. To have to sit in one place and think of a party in another raised emotions in him akin to panic. Yet it was equally true that if he went to the party, he soon tired of it. He tried of everything in possession; things lost their value with their change of title. He had wanted her to belong to him entirely, to give up her family for his sake, and once she had done so, he had thought her a poor fool. For if, fundamentally, he set a low price on himself, what price could he set on his belongings? As for the Hartley money and position, he had seen in them, with his peculiar combination of resentment and quick boredom, only the chance to make one of those splendid gestures of which he believed the good life to be made up: the gesture of contemptuous renunciation. But gestures, even splendid ones, became a bore, and it occurred to Dorcas that her husband might have already tired of renunciation.

That night she lay awake for a long time, thinking, and in the morning, early, she put on her wrapper and went down to the dining room. Her unexpected appearance had just the effect on her father that she desired.

"Dorcas, good heavens, is anything wrong?"

"Nothing at all." She sat beside him and reached for the silver bell. "I've come to have breakfast with you. There's something I want to discuss."

The paternal gaze blurred as she opened her subject, and she sensed the re-emergence of the senior partner. She was determined, however, to be as stubborn as he. If he had a daughter, she had a son; it made them equals. She could never win an argument with Robin, but she knew that in scenes she was apt to prevail. With her father she sensed that just the opposite might be true.

"You're always telling me that some day I'll be a limited partner in your firm. That some day I'll have this or that. But 'some day' means very little to me. I've got a husband who's full of talent that he has no time to use. You once told me that publishers were people who didn't have the guts to live in attics and write. Well, Robin might have done that, if it hadn't been for me and little Derrick."

"But you and little Derrick were responsibilities that he assumed. He knew what he was doing!"

"Daddy, that's just talk, and you know it. One doesn't 'assume' a responsibility like marriage. I wanted to marry Robin, and I pulled it off." She gave a dry little laugh that surprised them both and perhaps even shocked him. "The poor boy didn't have a chance."

"That isn't the way *I* got married."

"I know it isn't. But it *might* have been. If Cousin Geraldine had been let alone." She stared at him boldly, though with a pounding pulse, and, for once, he looked away. "Things have happened to Robin, and they've happened because of me. It won't take much money to set them straight, and I want you to give it to me. I know all your opinions about in-laws and grown up children, and I don't give a hoot. I need the money, and I'm asking you for it."

How easy it was! She could hardly believe it, and in the exultation of the moment she almost forgot her objective. But Derrick did not. He stared back at her so long that she began to wonder if those hard gray eyes were taking her in at all. Was he calculating the amount? Whatever it was, it could hardly matter to his exchequer. Only to his conscience. And then she felt a small damp chill near her heart that he should be thinking so hard.

"All right," he agreed suddenly. "If you will let me do it my own way."

"How will that be?"

"You'll see tonight. Didn't you say Robin was coming for dinner?"

She underwent a violent reaction that night when Robin appeared in her room as she was getting dressed, smiling and armed with a huge bunch of red roses. He made such a fuss over her and the baby that she burst into tears.

"No matter what I do," he protested, "I seem to get a liquid reaction."

"Oh, Robin!" she murmured and flung her arms around his neck.

Dinner was gay, even a bit hysterical. Although they were only four, and Ida drank scarcely more than a sip, Derrick opened two bottles of champagne. He toasted the baby; he toasted Dorcas; he even toasted his son-in-law.

"I have a confession to make," he announced in his easiest, most friendly tone. "I'm beginning to see that certain ideas of mine may have been too rigid. Life has a funny way of getting back at people whose ideas are too rigid. It has a way of tripping them up."

Robin finished his glass and held it out to the bottle which his father-in-law reached over to him. "And that's happened to you, sir?" he asked politely.

"Exactly. It happened to me. Tell me, Robin, is it true you're writing a novel?"

"Oh, when I find the time. Of course, it's just a weekend proposition."

"Of course. And one of these days Mr. Hitler is going to start a war, whether he means to or not, and sure as shooting, we're going to find ourselves in it. Which will mean further delays for your book. And by the time it's all over and you're out of the service, who can tell? You may have lost the inclination. That book may never get written."

"I imagine the cause of literature will survive," Robin said pleasantly.

"But it might not," Derrick insisted soberly. "It might not. And what really bothers me is that here we are, a family at last united and happy, with enough money to allow us all to pursue our serious goals. If you, Robin, a brilliant young publisher who has proved a dozen times over that he can support his family, are not to be allowed to finish what might be an important work of fiction because of *my* scruples, or because of *your* scruples about my scruples, I think we are both very much to be blamed."

Robin put down his glass abruptly. "How do you mean, sir?"

"Well, damn it all," exclaimed Derrick, hitting the table with his knuckles, "I simply mean that you should resign from the Brandon Press and do me the courtesy of letting me pay your salary until such time as you have completed your novel!"

Robin fixed his gaze on Dorcas, and she saw, with a suddenly sinking heart, how interested he was. For it all now seemed too easy, too pat to her. There was something shocking about the speed with which her father cleared away the underbrush that had kept her from him. As he moved closer, in long, easy strides, with that swinging scythe, she had a sudden, terrible sense of what might have been concealed in that torn, tossed underbrush.

"It's certainly a handsome offer," Robin murmured. "What do you think, Dorcas?"

"Well, I think your career as a publisher is important, too," she answered and saw his eyes instantly darken with dissatisfaction.

"We can always go back to publishing," her father remarked with a little grunt, eying her suspiciously. "Particularly if we're prepared to make a small investment in the firm. But now that we've finished dinner, I suggest that the gentlemen withdraw to my study and continue the discussion over a brandy and a cigar."

Upstairs in the living room Dorcas appealed to her mother as the latter turned to her needlepoint.

"What would *you* do, Mummy?"

"Well, it's really Robin's decision, isn't it?"

Dorcas reflected despondently that no woman married so long to her father could be expected even to imagine a man who did not make his own decisions about his own career.

"The trouble is it was my original idea," she confessed. "And now I've got cold feet. Daddy has such a way of taking things over. I stuck out a finger, and my whole arm's gone."

"But is it really such a vital decision? Don't we give too much weight to these money matters? The more I think about it, the more it seems to me that Aunt Dagmar had the right attitude. The only thing to do with money is to make yourself comfortable."

"But Aunt Dagmar's money was her husband's not her father's."

"I doubt if Aunt Dagmar would have cared whose it was."

"But I do! It's the difference in the generations."

When Robin and Derrick joined them, the former was smoking a big cigar and walking with a slightly unsteady step. Both, however, were smiling, and a pact had evidently been selected. Robin wanted to say good night immediately, but Dorcas insisted that he go with her upstairs to see the baby. In her bedroom she closed the door quickly and turned to him.

"It's all agreed, then?"

His eyes immediately hardened. "Do you object?"

"Only to the speed of the whole thing."

"You have no faith in my novel," he said with sudden petulance. "You never have had."

"I confess I distrust my father's sudden faith in it."

"What do you think he's trying to accomplish?"

"I wish I knew."

"Dorcas, my dear, this is absurd." He smiled and came over to put his hands on her shoulders. "You're so overwrought you can't even appreciate the poor man's simple gesture of generosity. Why, just because he was once a Philistine, must we condemn him to be one forever? Everyone knows that having a baby knocks your judgment out of whack. In your case it's revived all your old suspicions of your father. Perhaps I made a mistake in letting you come here. Perhaps you should have come straight home. Anyway, when we get into our new apartment, everything will be all right."

Dorcas allowed herself to be consoled and decided that all might still be for the best. After all, her father and Robin were at last agreed about something. She turned her energies to the search for an apartment and, as soon as she was well enough, spent long pleasant mornings with her mother, looking over the market. She finally found what she wanted on Gracie Square, with Carl Schurz Park nearby for little Derrick and a big nursery with a gay wallpaper of rabbits and elephants that had a beautiful view over the East River. She was so happy about it that she wondered if there might not be more in Aunt Dagmar's formula than she had supposed. Perhaps all she had to do in making decisions was to substitute her baby for herself. If she could just succeed in making little Derrick really "comfortable," how much did her doubts and fretting matter?

Robin rented a room on Third Avenue in which to do his writing. He said that he could never write at home with a baby and the telephone, and he added the comment that the atmosphere of Gracie Square was too rich for his muse. He left the apartment at ten and sometimes did not return until late at night. The subject of his novel was his father's life and suicide, and there were to be several chapters about the son's dilemma over the insurance policy. Dorcas thought it sounded like promising material, but after the first month it became apparent that it was not going well.

"Why don't you just grit your teeth and write it all out, so many pages a day, until it's finished?" she asked on a morning when he seemed particularly despondent. "I know it might all be very bad, but at least you'd have something to work on and revise."

"Do you think writing a novel is like writing a prospectus for stocks and bonds?" he cried indignantly. "I declare, you're a worse Philistine than your father!"

"I thought we'd ceased to regard him as one."

"Then you've taken his place!" Robin arose from the breakfast table to stare down on the turbulent grey of the East River. "I might have known! A few weeks on Gracie Square, and you revert to basic type. The lady bountiful who despises modern fiction but wanted a 'lit'ry' man for a husband!" He threw up his hands as he warmed to his argument. "Imagine my having been fooled for a minute! My simple role was to give you the opportunity for a divine row with Daddy. And then to provide you with a child whom you could name after him and have an equally divine reconciliation. Finis, Robin! Your time to bow out, boy!"

"Why don't you put that idea in the novel? It might make quite a good twist."

"Don't think I *won't!*"

"Well, at least, you can't say I haven't afforded you inspiration." Dorcas glanced at the clock. "I have to take Derrick out. Aren't you going to work today?"

"Are you now the overseer of your father's fortune?" he demanded furiously. "Are you afraid he isn't getting his money's worth out of the poor hack writer? Shall I put up a time clock? Or bring you the sheets each night for your inspection?"

"I only thought it might help you to talk it over," she said with a shrug. "If you want me to shut up, I'll shut up."

"Nothing helps me! Not even the panacea of your proposed silence!"

Robin became moodier and moodier. Invitations for weekends, which he would never have previously accepted, he now grabbed at eagerly, and if Dorcas could not leave the baby, he would go alone. He had to have a "change"; he had to "discuss the book" with somebody; he had to have "another look" at Westport or Sharon or wherever it was, because of a chapter that was now to be set there. Every sudden whim that struck his fancy, the yearning for a movie in the middle of the day or a night club in the middle of the night, had to be promptly gratified and then justified as the search for raw material. Dorcas tried for a while to keep up with his nervous activities, but the baby, whom she breast-fed for five months, had a first lien on her time, and when that was over, Robin had already adapted himself to his semi-bachelor life and showed little disposition to share it. It was better for his "creative thinking," he explained, if he spent a certain amount of time by himself. But "by himself," Dorcas ruefully concluded, seemed simply to mean without her.

There was heartache, of course; there were long, low dismal mornings, in which she sadly, and more and more resentfully, pieced together the selfishness that made up the pattern of his conduct to her, but little Derrick continued to compensate. He was a fat, strong, laughing child, with a comic resemblance to his grandfather, and he accepted greedily all the maternal attention that his own father spurned. Dorcas had hired a nurse, that she might have more time to spend with Robin, but when he failed to avail himself of it, she dismissed her and took over the care of Derrick herself. When Robin remarked that she was becoming a domestic drudge, they had their first real words on the subject.

"What else have you left me to be?" she exclaimed in sudden, blazing indignation. "Do you care anything for my opinions or even my company? What do you *expect* me to do with my time?"

"You might read," he said sheepishly. "Think of all the things you could read. You're always complaining that my literary friends won't talk to you. Well, catch up with them!"

"But I don't want to! Why should I read a lot of trash so as to talk to *your* friends instead of looking after my own child?"

His look of abashment took in the angry mother in the once submissive wife. "I thought you might want to help me out."

"Help you out? When you won't even let me type your manuscript!"

He made no answer to this, and she felt an immediate compunction at so easy a victory. For it occurred to her that she might have jabbed a knife in the tenderest of his wounds.

Perhaps the reason that he gave her no manuscript was that there was no manuscript to give.

But she had to get on with her own life. She would have shared a garret with Robin had he asked her; she would have turned her back on her father and his money had he merely solicited the gesture. But it was only too clear that the primary function of her father in Robin's mind was to serve as a target for his cruder jokes, and this was just as true after he had taken his money as before. Robin had simply changed his attitude from one that held money to be corrupting to one that held it to be unimportant. *He* could be above it, but she, apparently in his philosophy, could not. He continued to taunt her with the elevation of their standard of living, telling her that she could no more escape her background than a fly from sticky paper. Very well, she decided wearily. She would accept her background. She would no longer kick against the pricks. It slightly soothed her injured feelings to suspect that in the long run young Derrick would prefer the Hartley to the Granberry way of living.

Robin was startled when she announced that she had accepted her father's offer of the guest cottage at Oyster Bay for the summer.

"You don't expect me to commute, I hope?"

"Why should you commute? You'll have your own study there. Or, if you prefer, you can work in the big house. There's a room on the third floor with a beautiful view of the bay where you'd never be disturbed."

"Do you really think I could connect a single subject, verb and predicate on *that* gold coast? Why the very air would disintegrate any idea except a few old chestnuts already used by Scott Fitzgerald!"

"Stay in town, then," she said, a bit curtly. "But you surely don't expect me to keep the baby in the broiling city because of your theories about the air on Long Island?"

"*Other* babies, I believe, spend the summer in town. I've even heard on good authority that some of them survive."

Dorcas, as a mother, scorned to answer this. "You'll come on weekends?"

"I'll have to see how things go with the book."

She found, when she was settled in the cottage with her old nurse, Margaret, who had come over from the big house to help with the baby, that she had a sense of tranquillity tempered with relief. Was this how Robin felt when he was away from *her?* The little white cottage was clean and fresh and full of gay chintz; it had a modern kitchen, and Margaret was both consoling and efficient. Dorcas had quiet dinners every night with her parents and spent long, lazy days sitting on the lawn by the Sound, watching the sea gulls and the sailboats and rocking the baby carriage. It was peace, a rather inert peace, to be sure, but still peace. And the whole big shimmering place, her father's pride and joy, with its broad, close-cut lawns and its tall, gabled, slate-roofed manor house of purple brick, so evocative to her of stately colonial days on the James River, had always been dear to her heart.

But her sultry idyl was shattered one afternoon by the arrival of a haggard Robin who announced that he had burned his manuscript. Dorcas took him down to the beach where he could lie on the sand and shake and moan while she made little noises of consolation and poured him an occasional drink from a thermos. By evening he was quiet and seemingly resigned, and he even agreed to go to the big house for dinner. She told her mother on the telephone what had happened and warned her not to refer to it, nor did she, but her father, in the middle of what till then had seemed a pointless lecture about business, suddenly gave it a personal application.

"You know, Robin, I think I could make an investor of you. I really do. I think you have the nose for a good thing."

"*Me?*"

"Yes, it's hard to explain, but one has a feeling about these things. I'm not suggesting you give up your writing, or anything like that, but don't you ever get what they call 'writer's block'?"

"Do I! With me it's chronic!"

"Well, next time you feel an attack coming on, how about warming a desk in my office till it goes away? A bright fellow like you could pick things up fast. And who knows? You might even find you liked it. After all, you could be a weekend writer with me as well as with a publisher."

Robin stared at his father-in-law with wide semi-hypnotized eyes.

"You mean you want *me* in Hartley and Dodge?"

"Why not? Life isn't as tightly pigeonholed as you writers seem to think. You'd be surprised how much creative imagination you'd find downtown. Besides, some day that boy of yours is going to have a slice of my business, and I'd like to think you'd be able to help him with it."

To Dorcas her husband's expression had changed from wonderment to something closer to awe. Who, it appeared to ask, was this man who had so sublime a disregard for every principle as well as every prejudice? All of Robin's poor little artistic credo, his do's and don't's, seemed to run off like dirty water over the glazed steel of Derrick's basin.

"Do you think I might start tomorrow, sir?" he asked in a hushed tone.

"By God, you can start tonight!" Derrick exclaimed heartily. "You can come into my study, and I'll tell you about a little oil project we're thinking of going into."

When Robin and Dorcas returned to the cottage, he was silent and subdued, beneath an air of mild exhilaration that was only partly due to Derrick's brandy.

"I told you about the air down here!" he exclaimed. "It's made me a banker in eight hours time!"

"But, darling, it's only temporary," she said soothingly. "Just until you get started on your next novel. I think it's a wonderful idea. It'll take your mind off the old book and give you material for a new one."

"Temporary!" he cried, with a rather screechy laugh. "As if anything about your father could be called temporary!"

He refused to discuss it further, and the next morning he went into the city with Derrick on the early train. For two weeks he commuted regularly, an odd, deflated, silent Robin who drank five martinis before supper and went to bed directly afterwards. He behaved with a new respect towards her father, but with Dorcas herself he was increasingly moody and sour. He was now given to murmuring quotations from T. S. Eliot that were apparently relevant to his commute: "A crowd flowed over London Bridge, so many, I had not thought Death had undone so many." In less literary moments he uttered dark hints about zombies and the "living death." He refused to tell her anything about what he did in the office, but she gathered from her father that he was supposed to be occupied in reading statistical reports of electric companies. Whatever happened, she reflected with a dry discouragement, it was bound to be blamed on her, whether the failure of his novel or the failure of his job.

After the second week he telephoned from the office that the weather was too hot for commuting and that he was going to stay in town. She expected him for the weekend, but he did not come. The following week he telephoned only once, to complain about the laundry, and the week after, her father reported that he had failed to appear in the office at all. Dorcas simply shrugged, without even attempting an explanation, and her father, in his usual fashion, dropped the subject. But three days later he called at the cottage on his way home from the station, looking very grave.

"It should interest you to learn that your husband has spent the last two nights in the apartment of one Vera Stiles."

"How do you know?" she asked in a dead voice.

"I've had a detective on him for the past ten days."

Her head was spinning, but she could still accept it. "I suppose I'm not surprised. What do you think I should do?"

"I think you should divorce him."

She was intrigued by the distant roaring in her ears. "Isn't that rather drastic?"

"Strike now, child. The man's no good. He never has been. God knows, I've tried to see things his way, but what's the use? He's rotten through and through!" He slapped the table with the palm of his hand as his argument gained its crisis. "We've got to move and move fast. I want you to see a man called Mark Jesmond. For my money, he's the smartest young lawyer in town. Frankly, I'm trying to get him out of his firm into my business, but that's neither here nor there. Will you see him?"

"I don't know."

"Will you just see him? That's all I ask."

"I don't know!" She jumped to her feet with a little cry of delayed agony. "I've got to see Robin first!"

She found him, the next morning at noon, in their apartment. He had not shaved and was still in his pajamas, reading a newspaper. He did not even get up as she came in, and his smile combined resentment with hostility.

"I can see you know 'all,' as they say."

As she stared down at him, her whole body trembled with what she felt now must be dislike. For what else could it be? Could the wildest sentimentalist have still called it love? "I know a lot. What I'd like to know is what you want. What you plan."

"Why don't you ask your father?" he demanded sneeringly. "Doesn't he make all the plans for you and me? Isn't it his

Gilbert and Sullivan detective that I see at restaurants, hiding behind a false beard?"

"Can't we leave Daddy out of it for once? Can't we discuss this thing as it concerns *us* and us alone?"

"Of course not!" he cried, jumping to his feet. "How can we leave out God?" He slapped his forehead and strode to the mantelpiece, turning to face her in a rather stagy pose. "From the very beginning he has plotted to destroy me. Oh, I may be a sniveling, self-pitying failure, but there are still things I can see. For all my faults, I'm bright. I'm as bright as your father, even! I can see that he was smart enough to anticipate that, living on *his* money, I'd never be able to finish my novel. He knew that his greenbacks, like faithful little soldiers, could be counted on to do *that* job!"

"Why are you so sure it was his money?" she interrupted. "Can nothing ever be *your* fault? How do you even know you were cut out to be a writer? Maybe you weren't. There are other things in life, after all."

"That's right!" he shrieked, with a savage glee. "Be a good wolf cub and join Daddy. Tear me in pieces! How do I know you weren't in it with him from the beginning?"

"In *what*, for God's sake?"

"In the whole business of degrading me. Of course, once he'd killed my novel, the rest of the job was easy. All he had to do was turn me into a poor zombie of a commuter, so you could see me in Daddy's office, Daddy's office that *I'd* sneered at. He *knew* you had only married me to irritate him. All he had to do to crush your silly rebellion was to *approve* of me. My God, if ever a man was castrated, you see him now before you!"

Dorcas surveyed him with a new detachment despite the dead weight in her heart. She was even able to reflect on the points of possible truth in his crazy picture. But what did truth or falsehood, guilt or innocence, matter once a thing was over? There remained the obsequies, a decent period of mourning and then — and then a life with little Derrick.

"It must be my poor consolation," she said as she crossed the room to the telephone, "that Daddy and I continue to provide your imagination with such excellent literary material. Perhaps there will be a new book, after all." She dialed her father's number and gazed down at the river as she waited. "Mr. Hartley, please. His daughter calling." She sent a dry, cold stare across the room to Robin as she heard her father's voice. "Oh, Daddy? I think I'd like to see Mr. Jesmond after all. Could you arrange an appointment? Oh, he's with you now? Can I come down? How perfect."

The white walls of her father's square office gave out a gleam like his own burgeoning assurance. Three landscapes: a green field, a riverbank and cattle in pasture, executed with the mirror accuracy of the Barbizon school, testified to their owner's clear flat view of the universe. New York Harbor, spread out in the wide south window, blue and grey and smoky, might have been done by an intruding impressionist. Mark Jesmond sat at the gilded Directoire table that her father used for a desk and scratched his cheek. He was a man of rather less than medium size, with tousled brown hair and grey slanty eyes, who wore a combination of a rumpled old tweed coat and grey flannels that Dorcas had never expected to see on Wall Street. It went with his restlessness, his boyish, rustic, snub-nosed face, his air of the farm boy who had stumbled into Wall Street from the hills of New Hampshire to beat the toughest traders at their own game. For that was it, she decided as she eyed him apprehensively and told her tale. He was tough. He specialized in toughness. There was a dull gleam in those grey eyes that might have come from metal. Small wonder that her father liked him.

"So there we are," she finished with a deprecatory shrug. "I suppose the question is, what next?"

He put both hands over his face in a somewhat disconcerting gesture and dragged them slowly down, revealing first the long eyelashes now comically slanted, then the pulled skin of his eyelids and cheeks. "The first thing is to change the lock in your apartment. Mr. Granberry's clothes can be packed and left in the lobby. Don't worry. I'll take care of the details."

"But the apartment's his."

"No, it's not. Fortunately, that plan was never carried out. It stands in your name."

"But where will Robin go?"

"That's his affair. Let him go to that woman's. Why should you give him a home?"

Dorcas nodded slowly. "And after that?"

"I suggest we file the complaint for divorce tomorrow, naming Vera Stiles as co-respondent. There need be no publicity unless Mr. Granberry fights us. But I doubt if he will. We won't ask for any alimony. Simply for sole and absolute custody of the child."

"Oh, but I'd want Derrick to know his father!" she protested.

"That will be up to you," Mr. Jesmond said briskly, rubbing the tip of his nose with the palm of his hand. "My job is to see that you hold the big trumps. After that you can play your hand as you wish."

"But don't most people go to Reno or Mexico?"

"Most people don't get valid divorces. Your father wants you to have a binding decree here in New York, with unquestioned control of your child. All that we ask of Mr. Granberry is that he remove himself from the family picture. Neither his wife nor his child need ever cost him a penny."

And Dorcas, watching those eyes, knew that it would be

so. She was in her father's hands, the firm, dexterous hands of a master surgeon. Indeed, the whole procedure was rather like an operation. All she had to do was submit and lie back to be anesthetized.

"You mean I won't even have to *see* Robin again?"

"Why should you go through any more pain? It seems to me you've suffered enough from him."

She knew that it was cowardly not to see Robin and discuss it with him, but she didn't care. The luxury of a future without scenes was irresistible. She decided to obey her father and Mr. Jesmond in every instance, and went back to Oyster Bay where she and little Derrick moved into the big house and where a detective watched, night and day, to be sure that poor Robin made no move to steal, or even to see his child, or to harangue his wife with useless but painful complaints. Dorcas never answered the telephone herself, and the servants were told to hang up if Mr. Granberry called. Two envelopes, addressed to her in his handwriting, were returned unopened with a typewritten note that all communications should be made through Mr. Jesmond. It turned out later that Robin had offered to give up his son if an out-of-state divorce could be arranged and Vera Stiles's name left out of the proceeding, but Derrick was inexorable. A New York divorce was necessary, and a New York divorce was obtained. In the end Robin failed to appear, and Dorcas' petition was granted in full.

During the suit Mark Jesmond made several trips to Oyster Bay to confer with his client. He seemed, each time, disposed to linger when his brief business was over, and Dorcas took him once for a stroll around the place and once to the beach for a swim. He proved to have a surprising enthusiasm for the out-of-doors, and in the Sound he swam out so far from the raft that she became nervous and called him back. He talked incessantly, about himself and his ambitions, scratching his head and his sides as he did so, and he made as many disarming references to his poor childhood on a farm in New Hampshire as he did clumsy ones to the important people whom he knew. He was an odd blend of naïveté and worldliness, with a sturdy, down-to-earth farm boy's charm and the hard, dry eye of an old tycoon. He evidently sensed the uniqueness of his own mixture, for he constantly played it up. On the day that he brought her the final decree, they had cocktails on the terrace, and he toasted her new liberty.

"I hope it doesn't mean that you're going to be free of me," he added, and, astonishingly enough, he winked.

"Oh, no, we're old friends now."

"I think we are." And, even more startlingly, he reached over to put his hand on her knee. It was only for a moment, but it was a moment that paralyzed her. Before she had recovered herself, the hand was gone, and he was looking over the Sound and whistling a tune. Then he finished his drink in a gulp and got up suddenly to hit a croquet ball through the first two wickets on the lawn. She was grateful that his attention was distracted from her, for she was trembling in every limb. How could it be that this small, tense man, this cold and chattering egotist, with one crude, perhaps haphazard gesture, had aroused her lust as Robin had not done in the whole course of their marriage? For why else was she trembling, she asked herself in a sudden giddy twinge of shame? Why, except that she wanted Jesmond, wanted him as she had never dreamed she could want a man before? And all in two minutes! The screen door banged behind her, and she gasped with relief as her father came out on the terrace.

"Mark says it's all over, Daddy!" she cried, running over to kiss him. "I'm so glad. And so grateful to you for arranging everything!"

And she flung her arms tightly around his neck and burst into tears. Her father held her closely and murmured consoling things. He and Mark, of course, would find it entirely natural that she should be caught at such a moment in the backwash of an old emotion. But how could they know that she was weeping for the unhappy Robin who had been caught up in the net of his own weakness and cast out of it again by two remorseless fishermen to die a gasping death on the beach? How could they know that she trembled with remorse at her own passivity, at her own surrender to the first show of force, at her own itching need to cringe, like a dog, before the boy master with a whip? Robin, yes, she knew what a poor thing Robin was, but what chance had he had in the hands of as poor a thing as she?

PART V

Geraldine's Return

12

Geraldine: 1935

WHEN Freddy Brevoort died of a throat cancer, only a little past his fiftieth year, he left Geraldine a childless widow and, what was worse, a poor one. The trust fund which had maintained them both so comfortably in Paris and in Cannes, in two small tidy flats, with an Hispano-Suiza town car for Geraldine and a Bugatti racer for Freddy, went back, "in default of issue," as the latter's inconsiderate grandfather had phrased it, to Freddy's three sisters who, although all married to men of means, had shown a selfish indisposition to waive their rights. Geraldine succeeded only in drying up whatever impulses of generosity might have otherwise lingered in her family-in-law by suing them on the grounds that she had been defrauded of her widow's share. And so again she found herself without a rudder in a sea churned up by the malevolence of relatives, just as it had happened ten years before when Talbot Keating had discovered her diary and used it in their divorce proceedings to dodge a man's proper burden of alimony. It was Freddy, big and red and obtuse, yet so gentle of heart, who had then rescued her from gin and melancholia and taught her that the secret of idleness lay in routine. The decade of her marriage to him had been her one decade of peace. In a France which had then been the haven of irregulars, she and Freddy had maintained a regular schedule where newspapers, naps, drives, movies, cocktails and lovemaking had lapped against the beach of their calm like small, gentle, slapping waves. In the squall of tears and fruitless litigation that had followed the last horrible months of Freddy's illness, she had felt abandoned by all, by her dead parents, by her emptily cheerful brother, by his rich, hard, distrustful wife. She was already half intoxicated on the night when Ida's cable arrived, but not so much so that she failed to see in it her only salvation.

Hope you will come to us for the winter. Derrick arranging transportation and all details with Morgan's. Insist you worry about nothing.

And a scant ten days later she had been settled in the Hartleys' guest room on Fifty-third Street, coddled and crooned over by an Ida more suited to the role of nurse than to any other in which she had yet seen her. Lying in the big mahogany bed and gazing at the sentimental eighteenth century prints of "L'Enfant Egaré" and "L'Enfant Retrouvé" which Aunt Lily Trask had picked up at some long distant auction, she felt lulled by a past that had once seemed to her so strict, even censorious, and that now bore the linea- ments of some stern old governess, visited in retirement, and found, after all, to be sweet and dim-eyed and even rather clutchingly affectionate. There were meals, too, as regular as Freddy would have wanted, and afternoon drives in the Park and up Riverside Drive in a green, soft-springed limou- sine, and visits at teatime to relatives and family friends. She and Ida talked by the hour of their childhood, populat- ing the street with ghosts, and she found that nostalgia, like faith, *could* be cultivated and that it was pleasant to look back over the years to a girlhood that seemed to have some of the innocence and goodness and subdued melancholy of an American primitive.

But Ida was not Freddy, after all. As he had been essentially calm, so was her cousin essentially nervous, and Ida's nervousness had been bound ultimately to infect the peace of this new retreat. Geraldine was first irked by the atmosphere of ceaseless supervision. Ida, who obviously considered her an alcoholic, deeply disapproved of her habit of bedroom drinking. She even disapproved of Geraldine's modest little efforts to make her bedchamber a more feminine abode, with a pink-skirted vanity table and a bevy of big floppy dolls with parasols and crinolines. But how in the name of thunder was a lady expected to live surrounded by dark mahogany? There was even a shaving mirror on a mahogany stand in the bathroom and photographs of fraternity groups from Uncle Gerald's class at Yale! And would it have ever occurred to Ida that a guest might like bath salts, and something more exotic than Ivory soap? It was obviously a perverse fate that had wasted a fortune on her cousin and left herself so poor.

Their first sharp words, however, were not occasioned by interior decoration but by Hugo. He was a short, bright, waspish black-haired young man, with glittering eyes in a frog-shaped face, who went to Yale, probably because his father had gone to Harvard, and came down to New York every weekend. Geraldine enjoyed asking him about his girls and his parties and telling him of the stormy years of her marriage to Talbot Keating. He would knock at her door when he came in at night, and if she was still awake, reading a detective story, as she usually was, he would bring her a nightcap. It was one of these sessions that Ida interrupted, appearing in the doorway in her nightgown, a pale moon of disapproval.

"Hugo, hadn't you better go to bed? You know you have to go back to New Haven early in the morning."

"I thought I'd sit up till traintime, Ma," he replied easily. "Can I get you a drink? Cousin Geraldine and I were talking about Paris after the war. Did you know she knew Hemingway?"

But Ida did not seem to hear his questions. "Hugo, please go to bed!"

"Don't you think I'm getting a bit long in the tooth to be sent off that way?"

"Hugo, *please!*"

When he saw his mother's tears, Hugo rose immediately, made a little bow to Geraldine, winked and left the room without a word.

"What a fool you are to treat him that way!" Geraldine burst out in a voice whose anger startled herself. "Do you want to make him despise you?"

"I don't want him to see you drinking when I've told him you're not meant to."

"Really, Ida, you're a period piece! That boy knows far more about life already than you ever will."

"That's just what I'm afraid of. He knows too much about things that won't make him happy."

"Who are you to be the judge of that?"

"Well, have they made *you* happy?"

"I've had a lot of hard luck. We're not all blessed with your good fortune."

"Hard luck?" Ida's query had a scorn that only the late hour and maternal concern could have elicited from her. "You haven't had *that* much hard luck."

"I suppose it wasn't hard luck to lose my husband from cancer!" Geraldine cried angrily. "I suppose it wasn't hard luck to have his sisters steal my money!"

"It was *their* money," Ida retorted. "It was as much their money as if their grandfather had willed it to them directly."

"If you have nothing better to do than make yourself disagreeable, why don't you go to bed?"

Ida left, like Hugo, without another word, and the next morning at breakfast she was her consoling, solicitous self again. But there was a difference, from then on, in their relationship. Geraldine could not forgive her attitude about Freddy's sisters. This seemed to her a basic issue in the question of whether or not a person really cared about her. Even Derrick, who was surely a hard enough man of business, had taken a less dogmatic position. He, at least, had shaken his head and agreed that she had been badly used.

Derrick, indeed, had been perfect. There had been nothing in his grave, courteous, sustained air of hospitality or in the continuing sympathy of his questions about her health and spirits to suggest the least lingering resentment of his treatment at her hands two and a half decades before. And to make matters even better, the occasional gleam in his fixed stare gave play to the exciting suspicion that her old attraction for him might not be entirely dead.

He took over her tangled affairs and quickly unraveled them. His only requirement was that their business discussions be held in his office. She chose to read into this the natural desire of a self-made man to be seen in his glory by the woman who had spurned him when poor, and she understood and sympathized. Besides, she loved the air of moneyed masculinity of the vast new offices of Hartley and Dodge on Broad Street. Derrick had hired a decorator, but it was easy to see that he had not given her a free hand. The entrance hall had the green walls, the Sheraton armchairs and the dark Dutch landscapes with ruminating cows that were coming into fashion for investment houses, but Geraldine thought she could make out Derrick's influence in the wide, white chaste corridors and the heavy bronze plaques that bore the names of the partners by their doors. Each time he summoned her at noon, talked to her gravely for twenty minutes and then took her to India House for lunch.

"The thing about money," he warned her when she spoke of Freddy's trust, "is to know when you're licked. The greatest disasters come in trying to retrieve losses. My lawyers advise me that you will not prevail against Freddy's sisters. So be it. Let us concentrate on making you comfortable with what you have left."

"But can you? It's so little."

"That's *my* problem."

"Oh, Derrick, how can I ever thank you?"

"By having lunch with me once in a while. Like this."

She blushed, she hoped, prettily. "I don't know if you ever read Edith Wharton. Ida and I used to love *The House of Mirth*. The heroine lets a married man speculate for her, and then he demands a reward that she has not anticipated." She laughed, a bit nervously, to make light of her reference. "She finds herself hopelessly compromised. Of course those were prehistoric days."

"But was he speculating with *her* money? Or with his own and pretending it was hers?"

"I don't remember. Does it matter?"

"Of course it matters. When a man speculates with a lady customer's money, the relationship is entirely professional. There can be no question of compromising her."

"Forgive me. I was being silly."

The smile that he gave her was enigmatic, and she even decided that it might ultimately be necessary to be more guarded in her talk. Yet the weeks passed, and Derrick said nothing that he could not have said in the presence of Ida. When the latter went off to Stonington for a weekend on an errand for old Aunt Dagmar, and Derrick suggested that he and she dine out at a new French restaurant, it seemed like the most natural thing in the world. As she sniffed her plate of steaming mussels in an alcove paneled after Fragonard, she reflected how little it really took to make her contented.

"What is Ida doing in Stonington?" she asked.

"She goes up regularly to inspect the old Denison house there. Aunt Dagmar has an obsession about the caretaker being a drunk."

"But Aunt Dagmar's half ga-ga!"

"Her word is still law to Ida."

"Ida is wonderful," she mused. "I wish I had her sense of family responsibility."

"No, you don't." Derrick's reply was unexpectedly curt. "You've always laughed at Ida and her sense of responsibility."

"*Derrick!*"

"Well, haven't you?"

"Certainly not. Ida is made out of different material than I am, that's all."

"Material you laugh at, that's just the point."

"Derrick, what are you driving at?"

"Simply this. I've been surrounded for years by an attitude of false admiration and false pity for Ida. I've come to believe it's a way people have of saying they don't like *me*. But I want *you* to like me, Geraldine."

"I do like you. I like you very much."

"You know what I mean."

She felt a little shiver as she glanced at those fixed grey eyes. He was so extraordinarily immobile, like an ivory Buddha.

"I wonder if you really appreciate Ida," she murmured.

"Of course I appreciate Ida. In fact, you might say she's my hobby. Ida fascinates me. I've never been able to make the least dent in the wall of her preconceptions."

"Perhaps you haven't really tried."

"Perhaps not. But if I had, one or the other of us might have been smashed. And I'm not at all sure it would have been Ida."

"You always think in terms of smashing things, Derrick. It's hardly the way with women."

"You mean I've frustrated Ida? Very likely. But she's been frustrated a long time. She must be used to it by now."

"A woman never gets used to it!"

"*You* wouldn't," he retorted, and an almost playful note crept into his flat voice. "But then you're not Ida. You haven't forgotten you're a woman. Men to Ida are basically irrelevancies. As long as she had her old house on Fifty-third Street and enough money for her charities, she'd never notice if I was gone. She could run errands for her old aunts until the last of them was laid away, and then be Aunt Dagmar herself."

"You surely don't mean, Derrick, that you're thinking of *leaving* Ida?"

"That depends entirely on you."

There was no mistaking him this time. It was going to be a giddy evening. "Upon *me?*" she gasped. "You mean, upon my advice? Well, surely, you don't think I'm going to advise you to leave poor Ida now, after all these years . . ."

"Look, Geraldine," he interrupted brusquely, "let you and me understand each other. In case we don't already. I've never forgotten you, and I think it unlikely, at my age, that I ever shall. I've turned the half-century mark. Some people call it the dangerous age. I call it the age of resolution."

The waiter was again hovering, and as he discussed the sauce with Derrick, who was a methodical and painstaking gourmet, she had a few moments to catch her breath. She found it exciting to suppose him a man who would not anticipate his physical possession of a woman by so much as a pat of her hand. A man who could break off a proposition to give a waiter minute instructions. She remembered *Wuthering Heights* from her days at Miss Irvin's and how she and Ida had thrilled at the hardness of Heathcliff.

"I said it was the age of resolution," he repeated as the waiter went off. "Don't you think it can be that?"

"What must we resolve?"

"We?" He smiled for the first time, a smile that had the same faint mockery as his expression. "Do I take it that my feelings are reciprocated?"

"Well . . . really, Derrick . . . I hardly know what to say . . ." She took happy refuge in a little sob. "My poor Freddy hasn't been dead two months."

"I knew you *years* before Freddy. I have the prior claim."

"Claim?" she cried indignantly. "How can you talk about claims? A married man?"

"I may not always be that."

"You don't mean you'd ever actually divorce Ida!"

"No, but Ida might divorce me."

"Do you really think she would?"

"She's not the kind to hang on to a man. She's much too proud."

"Poor Ida!"

"Yes, poor Ida. But her real humiliation took place twenty-four years ago. You ought to know about *that*."

"It wasn't my fault!"

"Let us agree now, once and for all," he said in a sharper tone, "that everything that has happened or that is going to happen is *my* fault. Let it all be on my shoulders. They're broad enough. You are in no way to blame." He paused, as if silence would ratify. She was silent. "After Ida's former humiliation, the present will seem light enough. She is older, and she lives in a more understanding world. Besides, she will have the sympathy of the whole Denison clan. A throbbing sense of injustice and a generous financial settlement can do worlds for a woman in that position."

"What a cynic you are!"

"I take the world as I find it. But let us come to your part in the matter."

"Mine?" she asked in surprise. "But I have none!"

"I beg your pardon. You have no blame, for that is mine. But you have a part. If I do all this for you, what will you do for me?"

"I cannot be committed," she replied in what she hoped was a tone that combined dignity with the least hint of disappointment. "How can you expect me to be disloyal to Ida? I wasn't before, and I won't be now. All I can say is that if you and Ida should ever decide to part, if you should ever find yourself a free man, I might — I just *might,* mind you — be willing to pick up this conversation where now, I'm afraid, we must drop it. Is that fair?"

Derrick's laugh was now frankly mocking. "I'm afraid it's not! As I say, I'll take the blame, but I won't take everything. Suppose you squint for a moment at your own position. You are a widow of extravagant habits and inadequate means. You're still a beautiful woman, but you're forty-six years old . . ."

"Derrick! You churl!"

"Ida's little family book, my dear, is full of dates. Let us stick to the facts. You expect me, a man of property and family and of the best reputation, to incur the ignominy of the world on the mere chance that you will eye me with favor amid the smoke of my burnt bridges. No, Geraldine, life is not like that. I should have thought you would have learned by now."

"What must I do?"

"You must give me some tangible evidence that you are not indifferent."

She turned away from that maddeningly level voice, hoping that her pallor would not tell him the full story of her shock. It was degrading, surely, to be titillated by so matter-of-fact a treatment of things that should be romantic or nothing. "I suppose I can imagine what that evidence is," she muttered.

"I suppose you can. I own a brownstone on Sixty-third

Street — the second and third floors have been converted into a duplex apartment that is now vacant. It will be yours, decorated as fancily as you wish, complete with cook and maid."

She played for time, fussing with a cigarette and with his gold lighter. "And a key for you, I suppose?"

"No. I would take my chances that you would open when I rang."

"My dear Derrick, there are words for ladies who live in apartments paid for by men!"

"Words!" He grunted. "How women love them! I am simply trying to be honest with you. I will see to it that your capital is doubled, if not tripled. You will have a beautiful apartment, and everyone will say you were lucky on the market. Even Ida will be glad for you. Must all this be refused because Derrick Hartley, your investment counsel and cousin-in-law, occasionally calls to discuss the market at the cocktail hour?"

"Is that *all* he calls for?"

"In the eyes of the world, that will be all."

"And what if I say no?"

"Then our little idyl is over before it has begun."

She turned quickly and read conviction in his slowly repeated nod. "I suppose it wouldn't be so wicked if we got married later," she said doubtfully. "After you and Ida were divorced."

"I've told you. The wickedness will all be mine."

She sighed deeply. "Would you do me a favor?" she asked. "Could we say no more about it tonight?"

"I think we've said too much already. Let us enjoy our dinner. Will you allow me to order a bottle of champagne?"

"To celebrate? Certainly not!"

"To forget."

"What? My conscience?"

"No. Your approaching birthday."

"Damn you!" she cried with a burst of laughter. "And damn Ida's little book!"

She had to admit that he behaved handsomely for the rest of the evening. Not once, directly or indirectly, did he return to his proposition, and when he took her back to the house, he bade her good night at the door of her room in so perfectly a formal manner that, even in Ida's absence, she felt no need to lock her door. So many men would have fatuously supposed that any woman would have been secretly mortified, under the circumstances, had no attempt to open it been made! One of the enticing things about Derrick was that he was so obviously interested only in ultimate favors. To him there were no preliminaries. In love as in his business, he was a man who went straight to the point.

And what, she asked herself that night, when her lights were out, was the point of not coming to the point? Was it *her* duty to save a marriage that Ida seemed to care so little about? Were not the children grown up? And didn't Derrick have money enough for *everybody*? It was all very well to talk of family obligations, but who felt obligated to *her*? Had obligations kept Freddy's money from going to his sisters who didn't need it? Would obligations look after his widow?

"Derrick is perfectly right," she murmured to herself. "Ida doesn't *care*. She's never cared about anything, and life has filled her lap to overflowing. With all the things it has denied *me*: children, money, security. Why should I always be left out? Why should I have to drag myself about to cheap watering places, smiling at old widowers with gummy eyes? Or else begging a pittance from Scotty's rich wife? And probably being refused! No, if Ida can't hang on to her possessions, if they keep just tumbling out of her lap, how can she expect people not to pick them up? And if *I* don't, someone else will! Because Derrick is wrong. He *is* at the dangerous age. And I could probably get more money out of him for Ida than Ida could herself!"

But Ida's reproachful eyes still remained in her fitful fancy until, exhausted and gently weeping, she fell asleep.

The next morning before lunch she went across the street to call on Aunt Dagmar. Aunt Dagmar was in her middle eighties and had begun to fail in the past year, but her position as head of the family had never passed to another. She continued to live in Uncle Linn's French Renaissance house. His will had provided that it should go, on her death, with the rest of his estate, to Columbia University. In this way, he had claimed, she would be rich but unpestered by relatives. Now she sat every morning, apparently contented, in her chair by the big stone fireplace surrounded by the newest books that she never looked at and the embroidery that she never picked up. Wrinkled and brown, with hair as white as drawing paper, she had still some remnants of her ancient beauty.

"Aunt Dagmar," Geraldine began, coming straight to the point, "do you remember when you and Daddy made me give up Derrick? Because he was Ida's beau?"

"Derrick who?"

"Derrick Hartley."

"Oh, *Derrick*. Of course I remember. But, my dear, he'd even been kissing poor Ida. Right in the Metropolitan Museum, where anybody might have seen them!"

"And where anybody who hadn't was told by Ida!" Geraldine murmured, but Aunt Dagmar did not hear. "Tell me frankly," she continued, "do you think it has worked out for the best?"

"You mean Derrick and Ida?"

"Yes."

"Well, I suppose it has. I doubt very much if *you*'d have made him happy."

The old were certainly unexpected. It had never occurred to her that Aunt Dagmar would have viewed the question from Derrick's point of view. "Why not?"

"Because it's an art to be happily married to a selfish man. I know something about that."

"Is it an art that Ida possesses?"

Aunt Dagmar considered this. "I think in her own way, she may."

"But did you know at the time he was selfish?"

"I don't remember what we knew at the time. Why does it matter?"

"Because I find myself wondering if I was right to give in to you. Nothing has worked out in my life, and everything has in Ida's."

"But he kissed her in the Metropolitan Museum! Right where anyone could see them!" Aunt Dagmar paused, trying to remember something. "I believe it was in the Egyptian Room."

Geraldine sighed with exasperation. "It seems to me I had as good a chance as Ida to make him happy. *Then*."

"But, darling, Derrick could never have been happy without children. A rich man without heirs is like an unmilked cow. I know something about that, too. Of course your Uncle Linn had Livia, but she was worse than nothing."

"But Derrick couldn't have *known* that I wouldn't have children!"

"But you didn't, did you?"

Geraldine gave it up with another sigh and let the conversation revert to Aunt Dagmar's more usual topics: the finding of a new kitchen maid, the destruction of the house across the way, what Uncle Linn might have thought of

Franklin Roosevelt. She reflected ruefully how untrue it was
that the old lived in the past. They lived in the immediate
present, the minute-to-minute present, except when they retreated for a stately recess into a fictional past. As for the
past where Derrick had first proposed to her, that quiet
brownstone past, with its fussiness and its quibbling and its
love, how was it possible to bring *that* back? And why, really,
should she want to? Was it not better to forget it altogether
with its emotional tangle of stultifying family duties? Had it
not forgotten itself? Where were the Denisons of Fifty-third
Street, she wondered as she came out to the sunlight through
Aunt Dagmar's heavy grilled doors. Uncle Philip's house at
the corner was gone. A jewelry store occupied its site. Uncle
Willie's had made way for a parking lot, and her father's was
a night club, or perhaps worse. Everything in New York
reminded one of the prevalent dust to which, almost immediately, it seemed, one was condemned to return. If one
didn't seize that day, a contractor would.

She found Ida in the front hall, back from Stonington in
a rather buoyant mood.

"You've been to see Aunt Dagmar. How sweet of you."

"Well, after all, she's my aunt too."

"I'm sorry, dear. I suppose I do get a bit possessive about
her, living just across the street. Suppose I take you out for
lunch? Would that be fun?"

Of course it would not have occurred to Ida, had she enjoyed double Derrick's income, to take her anywhere but the
Park Club. Who but a benighted woman would not be
content with a vegetable salad and lemon ice, consumed in
the company of ladies, half of whose faces and all of whose
names were familiar? The whoop-whoop of female laughter
rose through smoke to a lofty ceiling decorated with tropical
birds. Geraldine, glancing restlessly about, saw two class-
mates from Miss Irvin's. They nodded and waved, and she

wondered, from the way their heads drew together, what horrors they must be saying of her. It was curious that even the girls who had been "fast" at school seemed now as settled as Ida. It was as if the New York female world had drawn together in a single dreary lump of uniformity to scorn Geraldine as a lonely maverick. Well, scorn, she would like to remind the members of the Park Club, could be a two-way street!

Her mood was not improved by having Ida, twice during their meal, rise from her seat to visit other tables.

"You're always talking about the way things *used* to be done," Geraldine observed crossly, the second time that she returned. "Surely, you know that table hopping is considered bad form."

"But I had to say a word to old Mrs. Kay about Annie's engagement. And to tell Miss Street and Cousin Ella Rhodes that our meeting at St. Luke's has been postponed."

"None of them seem to come to you."

"But, Geraldine, they're *older*."

"We're all still at school, aren't we? With old girls and new girls and medals and crushes. What is this very dining room but an extension of Miss Irvin's? And why should any group of women want to extend Miss Irvin's unless they've lost all hope?"

"Hope for what?"

"Why, for men, of course!"

"Geraldine, you're too absurd. At *our* age?"

"Of course at our age! That's just what I mean!" But the sharpness of her resentment was suddenly blunted by the notion that Ida's indifference might work to her own advantage. "How young do you start working on them?" she asked. "Is Dorcas a member?"

"No. But I think when her divorce is final, she may want to join. I doubt if poor Dorcas is going to be interested in seeing any men for a long time. She's been through a bit of hell, you know."

"Of course I know. Are you forgetting what I went through with Talbot?"

"Don't you think it's worse when there's a child?"

"Not when the child's a baby, like Dorcas'."

"I wonder if it matters how young or old the child is."

"Really, Ida! Suppose it's grown up!"

"Sometimes that only makes it worse. If Derrick and I were ever divorced, for example, it might completely disillusion Hugo. You can't tell. It might set him permanently against marriage. Of course it's purely hypothetical, but that's the reason, no matter what Derrick did, I could never divorce him."

Geraldine, looking suddenly up at the ceiling, thought that she was going to scream like one of the tropical birds. Could anybody have imagined such perverseness?

"It's only mothers who count, isn't it!" she exclaimed shrilly. "We poor sterile creatures can marry and divorce at will! I suppose you and Aunt Dagmar wonder why we bother with such technicalities? Why we don't simply flit from mate to mate and not intrude on the majesty of the law?"

"Geraldine, my dear, don't be a goose!"

Anger now convulsed her. If Ida wanted a fight for her husband, woman to woman, that was one thing. But to be frustrated, after all she had suffered, by one of Ida's dowdy, Park Club principles was too much to be borne. Was it possible that they had conspired to ruin her, this old-maid matron and her money-grubbing husband? Was *that* the revenge of Fifty-third Street?

"You've always resented me, Ida, and you still do! You resented me as a girl because I was prettier and had more friends and Aunt Dagmar preferred me! You resented her giving me my coming-out ball while you only had that dreary tea!"

"Darling!" Ida exclaimed, laughing in sheer surprise. "I adored your ball! I always admired you, and at times I envied you, but I never resented you. If I'd resented you, I wouldn't have asked you to come to me this winter."

"You only wanted to play Lady Bountiful!" Geraldine insisted with childish spite. "You wanted to have me, poor and bereft, dependent on your generosity!"

"I'm sorry if I made you feel that way," Ida said in a graver tone.

"And Derrick! You can't pretend you didn't resent my taking Derrick from you!"

"Taking Derrick!" Ida's eyes were limpid with shocked surprise. "But, my dear, do you think I can ever forget that it's exactly to your unselfishness that I owe my husband and children?"

Geraldine pulled a handkerchief from her bag and dabbed frantically at her eyes.

"There, dear," Ida continued soothingly. "I think it may do us both good to have a bit of a blow-up once in a while."

"Ida, please leave me," Geraldine murmured. "Just let me sit here alone a minute, will you?"

When Ida had gone, after hovering nervously about the doorway to look back at her, Geraldine took several long breaths until her incipient sobs were under control. She strove to keep her mind fixed on the one desperate resolution that would save her from being smothered in the stifling down of Ida's commiseration and Ida's principles. If she was to live, there was only one way for her, Geraldine, to live.

Outside the Park Club she walked to Madison Avenue and found a telephone booth. If Derrick were in, that was the answer. If Derrick were out . . . well, she shuddered to think. He was in.

"I've decided I'd like to see that apartment," she gasped, and leaned back against the wall of the booth, half in a faint, as she heard him telling her when and where to meet him.

The affair, like everything else in her life, including her brief conversion to the Catholic Church, turned out to be something of a disappointment. It was not that she found Derrick, after her first flurry of embarrassment at the abrupt change in their relations, an incompetent or clumsy lover. Far from it. He was deliberate, vigorous and forceful, just as much so as she had anticipated. But he was not romantic. In fact he seemed to go out of his way to be *un*romantic. He seemed to regard her nakedness more with the clinical eye of a doctor in a consulting room than with the rapture of a man who had been starving two decades for so privileged a sight. The good fortune that, after so long a period, had translated the Beatrice of his dreams to the Beatrice of his bed he took as much for granted as the good fortune which had brought him his Wall Street partnership and his membership in many clubs. It was hardly agreeable to Geraldine to feel like a piece of cheese which had fallen into the jaws of a patiently waiting fox or like another share of stock in the bursting Hartley portfolio. Nor was it agreeable for her to suspect, from the regular pattern of their meetings, that his interest was predominantly, if not exclusively, physical. He would never linger beside her after making love, but would get up briskly and dress and go to the bar table to mix a drink. In the desultory conversation that followed their brief moments of intimacy, he was apt to talk, rather boringly, about his daughter's divorce.

"The poor kid got herself off to a terrible start, but there's one blessing to the loose age we live in. At least, she can have a new try. If she could only get interested in Mark

Jesmond, I'd feel the whole wretched business might have been worth it."

"But don't you see, that's just her trouble?" she asked, exasperated, as she tied the cords of her dressing gown. "You expect her to do what *you* want. The poor girl has to make her own choice."

"Robin Granberry was her choice."

"Was he? I wonder. Maybe she picked him out of sheer reaction. Maybe you were as much the cause of Robin Granberry as you'll ever be of Mark Jesmond."

"I think I ought to know something about my own daughter!"

"I think you ought," she retorted, irked at the impression which he conveyed that she was not fit to speak of anyone as pure as Dorcas. "You seem to forget that I've been through the same thing myself. I, too, believe it or not, was once a disillusioned girl."

But at once he changed the subject. It was impossible not to notice that he always did so whenever she was about to speak of her divorce from Talbot Keating. Did he think that the topic might lead to the question of his own from Ida? She dared not ask, for the simple reason that she had no weapon left in the event of hostilities. She had delivered herself into the hands as well as the arms of this calculating man, and she shivered at the consequences of her rashness. If it had been foolish to imagine him a Heathcliff, it had been idiotic to imagine herself a Cathy. How could she have forgotten the fate of unhappy Isabella?

"I must be getting back," he said, rising as he finished his drink. "Ida's having people for dinner."

"Ida? Since when has Ida had people for dinner? You mean you're entertaining for the greater glory of Hartley and Dodge."

"Not tonight. This is family night. All cousins."

"Cousins?" she asked querulously. "And what about little Geraldine? Is *she* no longer a cousin?"

"Ida wanted you," he said calmly, lighting the cigar that he always carried in the street, "but I talked her out of it. I know how those things bore you."

What could she say? That boredom was better than loneliness? He never expected her to be lonely. So long as she was ready to make love on the two weekday evenings when he called, after office hours, entering the building through the back yard by crossing from another of his properties, she was perfectly free to do as she liked, even to go out with other men. Derrick was evidently not interested in the exclusive possession of what he briefly but regularly needed. His attitude hardly augured matrimonial intent.

When she really stopped to think of it, her only true pleasure in the affair lay in decorating the apartment, and even that was almost spoiled by Ida who insisted on helping her and on ransacking the family warehouse to furnish what the tabloids would have described (had she or they only known) as her husband's "lovenest." Geraldine consoled herself by reasoning that it was only a matter of time before Ida would have to face the facts and that it might help them both to behave in a civilized fashion at the crisis if they had kept up their intimacy to the last possible moment. And so together they picked out of storage old Denison pieces and Barbizon paintings and boxes of Waterford glass and went shopping for rugs and curtains and fought over colors and in particular over Geraldine's craze for mirrors, mirrors on screens, mirrors as table tops, smoked mirror panels in the bedroom, and for large, floppy dolls.

"But, darling, only tarts buy them," Ida protested.

Geraldine was always scrutinizing her cousin for the least sign of matrimonial discontent, but Ida struck her as almost smug in her matronly security. At last, Geraldine began to feel the approaches of panic. She wrote a letter to the lawyers who had handled her abortive case against Freddy's sisters, putting her situation as if it had happened to a friend and asking what legal redress, if any, existed. She had to wait for two weeks before she got their laconic reply, and then she blushed with shame and disappointment as she read between the lines of that cynical, pompous epistle how easily its author must have guessed the identity of her "friend."

"Don't you hate lawyers?" she asked Ida at lunch. "They dry-clean the romance out of life."

"Only if you send things to them."

"You mean you never would?"

"Not my life, anyway. They'll have to be satisfied with my death. That I leave them gladly. As a matter of fact, I'm taking care of it this afternoon."

"What on earth do you mean?"

"I'm going down to sign a new will."

"To disinherit somebody?"

"Not quite. Derrick and I are going abroad. He has a passion for making final arrangements before any trip. It makes for a rather gloomy start."

"Oh?" Geraldine's voice was low and flat. "I didn't know you were going abroad."

"Neither did I. Till yesterday. Wouldn't you like to come with us?"

Geraldine had fully intended to have it out with Derrick before there should be any intimacies that day, but there was something in his expression (no different, it was true, from other days) as he stood at the door when she opened it, coat on arm, hat in hand, that precluded discussion. He went straight to the bedroom after his usual brief, gruff salutation, and she found herself once more submitting to him with tears of resentment that the question of her readiness, or even her pleasure, should so little exist for him. Afterwards,

as he mixed the cocktails by the big gilt bar table that he had
bought on her birthday, he did not even notice the remnant
of her tears.

"I lunched with Ida today."

"Oh, did you?"

"She says you're planning to go to Europe. I was grateful
for the information."

"In the early fall," he confirmed casually. "As you know,
we've been worried about Dorcas. We thought it might be
a good idea to take her to France after the divorce. She's
awfully broken up, poor kid."

"I've heard all about it. Several times, thank you."

Derrick frowned at the implications of her tone. "She's
been through hell," he emphasized gravely as he crossed the
room to bring her her glass.

"Oh, hell, really! How you and Ida go on about it! Nothing has happened to Dorcas that she won't get used to. I
know I did. And what about *my* summer?"

"Why not come along with us? Ida'd love it."

"And carry on under her very nose?"

Derrick laughed easily. "I might give you the summer off."

The summer off! Her temples throbbed, and her mouth,
even after a quick sip of her drink, felt dry and rough.
"Derrick!" she exclaimed. "When are you going to tell Ida?"

"Tell her what?"

"That you want a divorce! Or shall I do it?"

His face was suddenly grim as he stared back. "I wouldn't
do that if I were you."

She rose from her seat in accordance with what she felt
should be the dignity of the impending scene. "I think it's
time you told me, Derrick, whether you have any intention of
going through with what I understood you to promise."

His grimness faded when he pursed his lips and put his
hands behind his back, as if she had simply asked him a tricky

question. "You must remember that Ida and I have been married a quarter of a century. One doesn't snap such old ties lightly."

"Lightly!" she cried. "When did we ever suggest that it be done lightly? The question I'm putting is, will it be done at all?"

Again he hesitated, and then, suddenly, his hands reappeared from behind his back. She saw at once that the fists were clenched. "No!"

"Thank you! And now will you please tell me one more thing. Did you *ever* intend to ask Ida for a divorce?"

"Never!"

She stepped back under the double impact of his defiance, as if he had pushed her in the chest. Taking a deep breath, she just managed to keep up her high, deliberate tone. "Then you *admit* you seduced me under a false promise of marriage?"

Derrick turned to the bar table with a careless shrug. As far as he was concerned, the scene was evidently over. "Isn't it a bit idiotic at your age to talk about seduction?"

The last of her dignity vanished with her wild burst of temper. "No!" she almost shrieked. "I *was* seduced. It was your revenge for what happened before you and Ida were married. You've been plotting ever since to make a whore out of me. To make a whore out of your wife's own cousin!"

"The day you became a whore was the day you married Talbot Keating."

"I loved Talbot!"

"The hell you did! You wouldn't know how to love. You sold yourself to him, and you've been selling yourself ever since. The only difference between me and the other men is that I don't pretend."

Now that the worst had come, now that hopes which had barely been hopes were shattered, now that a word had been used which she had dreaded all her life, she was surprised at her own fortitude. The only thing that seemed to matter was not her future, but her past. She drew herself up as she determined, whatever her disadvantage, to put in his place this churlish creature whom Uncle Linn had so rashly introduced into the family.

"There's another difference between you and the 'other men,' as you are crude enough to describe them. The others were gentlemen."

He opened his mouth as if to make a scornful rejoinder, but then paused and shook his head. When he spoke, there was even a hint of affection in his tone. "I grant I'm no gentleman. I don't pretend to be one. But that can make life so much simpler. You'll see. You and I should get on much better after this little blow-up."

"You can't, surely, mean that after what you've called me tonight, you actually still expect . . . ?"

"Wait a second, wait a second," he interrupted brusquely, "who called you what? *You* were the one who introduced that five-letter word. I have no use for labels. I'm too busy with the facts. And suppose you pause a minute and look at them. Ida and her whole family are coddling you as an inconsolable widow. I'm paying your bills and investing your money. Do you realize I've doubled it already? And what's more, there are no strings attached. You can see anyone you like. You can marry, if you want. Your reputation is at least as good as it was before I came into the picture. If ever a girl had her cake and ate it, it's you. Think twice, Geraldine, before you throw *me* over. You'll never duplicate a berth like the one you've got."

"It's charming of you to point out your generosity," she retorted icily. "But what does it amount to when it's based on a lie?"

"What lie?"

"The lie that you would marry me!"

Derrick threw his hands in the air. "For pity's sake, don't be so childish! Is adultery that ends in divorce any holier than adultery that doesn't? And, anyway, you don't really want to marry me. All you want is security. Why not? I understand that. My point is precisely that you're getting it. If you'll just go on the way we've been going, I'll triple your capital in a year!"

"Is this another proposition?"

"There you go, with your labels again! I know plenty of women, just as well born as you, who wouldn't mind listening to such a proposition."

"Would Ida?"

"Ida's different. You know about Ida."

"Well, I'm Ida's cousin! That's something you've never understood about me. Or perhaps about her, either. We were brought up under a code, and there are some things we just don't do. Perhaps the distinction between what is and what is not allowed is sometimes subtle, but it's always there. I wouldn't expect you, an outsider, to understand." Rising, she walked, with proud steps, to the door. She picked up his grey hat and dark blue overcoat and reached them towards him. "Good day, Mr. Hartley!"

"For good?"

"For good."

His smile was nasty now. "You seem to forget whose house this is."

"That would not be possible," she retorted, "with you here to remind me. You've always been the little boy from the small town with your nose pressed to the window of the great world. And no matter how much money you make, you'll always be that pushing little boy."

"The pushing little boy you tried to marry!"

Angrily she threw his coat and hat to the floor at his feet. "You're as common as dirt!" she retorted. "And you always will be. Common in your manners and common in your lovemaking!"

Derrick stopped to gather his belongings. "You're a fool, Geraldine," he said with a rueful shake of his head. "It may be true there was some revenge in what I did to you. You hurt me badly, years ago. But you can't see that what I did hasn't hurt you. Just the way you can't see that a great deal of real desire may be mixed up with that revenge. I suppose the only unique thing about you is that you've made a fool of yourself twice with the same man."

She flung herself back on the sofa when he had gone and sobbed for a quarter of an hour. Then, bored by her solitude and the sound of her own grief, she rose and spent an equal time at her dressing table, repairing the damage. It was gratifying, at least, to feel that the still beautiful face that stared back at her was once more the face of a Denison, a Denison of whom all the others could be proud. Then as she rose and surveyed her apartment, her eyes clouded at the prospect of having to leave it, and she felt a clutch of the old terror at the idea that honor might obligate her to give back the money he had made. But a moment later she tossed her head. Why should she? Was the money not hers? Legally *and* morally? Had he not said so himself? Were there to be no limits on the reparations demanded of a poor widow? Would even Ida ask them of her? Fortunately, she could never discuss it with Ida. And going back to her living room she sat on the sofa, a floppy doll tucked under each arm, and consulted her address book. Whom could she call at this hour, of all Freddy's friends who had said: "Let me know, Geraldine, when you're feeling better and have an evening free"? Some of them had meant, with their wives; some, perhaps, had not. She was reaching for the telephone, but she decided that she would first see if the martinis left in Derrick's silver pitcher were too watery. She needed to celebrate the restoration of the family honor.

13

Ida: 1936

IT HAD NOT taken me long to find out about Derrick and Geraldine; the latter had been too anxious for my enlightenment. I suppose it would have destroyed half her satisfaction in the affair had she been unable to throw it in the face of the younger cousin who had had the temerity to get all the things in life that Geraldine, now that it was too late, thought she had always wanted. And so it was impossible for her, even supposing that it was subconscious, not to bracket Derrick's name with each expenditure of new money in such a way as to drive my poor self-respecting little doubts out into the snowstorm of truth. She showed some of the cockiness that she had shown in the winter when she had first taken Derrick away from me, a cockiness that gleamed steadily, then as now, from behind the shabby old careless bead curtain of her perfunctory shame. I, too, was ashamed, but of minding her malevolence more than I minded Derrick's infidelity.

The muddy waters of my emotions were at their muddiest when the affair was broken off, for I found the end more distressing than the beginning. I had suspected from the increased acerbity of Geraldine's references to Derrick that a breach might have occurred, but I was not sure until the day when she poutingly told me that she had no summer plans.

"How about coming to Europe?" I asked her.

"You mean with you and Derrick?"

"Well, it wouldn't have to be with us. We could all meet in Paris."

"Do you think that would be wise?" Geraldine allowed a dreamy look to cloud her eyes as she stared over the tables in the Park Club dining room. "Paris, the city of love?"

"You mean, it would remind you too much of Freddy?"

Her cloudy gaze was faintly pierced by irritation. "The three of us in Paris? Surely, Ida, you've heard about two being company?"

This, I felt, was a cruder reference to the affair than my dignity, or what was left of it, could permit. "I'm sure I don't have to worry about that kind of thing with *you.*"

"Every woman has to worry about every other woman," Geraldine murmured, in the irritating drone that she used for her worldly-wise clichés. "You must never forget what happened the winter that Derrick and I first met."

"But that's ancient history, Geraldine!"

"The embers might be lying around still." She surprised me by placing her long white hand on mine. "Best not risk it, dear. Because if there's one thing I'm clear about in my mind and heart, it's that I could never hurt you. Never, never!"

I knew the note in Geraldine's voice when she was trying to be sincere. And if she had convinced herself that she could never hurt me, it could only mean that the affair was off, and if it was off, was I to be in the position, once again in my life, of owing Derrick to her? I didn't like it. I didn't like it at all. My ancient feeling of guilt at having come between the archetypes of male and female, at having prevented what had then seemed to me so innately fitting a union, returned in force, and I had to evoke in my fancy the loudest bray of the Denison laughter to avoid the pitfall of trying to induce my husband's mistress to return to him. I saw now in this unexpected twist of my perverse disposition the traps of Trask sentimentality and that it was possible, by dwelling too morbidly on imagined guilt, to play the pander in one's own home. There had been more, evidently, than just a sense of appearances behind the philosophy of my mother's family. There had been a deeper sense of human dignity than I appeared instinctively to possess.

I had pulled myself together, however, by the time we sailed on the *Paris* and was able to accept with a degree of equanimity the new attentions of a Derrick who seemed determined to make up for anything that I might have suspected. He walked on deck with me in the mornings instead of reading his financial reports, and at table he was full of breezy suggestions about wines and special dishes. It was as well that one of us should make a noise, for Dorcas, from the moment of our sailing, had sunk into an unexplained depression and now would hardly speak to us, sitting all day in her deck chair, staring at the sea and quitting our table abruptly after a few spoonfuls of one course. For once in her life, she was particularly resentful of her father, whom she seemed now to blame for all the misery of her divorce, and he made things no better by his jovial espousal of the suit of Mark Jesmond, who had left the law to become his right-hand man at Hartley and Dodge and who was now the rather grudgingly accepted beau of the boss's daughter. Dorcas criticized Mark incessantly, before and behind his back, but she still went out with him. I could not decide whether her current moodiness arose from regrets over Robin or indecision over Mark, and I thought it wisest, unlike her father, not to prod her. One morning, however, she brought the subject up herself.

"I'm so worried about Robin," she said, her eyes fixed on a lively sea. "I can't seem to picture how he'll get on alone. He's so helpless, really. How do I know he won't drink himself to death? Or worse?"

"People like Robin have more resilience than you think. Just when you've given them up, they come bouncing back."

"You mean Robin will come bouncing back?"

"Well, not to you," I assured her. "But I wouldn't worry about his killing himself. When I last saw him he was cheerfully planning to be married to that Miss Stiles."

"When *you* last saw him?"

"Yes. I went to see him in his hotel. I had some of your misgivings about what he might do. Fortunately, he made me feel like a fool. He was totally merry and gay. And the next day I sent him a check for a thousand dollars as a wedding present."

"*Mother!*"

"Well, why not? I always liked Robin, and of course he was utterly broke."

"Did you tell Father?"

"No, and don't you, either. I did it with my own money."

"Did you think Robin had *any* chance of being happy with that woman?"

"No. I doubt if Robin could be happy with anyone. But I wanted to see him off to a good start."

"Because I treated him so badly?"

"No, dear. Because I liked him."

I left her to brood, her relief at learning that Robin was not suicidal understandably soured by the insulting speed of his recovery, and her mind now free to concentrate on the more interesting question of Mark. However little I welcomed the idea of a rapid second marriage for Dorcas, it was beginning to be evident even to me that she was a woman who would find it difficult to exist for long without a husband. She was more sullen than usual that night with her father, and early the next morning, when we were entering the Solent, I suggested that he disembark in Southampton and do his business in London while we went on to Paris.

"There's no point trying to shake her out of this mood,"

I warned him. "She'll come around in time. For the moment she has to have a scapegoat, and it might just as well be you. Lord knows, I've had *my* share of it!"

The hotel into which Dorcas and I moved the next day was near the Vendôme where I had stayed more than thirty years before with Grandma, and there was nothing about our situation to make Paris seem less hard and grey than it had seemed to me then. Yet this time, despite everything, I loved it. I had traveled very little in my married life because Derrick, who had to travel continually for business, preferred to spend his vacations at home. I had lived a New York woman's existence of charitable committees, lunching daily at the Park Club with friends whom I had known since school. We met in groups to discuss books and philosophy and current events; we lunched on Thursdays in French and on odd Mondays to learn Italian. It was a life that has been lampooned in a million cartoons, but it had been comfortably full, pleasantly monotonous, and my consolation was that I wondered if the cartoonists in the jungle of their own lives had had so many glimpses of that rare bird, content. But to be in Paris, with an open car and driver, with no friends or duties, and with long days in which to see the history of France expressed in its monuments, was at least to know that the bird had once been there. I remembered old Mr. Robbins and his cult of Richelieu and reflected wistfully how close the years had brought us.

Dorcas was at first my somber companion on daily excursions to Versailles, to Fontainebleau, to Chartres, but in a week's time she protested that she had had enough and wanted to look up some friends from the Brandon Press who had established a short story magazine in Paris. After that I saw her only at breakfast and sometimes at dinner. Fortunately, Hugo turned up at our hotel on his way to join college friends for a bicycle tour of Germany. He was appalled at my solitary schedule and took me out to dinner at Maxim's to protest.

"Two women can't live in Paris together. It's a crime! I don't care how down Dorcas feels. Send her over to London to mope with Daddy, and let's you and me take a trip together. I can join my pals later. Hell, I see them all winter in New Haven."

"Darling, I'd be your ball and chain."

"Not so. I'd like to see you on your own for once. I'd like to see you *live*."

"What would I have to do to live?"

"Well, you wouldn't have to make eyes at a gondolier. Or go to the Beaux-Arts Ball in a fig leaf!"

"Hugo!"

"Isn't that what you think people mean by living? All you old girls at the Park Club? I just want you to go on a motor trip. With me. No big car. No chauffeur. No plans. We'd stay at each place as long as we damn pleased and no longer."

"Your father's spoiled me for that," I said, shaking my head. "I'd be lost without a timetable."

"Oh, Ma," he said disgustedly, "you never have any fun, and it's getting later all the time."

Hugo, unlike his father and sister, had never taken me for granted. I was always a person to him as well as just "Mother," pronounced in a tone of understandable protest. Hugo deplored me, criticized me, shouted at me and even at times hurt my feelings, but there was always juice in our relationship. It was not unlike the relationship that I had had with Christopher, except that Christopher had been gentler than Hugo and had cared about me less. Hugo cared about very few people, but I think I had a fixed if narrow bench in the hallway of his suspicious heart. As for my own heart, well, it was absurdly full of Hugo. I was always watching myself to be sure that I would not embarrass or oppress him with the abundance of my feeling. I was even terrified that he would persuade me to let him ruin his summer, and I was actually relieved when he was safely on his way to Germany.

I had reason to question the true identity of Dorcas' publishing friends on the day when I came back to the hotel at lunch time, having expected to be gone until evening, and found Mark Jesmond sprawled on a sofa in the lobby. Even abroad he wore the brown coat and grey flannels which, with his rumpled hair and shrewd, grinning boyish face, wizened a bit as such faces become after the age of thirty, seemed to have as little reference to France as the morning mail at Morgan's.

"What a pleasant surprise, Mr. Jesmond," I greeted him. "Have you come over on business for Derrick?"

"Well, that's the usual excuse, isn't it?"

"I hope you don't let him hear you say that."

"Oh, I think I can count on Derrick to forgive my real motive."

He looked at me in rather roguish manner as he threw off his employer's Christian name, and I inferred that he wanted me to go on.

"What is your real motive?"

"To marry your daughter!" he boomed at me suddenly, with a brazen grin.

I studied that grin carefully and noted how little humor there was in it. "That *is* a surprise," I said calmly. "Whether pleasant or unpleasant remains to be seen. You implied that my husband knows?"

"Oh, yes, I have *his* blessing."

"And Dorcas'?"

"Well, she wasn't exactly averse to the idea in New York," he said with another grin. "But I don't know about Paris. What's been going on over here?"

"Mr. Jesmond," I said sternly, to reprove his note of accusation, "may I ask if you're interested in *my* blessing?"

"Very much so. As many as I can get!"

"Then will you tell me why you think you can make my daughter happy?"

"Here and now?"

"Where better?"

"Because I'm not a weakling, like Granberry. Because I know where I'm going and where I want to take her!

"You don't make it sound like a very attractive courtship," I observed. "At least not to my old-fashioned ears. But that's your and Dorcas' affair, not mine. I'm only interested that you're ashamed to tell me that you love her."

He flushed a mottled red and looked down at shoes which needed shining. "You're right, Mrs. Hartley. I'm an egregious ass. Of course I love her. I love her with everything I've got."

When he looked up and smiled, without grinning this time, it was a great improvement. "Thank you, Mr. Jesmond. I think we may get on. Yet."

At this point Dorcas walked out of the elevator and stopped abruptly as she saw us. Her mouth dropped open and then slowly closed, and the stare which she shifted from me to Mark changed from surprise to hostility.

"Well?"

"Your mother and I have been having a little chat," Mark explained. "I've been trying to win her over to our point of view."

"*Our?* I'm sure I don't know what you mean." She turned to place an unexpectedly protecting hand on my elbow. "Shall we go in to lunch, Mummy?"

"Wouldn't Mr. Jesmond like to join us?"

"No doubt. But I don't feel like joining Mr. Jesmond."

Mark simply grinned again. "I'm sure it's not your fault she's such a spoiled brat, Mrs. Hartley. She must have learned her bad manners with that long-haired literary crowd." He winked at Dorcas. "Goodbye, honey. I'll see you at drink time. Only try to be in a better mood, will you?"

Dorcas and I both stared after that jauntily departing figure, and when our eyes met, we looked away with the same impulse of embarrassment. It was as if her silence had been a consent to some intimate, almost unseemly gesture, which she would have liked to have hidden, but no longer quite dared to repudiate. Our constraint continued in the quiet hotel dining room.

"What I fail to understand is why you didn't tell me he was here," I said at last. "Have I ever in the least objected to your seeing him?"

"I didn't want you to be bothered."

"Bothered? But, my child, what do you think I came to Paris for, except you?"

"I know, Mummy, you've been a darling, but I can't talk to you about Mark."

"Can you to Daddy?"

"No." Her sullen shipboard look returned at the mention of her father. "Daddy's too much like him. Marrying Mark would be like marrying Daddy."

"Would that be so terrible?"

"Oh, Mummy, please!" Her voice rose with an edge of pain. "I don't want to hurt you. That's why it's all so difficult. Ever since my divorce I've seen Daddy with different eyes. I've seen what he's done to *you*. I don't want that. Would you want it for me?"

Dorcas' adoration of her father, however irritating, was far less painful than her disillusionment with him. It is never agreeable to seem pathetic to one's own child. "Have you considered that you might do better with a man like Daddy than I did?"

"You mean because I'd fight him?"

"No. Because you might believe in him."

She reacted to this with unexpected humility. "You think I'm so stupid?"

"Belief isn't a matter of intellect. There's nothing clever about *not* believing in a man like Mark."

She shook her head and sighed broodingly. "Perhaps. If that were all. But there's something else."

"About Mark?"

"About me. You'd never understand."

When I said nothing, but simply waited, Dorcas gazed about the high dark-paneled dining room and the silently chewing, elderly couples. "Well, we're in Paris, aren't we?" she said with a bitter laugh. "Maybe it's the place for such explanations. The thing, if you *must* know, is that my feeling for Mark isn't the kind to build a marriage on. It's too physical."

"Do you think mine for your father wasn't?"

She appeared to consider this apparently novel idea before rejecting it as irrelevant. "But Daddy was big and strong and handsome, and Mark is — well, to begin with he's smaller than I am. And he's funny-looking."

I began at last to sense how truly miserable she was. Dorcas had inherited all of my grandmother's capacity for sterile suffering. She had her father's literalness as well, but none of his toughness. When she turned her gaze impatiently to the window opening on the small graveled courtyard, I realized that I could not evade with any honesty the elementary fact that this perverse, proud, somber, stubborn creature was my daughter and was appealing to me. Appealing to me for the first time in her life. "Mark must be almost as near my age as he is yours," I suggested. "Which is why I can understand his attraction for you. He's very much a man, and that's not a quality one measures in biceps or toothy smiles."

"You mean *you* feel it?"

"Certainly I feel it."

There was jealousy as well as incredulity in her stare. "You mean you're *attracted* to Mark?"

"Well, I don't know if we need go as far as that. But I can understand *your* being attracted. He's a very attractive man."

Reassured but still gloomy, she debated the consequences of this. "He says he wants his answer this week."

"Why so soon?"

"He says if I won't marry him in Paris, I won't marry him anywhere."

"That's absurd."

"But if he means it, Mummy!" I was shocked by the way in which her eyes suddenly flooded with fear. "If he means it, and I lose him!"

"Darling, he can't mean it!" I shivered at the inward twist of my compassion with my exasperation. "Why are you so sure that you're not simply in love with Mark in the most ordinary, old-fashioned way?"

"I'm *not* sure," she exclaimed in what was almost a wail. "Was I in love with Robin? I thought so at the time, and look what a mess I made!"

"This strikes me as a much stronger thing."

"But how does one tell?"

I concentrated carefully on placing a tiny piece of butter on my Melba toast. "By going away with him."

Dorcas stared at me now with something like awe. "Going away with him?"

"For a few days. Nobody need know. Go to some little beach in Spain."

"*Mother!*"

"Well, I thought your generation was supposed to be so liberated."

"But not *yours!*"

"Must I remind you of the night you spent in Robin Granberry's apartment and flung in my face?"

"But we didn't *do* anything!"

At another time I could have laughed at her shocked expression. "Well, it's a pity you didn't. The only way you're ever going to make up your mind about Mark, whether you marry him or not, is by living with him. And if that shocks you, all I can say is that you're very easily shocked!"

"It shocks me coming from you," she insisted. "I can't imagine you doing such a thing with Daddy. Would you have?"

"Those were different days."

"Would you today?"

"In your position, I might."

"But, Mummy, I had no *idea* you were so immoral!"

"We live and learn."

An instinct told me that the only course was a fixed one, that apology or sustained defense might be equally fatal. I had taken from Dorcas her childhood image of me, and it was important that I should not hide it or even hold it too tightly, but that I should simply leave it quietly beside us on the table until she saw that it was only a doll with a painted smile and a body stuffed with straw. I finished my meal in silence as she brooded, feeling very Gallic and unlike myself. I remembered what Paris had done to Grandma. What in the name of all the household gods of Fifty-third Street was it doing to me?

Dorcas did not accompany me that afternoon to Compiegne, and when I returned I found her writing at a desk in the lobby, a small suitcase standing by her feet. She jumped up when she saw me and put an arm about my shoulders and held her cheek against mine.

"I was trying to slip out before you got back, you wicked old thing," she murmured. "I was writing you a note. Try to keep Daddy from running all over France with a shotgun, will you?"

Which turned out to be not so easy to do. Derrick came over from London two days later and was furious when I told him what had happened. He strode up and down the little sitting room, seeming absurdly loud and Yankee against the grey panels, denouncing Dorcas as a loose woman and myself as an unprincipled sentimentalist. Only when he said he would fire Mark did I intervene.

"I wonder why you think you're in a position to lecture me as if you were Cotton Mather. I would have thought that recent events might have disqualified you."

The most attractive thing about Derrick was his instant ability to face a loss of advantage. He ceased his pacing and actually smiled. "Did Geraldine tell you?"

"That is something that you and I are never going to discuss," I retorted firmly as I rose to answer the buzz of the hall door. "Silence is our only possible salvation." The page in the hallway handed me a telegram. It was postmarked from Santander in Spain and read: "Mark and I married today. Returning Paris Monday. Can we dine gala? Beg Daddy forgive moodiness boat. Madly happy and love to all. Dorcas."

I handed it silently to Derrick and watched his face light up. "By God, Ida, I hand it to you. You've really done it this time!"

"But what? Isn't that the question?"

"You've given her a second life, that's all! After she made hash of her first one."

"I wonder." I took the telegram and ruefully studied its text. "I wish it had taken her a little more than forty-eight hours to rush to the sanctity of law. I'm afraid she's aghast already at her own daring in going off with him. The next step will be for her to forget that she ever did." Seeing Derrick's impatient frown, I shrugged. "As her father has forgotten already."

When Dorcas and Mark, exuberant, and Derrick, glowing, were ready to sail for home, I surprised them all by saying that I was planning to spend a few weeks with my cousin, Elly Denison, Uncle Will's daughter, who had married an Irishman. They protested, but not too much, and in less than a week's time I found myself settled in an old grey shabby Georgian house in Galway where time seemed the only luxury. Elly was big and cheerful, like the other Denisons, and her tweeds and red cheeks and blown grey hair went well with the Anglo-Irish hunting set of which she and her husband and six children were devoted members, but her particular asset to me at this juncture of my life was her impersonality. She would stride into my bedroom early in riding clothes, ask if I had everything I needed, and then I wouldn't see her again until dinner.

It was perfect. I would take her dogs out to stroll for hours on the windy moors until the early fall mists drove me in to the fire in the big library. I allowed the bleak, treeless, dune-green, hilly coast of County Galway to enter into my being until it seemed to me, when I strolled along the bluffs and listened to the roar of the Atlantic, that I had traveled as far as it was possible for a human to travel, at least from the brown gridiron city of my childhood, and was perched now upon the very border of the known world. I wanted to think that I was merging with the countryside like an old woman in black, sitting outside a white thatched cottage and chewing a pipe, but I could never quite fool myself. All that was really happening to me was the self-indulgence of detachment. Detachment from my little curriculum of self-appointed tasks. In the evenings now, when Elly and I chatted about the past, Fifty-third Street seemed as unreal and as quaintly entertaining as a novel by Jane Austen. Only when she made a bitter reference to Geraldine, whom she had always detested, was it again the street of my education, seen now with more perceptive eyes.

"She behaved like a bitch to you over Derrick — you can't deny that."

I shuddered to think what Elly, who was referring to the events of 1912, would have thought of the events of the preceding spring. She would never have understood that, according to my old, misleading lights, Derrick and Geraldine, by their affair, had given me back the freedom of which they had robbed me, years before, when she had rejected him. They had relieved me of the burden of obligation which I had so long and so uneasily carried, with the result that I had not been truly conscious of the wrong which their affair had done me until they had given it up. It was Derrick's attitude of fumbling apology on board the *Paris* that had made me see him for the first time as less than cold and self-absorbed, as less than a man who put a large career ahead of nation and family, but as actually shabby, as a mere small lying creature whimpering for his wife's forgiveness for a sin that he had been frustrated from committing. And Dorcas, by having been his pupil, had suffered in similar, if not in equal fashion, according to my now sterner estimates. I could stay with them and help them and be, indeed for the first time, an active agent in their lives, but in doing so I was descending from an elevation whose pinnacle, looming above me in the dissolving mist of my preconceptions, had an outline perilously similar to the lofty peak which I now identified with contempt. It might have been this very peak that I was fleeing on the moors of Galway. If I dared not look over my shoulder it was probably that I feared the fate of Lot's wife.

How long I might have stayed in Ireland without Hugo's

cable I do not know. "Are you never coming home? Please remit explanation attraction Galway, Connemara. Park Club and I concerned your protracted stay."

I sailed from Cobh, and a week later I was seated on a trunk on a cold pier, listening to Hugo while we waited for customs. Derrick was in Chicago with the Jesmonds for a convention of investment bankers, and Hugo had journeyed down from New Haven to meet me.

"Cousin Geraldine was coming, too, but when I called to pick her up, she was in no shape to make it."

"Oh, darling, has she been drinking again?"

"Unless it was an excuse not to come. In which case I must admit it was a pretty good act."

"It seems so drab to come back to all that," I said with a sigh. "You'd have loved Ireland."

"Nobody drinks there, I suppose."

I asked him about Dorcas.

"Oh, she's blooming!" he exclaimed with a cheerful, if malicious laugh. "It's Mark this and Mark that, and have you *heard* what Mark's doing, and, Daddy, *when* are you going to make Mark a partner?"

"But doesn't Daddy want to make Mark a partner?"

"Oh, sure, but in his own good time. Women like Dorcas are terrors. When they finally get hold of a man who can satisfy them, they'll cut up the rest of us into patches to darn his socks!"

"You're crude."

"But accurate. What did you think you were up to in Paris? Forging a weapon against Daddy out of his own protégé?"

"You're being perfectly absurd," I protested. "Your father was all for that marriage from the beginning."

"Because he didn't *know*."

"Know what?"

"What it would do to Dorcas!" Hugo exclaimed gleefully. "But *you* did. I've always suspected that was a bit of a fiend behind that docile matronly brow. What are your plans for me? Had I better start running now?"

"Oh. darling, all I want is for you to be happy," I murmured, looking disconsolately down the long line of trunks that seemed to shiver in the cold grey of the wharf. It had been cold in Galway, but that had not been the grimey fall coldness that hangs about man-made things in a Manhattan out-of-doors.

"Well, keep your fine Italian hand off Hugo," he warned me. "Hugo's doing fine!"

And so perhaps he was. But why then had I come home? The brief flurry of activity that had followed the end of Geraldine's and Derrick's affair was now ended, and I faced, with a rueful sense of anticlimax, the resumption of my old life. Dorcas had returned, on a more solid basis, I hoped, to the preoccupations of matrimony, and Derrick had returned, after what I guessed to be a final diversion, to the joys of money-making. Hugo had his own bright eyes and his own bright future, and nobody needed me. Nobody, apparently, but Geraldine, and Geraldine I had little enough wish to help.

Yet I helped her, or at least I went through the motions. Geraldine, I often speculated in the years that followed, seemed to have been born to prove to my only too credulous soul how little we can do for other human beings. I sat with her; I laughed with her; I reminisced with her; I agreed with her. I did everything but drink with her, and that, in the last analysis, was the only thing she really wanted of me. Geraldine hated me, and for the next fourteen years I presented a bland, fatuous, smiling target for her hate.

As she grew worse, she took less and less pains to conceal her antagonism, and yet she clung to me, for she had alienated all the rest of the family. She could never descant enough on the injustice of life that had brought me so much and her so little. She remained to the end the little girl who has come down with a bright face and bright flowing hair to find in her Christmas stocking a switch and a book of sermons while mine was crammed with packages that I dared not open. To me she presented the constant illusion of an opportunity to make up at least to one Denison what I had failed to give the others, and the reminder, equally constant, that it *was* an illusion. It accorded with my sense of justice that I should have to wait until her death for the cloudy release of being a survivor.

PART VI

Hugo in Love

14

Hugo: 1950

H ugo's apartment, on the top floor of his parents' house, was a storehouse of the treasures which a shrewd eye in the auction business had enabled him to pick up. Indeed, the only thing in common between the Japanese screen, the Italian primitive triptych, the Greek head and the giant Dresden porcelain boar was that they had been purchased by a man whose love of bargains encompassed no corresponding need of harmony. Hugo let his acquisitions speak for themselves, furnishing his rooms with the odds and ends for which his parents had no further use below. What the odds and ends looked like hardly mattered, for he never entertained there. When he had to make a bachelor's token return for the quantities of hospitality that were lavished upon him, he did so at the Knickerbocker Club or at the Pavillon, and was always careful to include at least one customer of the Denison-Adler Gallery to ensure the tax deductibility of his check. As he lived at home and entertained on the nation, his salary was available for art and for clothes.

He could have gone back, after V–J Day, to Hartley and Dodge, where he had made a brief start in 1940, accepting his father's offer of employment with the careless shrug of one who knew that war was coming. But after four years of destroyer duty in the Pacific, years that had given him, for the first time in his life, though he would never admit it, the sense of a job well done, he found the New York scene, and particularly his father, so absurdly unaltered, so ludicrously unaffected by those thousands of drowned bodies in the Pacific, as to repel him. He was already thirty in 1945 and knew what he wanted, or thought he did: elegance and order and small talk and women and *no* commitments. He wanted to do little things well, but he wanted everyone to know that he could have done the big things well, too. Indeed, he wanted the people who did the big things to recognize that his own choice was a pointed reflection on theirs. Hugo had become even pricklier with the years. He was always suspecting the men at his dinner parties of sneering, as he was sure his father did, at his job in an auction gallery. What difference, he would snarl to himself, did it make to *them* that Denison-Adler, after a long period of eclipse, was regaining its old position among the galleries of the city? Did it not deal in paintings and bric-à-brac and old furniture, women's matters? Was that a field for men, like oil and steel and zinc and celluloid?

It was his habit in the morning, before going to work, to stop for a minute, two floors below, and chat with his mother. Ida was at her best at that hour, before the anxieties of the day had settled upon her. Sitting in bed in her wrapper, sipping coffee, her lap full of letters and newspaper, she was least feminine in a setting where another woman might have been most. But it was before she had put on her clothes and her powder and neuroses that Ida's intelligence and curiosity, both qualities essentially neuter, were allowed to function at will. With the long brown cheeks and haggard eye of the early waker, she looked almost gaunt in her inappropriate pink.

"How was your dinner party?" Her question was safe. He had always been to one.

"They talked the wrong way," Hugo reported briefly. "I ate most of my meal in silence between two female backs."

"You seem to have a bit of trouble with that. Maybe you scare your dinner partners off."

"I *think* I know how to talk."

"That's just it. You talk too well. Ladies at dinner parties distrust men who talk too well."

"You suggest, then, that I become a bore?"

"Or stop going out so much."

Decidedly, he reflected, she had become tarter since Cousin Geraldine's death. In the perpetual tug-of-war of their relationship, it bored him when she agreed with him and irked him when she did not. "What do you expect a lonely bachelor to do with his evenings?"

"You might take a course." She went so far as to hand him, from the pile of her mail, a list of lectures at the Metropolitan Museum. "Was Mrs. Tyson at your party?"

His hand was raised to throw the pamphlet back on her bed, but surprise made him pause and scan it. "Why do you ask?"

"She's been mentioned as a trustee for Miss Irvin's School. I was wondering what you thought of her."

"What *I* thought? Isn't Grinnell Tyson one of Daddy's partners?"

"Yes, but there are so many of them now. I barely know her. I thought she was a friend of yours."

Hugo pondered the question of Miss Irvin's School. He knew that he would never make headway against his mother's loyalty to women's groups. It was on such, after all, that the basic defense of her life had been erected. But how in her wildest dreams could she imagine Kitty that type? "Isn't all that school board business just compensation for frustrated women?"

Ida did not even do his attack the honor of looking up from her newspaper. "How like you to assume that if a woman accomplishes anything, she's only filling a void left by a man."

"Well, *isn't* she?"

"Naturally." She turned a page and shrugged. "If she

were happy, she'd stay at home and do her fingernails. Isn't that your picture of us?"

"It's my picture of Kitty Tyson."

"Really? But I gathered from your father that she was rather pathetic. That Grinnell was something less than a faithful husband."

"Maybe she's something less than a faithful wife." He watched her out of the corner of his eye as he said this, but she was inscrutable.

"Then, of course, she won't do for our board. I'm sorry. I hadn't heard she was that kind of woman."

"Oh, Ma! Do you still believe in different kinds of women?"

"I believe in decent ones."

"Decent or inhibited?"

"What does it matter what I call them? You know perfectly well what I mean."

Hugo had learned from a psychiatrist whom he had consulted after the war that it was a common delusion of the libertine to regard every woman as loose except his own mother. But what about the mother's delusions? Was it not rather bewildering for the libertine if she had for her own sex her son's delusion about *her?*

"I'd better be getting to the office," he muttered.

"Are you doing anything Friday night?"

He hesitated. She was always trying to tie him up for her dinner parties which she always weighted down with relatives. "It so happens that these very Tysons want me for the Nurses' Aid Ball."

Ida's face continued elaborately expressionless. "You're committed, then?"

"Not if I don't choose."

"Minerva Denison's taken a table and wants you desperately. It's an older group, but Alfreda will be there. She's really a most attractive girl."

"Oh, the girls *you* find attractive!" he moaned. Yet he considered it. Minerva Denison was old and ugly, but she was also rich and gay. She and her young daughter followed the world of fashion from Palm Beach to Bar Harbor and lived in large hotels. The childish fallacy that such people were glamorous, though long recognized for a fallacy, still stuck in the top of his mind.

"I'd really appreciate it if you would," his mother pursued. "Minerva's always asking me to do things, and I can never get your father to go."

"I object to being used to pay off your social obligations, but I suppose I might have a whack at it. How old is the girl?"

"Twenty-one. And really such a darling."

"A bit young for me, isn't she?"

"Just the right age. And only a second cousin."

"Poor Ma!" he exclaimed as he got up, "what a pity we're not French. You and Cousin Minerva would have worked it all out in advance. The dowry and the date of the wedding and even where Alfreda and I would go on our honeymoon." He paused as the idea struck him. "Or *have* you?"

"You're perfectly ridiculous," she retorted in a tone of such complacency that he began, quite seriously, to wonder what she *had* done.

The Denison-Adler Gallery was housed in the same building that had housed it since 1892, when Hugo's great-uncle, Philip Denison, and Herman Adler, a Swiss art dealer, had founded it with a loan from Linnaeus Tremain. It was a large, grim, brown cube, with a few small half-circle windows, vaguely inspired by the Palazzo Strozzi in Florence, and it stood just off Lexington Avenue on Fifty-seventh Street. A modern structure was needed, and a site farther uptown, if the present prosperity of the business was to continue, but control had long passed to a handful of penurious

Swiss stockholders, and the Denison shares, sentimentally retained by members of the family in memory of Uncle Philip, was not sufficient or sufficiently organized to permit Hugo to force his will upon the firm. The Adlers regarded him with mute admiration and mute fear. Since he had come to the gallery five years before, he had worked successfully in every department, preparing accounts and catalogues and even swinging the gavel on auction days, but more recently it had been inevitable for the management to use him, with his connections and his aggressive good manners, in the front office to deal with a clientele which included so many of his friends. How long, the Adlers wondered, could they hold him and still hold control?

Hugo enjoyed their concern. He had no ambition to run the business; he had picked it because he had a start there, because it irritated his father to see him an auctioneer, because the hours were regular and because he enjoyed seeing and handling beautiful things. He despised the slow, cautious, fat Herman Adler III and loved to make scenes in his office, demanding new policies and higher pay, and allowing himself, after much bluster, to be bought off by a small concession or a bonus or even by the opportunity to pick up a bargain from an estate before the auction inventory was completed. But his greatest pleasure in the business was in the display rooms with their changing shows, and no morning passed that he did not stroll through them, catalogue in hand, to check the descriptions and arrangement.

Only an hour after his talk with Ida, as he was making his first round, he caught sight of the graceful, diminutive figure of Kitty Tyson bending over a glass case in the book and manuscript room. She was hatless, and her hands were plunged in the pockets of her black, flare-skirted coat. It always amused him that a woman who dressed with such art could seem as careless as a college girl, unless, of course, that was precisely the goal of her art. Kitty with her small black ring curls and her large beseeching blue eyes, her little upturned nose and her air of wistfulness, was always in danger of seeming as cute as her name. Yet she could dispel the impression, just as it was hardening to a judgment, with a quick, cagey glance that opened vistas into her understanding of people's misunderstanding of her. Kitty cajoled a world to make it forgive her for being more than she appeared.

"I never think that beautiful ladies and old books go together," he said as he moved up behind her. "Like Dorothea in *Middlemarch.* Or don't you know *Middlemarch?*"

It was their game, on meeting, to start each conversation as strangers.

"I was supposed to read it at school, but I don't think I ever did," she replied, without turning around. "Anyway, I don't want a book. I want a picture. A beautiful, beautiful picture."

"You mean you want to *bid* on a picture. This isn't a shop, you know."

She turned now and nodded submissively. "I mean I'd like to bid on a picture."

"What kind of a beautful, beautiful picture?"

"How do I know till I see it?"

"Well, come find it, then. You're in luck. We've just hung the Whitlock pictures. Collector's 'musts.' Monet, Piscasso, Vuillard, Walter Kuhn, Braque, Rouault, Matisse and Dufy. The very pick of the fashion!"

He led her into the main gallery where a dozen persons were studying the Whitlock collection and took her up to a tiny smudge of canvas in a large gilded frame, a blurry rose by Renoir. "Just the thing for the little table by your favorite armchair. A shaving from the floor of the master's studio. A scraping from the palette of genius."

Kitty moved closer to squint at it. "One forgets how badly

they could paint when they wanted to." He followed her as she toured the room, pausing longest before the Vuillard.

"Well, of course, that's a beauty, but the rest . . ." She shrugged. "Tell me, was it a banker's collection?"

"How did you know?"

"Because there's one of everything. What Grinnell would call a diversified portfolio. But he must have been stingy. He got all the bad ones, didn't he? Poor man," she mused, looking about in final review. "I wonder if he had any fun with it. Or did he do it all with an agent? What would he have bought fifty years ago?"

"Fake Rembrandts and bad Lawrences."

"And fifty years before that?"

"Oh, then, he might have had fun. With Landseer dogs and stags and Alma Tademas and seraglio scenes. Before taste was king. As a matter of fact, we have a rather fine Landseer that just came in. Would you like to see it?"

"Tomorrow. I only dropped in to see if you'd made up your mind about Friday night."

"Oh, yes, I'm sorry. I promised Ma I'd go to Minerva Denison's."

There was a pause as she fitted the name into the puzzle of his family. "That's Mrs. Scott Denison, isn't it? A widow? A cousin?"

"Not close. But you know how Mother is about family."

"Ah, yes. And there's a daughter, too. Surely, there's a daughter?"

"There is, apparently, a daughter."

"Apparently." Her tone gently mocked him as she moved back along the wall and paused, with the faintest air of conjecture, before an angry factory by Leger. "And you had told me that you might have to go to Chicago."

"Well, it seems I don't."

"Then Mrs. Denison's invitation came *after* mine?"

"Oh, come now, Kitty, don't go on about it. It was a very little thing for Mother to ask."

"To give up my dinner? Thank you."

Hugo stared in surprise. The essence of Kitty, the very *point* of Kitty, was precisely that she never acted this way. "What's come over you?"

"Does it never occur to you that there may be limits to my enjoyment of being taken for granted?"

"But why suddenly make an issue of old Minerva?"

"Your mother's made it, not I." She turned around with a new look of stubbornness in those usually docile blue eyes. "It was *she* who made you give up my dinner. And with malice aforethought!"

"Kitty, you're being ridiculous!"

"I'm not!" she insisted with a sudden, tight little passion. "I *know* about mothers. I'm sorry, Hugo, but I don't like them. I didn't even like my own. Your mother wants you to marry that Denison girl. She's plotted it all out, and she'll succeed, too!"

There was nothing to do with so unprecedented an outburst but to treat it lightly. "It can hardly be malice," he said with a shrug. "Only this morning Ma was talking about you for her school board."

"Exactly! That will be my consolation prize. Oh, she's deep, I tell you." Suddenly she was pleading with him, her hand lightly on his arm. "Please give up Mrs. Denison's dinner for me, Hugo. Will you?"

"But it's all so absurd!"

"I've never asked you to give up anything before!"

"Well, of course, if you insist," he said angrily. "But I think it's most unreasonable of you. And selfish!"

"Thank you, darling," she interrupted in a quick whisper. "I *do* insist. Thanks a million. And now I'll go and let you work."

Before he could stop her, she had crossed the gallery and was out the door without even turning to nod goodbye. He cursed to himself at the thought that his mother would have already telephoned his acceptance to Minerva Denison. Women!

Their affair was nearing the end of its first year, and his ardor was considerably dimmed. Yet he was fair enough to admit that it might have been dimmed by her having been so exactly what he had thought he wanted. He had visualized a mistress beautiful, well dressed and widely admired, who would send him covert understanding glances across the drawing rooms where they would meet, who would lunch or dine with him, on selected occasions, in quiet, out-of-the-way places and who would come, veiled and silent, to a secret rendezvous. He had wanted, in other words, mystery, efficiency, ease and tact, all of which Kitty had been able to provide, and without experience, too, for he had believed her when she told him that he was her first lover. But in becoming his dream girl, she had condemned herself to the insubstantiality of a dream.

Oh, yes, she loved him. There was no minimizing that. But how long did a man have to be grateful for being loved? And was she not proving at last — she, whose chief virtue had been that she was always different from other women — the banality of the ages, that love *had* to become exclusive? Was it not the real Kitty he had just seen, and was not the self-effacing creature of the past year an artifice? Life was crammed with the inevitability of being possessed, hugged, stifled, and what but that had just happened to him in his own place of work, early, on a business morning? It was intolerable, as intolerable as Grinnell Tyson's friendly handshake and condescending offer of brandy and cigars, the little gestures of the older adulterer who hopes to prevent the younger from tiring of what has so long tired him. It was

essential that Kitty should learn, if she wished to continue
their present arrangement, that a lover must have at least the
freedom of a spouse!

Minerva Denison's dinner was hilarious from the start, as
warm and crackling as the fire under her massive marble
empire mantel. She was a woman who understood the importance of cheerful beginnings. She lived in a crisp new
apartment hotel with a crisp new living room, all white and
yellow, with dark, seventeenth century canvases of flowers
and dead game hung between french windows overlooking a
dusky, winking Central Park. Minerva was one of those rare
women who entertained well without fussing. She might have
had her chairs rejoined and her rugs cleaned every winter,
but she would not even turn her pink head or gaunt frame
at the sound of a broken glass.

"Now, here's a good boy who's not ashamed to come on
time!" she cried, extending two long brown arms to greet
Hugo. "Bless me, dearie, if I don't see Denison written all
over you. I'll bet you like parties and girls and horse races.
Give me a kiss, honey. We're close enough kin for that. And
then go over and talk to my little girl. She's been dying to
meet you."

Alfreda was not big and bony like her mother, but she had
the same outward manifestations of enthusiasm and energy.
She was basically a rather plain girl, with a long Modigliani
face and a small hooked nose, with a bit of twisted mouth and
an oval chin, but everything that could be done to improve
her looks had been done. She had the brightest teeth and the
most beautifully waved blond hair that Hugo had ever seen,
and her small, lively tan eyes popped at him from under
arched, plucked brows. She seemed not only ready to laugh,
but to be laughed *at*.

"Do you like my new dress, Hugo?" she began at once.

"It cost a fortune, and I'm wearing it just for you. Because I'm too lucky for words to have a handsome cousin who's kind enough to take me to a dance and introduce me to everybody. You will, won't you? Mummy tells me there's nobody you don't know."

"Well, I didn't know *you*. So you see what a poor crumb I am."

"Ah, but you know me *now*. Or you will." She led him to a corner and a sofa that would hold only two. "Let me start by telling you about myself. I take courses at Columbia. Serious ones, too. I do best with precise subjects, like dates and figures and where things are. I'm an only child and I've probably spent too much time in Europe. I love parties and people, but I'm bored with boys my own age."

"You prefer old men like me."

"You're not old; you're thirty-five," she retorted promptly. "I looked you up in Cousin Ida's family book. I consider that the perfect age for a man. I shouldn't dream of marrying anyone who was a day younger. But don't worry. I won't try to marry you. Mummy tells me you're madly in love with that beautiful Mrs. Tyson, and I think it couldn't be more romantic. I'll just have to think of you as an older brother."

"Mrs. Tyson?" Hugo queried. "What Mrs. Tyson? Surely not the one who's married to a partner of Daddy's and has two girls in boarding school?"

He understood from her baffled look why she did badly in the more speculative subjects. "I mean Mrs. Grinnell Tyson," she complained in the tone of one who at a store counter spots a defect and wants her money back. "Isn't she the one? Mummy seemed so sure." As he shook his head slowly, with the air of a man groping for a clue, she had a happy inspiration. "Oh, I see! You're shielding her. I think that's so gallant! Anyway, I don't think of her as old, any more than I do you. You see, my mother was over forty when I was born. It gives one a different point of view."

"Do you intend to wait for the same period before embarking on family responsibilities?"

Again he had pulled her up too short. "Now, why do you ask that?"

"Because if you and I were to marry, it would mean that I couldn't become a father until my fifty-fifth year."

"But I could never marry *you!*" she exclaimed, as astonished as if he had made a serious proposal.

"Why not?"

"Oh, oodles of reasons. We're cousins, in the first place, and then you're in love with Mrs. Tyson, and, anyway, it isn't my idea at all. I've figured everything out. You're to be a perfectly divine friend, and it would spoil everything if we married."

"I don't know," he protested, a bit piqued by her air of conviction. "I might be a perfectly satisfactory husband."

"Oh, no, no, no!" She shook her head emphatically. "You're not the type at all. Not at all!"

"What is the type?"

"You won't laugh?"

"Cross my heart and hope to die."

She eyed him suspiciously as he moved a finger diagonally across his shirt front. "Well, he wouldn't have to be in law or business or anything like that. As a matter of fact, he wouldn't even have to make money. I figure I have enough for two."

"How gratifying. For him."

"Now don't be sarcastic. I'm simply trying to be truthful. Don't you think it's more fun when people are truthful?"

"By all means. Please go on. You still haven't told me your type of man. All I know is that he can be poor."

"Well, I'd want him to be in public life. Not necessarily in elective politics. He could be a career man."

"In the Bureau of Weights and Measures, for example?"

She giggled. "Well, of course, what I'd really like is to have him in the State Department."

"As Secretary?"

"Now you *are* laughing at me. No, if I thought he had a future, he could be the lowest of the low. There! I've told you my ambition, and I'm sure you think me a total ass."

"Oh, no. I think you're honest. Which is a million times rarer. Which perhaps even justifies you. But tell me: is that why you want an older man? So you can be sure he's already launched in the right direction?"

"That's it. The young are so risky."

"But they can always be shed."

"Oh, I shall never divorce." Her gravity now struck a deeper note. "I'm like Mummy, a one-man woman. That's why the choice is so terribly important."

It was peculiar how quickly her candor effaced the crasser aspects of her silliness. She made him think of a brilliantly plumaged tropical bird, exotic despite a plain, quaint, honest face. She was intense, literal and probably dull. But he also suspected that if the man of her ultimate choice fell short of her goal, she would be a good sport about it.

At the ball he was unreasonably irked by the perfect discipline that kept Kitty from casting even a glance in his direction as he danced with Alfreda. He wanted her to see that he was not in the least apologetic.

"I see your beautiful Mrs. Tyson," Alfreda observed. "I'm sure she's disconsolate. Why not pop me back at the table and go join her?"

"I'm quite happy, thank you."

"Faithless man! But, then, of course, that's what everyone says about you. I suppose you're aware that you have an absolutely foul reputation?"

"But I'm a lamb, Alfreda! An absolute lamb!"

"It's not true, then, that Mrs. Tyson is disconsolate?"

"Oh, that's all over and done with."

"Goodness me, did anyone hear a cock crow?"

Just then they were cut in on, and as Hugo watched her move across the floor with her new partner, fitting herself neatly but somehow not provocatively into his embrace, he saw that she was talking again, and with the same awkward animation. It gave him the feeling that he and Alfreda and this other man were automatic figures, turning around and around on top of a music box. But this feeling changed in degree as he continued to watch them, from amusement to irritation and finally to something closer to actual anger. It might seem absurd to be angry that a girl whom he had just met should be as attentive to one partner as another, but Hugo was too old a hand in the business of women to waste time repining about such absurdities. They meant one thing, and one thing only, and although he was startled at such immediate evidence of sexual attraction to that bobbing figure across the room, he knew the futility of denying it. It then occurred to him that everyone had taken this girl with the utmost seriousness from the beginning, his mother with her arcane hints, Kitty with her unprecedented accusations and even old Minerva with the warmth of her initial greeting. Were they, as women, acting out their ancient, predetermined roles, his mother, a silent robed figure walking in from the wings and pushing a young bride before her, and his mistress, in the back of the set, drowning herself like a perverse lemming in a jealousy which she knew to be fatal to his affection? Or was it rather *he* who had set them all in motion? Did they sense, by some female instinct, that he had reached the mating point, a jaded Victorian bachelor, complete with opera cape and opera girl, ready at last to retire to his county with a well-endowed virgin whose pertness must be no stain on her purity? But how fatuous could a man be? Shaking his head to dispel such foolish thoughts, he crossed the floor to cut back on Alfreda.

"Even *I* know you ought not to cut back on the man who's cut in on you," she protested.

"Those are debutante rules. You're not a debutante any more."

"Thanks for rubbing it in! It happens that I was having a most interesting talk with that gentleman."

"He's a dope. Forget him."

"Forget him? Dearie, he's one of Mummy's guests, I ——"

Again Hugo felt a hand on his shoulder, and he turned angrily to find Teddy Allen, with a constrained grin, and Kitty Tyson, at his side.

"Look, old man," Allen was saying, "Kitty suggests we do what used to be known as a double-cut. It's the only way I'll get a chance to have a word with my old friend, Alfreda. I have to catch the midnight to Washington."

Allen was a bachelor of Hugo's years, in the State Department but attached to the United Nations. They were "extra men" on the lists of the same hostesses, and Hugo detested him on the mere suspicion of a tendency, among their common acquaintance, to bracket them. He turned abruptly to Alfreda.

"Do you know this man?"

"Oh, but of course!" she exclaimed with a startled laugh. "Where would Mummy and I have been, the winter we spent in Washington, without Teddy?" She smiled at Allen. "You see, I've grown up since."

"Flowered, my dear, flowered."

As they moved off together over the floor, Hugo stamped his foot. "Flowered! What a filthy term!" He spun around on Kitty. "What the hell made you do that?"

But even such roughness could not disturb her self-possession in a public room. Her eyes expressed nothing but sheer surprise. "Why I thought, poor man, that your duty dance with your little cousin had gone on quite long enough!"

"How kind of you. But it so happens that it wasn't a duty dance at all. It so happens that I *like* dancing with my cousin!"

She turned her gaze to Alfreda and Allen who were talking, both at once, with great liveliness.

"At least, *she* doesn't seem to mind."

For a moment he was so angry that he considered walking off and leaving her. But in the next moment he realized that there might never again be a better chance to make his position clear, and taking her firmly by the elbow he guided her back to her table, now deserted by her guests on the dance floor. They sat in a rather severe silence while he drained off half of somebody's champagne glass.

"I want to be very serious," he began. "There's a matter I've been meaning to discuss with you for some time."

"It must be terribly important to make you look so grim. And to need so much of poor Teddy's champagne."

"Ugh! You mean that was *his* glass! You asked *him* to your dinner?"

"He was kind enough to fill *your* place at the last minute."

But her reproach was simply evidence that she, too, considered Allen as his logical substitute, and he became still angrier. "Look here, Kitty, I want you to get one thing straight. I'm not going to be at your beck and call. There's no point in our relationship if it's going to be as tight as a marriage."

Her eyes expressed only a vague wonderment, perhaps as to what marriage he was referring. "Have I ever claimed it should be?"

"So if I want to dance with Alfreda Denison," he pursued, "or go out to dinner with Alfreda Denison, I must feel absolutely at liberty to do so."

"As indeed you are."

For just a moment he felt deflated, but then he reflected that her tolerance was only a woman's ruse. "Well, so long as it's perfectly plain," he concluded with a shrug.

"It seems to me," she retorted, with an at last quickening resentment, "that you've been doing exactly that ever since we met. The only difference is that now you throw it in my face."

"Is frankness throwing it in your face? Is simple honesty throwing it in your face?"

"Hardly," she said dryly. "As you will see when I show you what those qualities really are. Let us *be* frank, Hugo. Let us *be* honest." She glanced at his glass and then at her own which she had placed face downward. "Do you mind if I have a sip of your champagne? Or of Teddy's? Whosever it is?"

Hugo watched, with a first pang of contrition, as she touched her lips to the rim of the glass. He had never seen her need even a sip before.

"I want to tell you," she continued in a graver tone, "that you're as free as you could possibly wish."

"Meaning what?"

"Meaning that you're free to see Alfreda and dance with Alfreda . . . and marry Alfreda, if you like."

"Aren't you making rather an issue of it?"

"Weren't *you?*"

"But marrying her! Why must women always go to such extremes? If you will recall my exact words, I was merely trying to point out . . ."

"Don't play the lawyer with me, Hugo," she interrupted with sudden impatience. "I can read all that small print. And I'm perfectly aware that your sudden interest in this new cousin means that you're bored with me. Or is that throwing things in *your* face?"

"You don't think you're taking a rather extreme position over a rather small matter?"

"Perhaps. But then my life has been made up of small matters."

"Thanks!"

"And now don't play the injured and scornful lover!" she exclaimed bitterly. "Spare me that, too. We both know perfectly well what you want. To keep me on ice while you roam the field. But I won't be shared, Hugo! I won't be a handy odalisque during the dry courtship of an immaculate cousin. You're not the only one with pride!"

Hugo began to realize at last, from the new note of passion in her tone, all that he might be giving up. And then he saw, in a sudden, brilliant, horrible flash, that Alfreda was precisely everything he *didn't* want. Was it not the worst of man's perversity that he should know himself perverse? He leaned forward with a sigh, his elbows on the table.

"Honestly, Kitty, I don't know *what* I want."

"That's because I'm behaving so well. It's really rather bitchy of me. It's kinder, in the long run, to make scenes."

"You spoil me."

"I always have. But when I think what you'll go through with that little cousin of yours, I can almost find it in my heart to be sorry for you. *She* won't spoil you. There." She spread her fingers on the tablecloth and contemplated her scarlet nails. "I *have* been bitchy, after all."

Even in the fall of his spirits he was conscious of a small, blurred resentment that she should have so turned the tables on him. "You almost convince me that you have," he said with an irritated shrug. "What else can I say?"

"You said once that women never knew how to end things. I've always been determined, when the time came, that I would prove you wrong. I shall go home now. I'll tell Grinnell I have a headache, and I'll have a good cry, which should make me feel much better. Don't come to see me until I write you. When I have myself quite under control, I'll ask you to dinner. And then, perhaps, we may learn the hardest thing of all. How to be friends."

The music had stopped, and the dancers were returning to their tables. He saw Grinnell Tyson and a lady in blue coming across the floor towards them. He stood up.

"Kitty, do you know something? Do you know you're a rather great woman?"

"Don't be sentimental, Hugo!" she said sharply as she turned away from him. "Don't spoil a perfect record!"

15

Hugo: 1950

HE WAS FREE now to devote all his time to Alfreda, which he did in a flurry of attentiveness, as if the very magnitude of Kitty's sacrifice required that not the least portion of it be wasted. He wrote Kitty that he looked forward to embracing her wise and kind offer of friendship and would telephone her when a "decent interval" had elapsed. He then proceeded to put her completely out of mind. Life with Alfreda was silly and crowded, but it was as hectic as it had promised. She and her mother loved to see large numbers of people and to do large numbers of things, largely, it appeared, for the pleasure of discussing them afterwards with the faithful clique that foregathered daily at the cocktail hour. Hugo was amused by the enthusiasm sustained by mother and daughter over matters which, according to universal experience, were supposed to pall. It was unthinkable that anything should ever spot the silks and satins of their apartment or disarrange the little row of Minerva's pink brow curls. Old age was never mentioned in their living room, and sickness rarely. Decay, like dust, was banished from the premises.

"What's the point of having people in for cocktails *every* day?" he asked Alfreda once. "Do you really think it will bring you nearer your goal?"

"You mean my diplomat?" She was not in the least abashed by the crudeness of his reference. She had given him his chance to label her as silly, and when he had not done so, she had taken for granted that he accepted her in every particular. She had a way, he was beginning to see, of creating allies by her very faith in them. "Why not? How does one meet people except at parties? That's how I met Teddy Allen. And that's how I met you!"

He laughed scornfully. "You're barking up the wrong tree with Teddy Allen. He'll be lucky if he ever gets further than Protocol."

"Now why are you so sure of that?"

"Because, my dear, I've made a study of the ladder of fame."

"You don't seem very interested in your own rung on it."

"Is that a dirty crack?"

"Oh dearie, of course not!" she exclaimed, abashed by the sudden flare of his hostility. "I just meant that you didn't seem to have that *kind* of ambition. Why should you? It's perfectly fine to be taken up with the sale of beautiful things. Honestly, I mean it!"

Hugo looked at her suspiciously. He was not a bit sure that she cared about beautiful things. She lacked the smallest inclination for the abstract or philosophic. Her alert eye went straight from the general design to the specific detail, as her mind raced to the nearest pigeonhole. "I get it!" was the phrase most often on her lips. She seemed bent on reducing the wilderness of observed phenomena to an ordered garden with white labels tied to the stem of every flower. But once defined there was an end to a subject; Alfreda was ready and eager to move on to the next. She saw no point in dallying, in turning things over, in pondering their implications. Nor, in truth, did Hugo, but the exaggeration in her of his own intellectual bad habits made him uneasily aware of the toll of their kind of bright, picking mentality. And it exasperated him that everything he tried to teach her was immediately drawn through the tight sieve of her preconceptions, so that only what she had already believed remained.

"Let's have another bottle of wine and skip the silly party," he suggested one night at a restaurant where they were dining before a reception at Irene Trask's. "I have it on the best authority there won't be even a consul there."

"But I *want* to go to the silly party."

"Doesn't the law of diminishing returns exist for you?"

Her glance seemed to deplore the irrelevance of his male habit of speculation. "Not till I've got what I want!"

He was careful not to betray the effects of her still growing physical attraction for him, except for an occasional gesture, confident but at the same time ambiguous. He would reach over to take her hand in his, in parody of an uncle, when he lectured her about her hasty enthusiasms for people or her bad taste in art, and if he helped her into a cape or a fur piece, he would allow his fingers to linger a moment about her shoulders. He knew that there could be no question of anything but marriage with such a girl — she *thought* only in terms of marriage — and he was still a great distance from any such commitment. She accepted his gestures, but seemed to regard them as mere manifestations of the type of demonstrative friendship that her little group espoused. So far as Hugo could make out, the bright hard sun of female influence on her life had yet to be darkened by a male cloud.

In the taxi that night, taking her home from the Trasks' reception, he tried to reassert the crumbling illusion of his authority with a kiss.

"Aren't you rather stretching your role of guide and mentor?" she demanded, moving promptly to the far end of the seat.

"Oh, hell, what's a little kiss. A good-night kiss? You'd probably give as much to any crummy sophomore."

"I don't happen to go out with crummy sophomores, thank you."

"Well, aren't we cousins? Doesn't a cousin rate a cousinly kiss?"

"Very well. I'll give you a proper cousinly kiss when I get out of the cab."

Which she did. As they drew up at the entrance of her hotel, she moved quickly over to give him a dry peck on the cheek. Before he could catch her in his arms, however, she was out of the taxi and greeting the old doorman with the mannered graciousness of an English princess visiting a settlement house. He had to admit that she knew how to keep her pigeonholes straight.

But the little scene in the taxi, however inconsequential at the moment, was, only a few hours later, to change his life. Back in his apartment he lay restlessly awake until the early morning and finally got up to smoke cigarettes by his open window and to conclude in disgust that the oldest and tritest and stupidest thing in the world, love, romantic love, *valentine* love, had finally happened to Hugo Hartley. And *when* had it happened? Why, precisely when his favorite novelist, Proust, would have predicted it: at the exact moment when it had struck him that Alfreda's feelings for him were those of a devoted cousin and nothing more! This shattering perception had made him the instant prey of a host of violent fantasies about a girl who had neither looks nor charm nor genuine intelligence, a girl who was fundamentally a goose, and a stubborn, calculating goose at that! O omniscient Proust! O master psychologist! What did she have but youth, ordinary, smooth-skinned, fungible youth? It was only, he knew, because he was losing his own that he valued this commonplace and semi-precious jewel above all the treasures of Kitty Tyson. But what good did knowing do? Was he any less enslaved? Was he any less agog than a child in a trinket shop? And what would Alfreda extort in return for her bauble of youth? What but a lifetime of service!

"All right!" he cried angrily out the window. "I'll marry her, by God! And *then* we'll see!"

He laughed wryly at the picture of what his mother's pleasure would be if his words were carried down to her bedroom window. Then he went to bed and slept.

When he awoke he jumped up as if the day might not be long enough for all he had to do. For he was perfectly clear all over again that he *did* want to marry Alfreda. Why not? Was he the first man who had fallen in love with a woman who was his intellectual inferior? What woman, after all, was *not?* The point was simply that he wanted her, and what was that but the basis of marriage? Would she have him? Oh, yes. In time. She was a girl to distinguish carefully between a proposal and a pass in a taxi. And, after all, how many proposals did a plain, silly girl, even a rich one, get? But he was determined about one thing. There would be no further display of emotion on his part until she had evinced some on hers. It did not have to be much, a lingering look, an enigmatic smile, a hint of pressure on the hand, anything that would pull the scantiest veil of sex over her bold, neuter conception of their friendship. His pride, his dignity, his very success required at least so much. He would be assiduous, he would be constant, but he would be scrupulously correct. He would confine himself to her silly circle; he would be Swann among the Verdurins. And, touched by the picture of a man of his parts torn from his own fascinating world by passion, he took a pad and pencil and drew up a program before breakfast.

In the following weeks he carried it out to the letter. He divided his social engagements into those where he might expect to meet Alfreda and those where he might not. All of the latter he ruthlessly canceled. New invitations he treated in the same fashion, except that he did not scruple to inquire of a hostess in the first category: "By the way, you don't happen to be asking Alfreda Denison, do you?" One or two of them took umbrage — his aunt, Irene Trask, went so far as to remind him that she did not keep a disorderly house — but the others were amused and usually invited Alfreda. At the least hint of romance the toughest of the old girls became misty-eyed.

He never deviated from his cardinal rule of conducting himself with absolute circumspection towards Alfreda herself. He knew by the apprehensive look in her eye when she found him next to her at dinner that she had been advised by her friends of his now assiduous pursuit. He would then hope, by confining himself to a polite discussion of any matters in which she showed an interest, to substitute bewilderment, or, better yet, disappointment, in the place of constraint. To act the lover, in other words, to every eye but her own, seemed to him the surest way of bringing her to terms. But he found to his disgust that she parried subtlety with bluntness.

"I never thought you and I were going to have such a pleasant friendship," she told him one night, "after that awkward little business in the taxi."

"Pray don't mention it."

"Why not?"

Why not indeed? He swore under his breath. "Because I made a fool of myself. It's a thing that happens to old bachelors. We grow too cynical. And too conceited."

"You mean you've gotten over it? I'm *so* glad! It isn't true, you know, that all girls like to be pawed."

"I mean," he said, with as much dignity as her choice of verb had left him, "that, whatever my feelings, they are now under control."

"That must be such a relief to Mrs. Tyson."

"I told you that was all over and done with."

"Ah, but *is* it? You implied as much when I first met you, and that same night I saw you across the room having the longest heart-to-heart with her!"

Hugo gazed into those round, tan, startled eyes, so bright now with curiosity, and at those small, scarlet pursed lips, so tensely ready to burst open in either dismay or laughter, he could never be certain which. Surely it was encouraging that she should speak of Kitty Tyson and that she should have watched him that closely. According to Proust, his own ardor should now be abated. Yet he did not find it so. He closed his teeth gently on the tip of his tongue as a dark fantasy of possession filled his mind, of gripping those twitching white shoulders until she screamed.

"That was the end," he said in a low, sad tone. "That was when I broke it to her."

"Broke *what?*"

"That it was no longer possible for me to offer her my exclusive devotion."

"And you waited to tell her at a party? Where she couldn't make a scene? I think that's the meanest thing I ever heard!"

In his fantasy Hugo moved that grip from her shoulders to her throat. "Kitty doesn't make scenes."

"The more fool she! How else are we poor women to protect ourselves? And who, do I dare ask, is to share that devotion no longer exclusively offered to Mrs. Tyson? What great lady is next on the list?"

Hugo was too astonished to speak. Was it possible that his entire campaign had simply gone unnoticed? In her absurd determination to treat him as an older brother, had she been able to blind herself to everything but that pass in the taxicab? It seemed incredible, but he reminded himself that women like Alfreda *were* incredible.

"I'll thank you to leave my private life alone!" he snapped.

"Oh, honey, I'm sorry! I thought you wouldn't mind a little tease. Don't you realize that girls like myself are absolutely *fascinated* by that kind of thing? It's all so wicked and wonderful!"

"I suggest we change the subject," he retorted coldly, "and discuss whether you'd look better in your green satin or your red crepe de Chine at the Boys' Club Ball."

"Oh, which do you think?"

But if her independence of mind and professed ignorance of the state of his emotions was galling to him, her loyalty was worse. It seemed to him now the same that she might have shown to some soft, sad, grey former instructress, an aging mademoiselle, taken once a winter to the matinee of a visiting French company. It never crossed her mind that he, any more than the mademoiselle, might lose interest in her dresses and parties. It was particularly humiliating for him to discover, when he asked her now to dine, that she wanted to join friends afterwards, or go to a party, or even a movie. She would put it tactfully that she did not want to waste one of his evenings, but he suspected that it was not the waste of his that most concerned her.

One Monday, when he telephoned to arrange to meet her during the week, he found all her evenings gone.

"What about Friday?" he asked peevishly. "I thought you told me you were going to be in Friday."

"Well, that's just it, dearie, I am. I promised Mums I'd stay home. Even *she* thinks I go out too much!"

"But a quiet dinner with your old coz isn't really going out. We can have cocktails with 'Mums' first."

"I *promised* her, Hugo."

"Oh, damn your promises!" Everything in his little office, the pale early spring sunlight through the window, the smudged grey of the walls, even the redeeming Ingres drawing over his desk, seemed of an equal vapidity. He had to be shored up in this tight little box of commercial nothingness while *she* could go anywhere! And yet her going anywhere was as stupid as his staying in his box. Hers was merely the larger one into which his, in Japanese style, neatly fitted. What a life! "Damn it all, Alfreda, if you don't want to see me, you only have to say so! I'm not the intruding type, you know!"

"Oh, honey, how can you even think it? You're my friend of friends!"

"I'm not so old I can be treated like an uncle," he grumbled.

"An uncle! But you're my wolf of wolves! The most adorable extra man in town! I tell you what. Come dine with Mummy and me on Friday. She'd love that. And maybe you and I can slip out afterwards and go to the movies."

He had to be content with this and mollified by what he hoped was the sincerity of her tone. He had to go on dreaming of a future where he might have the privilege of knocking into her stubborn head the simple idea that her delights would be provided by him and him alone. For he had not given up hope that Alfreda would ultimately regard the conquest of so confirmed a bachelor as the crowning achievement of her silly social career and one that might appropriately mark her retirement.

It came as a shock, therefore, on Friday night to discover that Minerva Denison, who he had imagined himself rescuing from a solitary widow's supper, was giving instead a dinner party for her own noisy group. He found himself seated between two old girls who gossiped across him as if his masculine charm were nothing but a clothesline. Moodily he drained his glass of wine and contemplated the melancholy picture of his degradation. Perhaps it was beginning to be a bit too much like *Swann's Way*.

After dinner, when the gentlemen joined the ladies, he went promptly to Alfreda's side.

"I want to play backgammon," he insisted. "Over there in that corner. And I won't take 'no' for an answer."

"Honey, it's not friendly. Mummy expects us to help out."

"I *have* helped out. I've been a bowl of milk for two old tabbies, and I'm lapped dry."

She stared at him for a second and then uttered a cry of laughter. "You poor sweet! I guess you have earned it. Come along."

They sat in the corner before a table whose ivory surface was shaped as a board and arranged the red and black disks. But Alfreda, for once, was more interested in talking. About to throw her dice, she put down the cup.

"Shall I tell you something really exciting? Can you be discreet?"

He slapped one of his disks on top of another in a quick gesture of apprehension. "*Now* what?"

"It's possible — mind you, *just* possible — that I may be on the track of my man."

In the instant crash of his spirits there was no chance to dissemble. "Your Secretary of State?" he asked sharply.

She giggled. "Well, just possibly."

"Who?"

"Teddy Allen."

For a moment he was so angry that speech was impossible. He simply sat and glared at her. Then he swallowed and moistened his lips and at last began, in a low, hissing tone: "That mildewed old faggot? If you're going to pick a failure, at least pick a man. Women like you are fantastic. Absolutely fantastic. It's not only that you can't spot a winner. You can't even spot someone who'll be good in bed. Or don't you care about vulgar things like that? Don't you care about anything but Georgetown cocktail parties. *God!*"

Alfreda looked at him with a petrified expression in which horror and amusement were equally mixed. "Are you out of your mind?"

"Everyone seems crazy to the mad!" he exclaimed in a louder voice. "I never heard of such a thing! And does your silly old mother approve?"

"Everyone seems silly to you tonight," she retorted angrily. "Please keep your voice down, or I'll go back to the others. And now to your wild accusations. How dare you call Teddy a pansy? You know it's the grossest libel."

"Why hasn't he ever married?"

"Why haven't *you?*"

"Because I like too many women. Not too few."

"I could name two women with whom I happen to know he's had affairs."

"Bully for Teddy boy! What an old stud!"

"Will you be quiet!" She glanced quickly in her mother's direction. "Will you admit you have no reasonable grounds for calling him a pansy? Come, Hugo. Be fair!"

"Well, if he's not, he might as well be. He *looks* like one."

"He does *not*. To me, anyway. And I have it on reliable authority he's about to be made First Secretary in Rome. He'll be an ambassador at forty."

"On your money!"

"Hugo, you're way out of bounds tonight! Teddy has more money than I do."

"Oh, who *cares?* If you wanted somebody young and handsome, I could put up with it, but if you expect me to stand by and watch while you set your cap at that mangy old epicene . . ."

"Hugo!"

"My God, you'd do a thousand times better with me!"

"With *you!*" She sat up straight and caught her fingers to her mouth.

"Yes, me! Why not me? At least I love you!"

"*Hugo!*" There was no misinterpreting the astonishment in her eyes. "Honey, do you know what you're saying? Are you drunk?"

"Of course I'm not drunk," he retorted, furious. "What's so strange about my loving you? And how could you miss it, you silly ass! Why do you think I've been calling you up every day? Why do you think I keep coming to lousy parties like this one? Do you think I'd be seen dead with these old crows if you hadn't turned me into a pail of slop?"

"Oh, Hugo, Hugo." She refused to meet his eyes, but stared down at the board and ruefully shook her head.

"What's wrong? Am I so ridiculous?"

"Oh, it's not that. Darling, I'm sure you'll make some girl the most divine husband in the world." She leaned over the table to put her hand pleadingly on his. "Only, honey, I haven't thought of you that way. It's all too sudden. I can't just turn myself inside out."

"You could if you wanted to!"

"Ah, but that's just it! I *don't* want to. I don't want to at all! I could never let myself fall in love with a man like you. What's discipline for?"

"A man like me? What do you mean, a man like me?"

"Well, sweetie, you're absolutely charming and the best friend in the world and all full of know-how about people and things — you really *are* — but, honey, you're like a beautiful dessert of ice cream and spun sugar, you'd never do for every day."

"What's wrong with ice cream and spun sugar every day?"

"Darling, it just wouldn't *do*." She hesitated. "Shall I be frank?"

"By all means."

"Well, honey, let's face it, you haven't one tiny scrap of ambition, and I'm riddled with it. We'd be the most ghastly couple. You'd be perfectly content to go on forever in that auction gallery as long as you could go to all your parties."

"You accuse *me* of caring about parties!"

"Pots just *will* call kettles black, won't they? But I look upon parties as a means. To you they're an end. You'd be willing to play second fiddle to a bunch of Swiss art dealers for the rest of your life, if you could put on a black tie every night and be charming."

It was shocking and detestable to find that he had been judged by the very jury that he had thought he was charging. "So that's it!" he cried bitterly. "I'm not good enough! I'm not even as good as Ted Allen!"

"Dearie, you make me sound so brutal, but what can I say? I know what I am and what I want. At least that way I don't hurt anybody. As a couple, we'd be ridiculous. Which doesn't mean for a minute that you're not the sweetest, darlingest friend in the whole wide world . . ."

"Oh, shut up!"

He got up and strode to the hall. He did not even stop to bid good night to Minerva who was staring after him. Alfreda followed him, pleading.

"Hugo, please!"

"Good night!"

They stood in the foyer, stupidly side by side, before closed doors, waiting for the elevator.

"I can't bear to have you leave this way!" she wailed.

The doors at last opened.

"Good night, Mrs. Secretary," he growled as he almost leaped into the elevator.

On Saturday morning he was too tired and disconsolate to plan his usual game of squash at the Racquet Club, or a ride in the Park, or even a visit to a rival gallery. He could not face the prospect of his father at the breakfast table, so he boiled an egg and brewed coffee in his own kitchen and then dressed and went down to see his mother. But she was about to go out.

"You look tired, dear."

"Don't say that!" he snapped. "It makes me feel worse. Where are you going?"

"I'm taking the dogs to the Park." She had a small dachshund and a large, very old, half-blind bulldog that she took out every morning.

"Can I come along?"

"Of course. But won't it be rather dull for you?"

"I'll be the judge of that."

There was just a touch of early spring in the air. The grass was damp and brown, but with a hope of green, and the sky was a mild, apprehensive grey. The paths were full of muddy puddles where here and there a sparrow splashed. Hugo's head ached from the whiskey of the night before, and he felt low and heavy and wanted to weep. How ridiculous! When had he last wept? Could he even remember?

"How are Alfreda and her mother? Have you seen them lately?"

He repressed a shudder of irritation. But what else, after all, had he wanted to discuss? "Alfreda is very well," he answered in precise, sneering syllables. "She thinks she may at last be on the trail of a man who will satisfy her inordinate ambition. A statesman who will be a proper host at her parties and still find a few spare moments to guide his nation through an atomic era."

"You don't mean she's engaged!"

"No. I mean that her eye has alighted on the man whom she may ultimately dignify with her choice."

It was like Ida not even to ask who the man was. "I had so hoped it might be you," she said sadly.

"Me!" He laughed shrilly. "A poor little art peddler!

For the great Miss Denison! Surely, Ma, you forget yourself."

"Is that *her* idea? That you're not good enough?"

"That I lack ambition."

"She's quite right. You do."

Her matter-of-fact tone gave a sharper sting to the words. Hugo came to an immediate halt, and Ida was several paces ahead when he cried: "Ma! You too!"

She paused and pulled back the old bulldog which was trying to drink out of a mud puddle. "You've led a worldly life with worldly people," she pointed out. "You've even sneered at those who didn't. Why should you complain now if Alfreda has the standards of your set? At least she's honest."

"You defend her! *You!*"

"I don't defend her. I try to explain her. Why shouldn't she have a preconception of the kind of husband she wants? And if you care about her, why shouldn't you go a little way to meet her?"

"I?" he almost shouted. "You expect me to give up my business career and beg an allowance from Daddy while I try to shoehorn myself into the State Department? And all for a snotty little girl who sees life as a series of canapé trays? No, thank you!"

"She wouldn't require all that. You don't understand women. No, you don't, darling, for all your conquests. If you became head of your gallery, or even a vice-president, I'm sure it would do the trick. It's only the idea of your not caring that she really minds. And why shouldn't you care? You could easily get ahead if you wanted. You might even . . ."

"You too!"

"Why too?"

"You agree with Alfreda! You think I'm a lazy bum!"

"That's ridiculous, Hugo."

"It's true!" he cried passionately. "I thought *you*, at least, were different. But you're as bad as Daddy and Dorcas. You think I'm nothing but a society butterfly!"

"Darling, you're being totally unreasonable."

"And, by God, none of you have any idea what it *takes* to be a society butterfly! I'd like to see Daddy try it! But why do I talk to you? What matters in your philosophy but for the men to get ahead and the women to raise babies? Talk and art and love and music and beauty and everything that gives life the least point count for nothing! *Nothing!* Well, I'm through with the lot of you! I'll go my own way from now on, thank you very much!"

"When have you not?"

"Can't you see I'm serious?" he demanded furiously. "How can you go on making fun of me? I don't know what's come over you, Ma. Ever since Cousin Geraldine jumped out that window, you just don't seem to have given a damn about anything. Good day!"

He was walking rapidly away when he heard her call "Hugo!" and turned. She was smiling!

"Thanks for walking with me."

He did not deign to reply, but strode on hurriedly until he was out of the Park. His holidays were always so carefully organized with exercise, reading, dressing, calling, shopping, writing in his journal, or even thinking, that when he found himself at once without engagements and without a purpose, he felt so empty and restless that it was impossible to remain in one place. The props on which he had bolstered his life were numerous but interdependent, and not one could be pulled out without shaking the balance of the whole structure. If Alfreda despised him, then everyone must despise him, including his ungrateful mother whose champion he had always considered himself. And was he not worthy of being despised, a foolish gadabout, a dealer in trinkets, with a collection that, in the last analysis, was nothing but a pile of junk? Even his prize, the Watteau drawing — what was that but a thin little sketch dependent on the luster of its supposed creator's name? He would sell the works and go to Paris and sit in a café, or to Majorca and sit on a beach, or maybe to the Orient. In the meanwhile he went to three movies, staying a half hour at each, and visited the observation tower of the Empire State Building and the zoo. In the middle of the afternoon he made a long visit to the bar of the Knickerbocker Club, and it was not until five that he arrived at Kitty Tyson's.

She was alone with a tea tray and expecting nobody. It was one of those perfect coincidences that he always claimed never happened in New York. Grinnell had gone to his brother's in New Jersey for the weekend. Hugo thought he had never seen her looking so beautiful. There was a dignity and serenity to her green-velveted, late afternoon loveliness that made the ambitions of Alfreda seem shrill and childish in retrospect. Secretary of State indeed!

"I'm glad you came," she said as he sipped his tea. "I'm glad you didn't wait till I sent for you."

"Should I have?"

"Don't you remember? But never mind, of course you don't. The thing is that I'm just beginning to realize how much I shall need friends."

"Has something happened?"

She gazed into the fireplace. "Grinnell has asked me to give him a divorce."

He held his breath. "Because of . . . us?"

"Oh, no. Not in the least." She shook her head a bit ruefully at the mere idea. "He wants to marry his Olive, that's all. At long last. He was very nice about it, really. The settlement he offered was quite handsome. I get this house and the children and an income for life. Even if I remarry."

"It's the least he could do."

"Ah, no, Hugo, be fair. Give the devil his due. It's hard for Grinnell to part with money."

"Then what are you waiting for? Grab it!"

"But that's just it. What you once said to me. That we women can never make an end of things. The moment Grinnell made up his mind to go, everything in me reached out to pull him back. It wasn't love. I doubt if it was even habit. It was just a basic, atavistic fear of losing my man."

"You'll be all right. You're young enough and pretty enough and rich enough. You'll see."

"Will I?" She shook her head. "I've always taken it for granted that people would ask me to their parties. Now I shall learn what it is to be a single woman. I can hear those voices on the telephone already: 'Oh, Kitty, darling, I'm *so* sorry, but could we put you off for the eleventh? Johnny Jones has given out. Thanks, darling, I *knew* you'd understand.' I'll have to learn to be nice to all the right pansies unless I want to sit home, night after night, and eventually be an object of pity to my daughters when *they* start going out. Oscar Wilde said that to be in society was simply a bore, and to be out of it, simply a tragedy. I used to think that such a silly saying, and now it seems to me an eternal verity!"

As Hugo gazed about the soft, familiar room, with its harmonious blend of Chinese objects, of dragons and bird panels and silver junks, against the chaste dignity of English things, as if the trade of the eighteenth century had been the gentle accomplishment of gentle decorators, without guns or storms or opium, he reflected that the world that Kitty had made was better than that of many who sneered at it. He began to speculate that if the room was an appropriate setting for a Mrs. Tyson, it might be even more appropriate for a Mrs. Hartley, a serene, loving, satisfied Mrs. Hartley, always grateful to her husband, with two pretty girls in matching dresses, affectionate, respectful, a ready-made family, with contagious diseases and adolescent tantrums behind them. Why was that not a picture of which any man might be proud? He rose and walked to the window and looked at the little yard with its neat gravel and pink marble fountain and benches. It would be ideal for cocktails later in the spring. And then he turned to the big, Renoir-inspired portrait over the mantel of Kitty and her daughters, with black eyes and pale faces and furs and flounces, at which he had so often laughed, and imagined himself in a velvet evening jacket with embroidered slippers, raising a glass of brandy as he pointed out its defects in humorous but proprietary tone to a friend, to Minerva Denison, to his mother. And Kitty, after all, might still have a child.

"I wonder if it'll be as bad as you think," he said.

"Oh, yes. The best I can hope will be to be asked occasionally to the Hugo Hartleys'. When Alfreda's having one of her larger dinners."

He winced. "Alfreda's after bigger game than I. Her husband will have to be a famous diplomat."

"So? Poor man."

"You mean because he'll be married to Alfreda?"

"No. Because she'll always compare him to you."

"What a romantic you are, Kitty. Why do you assume that Alfreda's in love with me?"

"Aren't we all?"

He walked now to the bar table and poured himself a drink of straight, warm bourbon. He took a long sip before he turned to her. "Do you think I'd make a good husband?"

She returned his gaze without flinching. "Not very."

"Why not?"

"You'd be cross and fussy and dictatorial."

He threw back his head with a peal of laughter. "Oh,

you're shrewd, you're shrewd! How do you manage it?"

"What?"

"Never to be eager. Never to be stupid. Never to be vulgar or egotistical. Go on, please go on. I promise you, it's working!"

She said nothing and sat motionless, but for the first time in their relationship he noticed something like a glitter in those blue eyes. He walked over to sit on the sofa and place a hand on her knee.

"Do you think you could put up with a husband who was cross and fussy and dictatorial?"

It was her turn to laugh. Her laugh was not a peal, as his had been, but there was a hint of abandon in it. "God knows I'm used to it!"

"That's right," he murmured as he leaned over to kiss her. "That's it. Keep it light. Keep it light."

Upstairs in her room, half an hour later, Hugo was aggressive, almost violent, in his lovemaking. He did not scruple to imagine himself in Alfreda's arms, taking his revenge for her foolish preference. The passionate response of his actual partner he translated in terms of Alfreda's reluctant surrender to his rape. But later yet, in his own apartment, the memory of Kitty's love and the healing balm of her dependence comforted him and stayed with him until he fell asleep.

It was not until he awoke in the early morning that he was aware that the leaden feeling about his temples was not a hangover but depression. He rose from his bed and went to the window to look down on the grey deserted street which in the foggy morning struck him suddenly as an Utrillo, a painter whose work he had never liked. As the events of the previous evening began to march through his mind, at first with a slow, halting, muffled tread and then, suddenly, with a cacophonous blare of trumpets, he realized to what a pass his absurdities had brought him.

"Hugo Hartley!" he cried aloud. "You may as well pitch yourself out the window like Cousin Geraldine!"

The sound of his voice roused him to a completer consciousness, and he laughed bitterly. It served him right! The whole damn thing served him right! Had not Swann married Odette only after he had *ceased* to love her? And after all of Hugo Hartley's vaunted independence, all of his boasts and sneers, had he not been driven into making a fool of himself by a silly girl who preferred an ass like Allen? Get out of his proposal? Of course he could get out of it! But it would be just exactly his ironical and appropriate punishment that for once in his stupid life he could be a gentleman!

PART VII

The Emergence of Ida

16

Ida: 1950

I HAD ALWAYS admired Minerva Denison. I suppose it is elementary that we admire those who least resemble us, and she struck me as my opposite in every significant respect. She stood up to life and beat at it, as one might beat at a rug. It was hard for her to keep her hands off things; she always felt compelled to give people, as well as situations, a remedial tweak or a twist. The appearance of life was never so good that she thought she could not improve on it, and improve on it she usually did. For Minerva, despite her beautifully waved pink hair, or blue hair, or even, at times, green hair, despite the studied elegance of her apartment, despite her passion for parties and night clubs, was a mound of horse sense. The large brown, round face, in which the tiny features and small piercing eyes were almost lost, and the large round figure, more compatible with one's idea of a cook or mammy than a lady of fashion, were more expressive of her real character than the cosmetics and silks with which she sought to disguise them. Minerva was a common enough phenomenon among American women. In parlor comedy she is usually depicted as having a heart of gold and a genius for the practical solution of the love problems of younger characters. In actual life she had . . . well, a *fairly* golden heart.

She had certainly adored my cousin Scotty. He had been the only human being, beside the tax collector, who had ever managed to separate her from a substantial portion of her fortune. The self-made woman of her era (and Minerva, although born an heiress, had tripled her inheritance) was impregnable except, in middle life, to sex. In the first year of her marriage she had allowed Scotty to throw away a quarter of her capital on an Arizona ranch. But that could only happen once. Thereafter she snapped shut her pocket-book and doled out to him a liberal allowance for clothes and clubs and sporting cars, reducing it in the periods when he was drinking too much. But she was shrewd enough to exercise her conjugal control in a way that Scotty never resented. One doesn't, after all, resent a nurse, particularly, a strong, devoted, sensible sharp-tongued nurse. Scotty, under her care, lived several years longer than he had any right to expect, and Alfreda was brought up unaware of her father's failings. It was a tricky job, but Minerva pulled it off.

I think she liked me from the beginning, perhaps because she knew that as a girl I had had a crush on Scotty. Geraldine, I am sure, must have taken pleasure in telling her so, not guessing that Minerva was the kind of woman who wanted other women to love her husband. At any rate, she liked me and none of the other Denisons. One might have thought that, being so gregarious and party-loving herself, she would have found them congenial, and so, at an earlier date, she might, but at the time of her marriage to Scotty Aunt Dagmar's generation was mostly dead, and the survivors found Minerva plain and what Uncle Victor called "dumpy." Her actions had style, but not her appearance, and the Denisons cared a great deal for appearance. I, of course, did not, and she and I were immediately at ease with each other. I never criticized her; I never expected things of her, and it never bored me to dine with her and Scotty when the latter was tight. Better yet, I always struck her as being exceptionally in need of good advice and never took it, which meant that through the years we had an unfailing topic of conversation. Ultimately, I think I came to represent to Minerva the only family, outside of Alfreda, that she really had. With me she came as near as she probably ever came to relaxing the elaborate façade of her seeming good humor. With me she could enjoy the luxury of being cross.

She was very grumpy the day she told me the news I had been dreading. Minerva believed that misfortune was apt to be one's own fault and that one should be scolded for it. She had asked me to come to lunch ahead of her other guests, to have time to reprimand me.

"What's all this I hear about Hugo?" she began straight off when the maid had given her a very pale martini and me a glass of sherry.

"You must tell me."

"Oh, Ida, haven't you *heard*? Where do you live, anyway? He's going to marry Kitty Tyson. Everyone's talking about it."

I was grateful for Derrick's example, through the years, in maintaining a mask of calm. "I thought she already had a husband."

"Well, so she has. But she won't when the lawyers get through. It's only a question of how much Grinnell will have to give her."

"Those questions can be very serious ones to Derrick's partners."

"Really, Ida, how can you take it so glibly? Don't you *care* who Hugo marries?"

"Of course I care. I was just wondering why *you* did."

"Well, after all, aren't we family?"

"I mean, why do you object to Mrs. Tyson? She's rich and beautiful and what they call well born. Aren't those the qualities that your group admires?"

"What has my group to do with it? I'm thinking of *you*.

Do you want an old bag of used goods for your favorite child? And don't tell me he isn't your favorite child. I *know*."

"Ah, well." I shrugged, hoping that my features were still inscrutable, however fevered my mind. My first impulse was to take Minerva into my confidence and talk the whole thing out. But that was the way I had always behaved. Chat, chat, the eternal chat, the cozy confidence with the understanding friend that made even disaster a staple for future exchanges. The negation of life that came from reducing it to the grade of a mere topic, an undulation in the atmosphere between two human beings who might cease to recognize each other without the bond of anecdote. As if talk could save me! I felt suddenly as if I had picked up thirteen cards at a table of experts and had to do my thinking while I arranged my hand. "What can a mother do?"

"Plenty. If Alfreda were going to make such an ass of herself . . ."

"But Alfreda's a girl."

"What difference does that make? I tell you, Ida, you have a whole arsenal of weapons that you've never even peeked into. Well, *peek!* Reach in, dearie, and fight for your life!"

Fortunately, the next of her lunch guests now arrived, and in ten more minutes there were as many ladies gathered in Minerva's living room. Her friends were always polite, but I knew how little congenial they found me. I had no interest in facials or hair, or in resetting jewelry, and I could not join in the violent shrieks of laughter that punctuated their gossip. Yet, being worldly women, they had a certain respect for the social position I *might* have had. "Now if *I* were Mrs. Derrick Hartley," I could read in their curious, appraising stares, "I wouldn't wear that dull black suit or those seed pearls, and I'd certainly do something about my grey hair. And I wonder if I shouldn't find better places to lunch than Minerva

Denison's!" They left me to myself, on the outskirts of their circle, and that day, at least, it gave me a blessed opportunity to think. For I was beginning to make out that the reason Minerva was so upset was precisely that she, like myself, wanted Hugo to marry Alfreda. It was obvious, when one stopped to consider it. Hugo was older and experienced, and Alfreda needed an older and experienced man. He was bright and talented and able to hold his own in any world — all qualities dear to Minerva's heart. And then, too, there was Derrick's fortune. In the past I would not have hesitated to entrust my case to Minerva. I would have proceeded timidly into the thicket of maternal intrusion on the lives of others behind her broad back and stoutly wielded machete. But now I paused. If *two* mothers were in favor of a match, and one as unsubtle as Minerva, what chance had they with game as slippery as Hugo?

I took a big sip of sherry as I saw Alfreda come into the room and then beckoned to her.

"Cousin Ida, what fun!" she exclaimed in her animated style. "I came down early from Columbia because Mummy said you might be here. I'm so glad!"

I scrutinized her carefully. Why should I, who never gambled, have been so sure that there was sense and character behind her manner? Was it simply that she was my mother's great-niece? I told myself again that Hugo loved her. If I lost sight of that, I was lost.

"My dear, how sweet of you. But then Minerva's cook can't be matched on Morningside Heights."

"Ah, but I'm on a diet."

"You, Alfreda? You're too thin now!"

"One's never too thin."

"Now you sound like my Hugo," I ventured. "He's impossible about women. Heels can never be too high or eyebrows too plucked or waists too narrow."

"While *he*, of course, has a man's disposition to eat what he wants and do what he likes!" There was a distinct vibration of resentment in Alfreda's banter. "By the way, how is dear Hugo?"

"I thought you could tell *me*. You can imagine how much an old mother knows of that world."

"Or a young cousin."

"But you and Hugo have so many friends in common!"

"Mrs. Tyson doesn't happen to be one of them."

"Oh, Mrs. Tyson." I shrugged, with what I hoped was a brave show of carelessness, and even tried a French phrase. *"Que voulez-vous?* A man on the rebound is always going to make a fool of himself. I don't take Mrs. Tyson seriously."

"You don't?" Alfreda, usually so restless, seemed quite rigid with astonishment. "I imagine she'd be very sorry indeed to hear *that*. But who, pray, is Hugo rebounding from?"

"Who do you think?"

"Surely you don't mean *me!*"

"Who else?"

"Oh, Cousin Ida!" Alfreda's startled eyes seemed about to fill with tears, and I felt at once that I had been right in all my estimates. "Now, you're going to make me feel badly!"

"Why should you feel badly?" I demanded. "On the contrary, you should feel very proud. In fifteen years of playing the field Hugo's never once fallen in love. Never once! And now he's in up to his neck, and it serves him jolly well right. I've warned him again and again that one day a smart girl would come along who'd have the sense to turn him down flat. As a revenge for all of her sex! Well, now it's happened, and I'm delighted. It'll be the making of him!"

Alfreda's blankness was all that I could have asked. Surprise and concentration had drained everything else out of her thin, pale face. "Then you really think he won't marry Mrs. Tyson?"

"Never! He may be off his head, but not that far off. He'll take it out in other ways. I shouldn't be surprised if it made him president of his company. Oh, he's lazy, my Hugo, but he can work when he wants. And, of course, he's bright. He'll have the greatest auction gallery in the country one day, and it will all be thanks to you!"

If Minerva had been waiting for my signal, she could hardly have announced lunch more opportunely. I smiled brightly and pleasantly at Alfreda, as though our little discussion had been quite completed, and rose to go into the dining room. At lunch, I talked with unwonted animation and even joined in the general discussion about Minerva's new masseur. But I observed out of the corner of my eye that Alfreda was pensive, and I resolved to telephone Mrs. Tyson immediately after lunch. There was no telling how long I would have strength to sustain my chosen role.

When I had followed the pretty, polite little maid upstairs to the living room and found myself alone with Hugo's mistress (for so, in my perhaps old-fashioned way, I thought of her), it was all suddenly more difficult than I had expected. The room was even more perfect than I had feared, and Mrs. Tyson, seated before the Georgian tea service in a black Chinese robe with embroidered scarlet egrets, her small, deft fingers at work, turning on the flame, pouring hot water into the pitcher, picking up the sugar tongs, might have been the smiling, gentle, implacable favorite concubine, momentarily soothing the old, discarded wife. I wondered uncomfortably if what I had always considered as merely silly and kittenish was not essentially feminine. Or, essentially — and to use a word I never used — sexy. If we were going to battle over *that,* it seemed that the weapons must all be hers.

"I don't know how to begin," I murmured. "I seem to be nothing but nerves."

"Oh, so am *I!* I'm so glad we both admit it. How do you like your tea?"

I watched as she poured my cup and saw that she was not putting on her nervousness. She was clearly glad to have something to do with her hands.

"It's the second act of *Traviata,* isn't it?" she continued, her eyes and hands still busy. "Except this time it's the tenor's mother who's come. His father, no doubt, is too busy. Or perhaps doesn't even know. Or very much care." She looked up at last with a small rueful smile. "Of course you want me to give him up."

"I want you to give each other up."

"Thank you!" she exclaimed, with the faintest hint of mockery in her tone. She was not, after all, to be obsequious. "But I don't signify. Hugo is all that matters to you. How could it be otherwise?"

"You must matter to yourself, my dear."

"Or learn to," she agreed, nodding. She was silent a moment as she stirred her tea. "Yes, perhaps I must." She glanced at me now with a sudden, shy curiosity. "You know, Mrs. Hartley, what my first instinct was when you telephoned? To try to charm you. To try to win you over. That's why I put on this Chinese robe. I wanted to seem so cute and homey, with my tea set, and my little fire. But now that you're here, and I look at you, I begin to see things more clearly. If Hugo and I marry, you'll never forgive me, will you? And if we don't — well, I suppose I'll never forgive you. So there we are. We're doomed to be enemies. It's a pity, isn't it? Because otherwise I think we could be such friends!"

"We can still try to understand each other."

"Oh, I guess we'll do that." Her shyness was gone already, and there was a little girl's stubbornness in her sudden pout. "So long as you see, from *my* point of view, that nothing

matters but Hugo's wanting to marry me. It's the only thing
I've ever really cared about in my life." She closed her eyes,
as if to shut me out, before repeating slowly: "The only
thing!"

"But it's not true."

She stared. "What isn't?"

"That Hugo wants to marry you."

She regarded me for a moment with eyes that were half
frightened, half quizzical. "I wouldn't have thought you
could hit so hard," she breathed. "But he's asked me, you
know."

"Yes, but . . ."

"There's no but!" she cried, almost in panic. "He's asked
me to be his wife! Why should I listen to you? If he doesn't
want to go through with it, all he has to do is to come and
tell me. Why not? What rights do *I* have? He doesn't even
have to come. All he has to do is stay away."

"Ah, my dear, isn't that just the reason that he won't?
That you have no rights? Isn't that just what gives him his
obligations?"

Her face clouded over. "You don't know Hugo."

"One of us doesn't."

"Well, I won't fence with you," she replied, turning away
as if suddenly weary of it. "I'm sure you're too smart for
me. Like Hugo. But I can't give him up. If he gives *me*
up, that's that. But if, after my divorce, he comes to this
house and says: 'Kitty, shall we go down to City Hall and get
married?' I'm going. That's all there is to it, Mrs. Hartley.
I'm going. It's ridiculous for you and me to pretend otherwise. You know I'm going!"

"You think, then, you can make him happy?"

"Hugo has taught me that women in love don't care about
making men happy. Perhaps he's right. Perhaps they care
only about possession. But I *think* I care about Hugo's

happiness. And why shouldn't I add to it? Am I such a horror?"

Even at that moment, and even feeling as I felt, I was intensely aware of her charm. She was, indeed, a rare creature. Yet she was right. What did I care about rare creatures?

"Do you think he can be happy without children?"

She did not move, but her voice dropped to a whisper. "What makes you assume he won't have any?"

"I assume that, if it had been possible, you would have had more than two. Everyone knows how much Grinnell wanted a son. Isn't that the reason he's going to marry Mrs. Taylor?"

Mrs. Tyson had turned very white. "You don't pull your punches, do you?" she murmured. "But it may be different with Hugo. "Yes!" she exclaimed, turning on me with glittering eyes. "With Hugo it may well be very different!"

I was silent. I found it very distasteful to have her physical life with Hugo flung in my face, but I had certainly provoked it. Staring into the fire, I thought hard, as hard as I had at Minerva's. I had come armed with the weapons of reason only to blunt them against a wall of passion. But Minerva was right. I had barely begun to turn over the contents of my arsenal. And then, of a sudden, I heard myself talking, and I moved into the light-filled circle before the black pit exposed by parted curtains. It was no doubt significant that in starting, as I thought, to "live," my first metaphor should have been of a stage.

"I shall not ask you to give him up, then," I was saying. "That, manifestly, would be absurd. I shall simply ask you to give me a little time."

"But Mrs. Hartley, time is precious!" she protested. "Time is on your side! How can you ask *me* for it?"

"A very little time. Only a month. You must be very unsure of yourself if you won't give me a month."

"Every woman's unsure of herself," she retorted. "And why should you need a month? You have a month. More, probably. I can't go to Mexico until Grinnell's signed the separation agreement."

"But mightn't he sign it any day?"

She shrugged impatiently. "I suppose it's possible. I don't know."

"And if he signed it today," I pursued, "couldn't you go to Mexico tomorrow? Couldn't you be divorced the day after?"

"But it's so unlikely! If you *knew* how slow Grinnell was about money matters!"

"But it's still possible," I insisted. "That's why I want you to promise me to wait a month before you go."

"But *why?*"

"That's my affair."

"I mean, why should I do it for *you?*"

"Not for me. For the sake of our future relationship. I promise you, Mrs. Tyson, that if you do this for me, I will be a good mother-in-law to you. If you and Hugo marry."

"*If!*" She stood up now and raised her hands awkwardly to her temples. She was evidently so unused to physical demonstrations that she had no accustomed gestures. She was clumsy, pathetic, like a walking doll with a broken spring. "But you obviously have some ghastly plot. Why should I help you? Why should I give you the rope to hang me with? No!"

"One month. Only one." I, too, was standing.

"No, I'm sorry, *no!*"

"Then I must insist." My heart beat furiously as I delivered my ultimatum. "Otherwise Derrick will have to ask Grinnell not to sign your separation agreement for a month." I paused. "Under penalty of his withdrawing from the firm."

She turned away, her hands clasped in despair, and walked slowly to the window. "What can I do?"

I watched her remorsefully. For the first time she struck me as having some resemblance to myself. My old self. For I, too, in earlier days, might have been naïve enough to believe that a woman having the power of which I had boasted would have been content to ask for so little. How easy, after all, it had proved to shoot my dart between the ribs of that beautiful frame. And what a peculiar and horrid feeling it was to be for once on the side of the strong, of the Derricks of this world! Particularly when one's strength was a lie. For Derrick, I knew, would never have endangered his relationship with the least of his partners to get me my month. I had become, like him, a monster.

"A month, then," I said as briskly as I could. "May I trust you for a month? May I have your word?"

"The word of one gagged and bound?"

"Please."

Her back quivered impatiently. "You have it, then."

"Goodbye, Mrs. Tyson."

"I suppose you don't want me to tell Hugo?"

I paused, but I was ready for this. "You must follow your own judgment on that. *After* you have decided which of us it would help most if you do."

In the same excited mood in which I had left Minerva's lunch I went directly from Mrs. Tyson's to a telephone booth where I called Mark Jesmond. He was in conference, but his secretary got him out.

"I want to see you," I said abruptly. "And I don't want Derrick to know about it. It's a question of investing my money. May I come downtown?"

"I'll come up. Shall I go to the house?"

I glanced at my watch. It was late, and Derrick might come in while he was there. "No, could you meet me at the Park Club? I'll only keep you a minute."

I had always had a curious relationship with Mark. He had been quick to make out, in the early days of his courtship of Dorcas, that I counted for nothing where Derrick or Derrick's firm was concerned. He was, however, a suspicious person, and he had been troubled by what he considered the potential behind my passive disposition. He had taken in that I was not dumb. Mark, like all people of undeveloped heart, had to have a scheme to govern every relationship in life. With me it resulted in an attitude of elaborate respect that sometimes bordered on the sarcastic and that was in noticeable contrast to the casual treatment that I received at the hands of his wife. But as the years passed, and as Mark never observed the smallest attempt on my part to unseat him as Derrick's major domo, and as he had many occasions to appreciate my help in smoothing over Dorcas' emotional crises, he began to relax and even, ultimately, to enjoy my company. Mark had been so violently competitive all his life, so sure that the world would yield him nothing that he did not snatch, that it must have been oddly soothing, for a change, to discuss his fears and hopes with a detached but listening woman who accepted him without being fooled. Indeed, there were moments when I suspected that Mark credited me with plumbing his nature to the depths and of being as great a cynic as himself. Such moments were signalized by what I interpreted as a conspiratorial wink.

But there was no time for his demiconfidences that afternoon in the stiff, still little parlor at my club where I received him. We sat in a corner in two high-backed chairs, and Mark, who loved to sprawl and slump and who hated a female atmosphere, semed as tense and briefly motionless as a ruffled bird.

"It's about my Denison-Adler shares," I began. "I've come to a decision."

"You want to sell them?" He nodded his own affirmative

answer. "Good. I've always said they were a poor invest-ment. It's the kind of business where you must either con-trol or get out. I know you've had sentimental reasons for hanging on to them, but sentiment is a poor business-man."

I waited until he had finished. "You said control or get out. I think that's good advice. I want to control. Oh, not just me, of course. All the Denisons together."

Mark rubbed his mouth and chin with the palm of his hand, a sign of cogitation. Like Derrick, he hated to betray surprise. "Have you had a tip?"

"Let's put it that I have. Do you know how to go about picking up the necessary stock?"

"Part of my job, part of my job. To know every company in your portfolio." I knew, however, that Mark would have said this even had he never considered Denison-Adler be-fore. "As a matter of fact, one of the Adlers, Leonie, just died. Yes, we might pick it up. Let's see, how much would we need? There are about nine thousand outstanding shares, is that it?"

That was the thing about Mark. When you most thought he was bluffing, it turned out that he wasn't. "Ten," I re-plied, for I had already reviewed the matter with Christo-pher. "As you know, I have twelve hundred shares. My brother Christopher has two thousand. He's only kept them because of Hugo and because I've asked him to. Minerva Denison has another five hundred. Hugo has three hundred. I figure that, between us, we only need another thousand for control."

Mark made some jottings on the back of his newspaper. "That seems to be it. But, of course, the moment you start buying, you'll drive the price up."

"Can't I do it in a broker's name?"

"Of course. But even so, in a small company, the least

activity in the market will tip off the management. It may cost you a packet of dough before you're through."

"What do you call a packet of dough?"

Mark scratched his head and made more doodles on his paper. "Hard to say. It depends what resistance we run into. But I know a bit about the company. I doubt if the stock would more than double. But at that it would cost you two hundred and fifty grand."

"Very well. Two hundred and fifty."

"Mrs. Hartley! May I ask what you propose to use for money?"

"You can sell what I have that's not in trust and borrow the rest. Against my inheritance from Geraldine."

"Aren't you plunging rather deeply?"

"Suppose I am. I know what I'm doing. You needn't worry. I've thought it all out."

"But, Mrs. Hartley, I *must* worry. Please remember that I'm not only your son-in-law, but your financial adviser."

"Yes, and I respect your financial advice. Extremely. But, you see, today, I'm not asking for it."

Mark smiled the fixed little smile that he reserved for combat. "Even so, it's my duty to warn you that this may be a rash step."

"I can always go to my brother."

His smile widened instantly to a grin. "In other words, I must put up or shut up? Is that it, Mrs. Hartley?"

"Well, I'd never express it so rudely. But I'm absolutely determined to do this thing. And I've come to you because nobody would be smarter about picking up the shares for me. But if you won't do it, I shall have to go to others, that's all."

Mark now laughed and, leaning over the table, scratched the top of his head with all ten fingers. It was a most unattractive gesture.

"If it's possible to get your stock," he exclaimed, looking up, "I'll get it for you. But don't blame me if you're sold out on your own auction block! With Hugo at the gavel!"

Mark was good to his word. When he gave in, he gave in gracefully, for he correctly assessed that my determination was something new and serious. In the following two weeks he telephoned me every morning to report his progress. He had started off with a great coup, having picked up three hundred shares from the Leonie Adler estate at considerably less than true value, but immediately afterwards the market stiffened, and soon it appeared that control of the gallery was going to cost every penny that he had anticipated. In addition, he had to communicate with Minerva and my brother to be sure that they did not dump their shares. I became so nervous that I could no longer concentrate on anything. All of the capital of my resolution seemed to have been expended in a single afternoon. I accepted any chance invitation for cocktails in order to avoid meeting Hugo at home. I was in terror that he would cross-examine me about Mrs. Tyson or Alfreda before I should be in a position to confront him with my plan. I do not know what might have happened had he not been sent at just this time on a business trip to Boston. Never would I have believed it possible that I should have contemplated with such satisfaction the departure of my favorite child.

On the night of his return, a week later, he dined with Derrick and me. He rarely so honored us, for his social calendar was very full, and family evenings were apt to be constrained. Derrick always tried to prove that he was not an indifferent parent by pushing the conversation into the field of galleries and pictures, and Hugo, sensing immediately the basic contempt under his father's casually expressed curiosity, inevitably bristled. That night, however, Derrick at least forbore till dessert.

"I see Archie Sturtevant is dead. He had quite a few old masters, didn't he? I suppose you'll be picking them up now and selling them at triple value to some fool Greek."

"Fakes," Hugo said briefly without looking up from his plate. "The lot of them. I know the collection."

"You mean, you've dined there?"

"You ought to know by now, Father, there are very few houses where I haven't dined."

"I never see how you return your obligations."

"I don't regard the Sturtevants as an obligation," Hugo retorted loftily. "If it is, I discharge it by going there."

"And by calling their pictures fakes?"

"Well, if they are, they are. That's a matter of principle. I quite realize that stockbrokers are more moral than other people, but we dealers have our little game, too. And little games have little rules."

"I wasn't casting aspersions on dealers, Hugo."

"Of course you were. You always are. But it's quite all right. You needn't worry about *my* feelings. I have learned to be stoical before the rumble of paternal anathemas."

"You take me for granted," Derrick protested, irked. "That's one of the reasons I'm the way I am. You *all* take me for granted."

"And what's wrong with the way you are?" Hugo looked from Derrick to me with an air of bright surprise. "I *like* the way you are. You and I regard each other from the top of fortified turrets. We're both well defended, so we don't fear a sortie. Occasionally, under a flag of truce, we talk. It's as much as most fathers and sons can say. What I respect about you is that you've never pretended we had more than that."

I thought that Derrick would lose his temper at this, but

I underrated him. It was even possible that he took Hugo's analysis as a compliment. He simply grunted and returned to the original subject.

"Does it matter if the pictures are fakes," he continued, "so long as they're beautiful to look at?"

"My dear father, surely you know that authenticity is everything today?"

"Do you mean that if you had the choice of a bad Renoir or a beautiful attribution ...?"

"I'd take the bad Renoir," Hugo interrupted briskly. "Certainly. I'm a dealer."

"Then I suppose you went into the right business. We won't have to worry when your shareholders elect you president."

"You needn't be so sarcastic. I *may* be president one day."

"I'm not in the least sarcastic. I shall be extremely surprised if you're not elected at the next annual meeting."

"And what do you mean by *that?*"

"Simply that at the rate your mother's been picking up stock, she should be in a position by then to elect you."

So there it was. Mark had betrayed me. Had I really believed that he wouldn't? But as the atmosphere tightened around the table, as I felt, even with averted eyes, Hugo's burning stare on my cheek, I knew, with a sudden inner peace, that I was capable now of going through with what I had started.

"Mother! What's all this about?"

"Your father's perfectly right. I *have* been picking up Denison-Adler stock. Quite a bit of it. I think it's time control returned to the family."

"But you never told me!"

"She never told me, either," Derrick intervened. "The only reason I found out was that Mark thought it his duty to warn me how deeply she was plunging."

"I particularly told him not to!" I exclaimed. "I shall know better than to use Mark as my broker again!"

"Look, Ma! Will you kindly tell me what this is all about? Why do you want to control the gallery?"

I turned to meet Hugo's eyes, which were fixed on me with a startled, glittering stare.

"Because I want you to run it," I answered in a level tone. "When I have all the stock I need, I shall turn it over to you. With no obligation on your part. You can do anything you want to with it. You can sell it or give it away or use it for wallpaper. That's entirely up to you."

"But, Ma!" he protested, with a groan of mingled despair and appreciation. "You should have asked me before you started! How do you know I even *want* the damn gallery?"

"That's your affair," I insisted. "Mine is that I've made up my mind to give you the stock. Don't worry. I have my reasons. They might not seem adequate to everybody, but they seem adequate to me."

"Suppose I refuse it?"

"The shares will be registered in your name and mailed to you. After that, I shall have nothing further to do with them."

There were several moments of uneasy silence at this. Hugo was actually flushed, and I had time to reflect that my calculations had been exact. He was deeply moved. All his irritation, even his anger, at my unwarranted intrusion had dissolved before the realization that I was doing something for him and for him alone, something even at the expense of Dorcas and Mark.

"You don't care, then," Derrick asked me angrily, "that you're giving all your stock in Denison-Adler to *one* of your children?"

"You can equalize it in your will. My estate hardly matters compared to yours."

"But that means you're *forcing* me to write a new will! You're dictating the terms."

"Look, Dad," Hugo intervened, "as long as you've got to do your will over, why not take me out altogether?"

"How do you know you're even in it?"

"I don't. But as long as Mother seems stuck on giving me this stock, let it be my share of both your estates. Let me sink or swim with it. Dorcas will never miss it. Everyone knows you have millions."

"Everyone knows no such thing!"

"Oh, come, Dad, don't play games with me. If Ma wants to give me the gallery, what do you care? Keep your money for Dorcas. I don't want it. I don't begrudge Mark a penny of it. Obviously, you have more confidence in him than you've ever had in your own son."

Derrick glowered down the table at Hugo. There was a mixture of sincerity and impudence in the latter's tone that must have been hard for him to bear. "Maybe I've found him more sympathetic than my own son," he grumbled. "More considerate. More affectionate!"

"Maybe he's polished the apple more brightly!"

"Hugo!" I protested.

"I'll have you know I resent that, young man!"

But there was no controlling Hugo now. "What right has he to go blabbing to you what Mother does with her money?" he demanded. "What the hell business is that of his?"

"I think it's entirely natural for him to want to protect his wife's inheritance."

"His wife's inheritance!" Hugo sneered. "After all he's made out of your firm? After all you've given Dorcas? Mark Jesmond has one hell of a nerve objecting to anything Mother does for me. If I had a penny for every buck he's made out of both of you, I'd be a rich man. And on top of it all, he's angling for your job! Ask any of your sacred partners what he and Dorcas have been saying about *you!*"

"I think I can handle my own firm, thank you very much," Derrick retorted with massive dignity. "And if that's all the advice you have to give me for one evening, I hope you and your mother will excuse me while I retire to my study for coffee."

I waited until Derrick was out of the room and then turned in distress to Hugo. "You should *never* have said that about Mark wanting his job!"

"But it's true. I heard it at the Tysons'. The whole firm knows it."

"It doesn't make the slightest difference. You hurt your father's feelings. And what's the good of that?"

"Oh, shucks, he didn't believe it, anyway." Hugo put his elbows heavily on the table and rested his chin in his hands. "And why should I care if he does? Let him and Mark fight it out. He can cope with Mark."

"Are you so sure?"

"I'm so sure. But let's talk about you." He laughed, as if in despair of making sense of his subject. "Poor, dear, ridiculous, scheming old you. I know what you've been up to, mind you. I know all about your little ultimatum to Kitty. And your lunch at Minerva Denison's. And now this stock deal. Honestly, Ma, I don't know whether to laugh or cry. One resents interference in a mother. But interference on such a mammoth, such a gargantuan scale! There's something sublime about it. Something beyond resentment. My God, one can only gape before such a mother!"

"I'd do it all again," I said stubbornly.

"To have me marry Alfreda? To have me become head of an auction gallery and sell perforated wood to an idiot world as Louis XV? Is it so vital that I should do that? What's happened to you, Ma?" He gazed at me now in a speculative mood, slowly shaking his head. "When did you lose your doubts? Where on earth did you ever acquire this new serenity? Where did you learn to play God?"

"If you only *knew* how little it was that," I said with a shudder. "I'm nothing but a mass of frozen fears. But somewhere in that igloo there's one small candle of hope. No matter how much I tremble and chatter, it won't go out. Sometimes I think it's about all I have to live for."

"That I should marry Alfreda and live happily ever after?"

"Yes!" I stared at him gravely until the sarcasm faded from his eyes. "Yes," I repeated with a firmness that belied my desperation. "I may be an old fool, but I want the satisfaction of feeling that I've done one thing for one member of my family. I love you, my darling." When I saw the mist now in those hard eyes, I suddenly sobbed. We were to have a scene, he and I, for all his detestation of them. Well, why not? I covered my face with my hands as I sobbed again. "I love you more than anybody in the world. And if you marry Mrs. Tyson, I'll die, that's all. I'll simply die."

I looked up, after a considerable silence, and found him smiling.

"Well, I guess the least I can do, after that, is marry Alfreda!" he exclaimed. "Or at least try. In all good faith. I'm sure she won't have me."

"I'm sure she will!"

"Well, if she does, it's because you've sold me."

We both stood up, and I put my hands on his shoulders. "Hugo, dearest, you won't be doing it just for me?"

"Ah, now you're greedy." He took my hands and held them tightly in his. His old, cynical frown had returned. "If you really believe in a thing, why should it matter for whose sake it's being done?"

"Because it's for your happiness!"

"Yours and mine."

"Oh, no, darling, yours!"

"Can't I be allowed the pleasure of thinking that I'm doing something for my mother? After all, you care so much about doing something for *me*."

"Oh, Hugo!" I moaned. "Don't spoil it!" I saw with dread that his lips were tightening into the old look of suspicion. "You know in your heart that you love that girl!"

"Now who's spoiling it?" he demanded sharply. "Now who wants to have her cake and eat it? You've moved into my life like a bulldozer, and now you want to pretend that you haven't even been there. Or if you have, that your intrusion has been so subtle that I've never even been aware of your elfin feet! For what do you take me, a complete idiot? If you expect to maneuver men, do you think you can start at *your* age and with *me*?"

"Oh, Hugo, Hugo," I moaned again, but he was relentless.

"I want you to learn the courage of your convictions," he continued in the same bitter, deliberate tone. "I will go tonight to Kitty and break off with her. It will be a sticky business, but at least it will be brief." He smiled sourly, "I've done it once before, after all. And tomorrow I shall call on Alfreda and tell her that I'm turning over a new leaf. That I expect to become a great auctioneer and be appointed ambassador to Italy before I'm fifty. I shall then propose to her before the shock has worn off. And I will do it all for you."

"But will you be *happy*, darling?"

"Ah, now we want the moon!" He turned to the door and seemed about to depart without further word. But then he paused, For Hugo was merciful. Despite all his hardness he was the most merciful of my family. "Well, I'll tell you this," he said, turning back to me. "I'll tell you just this, and then bid you good night. I'll *probably* be happier than I would have been had you left me to my own devices. Probably. There. 'Probably' will have to content you. But what more, for the love of Mike, do you really want for your nickel? And since when have any of us spent more than that?"

17

Derrick: 1950

DERRICK sat moodily in his square grey office, late on a
Friday afternoon, and contemplated the surface of a desk
bare but for a spotless grey blotter, a clean crystal ash tray
and two photographs in twin gold frames, of Dorcas garden-
ing in a sloppy straw hat and of Derrick Granberry in football
clothes. Everything was ready for Monday morning; even
his secretary had gone. But Mark, with whom he was to drive
to Dorcas' that night, was keeping him waiting, Mark, who,
a scant few years ago, would have dropped any job in the
office so much as to light his father-in-law's cigar. Now, apparently, Mark found it more expedient to keep impressing
him with the burden of his work and responsibilities that interfered with such minor accommodations. Derrick impatiently jerked a drawer open to get out the weekly market
report and then slammed it shut again. Why should he have
to give any color to his inactivity? Why should he pretend
to Mark that he had *not* been kept waiting?

"I'll have to make him understand what a cocky little
bastard he's getting to be," he exclaimed aloud. "And I'll
have to make Dorcas understand it, too. If they think they
can talk about *me* behind my back!" He fixed a wrathful eye
on Dorcas' picture. The clumsy pose, the silly hat, that only
a month ago had seemed so lovable, struck him now as simply
clumsy and simply silly. "At least I have Derrick," he muttered, shifting his glance to his grandson. "Whatever happens, I don't think they can shake my hold on *him*."

He thought with a faint discomfort of the last years of Linn Tremain and how it had been necessary to wrest the reins of leadership from his shaking hands. But they *had* been shaking; that was the point. Derrick stared now at his own clenched fists, held stiffly up before his face. There was no trembling there, and when there was, he would be the first to see it. The worst of aging was in the false assumptions of younger people. He had always cared about details, but now, undoubtedly, his care was stamped as fussiness. Now . . .

"Are you about ready, sir?"

Mark, a coat over his arm, stood in the doorway, as if Derrick would, of course, have been waiting for him, as if he could have nothing to keep him so late on a Friday afternoon but the fact that he had made an engagement to drive his busy son-in-law to the country. Even Mark's "sir," which he always alternated with "Derrick," sounded sarcastic.

"I'll be with you in a minute. Sit down."

"But you say you have to get back to town tonight. We won't have much time for dinner if we don't go now."

"Sit down. I want to ask you something."

Mark strolled in and sat in the chair by the desk, putting his leg promptly over the arm. He always made himself ostentatiously at home. It was his way of subtracting from any excess of deference that might otherwise have been read into his manner. Somewhere, in the curly hair, grey now, before his fiftieth year, in the diminutive stature, the round stomach, the bright, staring eyes and the eternally rumpled suits, lurked the legal boy wonder who had come out of the woods to astound his elders and who paused now, undecided, at the threshold of an age in life that compelled him to choose another role. Mark, Derrick surmised, would pass directly to the judicial. From a pompous cherub he would become a dimpled Nestor.

"Two of the new men have desks in the research library," Derrick began. "I asked them why, and they said you put them there."

"Nothing escapes you long, does it, sir? I think those desks went in last night. You know what our space problem is. The alternative was putting them in the reception hall. But don't worry, sir. I'm working on it. I'll get my space, if I have to go up on the roof and hire the water tank!"

"That's not the point," Derrick cut in. "The point is that we should not take on new men till we have the space for them. I have always made it clear that the research library is only for research. Why was the problem not referred to me?"

"Oh, come, Derrick, you don't want to be pestered by every detail in the office, do you? Besides, you've been taken up with Hugo's engagement. I hated to bother you."

Derrick glanced keenly at Mark, but his face revealed nothing. Perhaps it revealed too little, as if he were trying to hide something. Two things struck him disagreeably about Mark's answer, first, that Mark knew perfectly well that he was very much interested in just such details, and second, that Mark knew equally well that he was not in the least taken up with Hugo's engagement.

"The assignment of office space goes to the very guts of office morale," he retorted, getting up to pace the carpet. "I thought you knew my principles about that."

"But, Derrick, it's only temporary . . ."

"It shouldn't even be that!" He paused to stare Mark down, but when he saw the gleam of repressed exasperation in his son-in-law's eyes, he turned abruptly and walked to the window. How well he knew that look, the look of the junior who must suffer patiently the rantings of his tiresome but ultimately to be replaced superior! He felt the anger thickening in his throat. Of course he ought to drop the whole foolish matter, but he couldn't. "I know that people look on me as a hard taskmaster," he grumbled, "but I have to be, if I'm to look after my dependents. People judge these things so superficially. Everyone thought old Linn Tremain was the soul of benevolence because he used to fill up his car with young men when he left the office. I never have. I like to use my drive home as a time to think. But Tremain never gave a damn what those young men were paid or how many were herded into a room or whether they ever got a decent vacation. He thought they were privileged to help *him* make money!" His sudden awareness that he had told all this to Mark many times before intensified his irritation. "Nobody bothers to remember that it was I who arranged the highest salaries and the longest vacations of any brokerage house in New York! Oh, no, a cheap gesture of generosity is all they care about, a charming smile, a 'Get in, my dear fellow, get *in!*' " And he waved his arm jerkily in crude imitation of his late uncle-in-law's courteous gesture.

"Well, if the lecture is over," demanded Mark with the sudden impertinence that he felt to be part of his charm, "shall we go to the country?"

At once Derrick felt the relief of the explosion of his temper. He knew — oh, how *well* he knew — that it was not a time for it, that it was late in the day and that he was fretted. But one had, after all, to have *some* indulgences. "You will oblige me," he said gruffly, "by seeing that those desks are removed tonight."

Mark had been in the Navy during the war, a lieutenant in the office of the Judge Advocate General, and he had a uniform answer whenever he wished to indicate that Derrick had been arbitrary. He would jump to his feet, salute and cry "Aye, aye, sir!" But now he did not even do that. Instead, he rose, with a faint sigh and a curious shadow of a smile, and walked to the door.

"I'll see to it, sir," he said quietly as he left the room.

Derrick, alone, sat back in his armchair and stared out the window over the vast panorama of the harbor. He wondered, detached, to whom it would matter if he should die there and then. It struck him again that it was not growing old that mattered, but having people *think* one was growing old. The moment Mark began to suspect him of fussiness and repetitiousness, he *became* fussy and repetitious.

"All done, sir." It was Mark again on the threshold, cheerful and smiling. "Shall we go now?"

Derrick was silent on the drive to Glen Cove as he completed his strategy for the evening. He had to find out if there was any basis for Hugo's rumor of the Jesmonds' treachery, and his plan was to ask Dorcas what the other office wives were saying about him. He had picked the best and the worst of them to ask her about. Evie Lockhart was the troublemaker of Hartley and Dodge. She drove her husband's career from the back seat, convinced that she was helping him with little sniping attacks on the senior partners at cocktail parties. Everybody, including her husband, realized that she was his greatest obstacle. Sophie Besant, on the contrary, married to a man who might well have competed with Derrick himself had it not been for recurrent nervous trouble, had been a model of tact and loyalty to the firm and had even assisted Derrick in persuading her husband to accept a position of lesser responsibility. If Dorcas' answers to what these women were saying did not vary in some marked degree, she would have to be lying.

His plan made up, he could almost enjoy the drive. Most of the miseries of life lay in indecision. Looking at Mark, he lit a cigar.

"I can never understand why a man as busy as yourself lives in the country."

"You know your daughter."

"But Dorcas would do anything for you, Mark. We all know that."

"She's happier in the country. She has her garden."

Did he mean it? Did he care? Derrick reflected that he still did not understand Mark. The Mark of the long low small-windowed farmhouse that cost a fortune in maintenance, and which he had stuffed with Americana too good for its interior, did not seem to go with the urban Mark who lived for his work and whose idea of relaxation was a baseball game followed by a night of drinking in a smoky bar. Perhaps it was because farmhouses and Americana were now so fashionable. Perhaps it was a relic of Mark's rustic New England youth. Or perhaps he really loved the house and simply wanted Dorcas to be happy. It was a mistake, Derrick reflected, to assume that cold people had to be always cold. It was a mistake that many persons had made about himself.

"I bet Hugo and Alfreda never bury themselves in the country," he remarked.

"No, they're real city mice."

"They're taking an apartment in Fifty-fifth Street, only two blocks away. Dorcas had better look to her laurels. A new daughter-in-law can be very attractive to an old man."

"Nobody's ever going to take Dorcas' place in your heart, Derrick, so don't kid yourself."

The assured ring of Mark's laugh brought back Derrick's darkest thoughts of the afternoon.

"I wouldn't count on that too much," he said dryly. He glanced at his son-in-law, but the latter appeared not to be listening. The big car was turning into his driveway, and they could see Dorcas on the lawn playing croquet with her children in the late spring twilight.

He had selected the moment when Mark was mixing cocktails which would give his son-in-law the opportunity, if he

chose it, to dodge any questions and leave them to his wife.
Derrick would know, of course, what to think if he did so.
And Dorcas, who had a light head, always lost what little
subtlety she had after the first drink. Seated in his accustomed chair by the fireplace under the serried rows of pewter
pots and pans, he did not even pretend to listen as she talked
about her girls.

"Dorcas, I want to ask you something," he inserted firmly
in the first pause. "And I want you to be very frank. I don't
relish talking about personal matters, but there are times
when it has to be done. Your mother has never taken the
smallest interest in the firm, and I have survived the few
persons who used to advise me. I must depend more and
more on you and Mark to keep me in touch, not with what's
going on — I think I shall always know that — but with
what people *say* is going on. Now that I'm in sight of seventy,
I can't expect . . ."

"But, Daddy, no one would dream you were a day over
sixty!" Dorcas broke in. "Mark and I never think of you as
old, do we, Mark?"

"I didn't say I was old," Derrick replied testily, glancing
at Mark's unturned back. "I never use that term. I said I
was in sight of seventy. I am. I'm sixty-six. The digit is a
fact. What others think about it is merely label. But labels
have their importance in this world. I can't expect people
to go on confiding in me the way they used to. I'm beginning
to seem venerable to them. Therefore, I'm going to need you
and Mark to tell me what people in the office are saying. Do
they think I keep too much in my hands? Do they think I
should accept a smaller share of the profits?" He paused
significantly. "Or do they think I should retire altogether?"

He had been careful to break the question into three parts,
which gave him time to study Dorcas' reaction. The first

thing he noticed was that she was evidently collecting herself. She was sitting very still, and her cheeks had turned a mottled pink. Her first movement had been towards Mark, but the sudden silence at the bar table where he had been mixing the second drink seemed to act as a warning, for she looked back at her father and even managed a smile.

"Who in the world do you think would be talking like that?" she asked in her own peculiar version of a light tone. "And who do you think would have the impudence to say it to *me?*"

"Evie Lockhart," he replied promptly.

The relaxed slump of Dorcas' shoulders followed too quickly not to be relief. And her laugh was too loud. "Mark, shall we *tell* Daddy?"

Mark turned around for the first time, with his habitual grin. "You mean about the boarding school? Yes, I think your father's big enough to enjoy that."

"Evie asks everyone how long you're going to keep us in boarding school. She says all the partners are like little boys with stiff necks from smoking up the chimney."

"And a jag from drinking cider after lights," Mark added.

"Do people agree with her?" Derrick asked, unsmiling.

"Well, you know how people are, Daddy. They always laugh at things like that. No matter how much they basically admire you. They're afraid of seeming stuffy."

"But do they talk generally that way?"

"Oh, *generally,* I wouldn't know."

"What about Sophie Besant? Has *she* said anything?"

Once again Dorcas glanced at her husband, and Derrick thought he caught the faint, half-irritated shrug of his son-in-law's shoulders, as though Mark were counseling his wife that the handling of her father, was, after all, her responsibility.

"Well, Sophie is devoted to you, of course," Dorcas began

more guardedly, "but she *is* rather a fuss-pot. She keeps taking me aside and murmuring how tired you look. And telling me how sorry she's always been that she didn't make Harold retire before the younger men started to laugh at him. Not, of course," she added lamely, "that anyone laughs at you, Daddy."

"They're still careful to hide it if they do," Derrick said dryly. He was convinced already that Hugo had spoken the truth. It faintly surprised him that where he had anticipated an almost unbearable spasm of pain, he should be feeling instead only the first tremors of what threatened to be a harmless, if nauseating anger. Dorcas with her mottled cheeks, her messy hair, her big, anxious eyes, had ceased in one searing flash to be his principal link with humanity. More simply, perhaps, she had ceased to be *he*, and what was not he had to be his enemy. Her worried eyes reminded him now of her mother's, and the wrath that mounted within him might have been only a bigger brother of the wrath which he had felt years before at Ida's clinging loyalty to the household gods of her childhood. But Ida, at least, had never preferred another man; Ida had never lied. Ida would never have twisted the innocent words of poor, loyal Sophie Besant, the one woman in the office family on whom Derrick could rely, into a warning that he should step down before he was senile. There was something horrible in Dorcas' crudity; it betrayed the violence of her eagerness to push her husband forward. She was too excited to concoct poisons; she could only reach for a club. She had even forgotten her initial position that nobody talked to her about her father!

"Such are the opinions of others." Derrick dismissed them in a hard, level tone. "Let us now get down to basics. What is yours? And what is Mark's?"

"You know mine, sir," Mark said in his easy drawl, coming across the room with the cocktail shaker. "I think you're as fit as you were the day I walked into your office and told you why you had to make me a partner!"

"Surely, Daddy, you can't think Mark and I would have any other opinion!" Dorcas grasped quickly at the cue so handed to her. "The only thing we worry about is that you're not having more of the good time you've earned."

"In what way?"

"Well, you never take a winter vacation, for example."

"I detest Florida, and I'm too old to ski."

"You've never taken one of those world cruises that all your friends go on now."

"To see Hong Kong from the deck of a steamer while I'm dummy? You know how I feel about *them*."

"You haven't even developed a hobby."

"My work is my hobby."

"But, Daddy, that's just the point. It *can't* be. Everyone should have a hobby *outside* his office."

"What's Mark's?"

Dorcas paused in momentary perplexity. "Well, if he doesn't have one, it's high time he did! Read any article about geriatrics. You have to *prepare* for retirement!"

"But suppose I don't mean to retire?"

"*Ever?*"

"Ever. Suppose I mean to die in harness like Uncle Linn Tremain?"

"Oh, but, Daddy, that's such a mistake!" She looked despairingly at Mark, but he had returned to the bar table to deposit the shaker. The very stolidity of that back seemed to warn her to drop the subject, but Dorcas was too excited to take his hint. Besides, she had taken a big sip of her second cocktail. "You should learn how to enjoy life while you still can. There's no point being obstinate about old age."

"But I do enjoy life."

"You can't expect to work forever!"

"I don't. One day, presumably, I shall die."

"You might think a little bit about Mummy," she said, almost crossly now. "Maybe *she'd* like to travel and see the world while she's still well enough to enjoy it."

"Your mother, like all her friends, may look forward to a long, healthy widowhood in which to enjoy such things."

"I mean, enjoy them with *you*. She was saying only last week how she'd love to see India."

"What are you proposing, Dorcas?" Derrick demanded in a sharper tone. "That I retire from business and orbit the globe?"

"Oh, Daddy, you're so extreme. I never said a word about retiring, did I, Mark? Of course you shouldn't retire. I simply suggested that you take more time off and enjoy yourself. What's so wrong with that?"

"Mark will tell you what's wrong with that, won't you, Mark?" Derrick exclaimed, allowing the first note of sarcasm to slide into his tone. Mark picked it up immediately and turned around to direct at his father-in-law the fixed, small smile with which he always covered embarrassment. "Mark knows that there's no halfway about these things," Derrick continued, staring at him. "When you're the senior partner of a firm like ours, you don't journey to India to see temples, do you, Mark? And you don't take time off to spend the winter in Florida. You either stay here and do the job or you turn it over to somebody who can!"

"Well, what's so sacred about doing the job?" Dorcas demanded stridently. "It isn't as if anybody was suggesting that you shouldn't remain on as a limited partner. Or that you should take your name out of the firm. Why should you do all the work at your age? Haven't you earned some rest? And, as for the profits, what earthly difference would a cut make in *your* tax bracket?"

"Oh, you're suggesting I take a cut, too?"

"Dorcas!" Mark interposed warningly. "Why do we have to get into that?"

"Because I asked her, damn it!" Derrick suddenly thundered. In the awed silence that followed his outbreak Dorcas looked in bewilderment from her father to her husband. She might have been wondering how she had been maneuvered in so short a time into a passionate espousal of the very retirement that she had just said she was not proposing. But neither Goneril nor Regan had subtle natures, and Derrick had seen, before it was too late, what would happen to his hundred knights.

"All I was saying," she grumbled, like a fretful child, "was that it's time somebody relieved you of some of the load."

"Somebody like Mark, for example?"

"Well, why *not?*"

"So there we are at last!" Derrick cried, rising from his seat. "You might have had the candor to tell me at the beginning. You want to get rid of me to make room for Mark!"

Dorcas' mouth became a dark circle of open dismay. "Oh, Daddy," she breathed in a horrified half whisper. "How can you even *say* such a thing?"

"I must say, sir," her husband echoed, "you're going a bit far."

"Not as far as I intend to go!" Derrick answered wrathfully. "I had very good reasons, before I came down this weekend, to believe that you had both been deliberately undermining my position in the firm. With hints here and insinuations there. If you had owned up to it, I should have forgiven you both. After all, I know what ambition is. I, too, had to clear out an older generation. But what I don't think I'll ever be able to forgive is what happened here tonight. The way you lied to me, Dorcas! And your nauseating hypocrisy about your mother's happiness! As if you'd ever thought one moment in your life about your mother's happiness!" He turned now on Mark, whose fixed, foolish little smile had become hard and stale. "And the way you let her do it!" he snapped at him. "The way you stood there and let her do it, despising her all the time for making such a hash of it. But you wouldn't stop her because you thought me so besotted a father I wouldn't notice! Well, you've miscalculated, Mr. Jesmond. For once in your life, you've miscalculated!"

The most terrible aspect of the scene, as Derrick recalled it later, was the speed with which all three of them adjusted to their new relationship. He had read that human beings were infinitely adaptable, but perhaps their adaptability was simply the measure of their superficiality. They did not love as dogs loved, or even as eagles. Dorcas was thirty-eight years old; for more than half Derrick's life she had been the person for whom he had cared most in the world, and yet in the course of a handful of minutes he could accept a situation where his paramount feeling for her was contempt and hers for him hatred. Worse still, there was more than acceptance in that moment of crisis; there was a certain wry satisfaction. Derrick was experiencing a dizzy, but not wholly unpleasureable sensation in being swept along by the hissing, churning tide of his temper; it was a catharsis in which cleansing and destruction were indistinguishable. He knew that the evening would be followed by heartache and loneliness, but this very knowledge made him reach for heavier weapons, as if to merit his hanging at least for a sheep.

"How dare you speak to Mark that way?" Dorcas cried shrilly. "Hasn't he been your slave long enough? Hasn't he had to put up with you in his home as well as his office? Isn't it enough that he's had to defer to you twenty-four hours a day for the past fourteen years? Why shouldn't he expect to succeed you after all that? Isn't it human? Isn't it natural?

You're the one who makes everybody seem mean and grasping by holding on forever!"

"Forever! At sixty-six? And in a firm that owes me everything? You ought to be ashamed to call yourself my daughter!"

"Your daughter!" she sneered bitterly, and Derrick would not have dreamed before that evening that her face could be so ugly to him. "What have I ever been to you but a possession? A convenience? Haven't I sacrificed my husband to you? My children?" Half hysterically she appealed to Mark. "Haven't I, darling? Haven't you told me so often enough?"

Mark, however, turned away abruptly, as though from an importunate child. "This is a private fight," he said peevishly, "between you and your father. Leave me out of it."

If anything could have made Derrick angrier, it was Mark's leaving Dorcas under fire. "There's nothing private about this fight, Mark!" he warned him. "You're in it, too. I want you to be quite clear that I have no intention of retiring while you're around to succeed me. And that I plan to remove you from the management committee tomorrow!" Derrick walked over to the table and struck it with his fist. "If I have to split the firm right down the middle, I'll split it! But I don't anticipate that will be necessary. I think I know, senile as you may consider me, on whose side most of the brotherhood will be!"

Mark gave a short, quick little sigh and then shook his head rapidly several times, as if to deplore his father-in-law's violence. He plunged his hands in his pockets and stared at the floor and finally whistled. It occurred to Derrick that it was the pose of a country boy who has just let a big fish get away. Yet surely this time it was genuine. What other fashion did Mark have of expressing so unprecedented a disappointment? He was simply facing the crash of the greatest hope of his life.

"Do you think we have to make all our decisions tonight?" Mark asked in a tone that was suddenly mild. "Over the stimulus of two rather potent cocktails?"

But Dorcas had been completely demoralized by Derrick's attack on her husband. She sank into a chair and buried her face in her hands. When she looked up at her father, the hate in her eyes was alarming. "You think you can get on without Mark?" she fairly screamed. "You don't know what you're about! All the customers, all the partners respect him far more than they respect you! You'll see!"

"Exactly," Derrick said grimly. "I'll see. We'll all see."

"He's done your job for years!" she went on in the same wild tone. "He's covered up for you, apologized for you, smoothed over matters that you've messed up! He's stood between your disgusting egotism and all the people who resent it. And now he's getting the gratitude from you that he might have expected. He's getting the treatment that Uncle Linn got, that Mummy got and that now I'm getting. What a fool I was ever to have expected anything more of you!"

"And what a fool Mark was," Derrick retorted brutally, "to have married *you* for the little he's going to get out of *me*."

Dorcas stared at her father in open horror and then again covered her face with her hands. She leaned over, and her big frame was shaken with dry sobs. Mark went over quickly to sit beside her; he put his arms around her and whispered something in her ear that Derrick could not catch. But she shook her head violently, and her sobs now burst out. Mark stroked her back clumsily; it was an odd sight. Suddenly he turned on Derrick, with more curiosity than dislike in his eyes.

"What a monster you are," he said in a soft, speculative tone. "What a real monster. Thank God in Heaven you've taught me not to care about the firm the way you care!"

He turned again to Dorcas and continued stroking her back, crooning low and indistinguishable sympathies in her ear. As Derrick watched dumbly, her sobs became louder and louder, and when she turned to fling her arms wildly around her husband's neck, he left the room. Hans, his chauffeur, was waiting in the front hall, and he wondered indifferently if Hans had heard. As the latter tucked his master warmly into the back seat of the Cadillac, fixing the rug securely about his knees with deft fingers, it occurred to Derrick that his servants cared for him more than any of his family did. At least he had always been happy in his relationships with underlings. They were simple relationships where each understood what the other expected. It seemed unreasonable to him now that family relationships could never be the same. Why, in a world that they themselves had complicated, did his children have to hurl his simplicity in his face? And confuse it with inhumanity? A monster? If he was a monster, the sea must be full of them. He closed his eyes to doze to the hum of the motor and the click of wheels on the parkway, but the sudden image of Dorcas' shaking shoulders made him start up.

"Hans!" he shouted.

Through the glass he could see his chauffeur's head turn in alarm, and the big car came to a quick stop by the side of the road. The sound of the traffic passing on their left increased to a roar. Hans was out of the car in a moment and had opened the back door.

"Sir? Are you ill?"

"Do I look ill?"

"Very pale, sir."

"It's nothing, but leave the glass down."

Hans rolled down the glass partition, and started the car. Back on the road Derrick felt better, knowing that he could now talk to Hans. He tried to doze, but once again he faced that vivid image. He clenched his fists.

"Hans!"

"Sir?"

"I had an argument with Mrs. Jesmond tonight. Did you hear us in the hall?"

"Oh, no, sir."

He was disappointed. He wanted to talk to Hans about it, but he could not bring himself to tell him. And certainly not to tell him how it had ended, with every inch of poor Dorcas' big body quivering in anguished pain. Oh, no, no, he couldn't even tell himself! He couldn't! And then, like a relieving tide, came the sudden anguish in the chest, the stabbing, biting, clawing pain in which Dorcas' image was lost.

"Hans!" he gasped.

The car skidded as Hans looked back. But then he turned again to the wheel, and Derrick was jolted to one side as they swayed off the parkway onto a side road. "The hospital in Glen Cove is the nearest, sir," he shouted. "We can be there in six minutes!"

Before Derrick lost consciousness, he was able to reflect how astonishing it was that his untutored chauffeur should recognize so quickly the symptoms of a heart attack.

18

Derrick: 1951

THE BALLROOM of the Park Club, with its three huge, scarlet-draped french windows and its three narrow crystal-ball chandeliers, had always been the symbol to Derrick of Ida's idea of a party. There frivolity and enthusiasm could be policed by a staff selected by a council of wise women. There the very curtains, despite their misleading color, acted as chaperons. It had been the scene of celebration of the Hartleys' twenty-fifth wedding anniversary and of Dorcas' debutante party. And now, despite his son's protests that to have his wedding reception in the room where he had gone to dancing class would be to fox-trot into marriage over the parquet floor of a childhood preparation, there was Hugo, in grey and black, standing beside his bride before the center window and smiling, rather complacently, in his task of shaking four hundred hands.

Minerva had been responsible for it, Minerva, a recent member of the club, who had long visualized the Park ballroom as the setting for just such a scene. But, however appallingly magnificent she might have been in pink organdie and pink hair, holding up the long line as she shouted greetings and threw kisses and waved her brown arms, it was perfectly evident to Derrick, posted opposite the bridal couple in his wheelchair, that Ida was the central figure of the afternoon. For it was Ida's club; she had lunched there, almost daily for thirty years; she had served as secretary and treasurer and on every committee, and now a good tenth of the resident membership must have been numbered among the guests. And Ida, in the long gray which most became her, seemed slim and dignified beside Minerva, and serene in contrast to the white, gesticulating figure of a daughter-in-law already intoxicated with congratulation. Yes, it was Ida's day, and Derrick begrudged her none of it.

A wheelchair was the perfect vantage point from which to view the party. The gleam of its steel accessories and the presence of a nurse at his side — even more obviously a nurse in the flower print that she uneasily, if festively, wore — kept all but the closer friends and family away, and those who spoke to him did so briefly. Yet he felt well, better than he had in weeks. The damage to his arterial system might have been such that he would never be able to work or exercise again, but that blow, like hovering death, had been accepted. Now he would live, in a relaxed, cynical, observing twilight, as long as it was decreed. Instead of battling his way upstream, he would lie in a sunlit pool and be fed flies. It was all very boring, but it had come as little surprise. He had been warned by his doctor two years before, a warning which he had communicated to nobody and which, after due consideration, he had decided to ignore. He had gambled on a longer respite, but he had no regrets. They had been two good years. The alternative would have been something not too different from his present existence. What would it have gained him to have started earlier?

The room before him seemed full of Denisons. All of Ida's family had gathered for this wedding of cousins. Old Mrs. Willie Denison, the last surviving aunt and senior widow of Hartley and Dodge, now in her nineties, was making her slow progress past the receiving line, on Mark Jesmond's arm. Derrick smiled at the speed with which Mark had taken over even the social duties of head of the firm. Behind the old

lady were her son and grandson, also partners. Who could
say that he had not repaid the Denisons for all they had given
him? But of course they had known he would. They had
known a good thing when they had seen it. They had made
greater use of him, in truth, than he had ever made of them,
and now that his use was over, they closed over him, like a
softly flowing, remorseless river on whose gliding surface his
washed rock had made its brief appearance. What else could
a lone rock have expected?

But what fallacies, what nonsense! If he went on in this
way he would end up as romantic as Ida and start borrowing
historical novels from the addled medical female at his side.
Who, after all, still owned the controlling shares of Hartley
and Dodge? Whose voluntary act had it been to give that
power of attorney to Ida? Could he not revoke it at will?
Could he not pick up the dropped reins whenever he chose,
even if the act of raising them should prove his last?

"Who is that wonderful old lady?" Miss Jonas exclaimed.
"She must be what the newspapers call a grand dame."

"She's my wife's aunt, and she's going to live to be a hundred."

"Isn't that something!"

"It's something for a woman to do. They like such mara-
thons. But not for a man. I thank the good Lord of bonds
and shares and Wall Street panics that He has numbered my
days."

"Oh, come now Mr. Hartley, you'll bury us all!"

"I may bury *you*, Miss Jonas, but only if I bore you to
death first. Now please don't talk. I'm thinking."

Ida smiled at him across the room and he nodded back. He
saw Alfreda nudge Hugo, and they both waved. It was wonderful how smoothly everybody got on now that Ida was in
charge. In the hospital Dorcas and Mark had paid him brief
but regular visits, and out of perfunctory conversation, sea-

soned with perfunctory smiles, they had managed to fling a
slender but passable bridge over what had first seemed an
unconnectible gap. Derrick had not had to be told that this
was Ida's price. He had divined that the Jesmonds must
have paid for Mark's senior partnership with their expressed
good will to Mark's father-in-law. And would continue to
pay. For Ida would never loosen the noose that her control
of Derrick's interests had enabled her to cast over their necks.
She had the tenacity of those who are late to act, the persistence of a benevolent Catherine de' Medici, called to power
after years of neglect. There had been the matter of young
Willie Denison's partnership and then the matter of pen-
sioning certain old clerks whom she had considered insufficiently provided for. And there would be other matters,
more and more, as time went on. Derrick chuckled at the
thought of how slim a chance poor Mark would have of
getting "Jesmond" into the firm name ahead of his own. He
would be lucky if Ida did not oblige him to restore to the
place of honor the "Tremain" which Derrick had deleted in
1924!

"Don't think too hard," Miss Jonas warned him. "It can
be very tiring."

"How do you know?"

"Oh, Mr. Hartley, you're a scream! You really are!"

Mark, with a smile that was like a clean bandage on his
wounded feelings, approached the wheelchair and began to
talk in a loud voice of Hugo's gallery.

"My coronary has not affected my hearing, Mark. Please
don't shout."

"I'm sorry, sir. I was just thinking, now that Hugo is
president, why wouldn't it be a good thing to stake him to
a new building? We might even reorganize his company
and issue more stock. How would that be for a wedding present?"

"Is it your idea to give Hugo a wedding present or to make money out of the auction business?"

"Both, of course!"

"Well, it may be an excellent idea, but my doctor says I'm not to be troubled with decisions. You'll have to take it up with your mother-in-law."

Mark flushed and moved away, but Derrick was beyond caring. He had to have *some* fun in his wheelchair. Dorcas, the matron of honor, a stalwart pole of blue chiffon under a floppy hat, still clutching her bouquet, now walked across from the receiving line to take her husband's place. Was Ida sending them over, one by one, like sentries?

"How does Mark enjoy being senior partner?"

"It's too soon to tell. But I hope you haven't been asking *him* that."

"And why can't I ask my own son-in-law if he likes being head of my own firm?"

"Because he'll think you're being sarcastic. Which you would be."

Derrick was amused at her total predictability. "Suppose I happen to be in earnest?"

"Mark's *always* going to think you're sarcastic. The only thing you can do for him is leave him alone."

"Aren't those rather harsh words for an old father?"

"They might be. If the old father cared." Her pebbly tone suspended the brief truce that had started in the hospital, and Derrick reflected that it was the first time they had talked alone, without the presence of either Ida or Mark. "But what's the point of pretending now?"

He shrugged, smiling. "Because I'm an old wreck. A lonely old wreck."

"Pooh. I don't feel a bit sorry for you. You've done everything you've wanted in life. I'd settle for a fraction of what you've had."

"Oh, I've had a lot." He nodded. "I don't repine. But does that mean I can't have anything more? Suppose I'm greedy? Suppose I want to die surrounded by loving children and grandchildren?"

"Surely, Daddy, you're not going in for a spiritual rebirth, too?"

He followed her glance to the receiving line where Ida was being kissed by old Mr. Dodge. Ida was never gracious about being kissed. She was putting her hand now on the old man's shoulder as if to restrain the hidden beast in him. "If your mother can begin over again," he demanded, "why can't I?"

"Because she can't, really," Dorcas retorted fiercely. "She can't make a new woman of herself at her age, and it's ridiculous for her to try."

"That's your credo, isn't it, Dorcas? That we're all condemned to our initial positions. That we make our beds once and lie in them forever. But don't you see, that's exactly what your mother is challenging? She says it's never too late."

"But it is!"

"Is it?" Derrick was really enjoying himself now. "It seems to me that she's making vast strides. This wedding today is all her doing. And so is my beautiful state of resignation at my illness. She may even teach Mark how to relax. I wouldn't put it past her. But perhaps you wouldn't want him relaxed at the price of owing it to your mother?"

She looked at him angrily. "What a nasty thing to say!"

"Oh, come, Dorcas, let's not you and me pretend. You hug your bitterness, as I hug my selfishness. Your mother's the only one of the lot of us who has actually tried to step outside herself. What we are beholding is the rarest thing in the whole world — a naked exercise of will power."

"A naked exercise of domination! She's always wanted to

rule the roost, and she jumped at the first opportunity. Which was your heart attack. She may have had to wait for years, but she was ready. God, was she ready!"

"If you're speaking of the firm, you forget it was I who gave her the proxies."

"Who else could you give them to? Who else could you trust? She saw it all coming, ages ago!"

"I wonder what her plans are for *you*, Dorcas. That will be amusing to watch."

"For me?"

"Yes. If your mother has decided to make us all happy, surely, she won't leave *you* out. Seeing how she goes about that job should almost compensate me for my enforced inactivity."

"I think Mummy will have the good sense to leave me alone."

"Why? You obviously think she's making a fool of herself. Don't people who do that always go on to make greater and greater fools of themselves? Oh, it should be glorious to watch!"

"You only say that, Daddy, to get my goat."

"And only because your goat is so easy to get." The incipient tears in her eyes provoked him. "Don't be so gullible, Dorcas. And *now* see what you've done! You've brought your mother to the rescue." Ida, indeed, was already headed in their direction. "Like a great general, she can spot dissension on her flank from the very heart of the fray."

Dorcas shook her head impatiently and walked off quickly as her mother came up.

"It's all right, my dear," Derrick said cheerfully, "we had only the briefest pass. I believe I pinked her."

Ida sat down in the chair beside him, her eyes watching Hugo and Alfreda who were being photographed. "It's very naughty of you. She's trying so hard to be good."

"I know. But you must remember how limited my diversions are."

"Alas, poor dear, I do."

"No, it's not poor dear. I really have no business being as happy as I am. I've been a shocking egotist for six and a half decades."

"We're all shocking egotists."

"That's what Dorcas thinks. She believes that you've taken my place, that's all. And that you've waited all your married life to do it."

Ida's smile was speculative. She turned her attention momentarily from the bride and groom. "What do *you* think?"

"Oh, I think differently. I think you're realizing the destiny that you elected as a child. I think you've become Aunt Dagmar at last."

"But I don't do things easily as Aunt Dagmar and Mother did. And the easiness is the whole point. Without that one is simply bossy and officious."

"Ah, but you see, their easiness was just your invention. The Denisons themselves were your invention. And you were very careful, being a guilt-ridden child, to invent an ideal that you could emulate but never approach. The Denisons, in your definition, were a crazy patchwork of inconsistencies. They had to be gay and lighthearted, even when they were being pure and dutiful. They had to be fearless, even when they were cautious. They had to be gallant and wear rubber boots in the house. They had to be endowed with all your terrors and yet never suffer from them. You made up the Denisons to prove to yourself that you were alone in the world!"

But Ida, apparently, could take anything now. Her smile deepened. "And why did I marry *you?*"

"To justify Geraldine's sacrifice."

"In giving you up? Was it so great?" She laughed cheerfully. "How little you still know of women! But, tell me, if all this was so, why have I changed? For I gather I *have* changed?"

"Because Geraldine's death exploded the myth of the Denisons. You saw the shabby reality."

"I saw Geraldine's shabby reality," she agreed quickly, "but then I always had. Geraldine was not typical of the family." For just a moment she brooded. "Oh, no, surely, she wasn't!"

He had gone too far, even in an invalid's game. "She had her share of the mythical qualities. Of the good ones, too, I mean. There's something I've never told you. It was she who broke off our affair. When she found I was never going to ask you for a divorce."

She looked at him in grave astonishment. "Is that a thing to discuss at Hugo's wedding?" But curiosity was too much for her, even then. "Do you imply it's a thing I should be *grateful* to Geraldine for?"

"No. But to her it was a matter of honor. She wouldn't be a kept woman. She was Denison enough for that."

Ida's laugh this time had a touch of the frantic. "Surely, our old Denison honor was something more than that!" Her eyes became softer, as she reflected. "Still, I see what you mean. Maybe it was something, after all. Poor, distracted Geraldine. Maybe she, too, tried. Or is that, too, my myth?"

"Your reality, my dear, is much finer than your myth ever was. If your mother and aunt could see you now, they would see that you had made something very beautiful out of the pieces and patches that they left you with."

"Beautiful pieces and beautiful patches," Ida replied, with tears now in her eyes. "And look at the crazy quilt I've made out of them! Oh, Derrick, you're a very good sport. Would Geraldine have made you happy?"

"Never! No woman could have done that. I sometimes think no woman could have lived with me but you."

She took his hand. "Can I build on that? Or would
Mother have called that a 'sloppy' question?"

"You? You can build on anything!"

They looked up at the sound of many feet and saw Hugo
and Alfreda coming across the ballroom to them followed by
the wedding party. Alfreda, as they drew near, hurried ahead
and threw her arms around her father-in-law.

"You poor, dear old darling, sitting there so patiently!
We're going to cut the cake now, but I had to come over
and give you a great big hug first!"

Derrick wondered, encompassed in white satin and lace, if
the glaze of Alfreda's good manners would be the icing on
Ida's cake. Why not? What was the harm of icing?

"Hugo," he heard Ida's voice, "wheel your father's chair
into the other room so he can see!"

And as Hugo, his bride clinging to his arm, slowly wheeled
the chair across the floor, the whole reception burst into applause. Derrick smiled to his left and right, like a sovereign
in a carriage. It was the least he could do for the woman
who was going to take care of him for the rest of his life.
Even at the end, he was getting things cheap.